A BONDED LEGACY NOVEL

ADELINE BRYANT

ISBN: 979-8-9993344-1-1 (eBook)
ISBN: 979-8-9993344-0-4 (Paperback)

Library of Congress Control Number: 2025913378

The story, all names, characters, and incidents portrayed in this production are fictitious. No identification with actual persons (living or deceased), places, buildings, and products is intended or should be inferred.

Book Cover by Sienna Arts

Edited by Clara Abigail

Published by Whiskers & Lipstick, Minneapolis, MN

First edition 2025

www.addiewrotethat.com

"Yeah. She's writing a book. There are good werewolves and maybe bad werewolves and they—" *He leaned in, whispering.* "Have sex..."

— my dear husband

Note to Reader

To the tender, the wrecked, the *curious*—

This story aches. It drips with desire and loss, with choices that don't come clean and love that doesn't come easy. You'll find soulmates, sex, and suffering.

You'll also find:
- Grief and mourning, including mate-bond loss

- Emotional manipulation and possessive behavior

- Parental death (referenced, not depicted)

- Mental health struggles (anxiety, panic, trauma responses)

- Estrangement and exile

- Graphic violence and physical injury (battle scenes)

- Death of secondary characters

- Raw, explicit intimacy (M/F, M/M, multiple partners, and power exchange)

And the Goddess who watches it all unfold...

These aren't just warnings, they're offerings. Take what you need. Leave what you must. And if you're looking for something that breaks you a little... Welcome to the pack.
   x Addie

Playlist

Running With The Wolves - AURORA
Howl - Florence + The Machine
Wicked Game - James Vincent McMorrow
Wolf - Highly Suspect
Wait - M83
Enchanted (Taylor's Version) - Taylor Swift
Risk - Gracie Abrams
Anchor - Novo Amor
King and Lionheart - Of Monsters and Men
Work Song - Hozier
War of Hearts - Ruelle
Rule #34 - Fish in a Birdcage
Mess It Up - Gracie Abrams
End of Beginning - Djo
Brother - Lord Huron
Like Real People Do - Hozier
Enchanted (Taylor's Version) - Taylor Swift (reprise)
I Found - Amber Run
The Yawning Grave - Lord Huron
Game of Survival - Ruelle
Bullet - Jared Benjamin
August - Taylor Swift
Heavy in Your Arms - Florence + The Machine
Arcade - Duncan Laurence
Exile (feat. Bon Iver) - Taylor Swift

The Night We Met - Lord Huron
The Wolves (Act I & II) - Bon Iver
Murder Song (5, 4, 3, 2, 1) - AURORA

LISTEN NOW

SPOTIFY

YOUTUBE

FATED

A Bonded Legacy Novel
Adeline Bryant

PROLOGUE

The Beginning

M oonlight was the first breath of creation. It flowed through the darkness, guided by Selene, the Moon Goddess. Her shimmering light lived and breathed, stretching across the land like a veil, seeking the untamed corners of the earth.

Selene's purpose was to shape life, guide it toward harmony by gifting the earth Her most beloved creation: Her children. With each step of Her journey, Selene's presence called out to the wild places of the world—where mountains soared towards the heavens, where ancient forests whispered secrets, where rivers carved stories into the land. As She wandered the realm, She noticed a missing link—an opportunity for a bridge between divinity and mortality, between light and shadow. And so, Her gaze fell upon the wolves.

She observed the creatures that roamed beneath Her luminous glow, drawn to their strength, loyalty, and fierce pack mentality. Their heads that tilted skyward when Her moon reached fullness. Their eyes, vibrant pools reflecting Her light, that held questions unasked. Their howls that stretched toward Her realm as if trying to touch something just beyond their reach. They possessed power but lacked wisdom, showed loyalty but not understanding.

One night, in the fullness of Her divine form, Selene descended upon a valley that resonated with Her essence. Towering cliffs reached up towards Her like supplicant hands. Wildflowers blanketed the valley, and a river of starlight cut through the earth. Here, She sensed the wolves moved differently, as if they had already tasted divinity. This sacred place would become known as Lunaris Sanctum, named after the river that carried moonlight within its depths.

As Her radiant light flooded the valley, it called to the wolves, drawing them forth from the shadows of the cliffs. And then, through the stillness, a wolf unlike any other emerged.

His coat swallowed the moonlight, darkness taking physical form. His eyes blazed like molten gold, challenging even the stars above. His paws pressed into the earth without sound, yet each footfall sent tremors through the air. His muscles rippled beneath midnight fur, movements fluid as shadow over water. The flowers bent away from his path—not in fear but reverence—as he advanced toward Selene. Though he exuded power, he did not bare his teeth or lower his ears. Instead, he stopped before Her feet and kneeled, not in fear but in recognition of something greater than himself.

"You see me," Selene whispered, kneeling before him. "Not as predator or prey, but as Creator, as Guide, as your *Goddess*."

She pressed Her hand to his brow, fingers sinking into fur that felt like captured night. "Through your submission, you shall become more," She promised. "You will be the first, the heart of what is to come."

From Her side, She drew a blade forged from pure starlight. Its edge kissed Her palm, and divine blood—silver like moonbeams—spilled freely into the earth. Lunaris Sanctum transformed before Her eyes, Her essence weaving into its very fabric. The ground trembled as Her blood seeped downward, silver rivulets forming patterns that glowed and pulsed with life. Runes unknown to mortal minds spiraled outward, etching themselves into stone and soil, while flowers burst into bloom where each droplet fell. The air grew thick with magic, shimmering visibly with each breath drawn.

The wolf watched, unmoving, as Selene rose and pressed Her bloodied hand to his chest. Divine energy surged through him. His spine arched as bones cracked and reformed, lengthening and reshaping beneath stretching skin. His howl of pain transformed midway to a gasping human cry. Fur receded in patches while his muzzle flattened, fingers emerging from paws even as his eyes retained their lupine sharpness.

Where once stood a beast now kneeled something new—muscles quivering beneath skin that could reflect both moonlight and sunlight, hands that could both kill and create. His transformation served as a bridge between worlds, the first step over a blessed threshold, the first of Her chosen.

Selene stepped back, studying him with affection. "You are both, and you shall lead both." Her words rang with prophetic certainty. "As wolf, you are Fenrir—unmatched in strength. As male, you are Caelum—bearing the stars in your blood. Both names are your truth, a reminder that you walk between earth and the heavens."

Caelum's eyes shone like gold in sunlight as he bowed, chest heaving, each breath a prayer of devotion. He trembled beneath the force of Her gift, divinity coursing through his veins. Selene watched as his body responded to Her power, his eyes widening with awe as he surrendered to Her will.

His pack, waiting at the hidden edge of the vale, eagerly approached, drawn by the power radiating from the transformed land. Save for one, they each submitted to Selene's touch and were granted the gift of a dual nature—wolf and human intertwined.

From this first pack, Selene's blessing rippled like waves on a still lake. She traveled from mountains to plains, forests to rivers, leaving behind marks of power. Each territory She graced became hallowed ground, giving rise to a new pack of Her children bound by loyalty to the moon and Her will. Each one another verse in Her song of creation.

She guided the alphas, chosen not just for their strength, but for their wisdom—leaders who understood that true power lay in service to something greater than themselves.

But as time passed, She noticed Her children's eyes straying toward the glittering human cities, their gazes reflecting not just curiosity, but hunger for something beyond Her gifts. Influenced by the ever-changing world around them, they built their own kingdoms and chased their own desires, consumed by a thirst for power that eclipsed their love for the moon. Where there once was unity now stood divided territories ruled by wolves who had forgotten their humble beginnings.

Generation by generation, Selene watched as their ceremonies changed. Ancient rites performed under moonlight gave way to elaborate displays of wealth. Mating rituals, once guided by divine purpose, became political tools for territorial expansion. The sacred power She bestowed upon pack leaders—power meant to guide and protect—twisted into instruments of control.

Alphas no longer served their packs but ruled them, demanding absolute submission. Those who refused to bow were cast out, forced to wander the wild places where separation from pack and purpose drove them to madness, their humanity withering as their wolf nature consumed them.

Each small change cut like a blade of starlight against Her heart.

Selene's luminous form dimmed as Her gaze fell upon the fractured lands, Her light extinguished by the sorrow within. Her children—Her beloved wolves—had changed. The purity of their connection to Her had weakened, and with it, the harmony of the world She had created and Her ability to reside in its domain. Her tears fell upon the earth like stardust, mourning the lost bond between Mother and child.

Yet, amid the darkness of Her sorrow, a single spark remained. A flame that bent but never extinguished—casting just enough light to illuminate a path forward when all else seemed lost—guiding Her to tend embers of devotion in Her children's hearts. While She no longer walked among them, Her light continued to touch their lands, Her whispers still carried on the wind, and Her presence lingered in their dreams.

Through the mating bonds, She hoped to guide them, not through force or control, but through destiny's quiet pull. A subtle reminder of what they once were and could be again. So into each blessed heart, Selene wove a thread of moonlight. An eternal connection that would call to its other half across any distance, through any darkness. These mating bonds would be Her eternal gift. A reminder that all Her children were meant to be united, even when territories and ambitions threatened to divide them.

And in their darkest moments, when greed and division threatened to consume them, Selene vowed to send forth a radiant light. A beacon of divine grace that could penetrate even the deepest shadows.

Some would resist, blinded by ambition or fear, turning away from Her brilliance, but She would persist, trusting in the bonds She forged, and waiting with eternal patience for Her children to find their way back into Her loving embrace.

REGIONAL COLLECTIVE OF PACIFIC NORTHWEST PACKS

IN DEFENSE OF OUR FUTURE.

121st Regional Summit

2026

IN HONOR OF THE MOON.

MARCH 5-7, 2026, 254 SELENE'S ERA

THE SUMMIT LODGE | COEUR D'ALENE, IDAHO

Please confirm your delegation and reserve accommodations by:
February 10th, 2026

For registration and lodging block access, refer to the enclosed packet.

REGIONAL COLLECTIVE OF
PACIFIC NORTHWEST PACKS

Greetings, Alphas,

On behalf of the Regional Collective of Pacific Northwest Packs, it is my honor to invite you to the 121st Regional Summit, hosted at the Collective's Summit Lodge in Coeur d'Alene, Idaho. For over a century, our summit has served as a sacred space for reflection, diplomacy, and interpack unity. It is a time to reaffirm the values that bind us, to confront the challenges that threaten us, and to strengthen the alliances that carry us forward.

This year's theme—In Defense of Our Future. In Honor of the Moon.—was chosen in response to the escalating rogue threat that continues to destabilize our communities. As incidents of unprovoked attacks increase in both frequency and severity, we are reminded that our strength lies not only in our warriors, but in our unity. In the sacred light of Selene, we must meet this moment together.

The Collective Council also wishes to acknowledge a concerning shift in ancestral patterns. Over the past two decades, we have recorded a noticeable decline in mating bond manifestations, as well as a marked rise in female first-borns within legacy bloodlines. While the Moon Goddess guides us still, the world around us is changing —and so too must we. In recognition of this, the Council has elected to expand this year's summit delegation criteria.

In addition to the traditional delegation structure—Alphas, Lunas, Betas, heirs, and three registered warriors—each pack may now send up to three additional guests, including beta-females and unmated she-wolves of rank or exceptional skill. Additional spots may be granted on a first-come, first-served basis following final registration.

We are also pleased to announce that, after forty-six years of separation, Crescent Fang—led by Alpha Caleb, grandson of Odin and direct descendant of Caelum, the First Alpha—will be returning to the summit on a probationary basis. The threat we face extends beyond our borders and our histories. It is the Council's hope that this reentry signals not only Crescent Fang's renewed commitment, but the beginning of a truly united Collective once more.

Finally, in lieu of the annual Heirs Basketball Game, a Memorial Run will be held to honor those lives lost to rogue violence in the past year. This sacred gathering will offer a moment of shared grief, shared remembrance, and shared purpose—as one community under Her watchful light.

We look forward to a summit marked by meaningful dialogue, renewed cooperation, and the continued guidance of the Moon Goddess.

May the Goddess's blessings shine brightly on your packs.

A. Voss

Alaric Voss | Silver Hollow Pack
Summit Planning Chair | Regional Collective of Pacific Northwest Packs Council

REGIONAL COLLECTIVE OF
PACIFIC NORTHWEST PACKS

Location:	Dates:
The Summit Lodge	Coeur d'Alene, Idaho	March 5–7, 2026, 254 Selene's Era

Room Block Availability:	Booking Code:
March 4 – 8, 2026, 254 Selene's Era	PNWSUMMIT2026 Instructions for reservation access and room assignments provided in secure delegate portal.

"In Defense of Our Future. In Honor of the Moon."

PURPOSE/AGENDA: The summit shall convene to discuss matters of shared defense, rogue activity, leadership transitions, and future alliances among the recognized packs of the Regional Collective of Pacific Northwest Packs.

SCHEDULE:

MARCH 4:	Delegation Check-in Welcome Reception
MARCH 5–7	Summit Sessions (10:00 am – 4:00 pm)
MARCH 6	Alpha/Beta Golf Tournament (afternoon) Memorial Run (evening)
MARCH 7	Closing Reception (evening)

Full session itinerary and attendee list provided upon check-in.

Approved by:

Alaric Voss | Silver Hollow Pack
Summit Planning Chair | Regional Collective
of Pacific Northwest Packs Council

January 17, 2026, 254 Selene's Era

REGIONAL COLLECTIVE OF
PACIFIC NORTHWEST PACKS

Invitations to the summit have been extended to all recognized packs in the region. Failure to appear may be interpreted as abdication of recognition from the collective.

BLACKWATER PACK | Bend, OR | 1905, 133 Selene's Era – present

POPULATION: 112

ANNUAL BUDGET: $13,328,000

INDUSTRIES: Education, History, R&D, Tourism & Hospitality, Beer

ALPHA FAMILY	Renford Blackwater	Eden Runa (unmated); Rhaenor* (17)
BETA FAMILY	Corbin Vale	Thalia Darian* (Nyla)
GAMMA FAMILY	Marius Holt	Emryn Solen* (Hestia)

RECOGNIZED AFFILIATIONS: Moonshadow | Greenridge (defunct) | Shadowpine (defunct)

BLOODSTONE PACK | Tacoma, WA | 1905, 133 Selene's Era – present

POPULATION: 231

ANNUAL BUDGET: $27,453,000

INDUSTRIES: Architecture, Healthcare, Law, Banking, Oil, Tech, Real Estate Development

ALPHA FAMILY	Darius Bloodstone	Althea† Kai* (unmated)
BETA FAMILY	Maxim Drayke	Hildi Magnus* (unmated)
GAMMA FAMILY	Talon Grant	Maris Elias* (unmated); Lyric (unmated)

RECOGNIZED AFFILIATIONS: Night Walker | Redridge | Silver Hollow | Blue Crescent (defunct) | Raven's Crest (defunct)

IRONCLAW PACK | Port Angeles, WA | 1905, 133 Selene's Era – present

POPULATION: 94

ANNUAL BUDGET: $11,172,000

INDUSTRIES: Healthcare, Real Estate, Masonry, Automotive, Milling, Agriculture, Wine

ALPHA FAMILY	Thorne Ironclaw (unmated)
BETA FAMILY	Halvar Stroud	Sonya
GAMMA FAMILY	Rowan Idran	Mikaela Ilya* (3)

RECOGNIZED AFFILIATIONS: Frostfall (defunct) | Blue Crescent (defunct)

REGIONAL COLLECTIVE OF
PACIFIC NORTHWEST PACKS

MOONSHADOW PACK | Portland, OR | 1905, 133 Selene's Era – present

POPULATION: 73

ANNUAL BUDGET: $8,708,000

INDUSTRIES: Defense, Fishing, Forestry, Healthcare, Manufacturing

ALPHA FAMILY	Raelen Moonshadow	Seraphina[†] Lena (unmated); Cian* (unmated)
BETA FAMILY	Aiden Solberg	Nerina Ryker* (unmated)
GAMMA FAMILY	Gunnar Fell	Maela Jace* (unmated)

RECOGNIZED AFFILIATIONS: Blackwater | Greenridge (defunct) | Shadowpine (defunct)

NIGHT WALKER PACK | Spokane, WA | 1905, 133 Selene's Era – present

POPULATION: 177

ANNUAL BUDGET: $21,069,000

INDUSTRIES: Hospitality, Tourism, Pharmaceuticals, Mining, Logging, Aviation

ALPHA FAMILY	Lucien Night Walker	Lydia Theron* (7); Altan (4); Elia (2)
BETA FAMILY	Malric Ashfall	Idris Kaelen* (5), Evelyn (2)
GAMMA FAMILY	Dax Arven	Renna Callen* (8); Soren (5); Aisla (4); Mira (2)

RECOGNIZED AFFILIATIONS: Bloodstone | Redridge
UNRECOGNIZED AFFILIATIONS: Crescent Fang

REDRIDGE PACK | Discovery Bay, WA | 1972, 200 Selene's Era – present

POPULATION: 128

ANNUAL BUDGET: $15,232,000

INDUSTRIES: Agriculture, Milling, Fishing

ALPHA FAMILY	Garrick Redridge	Ylva Niko* (15)
BETA FAMILY	Thurston Stone	Ylva Redridge Tessa (unmated)	Jasper* (13)
GAMMA FAMILY	Brannic Hill	Isolde Dariel* (17), Kaela (15), Joren (14)

RECOGNIZED AFFILIATIONS: Bloodstone | Night Walker

REGIONAL COLLECTIVE OF PACIFIC NORTHWEST PACKS

SILVER HOLLOW PACK | Yakima, WA | 1905, 133 Selene's Era – present

POPULATION: 142	ALPHA FAMILY	Aldric Silver Hollow	Eileen Riven* (Lira), Eira (17)
ANNUAL BUDGET: $16,896,000	BETA FAMILY	Cedric Halloway	Naela Nyric* (unmated), Lira (Riven)
INDUSTRIES: Agriculture, Forestry, Fishing, Education	GAMMA FAMILY	Fenrik Greystead	Brynn Garrin* (unmated), Illyra (unmated)
RECOGNIZED AFFILIATIONS: Bloodstone		

CRESCENT FANG PACK | Lakewood, WA | Inactive (eff. 1980, 208 Selene's Era)

POPULATION: 69	ALPHA FAMILY	Caleb Crescent Fang (unmated)
ANNUAL BUDGET: $24,633,000		
INDUSTRIES: Healthcare, Social Services, Education, Agriculture, Forestry, Hunting, Transportation, Carpentry, Electrical Engineering, InfoSec	BETA FAMILY	Asher Solan (unmated)
	GAMMA FAMILY	Varek Krell	Sienna
RECOGNIZED AFFILIATIONS: None UNRECOGNIZED AFFILIATIONS: Night Walker		

INACTIVE PACKS

DEFUNCT	BLUE CRESCENT	Spokane, WA
ROUGE INCIDENTS[†]	RAVEN'S CREST PACK	Graham, WA
	FROSTFALL PACK	Walla Walla, WA
	GREENRIDGE PACK	Heppner, OR
	SHADOWPINE PACK| Dalles City, OR
	EAGLECLIFF PACK	Jerome, ID
	STONEHEARTH PACK	Meridian, ID
	DENALI PACK	Sequim, WA

CONFIDENTIAL

Approved by: *A. Voss*
January 17, 2026, 254 Selene's Era

Alaric Voss | Silver Hollow Pack
Summit Planning Chair | Regional Collective
of Pacific Northwest Packs Council

CHAPTER ONE

CALEB

C aleb sat bathed in the fire's warm glow, its soft crackle and sweet scent of burning wood mingling with the musty aroma of old leather. His fingers skimmed the edges of a worn, leather-bound book—one of the tomes chronicling his pack's history piled high on his desk. His hazel eyes, piercing yet distant, lifted to the window.

As Caleb's thoughts drifted, his gaze swept across the moonlit landscape, the familiar contours of his pack's territory stirring something deep within him. Ancient redwoods and towering pines stretched beneath a star-studded sky. The forest floor undulated with gentle hills and hidden valleys, cloaked in a misty veil that danced and swirled in the night breeze.

Sighing, he shifted his attention back to his desk, where the Summit invitation lay like a challenge. Unexpected after decades of silence.

The packet had consumed Caleb's thoughts for over three weeks. The invitation should have been an honor, recognition of Crescent Fang's storied past. As Selene's first pack, they'd once been the heart of the region, but their influence waned as other packs pursued power and wealth.

The Regional Collective had evolved into something unrecognizable to Selene's original vision, and the Summit became a gathering of posturing pack leaders bargaining their power and influence to regulate everything from territory disputes to mating ceremonies, from resource allocation to modern pack laws.

While other packs submitted to the Collective's oversight, Crescent Fang's commitment to Selene's teachings led to their gradual withdrawal. What began as refusing to adopt new customs evolved into complete isolation. Other packs saw this as folly, but Crescent Fang saw it as a testament to their unwavering faith.

Caleb had never questioned the isolation of the pack he inherited. Until now.

A growing rogue threat loomed, a constant reminder of the danger that had been escalating for months. The report of the Denali pack's annihilation haunted him. Every wolf slaughtered in a single night. The territory reduced to smoldering ruins. Only bloodstained paw prints leading into the wilderness remained. The Collective's invitation proved the situation had escalated to a critical point.

Caleb's fingers clenched tighter around the book's worn cover. His eyes narrowed as the words blurred together, mind wrestling with everything the Summit represented. His breath caught in his throat for a moment before he forced himself to exhale, focusing on the task at hand.

A low hum vibrated through Caleb's mind as Fenrir, his wolf—a rebirth of his ancestor, Caelum's wolf—rose to attention.

"We should stay. The Collective is a distraction." Fenrir's words rumbled through Caleb's chest, a sensation more felt than heard. *"We can't risk the lives of our people—of the bloodlines."* The wolf's tone was edged with something deeper that Caleb couldn't quite decipher.

Caleb exhaled through his nose, his jaw tightening. *"We've stayed hidden for decades, Fenrir, and it hasn't kept us entirely safe. Perhaps it's time to reconsider our place within the Collective so we can better protect our bloodlines."*

A soft knock at the door broke Caleb's reverie. Asher stepped inside, smile making his eyes crinkle at the corners, his calm presence a balm to Caleb's frazzled nerves. The beta brought the forest with him—the scent of fresh pine sap and crushed cedar needles still clinging to his skin from when they'd raced through the western ridge that afternoon, Fenrir nipping playfully at Asher's wolf, Leif's, heels.

"You're still here." Asher leaned against the doorframe, a teasing glint in his eyes. "I thought I'd find you in bed, nose buried in a book by now—or even better, buried inside me."

Caleb leaned back in his chair, a genuine smirk forming on his lips. Asher's teasing brought a familiar warmth that momentarily quelled the anxieties shadowing his thoughts.

"I'm trying to make sure everything's in order before we leave. The council needs to approve my plans for pack management before I start handing out assignments."

Asher crossed the room, boots creaking on the wooden floor, and perched himself on the edge of Caleb's desk. His thigh brushed against Caleb's arm, sending a spark of electricity through his veins. Caleb's pulse quickened, throat going dry as fragments from that morning invaded his thoughts—waking up inside Asher's mouth, sheets tangled around his ankles, the rasp of stubble against his inner thigh, the way even Fenrir submitted to Asher as their bodies moved together...

Caleb forced himself from the memory. Though difficult to deny, Asher's lovemaking was a distraction he couldn't afford at the moment.

"That crease between your eyebrows gets deeper every time you look at those papers." Asher's voice softened as he squeezed Caleb's shoulder. "I know you feel the pressure of the pack's expectations and the unknown of the Collective's judgment, but I'm here to share that burden."

Caleb's gaze drifted to his beta. Warmth spread through his chest at the steady confidence there, but his stomach still twisted with unease. "I know that."

"And yet, you look like you're about to wage war instead of preparing for a summit."

The corner of Caleb's mouth quirked up. "Maybe I am."

Asher raised an eyebrow, expression a mask of incredulity.

With a sigh, Caleb ran a hand through his hair. "It's not just the Summit." He lowered his voice. "It's what it represents—the games, the politics our people have avoided for decades. With rogues closing in, one misstep could be disastrous—"

"You won't." Asher's voice left no room for doubt.

Caleb glanced up, meeting his beta's steady gaze. There was no doubt there, only unshakable confidence.

"And even if you stumble, we'll figure it out," Asher continued. "This summit isn't just about rogues or alliances. We're Selene's first pack—Her chosen. It's time to remind the others what that means."

Caleb's gaze drifted to the map of their territory, mind conjuring the faces of his pack members, their livelihoods, and the families dependent on his decisions. The enormity of that responsibility settled heavily on his shoulders.

Can I really do this?

"I'm an untested alpha who's barely navigating the oversight of our own pack's elders." Caleb drummed his fingers against the book. "I couldn't even convince the council to change our patrol routes. How am I supposed to stand among alphas who've been groomed since birth to maneuver in this political landscape?"

Fenrir paced the confines of Caleb's mind, hackles raised, claws scraping against his consciousness. *"We don't have to go. We can be strong alone."*

Caleb pushed Fenrir to the edge of his consciousness, feeling the wolf's displeasure like a cold spot between his shoulder blades. He swallowed hard, fears of inadequacy echoing back at him like a challenge. "What if I bring disruption to our people and danger to our lands?" The questions hung in the air, a tangible presence that pulsed with his own heartbeat.

"You're ready, Caleb. Trust me." Asher pressed his forehead against Caleb's, grounding him in the moment. "And you're not doing this alone. Whatever happens at that summit, we'll face it together. Like we always have."

Asher's words sank into him like sunlight into cold earth. The tension that had returned to Caleb's shoulders during their conversation finally broke. The vise grip around his chest that tightened with each moment spent studying the summit dossier dissolved, allowing his breath to flow freely again.

Caleb's doubts echoed a familiar uncertainty he'd faced as a teenager thrust into rapid preparation for his role as the future alpha after his parents' deaths. He'd faced the council's scrutiny as they'd questioned not just his ability to lead but whether the alpha bloodline should pass to Garreth, his father's beta. But Asher had stood beside him, unwavering, and faced them all down. His words had been a shield Caleb hadn't known he needed: *"Then it's a good thing he's not standing here alone."*

That truth remained unchanged, a constant that anchored Caleb with Asher's consistent confidence, just as it had all those years ago.

"Thank you," Caleb murmured.

"Always." A slow, knowing smile that hinted at pleasure ahead spread across Asher's face. "Now, let's get to work. The sooner we're ready, the sooner we can get to my originally planned evening activities."

As Caleb watched Asher review the schedule and directives, a sensation both familiar and frightening tugged beneath his ribs, waiting to be acknowledged.

Their bond transcended traditional pack hierarchy. Asher wasn't just Caleb's second; he was his lover. Their relationship had become a symbol of Crescent Fang's ethos, power flowing from partnership rather than dominance. Though not fated mates, they embodied Selene's intention: strength through unity, wisdom through balance.

Caleb exhaled, a small smile breaking through the tension. With Asher by his side, the Summit no longer seemed like a burden. It became an opportunity to remind the world of what the Crescent Fang pack—and Selene—stood for.

CHAPTER TWO

LENA

The metallic tang of blood flooded Lena's mouth as Cian's fist caught her jaw—a split second too slow on the dodge—sending a hot shock of pain radiating through her teeth. Her wolf, Elara, snarled beneath the surface, but something else caught her attention: the usual spark in her brother's attacks was missing. Instead, an undercurrent of anxiety threaded through his cedar-smoke scent.

"Getting sloppy." Cian's golden eyes—so much like their father's—caught hers. A forced calmness masked the edge in his tone. "You'll never make warrior status like that."

Elara paced just beneath her skin like a fever, the itch of fur almost breaking through as her instincts latched onto Cian's hesitation.

"He's holding back." The wolf's low snarl dripped with frustration. *"Push him harder. Make him fight like he means it."*

"You're the sloppy one." Lena feinted left, scenting the shift in Cian's balance, then drove her fist toward his exposed ribs. The satisfying thud of connection brought a grin to her face. Copper waves escaped her braid as she pivoted. She'd inherited their mother's beauty—the red-gold hair and sun-kissed freckles that set her apart from Cian's darker features—but when she pivoted for another strike, their father's signature move flowed through her limbs, mirrored in her brother's stance.

"Getting distracted, brother?" The corner of her mouth lifted.

"Never." Cian blocked Lena's follow-up strike but hesitated, a fraction of a second where his usual fluid grace stuttered. Not sharp enough. Not focused. Elara pressed closer to the surface, alert to the undercurrent of tension thick enough to taste.

A low whistle cut through the evening air.

"Cian, if she keeps landing those hits, you'll be the first alpha in history with a permanent limp!" Ryker called from the sidelines. The future beta's brown eyes sparkled with mischief, grin sharp as he laid back, lazily resting on his elbows.

Cian barked a laugh, dodging another strike from Lena. "I'd like to see you step into the ring with her and come out unscathed."

"Nah." Ryker ran a hand through his perpetually messy dirty-blond hair. "I'd rather keep this pretty face intact. Some of us need more than raw power to get by."

Lena snorted but didn't let her guard drop. The familiar banter couldn't mask the strange tension in the air. She felt it everywhere—in Cian's movements, in the way he studied her between strikes. As if he were trying to memorize something about this moment.

Is he testing me? she wondered. *Am I finally getting my chance to make elite warrior?*

Around them, grunts silenced as warriors paused to watch. They were always watching, always judging, the scent of their curiosity and assessment sharp as pine in winter. Their stares pressed against Lena's skin like a physical heat, prickling along her spine and tightening the muscles between her shoulder blades.

The alpha's daughter—watched and judged—not for my skill or strength, but for my potential value as a mate.

Elara snarled, driving Lena harder with every strike. *"Let them watch. Let them see."*

A flicker of movement pulled her focus, ears catching the sound of hurried footsteps. Jace jogged up, a teasing grin lighting up his face. "All right, Thing 1 and Thing 2. Break it up. Alpha Raelen wants to see you in his office. Now."

Cian lowered his fists, expression softening, but his jaw tightened ever so slightly. That same anxiety spiked in his scent.

"Don't worry, Lena." He wiped the sweat from his brow, leaning close. "It's nothing bad."

"You know what it's about, don't you?" Lena's eyebrow arched.

His smile turned crooked, usual confidence faltering. "Maybe." He glanced toward the packhouse, stance shifting subtly protective as his gaze lingered on her. "You'll see soon enough."

The walk to the packhouse felt longer than usual, each step heavy with anticipation. Pack life continued around them—warriors on patrol routes, pups racing through gardens, dinner scents wafting from kitchens.

Moonshadow thrived under their father's leadership. Alpha Raelen's tactical brilliance and diplomatic skill had created a respected force in the region. But with Cian poised to take over? Everything balanced on a knife's edge. The pack needed a smooth transition, especially with rogues threatening the northern territories.

Lena caught Ryker joking with Jace as they walked behind Cian. The future Beta and Gamma of Moonshadow, already falling into their roles—just like Cian would step into their father's. Everyone had their place.

Everyone except her.

As they climbed the front steps of the packhouse, Cian's hand caught her arm, grip gentle but insistent. "Whatever happens in there, you're ready for it."

Lena searched his gaze for any hint of what was coming, but her brother's expression held only that strange mix of pride and hope that made Elara whine in confusion.

She squared her shoulders and pushed open the door. Ready or not, change was coming.

The quiet atmosphere of their father's office greeted them as they entered. Raelen looked up from his desk, gaze warm but serious.

He gestured for them to sit. "I'll get right to it." Raelen leaned forward, hands folded on his desk. "Cian, you've spent the last year preparing to take your oaths. This year's summit will be your opportunity to step into the alpha role more fully."

Cian nodded, expression steady.

Raelen went on, "You'll attend the Summit as my surrogate. You'll represent the Moonshadow pack, participate in discussions with the other alphas, and begin solidifying your place as our next leader."

Pride swelled in Lena's chest for her brother, but under it churned a hollowness that sank like a stone to her gut. Elara's presence coiled tight against Lena's spine, ears pricked forward inside her mind, sensing more to come.

Raelen's gaze shifted to her. "And you, Lena. You'll accompany your brother."

Lena froze, heart skipping like a stone on water, mouth coated with cotton. She hadn't expected this. The summit—where pack leaders from across the region gathered, where alliances were forged and futures decided—was an event Lena had long been told would be critical if she ever took on the role of a pack luna or beta-female.

Lena blinked, startled from her ruminations. "Me?" The word came out softer than she intended.

"Yes," Raelen said firmly. "You've grown into a strong, capable she-wolf. The Summit is not just about leadership—it's about relationships, alliances, and understanding the larger dynamics of our world."

Lena shifted in her seat. "But why now?"

"This year's event focuses on defending our future while honoring our faith—addressing both the rogue threat and our community's changing dynamics. The northern and central packs will be watching closely given the attacks. With Cian coming into his role, some might see an opportunity to test our borders. Having both of my children there sends a message about Moonshadow's strength." Raelen paused, attention focusing entirely on her. "And perhaps you may even find your fated mate amongst the wolves in attendance."

"I'm not part of the pack hierarchy or a warrior." Lena's words came through gritted teeth as her wolf stalked beneath her skin, caught between hope and uncertainty.

Raelen's expression softened, but there was steel beneath it. "Your path may differ from your brother's, but it's no less important. The

Collective is considering changes to traditional pack hierarchies." He leaned forward. "With more female first-borns, they're debating formal leadership roles for she-wolves. Your presence could influence their thinking." He held her gaze. "You wouldn't just be proving yourself, Lena. You'd be opening doors for others."

Raelen hesitated, then added carefully, "And if you don't find your fated mate... Well, there are other options that would allow you to demonstrate your leadership in Moonshadow. We have many strong, loyal warriors who'd make excellent chosen mates. A chosen bond with Ryker or Jace could also strengthen our bloodlines and secure the pack's future, assuming neither of them finds their fated."

The suggestion tightened her stomach into a hard knot. A chosen bond would guarantee her place in Moonshadow, keep her with her birthpack, but Elara yearned for more—for that soul-deep connection that only a fated bond could bring.

Every wolf knew the stories, how Selene had split one soul between two wolves to create the first fated pair. Power. Destiny. Completion. Lena had witnessed it manifest—the sudden awareness, intertwined scents, wolves practically glowing with recognition.

Elara recoiled at the thought of a chosen bond. A phantom pain tightened Lena's chest until each breath came shallow and strained. The familiar faces of Moonshadow's warriors flashed through her mind, bringing comfort but no spark, no primal call that made her wolf sing.

Raelen gave her a moment to process, expression softening as he watched her internal battle. "I know it's not an easy thing to consider, but this summit will help you see the bigger picture. No matter what happens, you'll come out of it with valuable experience."

"I understand." The words came out soft and uncertain.

Cian reached out, squeezing her shoulder gently. "You'll do well, Lena. Trust yourself."

Lena nodded, thoughts churning with possibilities as she left her father and brother to continue their conversation. The summit presented more than just a chance to find her mate; it was an opportunity to chart her own course.

She understood the rogues' growing aggression threatened not just the northern and central borders, but the entire balance of power in the region. If she could prove her worth as more than a female just waiting for fate to decide her path, she might become the kind of leader the packs desperately needed in these uncertain times.

As Elara paced beneath her skin, muscles twitching with each phantom step, one question burned in Lena's throat like unshed howls: Was she ready for what waited on the horizon?

CHAPTER THREE

KAI

Kai Bloodstone stood at the edge of the ceremonial grounds, moonlight casting silver highlights across the sacred stones and catching in his dark, swept-back hair. The massive clearing, surrounded by towering cedars, hummed with an electric energy that matched his mood. Pine needles crunched beneath his boots while the scent of cold stone and aged incense filled his lungs.

His skin prickled as he reached the altar, broad shoulders tensing under generations of expectation. At twenty-four, every inch of his trained physique reminded him of what the pack demanded: the perfect future alpha.

Kai's fingers traced the ancient carvings etched into the altar's surface, the worn grooves still warm despite the night's chill, as if pulsing with the heartbeats of past alphas who'd taken their oaths on this very spot. In the moonlight, his striking green eyes—the unmistakable mark of the Bloodstone line—reflected centuries of tradition that would soon rest squarely on his shoulders.

Cold dread pooled at the base of his spine as he contemplated his future. Someday, he would stand here, taking the oaths to lead his pack. That moment felt both impossibly distant and terrifyingly close—the burden of legacy pressing against his lungs until each breath came with effort—the aberration of the ceremonial blade already slicing against his palm.

His wolf, Orion, circled the perimeter of Kai's consciousness, claws clicking against the foundation of his thoughts. Each movement sent ripples of tension down Kai's spine, muscles twitching beneath his skin as if phantom paws pressed into his flesh from the inside.

"Too quiet here." His voice rumbled through Kai's skull like distant thunder. *"Not enough action. Not our path."*

"You're as bad as I am." A humorless smirk twisted Kai's lips. "We'll get there."

But will I ever truly be ready for leadership? The question gnawed at Kai more than he'd ever admit.

The Bloodstone pack demanded strength, cunning, and vision—all qualities his father, Darius, wielded like weapons. Kai's fingers curled into fists as he remembered their latest confrontation.

"The delta rank would be fourth in the hierarchy, taking over security and the elite warriors," he'd argued, spreading the detailed proposal across his father's desk. *"It would free the gamma to focus on warrior education, pack communications, and guarding the luna. The responsibilities are too much for one person."*

Darius had barely glanced at the papers. "We've managed with alpha, beta, and gamma roles for generations."

"But our pack has nearly tripled in size since creation. Our challenges have evolved. The traditional structure doesn't—"

"Change for its own sake is dangerous." His father's tone had left no room for discussion. *"Our strength comes from the stability of our traditions, not from restructuring what works."*

It had been the same when Kai proposed mate integration in the hierarchy power structure. And his annual gamma retreat idea. Each time, Darius's response echoed the same theme: what had worked before would work again.

The pack needed evolution, not just tradition. The region needed a pack to lead by example. Why couldn't it be Bloodstone?

But his father saw only risk where Kai saw opportunity. Preservation where Kai saw innovation.

The crunch of stiff grass beneath his boots echoed in the stillness as he turned away from the ceremonial grounds, each step releasing the sharp, clean scent of early spring.

His father's towering silhouette waited on the packhouse porch. Arms crossed. Disapproval radiating from him like heat. The bitter tang of it hit the back of Kai's throat before he'd even caught his father's cedar-and-ash scent.

"Avoiding your responsibilities again, Kai?" Darius's low voice carried an edge that could cut steel.

"Just clearing my head." Kai forced the words out evenly. "It's been a long day."

"Every day is long when you're an alpha." Darius's eyes narrowed to emerald points. "The pack won't wait while you brood in the woods."

Orion bristled, but Kai swallowed his retort. Arguing with Darius was like fighting a tide—it only left you battered and exhausted.

"Understood." Kai brushed past his father into the warmth of the packhouse, swallowing unspoken arguments.

Familiar scents of roasted venison, caramelized root vegetables, and applewood smoke greeted him but did little to ease the tension coiling between his shoulder blades. The dining room buzzed with conversation, clinking silverware, and scraping chairs. The sounds vibrated against Kai's sensitive ear drums until everything faded when his attention locked on Ava.

Her sleek blonde hair caught the light like spun platinum, the scent of her expensive jasmine shampoo carrying across the room even before her laugh cut through the air—sharp and calculated, meant to draw every eye, vibrating at a frequency that made the wolf beneath his skin flatten his ears.

When their gazes met, her slow smile spread like honey, beckoning him closer. Kai hesitated as Orion's warning vibrated through his chest.

"She's trouble," the wolf growled.

"She's a force," Kai countered, though the words felt rehearsed.

He'd loved her since they were pups. Where others had scoffed at his ideas, Ava had always leaned closer, firing back questions and suggestions. As a survivor of a rogue attack that had decimated her birthpack, she understood the value of charting one's own path. Every vision became a shared blueprint, making fated bonds seem unnecessary when he'd already found his match in her.

At least, that was what he kept telling himself.

"*Strong, yes,*" Orion conceded. "*But not ours. She seeks her own power, not to build yours.*"

Kai crossed the room, shoving his wolf's doubts aside. Pack members straightened as he passed, their conversations dimming to whispers, chairs scraping as bodies shifted to make space, the subtle scent of submission and respect mingling with undercurrents of curiosity and assessment. Their attention never felt real—always tinged with obligation rather than genuine respect.

Ava, at least, never softened her edges. Her ambition matched his own, raw and unapologetic. That had to count for something.

"Off brooding again?" Ava's fingers trailed along his forearm as he sat beside her. Her perfume—floral and severe—overwhelmed the natural scents around them. "I swear, Kai, if you spent half as much time taking action as you do thinking, the pack would have already crowned you alpha."

"I'll take that under advisement." Kai claimed her beer and took a long drink, the bitter liquid cooling his heated thoughts.

Ava's smile widened, but something flickered behind her eyes that he couldn't quite read. She leaned closer, laughter like winter frost creeping across glass—beautiful but cold to the touch.

"*She smells of ambition and deceit,*" Orion rumbled. "*Her loyalty is to herself.*"

"Your ideas are bold and forward-thinking. You'll get there." Her voice dropped to a whisper as she traced circles on his arm, leaving goosebumps in their wake. "And when you do, I'll be right there beside you."

"*But will she be there* for *us?*" Orion pressed.

Kai nodded, acid rising at the back of his throat with each mechanical movement of his head. He needed to believe that Ava saw more than just a path to power in him. Years together, building a foundation brick by brick—surely that meant more than instant cosmic recognition. Yet doubt crept in when her smile felt practiced, when her touch felt more like a claim than a caress.

If I stumble, will Ava steady me—or will she search for another route to power?

As the evening wore on and Ava's commentary filled the room, Kai found himself drifting, memories overtaking him. His mother's voice, soft but certain: *"When you meet her—your fated—you'll understand what Selene intended for us all."* Even three years after her death, Althea's words haunted Kai. She and his father had embodied the perfect fated bond—their connection so profound it had sometimes made him feel like an outsider in their presence.

Despite the ambient noise of his surroundings, Kai couldn't silence the whispers of that memory or quell the persistent sense of disquiet it stirred in him. The familiar ache in his chest intensified—not quite emptiness, but something unsettled, unfinished.

The stories of fated mates were woven into the community's very existence, but Kai didn't want divine interference. He loved Ava. They'd crafted dreams together. Mapped a future. They were planning their mating ceremony for fall when they would seek Selene's blessing. The Goddess's approval of chosen bonds was rare, but Kai was certain She would recognize their genuine love and commitment to each other and the Bloodstone pack.

His mother's disappointed eyes flashed in his mind again. Her last words to him about Ava still burned: *"You're choosing a harder path than you need to, my love."* She'd never openly opposed them, but her gentle concern had sometimes cut deeper than Darius's outright disapproval.

"You can't outrun fate," Orion's voice was gentler now but tinged with longing.

Kai's hands clenched beneath the table, nails digging half-moons into his palms. His jaw tightened until he tasted the coppery tang of blood from where his teeth had caught the inside of his cheek, the sharp sting a welcome distraction from Orion's truth.

"Watch me," Kai replied.

CHAPTER FOUR

LENA

The crackling sound of the fire echoed through the quiet forest, its warm golden glow casting shifting shadows across Lena's face and the relaxed forms of Ryker and Jace seated on either side of her. Pine and wood smoke mingled with the earthy smell of damp soil and leaves, filling the air with a rich forest scent that clung to her skin and hair. Above the clearing, the trees creaked in the breeze. Their branches swayed like nature's own lullaby as cool night air carried whispers of the coming spring.

Lena's gaze fixed on the flames as she stretched her legs forward, thoughts wandering back to the discussion of mates. Her destined mate wasn't a son of Moonshadow—a bitter pill that had taken years to swallow—and the thought of leaving home made her chest tight. Regardless of Elara's protests, choosing a mate who would keep her in Moonshadow didn't seem so unappealing.

Her gaze drifted over to the pack's training grounds, now empty in the gathering dark except for memories of countless sparring matches and training sessions. She could almost see the warriors there still—their broad shoulders and lean builds, the way they moved with deadly grace. She'd fought alongside them enough to appreciate more than just their combat skills. Bonding with one of them—having a strong mate who would fight *beside* her, not just *for* her—wasn't the worst future she could imagine. At least then she'd know exactly what she was choosing, instead of waiting for fate to decide.

Her mind settled on Ryker and Jace next. The two constants in her life alongside Cian. They'd grown up together, training and causing trouble in equal measure.

But as mates?

Heat bloomed beneath Lena's skin, prickling outward until her cheeks burned. Her pulse quickened at the thought of them, that familiar tug beneath her ribs whenever they laughed or touched her. She'd yearned to mate with them when they were younger, but would choosing either of them now fracture what they've built? Was it selfish to want to maintain something already so perfect?

"You're awfully quiet tonight." Jace lounged against a log, poking idly at the fire with a stick. Firelight danced across his features, making his rust-colored hair look like living flame against fair skin. He looked both ruggedly handsome and boyishly charming even in repose. "What's on your mind, Thing 1?"

Lena rolled her eyes at the familiar nickname. "Just thinking." But she knew better than to expect that would satisfy him.

"About what?" Ryker shifted closer, wearing that particular expression that meant he wouldn't let go until he had something to gossip about.

She tucked a strand of hair behind her ear, weighing her words. "I talked to my dad today. I'll be attending the Summit this year...with Cian."

Ryker shot to his feet. "No way! That's awesome! You're going to love it. The meetings are boring as hell, but the parties are incredible! You'll get to meet wolves from all over the region. And Cian and I can show you around. Trust me, it'll be great." He bounced on his toes, practically vibrating with possibility. "Oh! And if Alpha's not coming, I might finally get in on some of that orgy action everyone always whispers about!"

Jace groaned, throwing his head back with a mock-suffering sigh. "Fantastic. Ryker gets to live his best degenerate life while I'm stuck here holding down the fort." His grin undermined his complaint.

"Someone has to keep the pack running while we're gone." Lena's lips quirked into a smile. "Who better than the future gamma?"

Jace sat up, tossing his stick into the fire with theatrical flair. "It's a travesty, really. Gammas get no respect. We're the backbone of the pack—training warriors, organizing patrols, keeping everything from falling apart." He spread his hands wide in exasperation. "And what do we get? No invitations to summits, that's what. There should be a summit just for us."

Lena and Ryker burst out laughing, and even Jace cracked a smile.

"Don't worry." Ryker clapped Jace on the shoulder. "We'll bring you back a souvenir. Maybe a nice 'World's Best Gamma' mug."

"Gee, thanks." The corners of Jace's mouth twitched despite his flat tone.

Their laughter rang through the clearing, but Lena's smile faded as she gathered her courage.

"There's more," she continued, voice softening. "Dad...said that if I didn't find my mate at this year's summit, I could choose a bond. Maybe with someone in the pack."

Jace's eyebrow shot up. Ryker, however, looked like he'd just swallowed silver.

"Like who?" Jace asked, leaning forward.

"He said there are plenty of warriors who'd make excellent mates, but he also mentioned..." She glanced between them meaningfully.

Ryker's jaw dropped with dawning horror. "Oh, no. No, no, no. He didn't."

"He did." Lena bit back a smile. "He suggested I could consider pursuing the chosen mate blessing with one of you—if none of us found our fateds, of course."

Ryker dragged a hand down his face. "I can't believe this. My dad is probably in on it too. They've been plotting our arranged marriage behind my back."

"Relax," Lena said with a laugh. "It's just an option. And honestly, you should be flattered. My dad thinks you're good enough for me, and you know I would be a kickass beta-female."

"Flattered?" Ryker's eyes bulged comically. "Lena, I love you. But as a mate? No offense, I'd rather be shackled in silver and sent to wrestle a rogue." His grin turned wicked. "Or have you forgotten the Incident?"

Lena groaned, burying her burning face in her hands. "Goddess, don't remind me. I had a complex for years about how you laughed at my lopsided nipples!"

Ryker doubled over cackling as Jace smirked, clearly enjoying her mortification.

"Hey," Ryker gasped, "I wasn't laughing at you. I was laughing at the logistics. I mean, how were we supposed to—"

"Do. Not. Start!" Lena snapped, but the memory flooded back anyway.

Lena had been breathless, flushed with excitement, adrenaline singing in her veins following their run. The scent of pine and damp earth clung to the three of them, mingling with something headier—the raw musk of pheromones thick in the air, a primal undertone that set her skin ablaze.

*She'd drank in Ryker and Jace, seeing them—*really *seeing them—their naked bodies a novelty, a secret treasure she was privileged to behold. She'd been mesmerized by their lean muscles. How sweat trailed down their skin like rivulets of moonlight. How their chests heaved with ragged breaths. By the obvious arousal hanging thick and heavy between their legs.*

Lena was so convinced that Selene had destined her for both of them. Elara had stalked beneath her skin that night, whining with anticipation, almost frantic with the need to claim what she'd believed was theirs.

At sixteen, she and Ryker had recently received their wolves, while Jace was nearly eighteen—the age when fated bonds were revealed. Lena couldn't fathom waiting two more agonizing years for fate to confirm what she already knew in her heart. That they were meant to share her, to claim her, to be hers.

She'd been shocked by her own boldness. One second: marveling at their sweat-drenched bodies. The next: grabbing their wrists, dragging them toward the packhouse and into her suite like a female possessed. "We're going to fuck," she'd declared with awkward determination, voice cracking on the last word.

The scene had been chaotic—overly aggressive kisses, her clumsy hands struggling around Ryker's erection, and Jace's inexperienced mouth fumbling between her thighs. Ryker couldn't stop laughing—about her nipples, about the way Jace's cock curved slightly left, about how the mechanics would even work.

Jace, however, had been fully committed. His pupils blown wide, cock engorged and dripping pre-cum as he took charge. "Ryker, lie down," he'd ordered. "Lena, you on top."

She straddled Ryker, back to Jace, but he'd halted her with a hand on her hip. "No, keep your back to him."

Lena frowned. "Why?"

Jace cleared his throat. "So, he doesn't have to, um...stare directly at your—uh..." He gestured vaguely. "Very... assertive *nipples."*

"Oh, come on, Jace." Ryker snorted.

"I swear to Selene, I will murder you both," Lena growled, though the fire in her cheeks made her threat less intimidating.

What followed could only be described as a train wreck. Limbs tangled, angles misjudged, and at one point, Lena's knee ended up somewhere that had Ryker letting out a strangled yelp and curling into the fetal position.

Just as they were both positioned at her entrance and started arguing about whether to thrust at the same time or take turns, the door slammed open so hard the windows rattled.

"What in Selene's name is going on here?" Cian's roar nearly took the roof off.

Lena screamed, scrambling for a blanket. Jace fell off the bed in his haste to not be there anymore. Ryker, who had been mid-laugh at Jace's misfortune, choked on his own breath upon meeting Cian's gaze and flailed, knocking over a lamp.

"Cian—get out!" Lena shrieked, dignity already in tatters.

"What the actual fuck are you doing?" Cian's face was a storm cloud, golden eyes ablaze with disbelief, rage, and what looked suspiciously like deep psychological distress. "Are you—are you trying to run a fucking train? On my *sister?"*

Lena groaned, pulling the blanket over her head. "This is the worst night of my life."

Ryker, ever the peacemaker, held up a hand from where he was half-draped off the bed. "For the record, we never got that far. We're still sorting out the uh...technical difficulties."

Jace, still on the floor, covered his face. "Kill me. Just kill me now."

Lena pulled herself from the memory, firelight dancing at the edges of her vision. The aftermath of the Incident had been...interesting. Lena's emotions had been a tangled mess of anger and mortification. She'd been furious with Cian for bursting in—for stealing what she'd believed was rightfully hers—but her anger had crumbled when she saw his face, looking every bit as mortified as she felt.

Ryker, shameless as ever, had brushed off the entire ordeal with his usual nonchalance. He'd laughed and joked—especially about her nipples: *"They're like a little team. One's just a little more ambitious than the other! It's inspiring."* Lena had been grateful for his efforts to diffuse the tension.

Jace, however... Something had shifted between them. Until she turned eighteen and they'd realized they weren't fated, an unspoken tension had lingered, a spark of attraction that had never quite fizzled out. Even now, Lena couldn't help but wonder what might have been if Cian hadn't interrupted them. If they'd been given the chance to explore the desire that had simmered between them.

Yes, the night had been a disaster, but also a turning point. She'd been trying to force destiny's hand, to reshape their friendship into something it wasn't meant to be. What they had now—this unshakeable bond that didn't require fate's blessing—was too precious to risk.

Jace cleared his throat, breaking her thoughts.

"Look, Lena. I know Ryker's an obvious choice—alpha-smart, beta-strong, blah, blah, blah... But don't sleep on your other option." He waggled his eyebrows with a wicked grin. "Sleep *with* me instead." He leaned forward, purring into her ear as he added, "The only thing better than raising our smart, diplomatic, and gorgeous pups would be *making* them. And trust me, you're going to *love* making them."

Lena barked a laugh, scooping up a pinecone and chucking it at his head. "Goddess, you're impossible!"

Jace dodged it with ease, catching the pinecone mid-air and tossing it aside. "I'm just saying," he continued, grin widening into something entirely too smug, "don't close the door on greatness, darling." His voice softened, teasing giving way to sincerity. "Seriously, though. You're going to be fine, Lena. Whether or not you find your mate, you'll make the right choice. And we've got your back, no matter what."

Lena shook her head, laughing despite herself. The earlier tension melted away, replaced by the warmth of their friendship. Ryker grinned, recovered from his mock horror, while Jace watched her with that steady certainty that always made things better.

They sat in comfortable silence as the fire burned low and night deepened around them. Their pack bond embraced them like the forest itself—strong, unspoken, and as natural as breathing. The future might be uncertain, but with these two and Cian at her side, Lena knew she'd never truly be lost.

Some bonds, she realized, were stronger than fate itself.

CHAPTER FIVE

KAI

Morning sunlight streamed through the windows of Darius's study, casting long shadows across the massive dark oak desk, worn smooth by generations of alphas who'd sat in this very room. The scent of books and polished wood permeated the air.

Kai watched his father review the stack of papers before him, noting how the silver threading through Darius's dark hair caught the light. Even in a simple cable-knit sweater, his father cut an imposing figure. Broad-shouldered and stern. Those distinctive Bloodstone green eyes, penetrating as ever, beneath strong brows. The creases framing his mouth deepened when he spoke, geography carved by decades of unquestioned commands. Lesser wolves still averted their gaze when those lines appeared.

"The annual summit is in a week." Darius's deep voice filled the room as he looked up from the papers, fixing Kai in his crosshairs.

Kai leaned back in his chair, the leather cool against his palms as he braced himself. "I know."

"You know," Darius repeated, voice edged with sarcasm. "But are you ready?"

Kai's shoulders locked into place, vertebrae stacking tight. "Of course I'm ready. I've attended every year since I was fifteen."

"Watching is not leading, Kai." Darius's words cut like steel. "This time, you won't just stand behind me. You'll speak."

"Speak?" Kai blinked, surprised. "What do you mean?"

His father set the papers down, folding his hands with deliberate precision. "Some of the regional alphas have decided to let their heirs take part as surrogates to prepare for their pending alpha ceremonies. Given our pack's proximity to the rising rogue threat, I must still attend, but you'll present our position on the northern border dispute. The abandoned Denali lands have become a point of contention. The alphas from Ironclaw and Redridge will be there to assert their claims. You'll argue for our interests."

Kai's heartbeat thundered against his ribs. This was his chance—to prove himself, to step out of his father's shadow—but the suddenness of it left his fingertips tingling, the taste of metal sharp on his tongue. "You trust me to handle this?"

"Trust is earned, Kai." Darius's eyes narrowed. "You think you're ready to lead this pack? Show me you understand the intricacies of regional politics, how to balance our hold and influence with the greater needs of our community. Prove that it's your time."

Kai met his father's gaze, determination hardening his spine. Orion's pride surged through their bond. "I will."

"Good." Darius crossed his arms. "Don't embarrass me."

A heavy pause filled the room before Darius continued, his expression unreadable. "There's one other thing you should know. Some packs are sending their unmated females this year."

Kai's stomach twisted. "Why?"

Darius's lips curled into a humorless smile. "The Collective wants to acknowledge the changing demographics in our community. They hope the she-wolves will learn from the lunas and beta-females in attendance and perhaps even find their mates." He fixed Kai with a steady look. "I think this may be a chance for you to find your fated as well."

"I don't want a fated mate," Kai said, the words worn smooth with repetition. "I want Ava. I trust Selene will bless our chosen bond because Ava is the only one I will ever love."

His father's alpha aura filled the room like a gathering storm. "I know what you want, but the pack needs strength. A bond with your fated mate will bring you into your power and could solidify alliances we need." He pounded a clenched fist on the desk. "The region faces tenuous times. The rogue attacks keep increasing and growing more vicious. Or have you forgotten how Ava came to join our pack to begin with?"

Kai's jaw tightened as Orion growled inside him. *"Fate again,"* his wolf muttered.

The stern lines of Darius's face softened. His shoulders slumped as he rubbed at his temples. "Look, I know you care deeply for Ava, but I'm not convinced she cares just as deeply for you." His father's voice carried the force of Bloodstone legacy. "I don't want to see you forsake your destiny and the vitality of the pack for someone who's not meant for you."

Kai rose, but Darius held up a hand, expression softening even further into something almost painful to witness. "My heart breaks for the loss Ava endured at such a young age."

The rare expression of vulnerability drained the resistance from Kai's limbs as he sank back into his chair.

"Yes, she is beautiful and smart." Darius's fingers drummed once against the ancient desk. "She has a strong will that would make for a fortuitous luna, but..." He leaned forward, voice dropping to barely above a whisper. "I sense she aspires to be Luna of Bloodstone more than she wants to be *yours*."

Kai remained silent, teeth grinding against the accusation. A bitter taste spread across his tongue as he fought to keep his breaths even.

Darius sighed. "The pack's future is my priority, but as your father, so is your happiness. As we've discussed, I will pass the alpha title to you on the equinox after your twenty-fifth birthday. If you haven't found your fated mate by then, I'll support your decision to seek the chosen bond blessing with Ava."

Kai nodded and surged to his feet. "I'll prepare for the summit."

"See that you do."

The study door slammed behind Kai with a satisfying bang that echoed down the hallway. Frustration simmered beneath his skin, threatening to boil over. This was supposed to be his moment—finally, a chance to prove himself. Yet his father's words about fated mates stuck like thorns in his mind.

Orion growled softly. *"You don't choose fate, Kai. She* does.*"*

"Don't start," Kai shot back, pinching the bridge of his nose.

Ava's laugh reached him before he saw her—sharp and confident, cutting through the air like a blade. She lounged in the main sitting room, surrounded by warriors eager for her attention. A familiar twinge of possessiveness tightened Kai's throat, even as Orion's disapproval prickled along his spine.

Her platinum-blonde hair cascaded like liquid moonlight over her shoulders, framing features as calculated as they were beautiful. The moment Kai entered, her pale blue eyes—cold and mesmerizing as arctic ice—snapped to his. The warriors scattered like leaves in a storm.

"There's my future alpha," she purred, rising with fluid grace. Every detail was seductive, from the black sweater hugging every curve to the way she'd painted her lips that signature blood-red—a color as bold as her ambition—to the slight sway of her hips as she approached. She moved like a predator stalking prey, the scent of her floral perfume intensifying with each step.

Kai didn't stop walking, but she fell into step beside him, fingers ghosting along his arm.

"Rough morning with the old man?" Ava gave his hand a gentle squeeze.

"Something like that."

Ava studied him. "You're tense. What did he say?"

Kai stopped at the back door, one hand braced against the frame. "He wants me to argue our position on the northern borders at the summit."

Ava's perfectly sculpted brow arched. "About time. Your mind for strategy is unmatched. Darius is finally recognizing what I've always seen in you."

"That's the easy part," he muttered. "The hard part was hearing him go on about fated mates again. He thinks I'll find her at the summit—that somehow my 'perfect bond' will be found in the middle of a parade of the regional alphas' unmated daughters."

Something flickered in Ava's expression as she tilted her head. "You know, the idea of fated mates...it's beautiful, in a way. A perfect bond, created by Selene Herself." Her voice wavered—a crack in her perfect façade that tightened his chest. "But it's also terrifying, isn't it? What if fate doesn't care about what *we've* built, about what *we've* fought for? What if it pulls *us* apart?"

"That won't happen. You're the one I want."

The hard light in her eyes dimmed, a sheen of moisture catching the light as her fingertip traveled the edge of his jaw, hesitating at the corner of his mouth. "I know, Kai, but fate... It doesn't play fair. Promise me you'll fight for us, no matter what." The edge in her voice made the hairs at the back of his neck rise.

"I promise." He caught her hand and pressed a kiss into her palm.

"So, what did you tell him?" Her thumb brushed across his knuckles before she let go.

"The same thing I always tell him." Kai's huffed. "That I've made my choice, and I trust Selene will bless our bond."

Ava's smile crept across her face, confidence radiating in her voice, though something about it made Orion seethe. Her hand pressed against his chest. "Exactly. We've built something stronger than chance, Kai." Her fingers danced across his collarbone. "Selene will see us for what we are: a strong match. An unshakable luna and her alpha. When the other packs see us together—see how we compliment each other's strengths—they'll understand why Bloodstone will thrive under your leadership."

Orion rumbled dissent, but Kai focused on Ava's touch.

"I'll prove myself, and in turn, prove to my father that you're the right choice," he said with quiet determination. "I'll show everyone I don't need some predestined bond to secure my future."

Kai started to tell her that Darius had promised to support their chosen mating if he remained unmated when he took his alpha oaths, but something stopped the words in his throat. A nameless hesitation, a shadow of doubt that flickered at the edges of his certainty. His wolf stirred restlessly beneath his skin, as if sensing the unspoken truth: part of him hungered for that wholeness his parents had shared, the completion that supposedly came only when joined with the soul Selene had crafted specially for his own.

"We'll show them," he said instead, the promise feeling both true and somehow hollow in the same breath.

"That's my future alpha," she cooed. Her smile widened as she rose on her toes, brushing her lips against his jawline—the touch tender yet somehow distant.

"She doesn't love you." Pain and protectiveness bled through Orion's snarl. *"You deserve someone who does."*

Kai stiffened, pulling back slightly, his wolf's words cutting deep.

Ava pulled back, searching his face with an intensity that made him want to look away. "Don't let him distract you," she murmured. "You've already proven yourself—the warriors respect you, the pack will prosper under your oversight, and you've never backed down from a challenge. Darius wants you to follow *his* path, but we're better than that. *You're* better than that."

Kai nodded, though doubt churned in his gut. Orion's disapproval continued to rattle through his bones, making Kai's teeth ache as if storm pressure had settled in his jaw.

"I need to get ready for training," he said, pulling away.

Ava's gaze lingered. "Don't let your father get in your head. You already know what you want."

Kai didn't respond. Instead, he pushed through the door. The cool air hit him like a slap, raising goosebumps along his arms as he strode toward the training grounds, his wolf restless beneath his skin.

"She isn't yours," Orion insisted.

"She will be," Kai answered, each step dogged. *"I'll make sure of it."*

CHAPTER SIX

CALEB

The morning air bit at Caleb's skin as he descended the hill, breaths steady and controlled from his early run. The rising sun caught in his chestnut waves, turning them golden at the edges and highlighting the powerful line of his jaw. Even at twenty-eight, he carried himself with the natural grace of a seasoned alpha. His broad shoulders and athletic build spoke to the legacy of his bloodline and years of training. Yet his hazel eyes held more thoughtfulness than most would expect from a young leader.

He slowed his pace as Erik's cottage came into view. Anxiety crept into his chest as he wiped sweat from his brow. Fenrir tramped circuits behind Caleb's ribs. Each loop sent ripples of awareness down his spine, vibrating through bone and sinew.

The cottage stood like a guardian at the edge of the main village. Centuries of moss and ivy softened its weathered stone walls. Smoke curled lazily from the chimney, carrying the familiar scent of Erik's morning tea—chamomile and something older, earthier. Caleb's hand hesitated over the carved wolf-head knocker. He blew out a breath and rapped twice.

"Come in." Erik's gravelly voice carried through the door, rich with decades of stories waiting to be told.

Caleb stepped into the warm cottage, drinking in the space that had always felt like stepping into Crescent Fang's living memory. Carvings of wolves adorned the mantle while shelves groaned under the weight of ancient books. A tapestry depicting Selene's blessing of the first wolves hung above the fireplace, its colors faded but its power undimmed. The air carried the subtle mix of aged wood, dried herbs, and dying embers that Caleb had always associated with Erik's counsel.

"Alpha." Erik rose from his chair with a smile that softened his time-worn features. Though the years had carved deep lines into his olive skin, pack members still straightened when he entered a room, a habit left from decades ago when he'd served as Caleb's grandfather's gamma. Now Erik watched Caleb carefully as he gestured to the waiting chair. "You're early."

A steaming cup of tea waited on the small table between them, its herbal aroma mixing with the cottage's familiar scents.

"Morning run was quicker than I expected," Caleb said, clasping Erik's extended hand. "I wanted to make sure we had enough time."

Erik chuckled as he lowered himself back into his chair. "I'd expect no less. You've always been thorough." He studied Caleb with a mixture of fondness and scrutiny that made hiding anything impossible. "You're nervous," he said.

Caleb's fingers drummed against his thigh before he stilled them. "I am. Fenrir's been...vocal. He doesn't think we should go."

"And what do you think?" Erik asked.

"I think..." Caleb's gaze fixed on the tapestry of Selene. "Fenrir's right to want to protect Crescent Fang. We're one of the last packs whose hierarchy directly descends from the first wolves." His fingers brushed absently over his chest. There, his bond with Asher pulsed steady and warm. "But Asher sees beyond our isolation. He believes these challenges—the rogues, the unrest—are signs the wolves need to return to grace. Asher thinks this summit is a chance for us to reclaim our place. To remind the Collective of Selene's gifts and what it truly means to be Her children. To show them She hasn't abandoned us."

The mention of his lover brought a wistful smile to his face, even as his thoughts tangled around their differing views. When Asher spoke, Caleb found himself leaning closer, not just as alpha to beta, but as a male drawn to the one who knew the shape of his nightmares and still believed in his strength each morning.

"And where do you fall between their views?" Erik asked, with a knowing grin.

"That's the problem. I don't know." His voice wavered, the weakness in his tone surprising him. "I trust Fenrir's instincts, but Asher has a way of making me see beyond my wolf's protective nature. He makes me wonder if there's more to gain than lose, reminding me that sometimes the greatest act of preservation is evolution."

Erik nodded, gaze growing distant as if watching memories play out. "You're not the first Crescent Fang alpha to wrestle with this. Your grandfather, Odin, faced a similar choice."

"When Crescent Fang withdrew from the Collective?"

"Yes." Erik's shoulders squared with pride even as lines of old pain shadowed his face. He reached for his tea, the steam curling between them like the threads of history itself. "Odin saw what the Collective was becoming—leaders more interested in amassing power than fostering community. He couldn't stomach the betrayal of Selene's teachings, the greed and ambition that poisoned the Summit halls. So, he pulled Crescent Fang away, to protect what mattered most."

"And it cost us our place," Caleb said tightly.

"It preserved our soul." Erik's eyes blazed with intensity, voice ringing through the cottage like a struck ceremonial bell.

Fenrir surged forward, the wolf's fierce pride in their lineage momentarily overwhelming Caleb's doubts.

"Make no mistake, Caleb. When the other packs abandoned Selene's teachings, it was *our* withdrawal that kept the true spirit of Her blessing alive." Erik's battle-scarred hand closed into a fist on the table. "Our isolation wasn't just a choice. It was salvation. The last bastion of what it truly means to be Selene's children."

Erik closed his eyes for a moment, hands clasping together as he gathered himself. When he spoke again, his voice had softened to barely above a whisper. "But yes, the cost was great. Over time, the world forgot what Crescent Fang stood for. Our wisdom became myth, our strength overlooked."

Caleb leaned forward, hands gripping the edge of the ancient table. "If my grandfather was right to withdraw, why should we go back now?"

A soft chuckle escaped Erik as he gestured toward the tapestry. "Perhaps Fenrir's right, and we shouldn't." His expression sobered.

"This isn't a decision for you alone, young Alpha. The elders have shepherded Crescent Fang's isolation for generations. Many will question whether you—still establishing your authority among them—should be the one to potentially reverse Odin's legacy."

Fenrir bristled at the implied challenge, a low growl building in Caleb's throat before he swallowed it back.

"The council has allowed you latitude in small matters, but this decision...it touches our very foundation." Erik's voice took on the measured cadence of ancient ritual. "But there's another perspective to consider. There's a belief, long held in Crescent Fang, that Selene's retreat wasn't abandonment. It was preservation."

"Preservation?"

Erik spoke with absolute conviction. "She withdrew to conserve Her strength, to prepare for a time when Her children would need Her most. A time when Her light would guide them home." He straightened, chest out, chin lifted. "Some believe that time is drawing near." The scent of cedar and old leather filled the silence that followed, while Erik's fingers drummed once—deliberately—against the worn wood of the table.

"I'm not the light," Caleb blurted, shaking his head.

"No," Erik agreed, a quiet snort softening his words. "But perhaps Fenrir's rebirth and participation at the Summit is the beginning of something greater. A spark." Erik relaxed in his chair, tone shifting to something more practical. "For now, your task isn't to decide the Collective's fate. It's to learn. Observe. Let them see Crescent Fang's strength and faith, not through force, but through presence."

The tension eased from Caleb's posture. This, at least, felt achievable.

Steam rose between them, carrying the earthy scent of herbs that tickled Caleb's nose as Erik continued, "Answer their questions honestly, but don't overcommit. Leave doors open, but make no promises." His tone grew firm. "And whatever you do, don't let their doubts shake your foundation. We know who we are, Caleb. Show them."

Caleb felt his wolf's approval rumble through his chest. His chin lifted, pride in his pack's heritage straightening his spine.

The shifting sunlight sent shadows dancing across the walls as Erik's expression grew thoughtful. Caleb leaned forward in his chair, recognizing the shift in his mentor's demeanor that always preceded his most valuable insights.

"The packs you'll meet... They're like threads in a tapestry, each one distinct yet part of a greater whole. Some you may recognize; others may surprise you." Erik reached for an old leather-bound book, its pages yellowed with age. "Take Blackwater, for instance. They're scholars at heart." A fond smile crossed his face. "In my day, they traded in knowledge like currency, listening more than they spoke. If you want insight into the archives, they're the ones to seek."

Caleb nodded, mentally cataloging the information.

"Then there's Redridge," he went on, a soft smile forming. "They were new to the Collective at the time—smaller, but unique. Their alpha and beta shared a mate—a fated trio." He chuckled at Caleb's raised eyebrows. "It raised quite a few eyebrows back then too, but Odin recognized their bond for what it was. Genuine."

A fated trio? Hope swelled in Caleb's chest at the possibility that Selene could bless him and Asher with a similar fate.

Erik's hand brushed over the book's worn cover. "Moonshadow was always known for its balance—walking the line between progress and tradition better than most. They blended modern innovation with devotion to Selene." His expression grew serious. "If you encounter them, you'll find wisdom there—but don't mistake their humility for weakness."

Fenrir's ears perked beneath Caleb's skin, snapping to attention. "You speak of them with respect."

"I do." Erik nodded earnestly. "Not every pack upheld Selene's values, though. Ironclaw..." He shook his head. "They were never satisfied with what they had—always seeking more land, more power, more recognition. Their ambition made them dangerous, even among allies."

"And our neighbors... Bloodstone?" Caleb asked, the cottage's warmth evaporating as a chill crept up his spine at the mention of their powerful neighbors.

"Ah." Erik's face sharpened with memory. "Rahoul, Darius's father, was a force of nature. His will was like a storm, driven by instincts he believed were Selene's whispers. His influence in the Collective was immense, and his pack reflected that strength."

He set the book aside and picked up his cup, draining the last drops before placing it down with the same careful precision he'd shown throughout their conversation. "Remember these dynamics, Caleb. They may have changed in your time, but history often repeats itself. Learn from them, but trust your instincts."

"And reintegration?" Caleb pressed. His wolf twitched with interest beneath his skin.

Erik's hand found Caleb's shoulder. His touch carried the wisdom of generations. "That's not a decision to make lightly. It's also not just yours. Heed Fenrir's warnings, listen to Asher's hope, consult with the council, and take your time, Alpha."

Fenrir's assent rumbled from the base of Caleb's skull down his spine. *"We go. We learn. We plan."*

"Listen to your wolf, your beta, and your heart," Erik reaffirmed, easing from his chair. "The three together will never steer you wrong."

Caleb stood, earlier nerves tempered by the elder's wisdom. "Thank you, Erik. For everything."

"Go well, Alpha." Pride warmed Erik's voice. "You will be tested, but you're ready."

The air felt different as Caleb stepped outside. The crisp chill no longer bit as harshly. His gaze swept over the familiar landscape. Uncertainty lay ahead, but a spark of purpose had kindled. He would face whatever the Summit held with faith, strength, and the unwavering support of those who believed in him.

CHAPTER SEVEN

KAI

The morning light painted Kai's suite in gold, but it was Ava's scent that drew him from sleep. The floral perfume she favored masked her natural fragrance. Curated. Just like so many things about her lately.

Her warm, bare skin pressed against his as her lips traced his neck with the kind of precision that came from years of their practiced intimacy. Her teeth grazed his pulse point as her hands mapped his chest.

"Good morning, my future Alpha," she purred against his throat. The title felt more like a claim than an endearment. She pushed closer, soft curves molding to hard planes. "I'm going to miss you, you know." Her teeth caught his earlobe, and the groan she drew from him felt like both pleasure and capitulation.

Kai opened his eyes, body already responding to her touch even in his sleepy haze. She'd been spending the night in his suite more and more as his birthday drew closer. Practicing. Preparing for the time where his bed would become their mating bed. She was especially enthusiastic last night, taking his mind off the Summit with her supple mouth and soft hands.

He knew he should rise, get ready to join his father for the journey to the lodge, but surely there was time for more of her.

Gripping her hips, Kai pulled her astride him and met her gaze. Her blue eyes shimmered with what looked like tears, but years in her orbit had taught him better. He'd never seen Ava cry without there being something she wanted.

She tucked her chin, hiding behind a curtain of soft blonde curls. He'd seen this exact pose before. The same vulnerable, subservient look she'd used during tense run-ins with his father over the years.

"What am I going to do without you for three whole days?" Her words dripped honey-sweet sadness as her hips rolled with calculated purpose, rubbing her ass against his growing erection.

Beneath his skin, Orion's hackles rose. The wolf's discomfort rippled along Kai's spine like someone dragging claws down his back.

"What if you find her?" she whispered. "Your fated mate. What if she's at the summit, and you forget all about me?"

The words "fated mate" struck like a physical blow. Orion surged forward with such force that Kai's fingers dug into Ava's hips. His wolf longed for their destined mate with a yearning that constantly clashed with Kai's resolve. A battle they'd waged countless times.

Kai shoved Orion's reaction aside. Sitting up to cup Ava's face in his hands, he forced her to meet his gaze. "Ava, you know that won't happen. I've told you a thousand times—I have no interest in pursuing a fated bond. I want you. *Only* you."

Her lips curved into a satisfied smile, though the glimmer of tears remained. "You mean that?"

"Of course I do." Kai's tone left no room for doubt as he brushed her hair back. His thumb traced her lower lip, watching her eyes darken at his touch. "You're the one for me, Ava. No one will change that. It is why I know Selene will bless our bond, because it's real. It's *ours*."

The words had barely left his mouth when Ava's entire demeanor shifted. The vulnerable, trembling female vanished, replaced by the fierce, unapologetic she-wolf he'd fallen for. The one who never backed down from a challenge. Who matched his own stubborn will with her own.

Her smile curved slow and predatory as she caught his wrist, pulling his thumb into her mouth. The wet heat of her tongue, the sharp scrape of teeth—it was a promise, and a threat wrapped into one.

Before he could react, she pressed him back into the bed with unmistakable intent. Her movements were liquid grace as she climbed his body with the assurance of a conqueror claiming spoils. Tangling her hands in his dark hair, she straddled his face, gazing down at him, ice-blue eyes blazing with lust.

"Good." Her voice was a commanding purr as she guided his mouth where she wanted it. "Then take a taste to remember me by."

Something primal ignited in Kai at her command—or perhaps at the challenge in her eyes. He wrapped his muscular arms around her thighs, spreading her wider as he pulled her flush against his mouth. The first taste of her electrified his nervous system, her arousal warm and intoxicating on his tongue.

Orion growled deep in his mind, the wolf's presence like waves battering against a cliff. *"This is wrong,"* he snarled, voice sharp and guttural. *"You give what should belong only to our mate!"*

But Ava's pleasure was a symphony Kai couldn't resist conducting. He took his time as he dragged his tongue through her pussy, savoring each tremor that ran through her body. Her thighs tensed against his cheeks as he flicked his tongue over her clit, alternating between feather-light strokes and firm pressure that made her gasp his name. The scent of her arousal clouded his thoughts until his wolf's protests became mere whispers against the storm of sensation.

"That's it, Kai." Her voice hitched as she ground against his mouth, hands tightening in his hair. The sharp pull sent sparks of pleasure-pain down his spine. "Just like that."

His erection bordered on painful, cock throbbing with each sound she made. Every gasp, every shudder drove him higher, made him want to prove something—to her, to himself, to fate itself.

"Goddess, Kai..." Ava's voice broke as she rocked against his face. "Don't stop."

The taste of her, the sound of her, the way her body trembled—it spoke to a feral need in Kai that even Orion couldn't fully deny. His hips ground involuntarily against the sheets, seeking relief. The friction was maddening, but not enough. *Never enough.* Years of toeing the line without ever fully crossing it had taught Kai exquisite control, but also left him with an ache that grew deeper with every intimate moment he shared with Ava.

He groaned against her core, the vibration making her shudder. His fingers found her clit as he licked and sucked with renewed intensity, urging her closer to the finish line. Ava's walls began to flutter around his tongue, hips jerking as the first waves of her climax built.

Coming into his sheets, Kai thrust his tongue deeper, coaxing her into her orgasm as he stroked her clit with precise, deliberate pressure. Her cries echoed off the walls—his name tangled with broken moans that triggered fresh waves of arousal through him. His free hand traced circles on the small of her back, grounding her as she fell through her release.

When she finally came down, quivering thighs braced against his head, Kai licked through her slit, savoring every drop. He pressed a final kiss to her clit before pulling back, face slick with her arousal. Ava collapsed beside him, chest heaving, a contented smile playing on her lips. The same smile she'd worn the first time he'd tasted her when they were young and sure they could defy destiny together.

Seven years. The thought came uninvited as he wiped his mouth and stared at the ceiling, the familiar cracks mapping their history together. Seven years of memorizing where to touch, how hard to press, when to stop—his body conditioned to approach the edge but never fall.

Kai's pulse spiked as he imagined finally claiming her, feeling her walls grip his cock instead of his fingers. The recurring fantasy was vivid: Ava's body welcoming him, taking him deep, sinking his fangs into her neck as their chosen bond blazed to life under Selene's blessing.

Orion's presence plowed forward with such force that Kai's canines lengthened involuntarily, pressing against his bottom lip.

"She isn't ours." The wolf's voice scraped raw against the inside of his skull. *"You dishonor our mate every time you touch her. Every time you let her touch you!"*

Kai closed his eyes, the wolf's dismay twisting like a knife in his chest. He loved Ava, but deep down, he knew Orion was right. What he shared with her was meant for someone else. Someone he hadn't met. Someone Selene had chosen for him. Yet, he couldn't bring himself to stop.

Ava curled into his side, breath warm against his chest. Kai wrapped his arms around her, pulling her close.

She tilted her head up, lips brushing his jaw. "Goddess, Kai...your tongue is sinful. I can never get enough of you."

Her words shot straight to his cock, leaving him aching and desperate to have all of her. Orion's accusations still echoed in his mind, but they only fueled his need to prove his wolf wrong. Kai's blood surged hot beneath his skin, and his alpha power crackled through him as his restraint snapped.

"*Present*!" The command tore from his throat, raw with equal parts desire and defiance. He would make her his. Mark her in his own way. Silence every doubt with the evidence of their connection.

Ava scrambled to comply, pride flickering across her features. The same look she'd worn when he'd first stood up to his father, when she'd whispered *"That's my future alpha"* like she truly meant it.

She presented herself at the foot of the bed. Head bowed, shoulders pressed to the mattress, back arched beautifully, pussy on full display for him. Kai caught the slight tremor in her thighs, the way her breath hitched not with anticipation but with something that looked like desperation—maybe fear. These glimpses of genuine feelings made it so hard to walk away from her. Made him believe their love could be enough.

Her submissive posture stoked the primitive essence in Kai's blood. He moved behind her, large hands spreading her cheeks to reveal her still-swollen sex, glistening with evidence of his earlier attention. Her willing surrender—a power no birthright could bestow—sent heat rushing through his veins.

His cock throbbed as he wrapped his fingers around it, torn by the urge to slide inside her—to obliterate boundaries they'd promised not to cross until their mating ceremony—and claim her. Instead, he leaned forward to taste her again, letting her still-trickling release coat his tongue like a brand.

Each lick was a declaration of ownership. Each moan he drew from her ammunition against his doubts.

He alternated between fucking her with this tongue and rubbing his erection against her clit. Her arousal slicked his length as he stroked himself, his movements growing more frantic, more defiant.

With each push through his fist, Kai tried to shove everything away—the looming summit, his father's expectations. A hollow ache in his chest whispered of something missing, making every touch feel like both victory and betrayal. The harder he tried to lose himself in the sensation of rutting against Ava, the more aware he became of what wasn't there—some indefinable connection, some spark that should ignite but never quite caught fire.

Orion pushed forward one final time, the wolf's anguish manifesting as a physical ache behind Kai's sternum, a vacant territory that no amount of pleasure could fill.

"This is not the bond Selene chose for us!"

The truth scorched his lungs, each ragged breath tasting of smoke and ash, but Kai was already too far gone, vision narrowed to a pinpoint of desperate sensation.

His orgasm hit like a tidal wave, pleasure warring with guilt as he pressed the head of his cock at her entrance. His release painted her flesh in thick spurts. Marking her with his seed momentarily sated his possessive alpha nature—the same territorial instinct that drove wolves to mark their lands, their dens, their mates.

Unlike the clear boundaries of pack territories or claiming bites, this marking was temporary. As futile as trying to carve his name in water and watching it disappear even as he wrote it. The satisfaction was hollow, never quite reaching his core. Pleasure without fulfillment.

As Kai's body shuddered in the aftershocks of his climax, Orion's presence softened briefly, a whisper of compassion threading through their bond.

The wolf understood Kai's longing. His need to belong to someone, but that understanding only made Orion's grief more profound—a reminder that no matter how many times he marked Ava like this, she would never truly be his to claim without Selene's blessing.

Ava's ice-blue eyes found his over her shoulder, satisfaction mixing with something sharper, more cunning.

"Mmm, Kai." Her lips curved into a smile that claimed as much as it promised. "You always know how to make me feel..." She paused, letting her words land with the precision of a well-aimed arrow. "Loved."

The word struck something deep inside him, its echo bouncing off empty walls. Even as Ava pushed back against him, content and mollified, he found himself listening for another sound, searching for another scent. Someone whose face he didn't know but whose absence left phantom pains like a limb he'd never had but somehow lost.

He pressed a kiss to the small of Ava's back, lips resting against her damp skin. For now, he would let himself believe in this. For now, he would ignore the growing tempest inside him and pretend that Orion's current silence wasn't more damning than his previous protests.

When Kai slid into the sleek limo an hour later, the evidence of his morning still clung to him—Ava's perfume on his skin, her taste on his tongue, unfulfillment aching in his chest.

His father sat surrounded by papers like a king presiding over court, the car's interior thick with the scent of leather and aged whiskey. The stark formality felt like a deliberate rebuke to the hedonism of his morning, to everything he was trying so desperately to prove.

"You're late." Darius didn't look up from his papers, each syllable cutting like a blade.

Kai settled into the seat across from him, forcing his jaw to unclench. "I'm here, aren't I?" His hands curled into loose fists in his lap, an ingrained habit after years of swallowing his father's disapproval.

Darius's green eyes—so like Kai's own—flicked up, sharp and assessing. "You smell like distractions."

The criticism hung between them, thick as smoke, carrying layers of meaning: weakness, failure, a son primed to throw his destiny away.

Kai pressed his tongue against his teeth, grounding himself in the lingering taste of Ava. He said nothing, silence thickening the tense air between them. His father's displeasure was nothing new, but today it struck closer to the barren space behind his ribs—to the doubts he'd just tried to bury in Ava's body.

Darius slid a folder across the seat, movements as precise as his words. "Let's go over the northern territory dispute." His tone shifted to the one that had brokered many pack treaties. "The Summit isn't just about the usual politics this year. It's about setting the tone for your leadership."

He reached over as Kai opened the folder, tapping one long finger against a map of the now-abandoned Denali lands. Darius paused, studying Kai's face. "The rogue attacks have some packs making moves to secure stronger alliances, stronger bloodlines."

The emphasis wasn't subtle. Darius's finger moved from the map to a list of attending alphas and their unmated children. "This is your chance to certify Bloodstone's continued position as the most powerful pack in the region...if you play your cards right."

Kai reviewed the contents of the folder, forcing himself to focus on the maps and boundary lines instead of his father's expectations that pressed down on him like a physical force. Territory disputes he could handle. Those, at least, followed rules he understood.

"How do you feel?" Darius prodded. "Prepared?"

The question carried that familiar edge—asking one thing while demanding answers to a dozen others.

"I've got it under control." For once, Kai's confidence wasn't forced. "Redridge's claim is tenuous at best. They don't have the numbers to stretch into a larger territory, and they can barely staff patrols for their current borders. And Ironclaw—" He tapped the northern boundary line. "They're overextending themselves. They've already taken over two abandoned packlands. Pushing to grow at a rapid rate will only weaken them. Establishing a neutral zone is the only logical solution."

His father's eyes narrowed, but something like approval flickered in their depths. "Good analysis, but don't get overconfident." Darius's approval vanished, gone as fast as it formed. "Ironclaw's alpha is cunning, and like any young alpha trying to prove himself, he's desperate. He'll exploit any hesitation and try to use your position as an heir against you. I believe Thorne's trying to replicate the success your grandfather had growing Bloodstone's hold in the central part of the region. I think he sees the Denali massacre as an opportunity. More land, more resources. A chance to grow his pack through territory and make Ironclaw more attractive for...strategic alliances."

The implication was clear. Marriage alliances. Territory exchanges. The politics of power that had governed their kind for generations.

Kai straightened, meeting his father's gaze. "There won't be any hesitation."

A faint smile touched Darius's lips. "I'm counting on it." He gathered the maps, sliding them back into the folder with care. "Speaking of alliances..."

Kai's stomach contracted into a tight knot. Orion's restless pacing beneath his skin made his muscles twitch. "I've already told you—"

Darius's raised hand cut through his protest like an alpha command. "I know what you've said, but I'm not asking for your opinion on fated mates. I'm reminding you of your duty to this pack—to our bloodline. Every Bloodstone alpha since creation has led with their fated by their side, their combined strength blessed by Selene Herself."

Orion hummed contentedly at the mention of their Goddess while the memory of Kai's morning passion soured further with his father's disappointment.

Darius leaned forward, alpha aura pressing against Kai's skin like storm clouds heavy with lightning. Where their power met, the air crackled with generations of Bloodstone strength—everything Kai's incomplete aura could be.

"You feel it, don't you?" Darius urged. "The limitation in your power? That wall you can't break through? Until you claim your fated mate, you'll never unlock your full potential as an alpha."

The words were another strike to the void in Kai's chest that he'd desperately tried to fill with Ava and their hope for a chosen bond blessing. His fingers dug into his thighs as the truth settled like lead in his stomach.

"You'll attend every social function," Darius continued, bitterness edging his words. "You'll speak to every unmated female. And if she's there...you will find her. The pack needs more than territorial strength to weather what's coming."

A chill ran down Kai's spine at his father's tone. Images of what the Denali massacre must have looked like flashed through his mind. The rogue attacks were increasing, growing bolder, more rapid, and his father's expression held something he rarely showed—fear.

"Bloodstone will need their future alpha to be at full power, and that means an alpha bound to his true mate."

The implication of Darius's words felt like silver in Kai's veins, but he forced himself to nod. "Understood."

The limo slowed as they approached the lodge. The sprawling timber structure rose against snow-capped peaks like an altar to Selene Herself. The crisp mountain air flowing through the lowered window hit Kai's lungs like absolution, sharp and clean, washing away the lingering heat and perfumed intimacy of the morning. Each breath felt like stepping closer to something inevitable.

Kai took in the surroundings: the line of luxury vehicles filling the circular driveway, the pack banners snapping in the wind—each one a declaration of power, of bloodlines, of destiny. Dread settled in his stomach at the sight of females gathering near the entrance. Their laughter and chatter vibrated against his molars until he had to consciously unclench his jaw.

Inside him, Orion rose to the surface as unfamiliar scents teased his senses. His sudden alertness felt like another betrayal, but Kai couldn't deny the primal instinct to search—to hunt—for that one perfect scent that would call to both wolf and male. A mélange of fresh fragrances carried on the wind—jasmine, vanilla, wild roses—but none of them sparked that soul-deep recognition his wolf yearned for.

Not yet.

He reached for his phone, thumb hovering over Ava's name. Normally, he would call to let her know they'd arrived—to tell her again he would miss her and remind her of how much he loved her—but Darius's sharp look stopped him. His father's earlier words echoed in his mind: *"An alpha at full power...bound to his true mate."*

Kai shoved the phone back in his pocket as he exited the limo and steeled himself for whatever lay ahead.

This is going to be a long three days.

CHAPTER EIGHT

LENA

The sun warmed Lena's face, wind tugging at her hair as the Jeep rumbled along the winding forest road. She sat in the back seat, trying to enjoy the warming pre-spring breeze, but her stomach twisted into knots that tightened with each mile closer to the summit. Ahead, Ryker leaned his elbow out the window, sunglasses perched casually on his nose, while his father, Beta Aiden, drove with an air of calm authority. Her brother, Cian, sat beside her, his commanding presence filling the vehicle even in silence.

Lena's thoughts were a storm of contradictions as she stared out at the endless stretch of trees. *Find my mate and leave everything behind? Or stay and choose from my packmates—perhaps someone like Holden with his steady hands and kind heart? Either way, will I be valued, or merely tolerated?*

She glanced sideways at Cian, scrolling through his phone with the casual ease of someone who had his future perfectly planned. Being twins had once meant sharing everything. Same blood. Same strength. Same potential. While Selene had marked his path clearly, she'd left Lena's future as uncertain as a morning mist. The irony wasn't lost on her. They'd shared a womb, shared their first breaths, first steps, first shift. Yet at the age of twenty-four, fate had given them vastly different destinies.

"So." She hesitated. "What happens if I meet my mate? Would I have to leave Moonshadow right away?"

Cian looked up from his phone, his expression softening. "Not necessarily. Every bond is different, and every pack has its own traditions. The most important thing is that you and your mate will make sure you're where you're meant to be. If your mate is an heir or an elite warrior, you would likely join him, but who's to say he wouldn't join us? Moonshadow has always been your home, and it would take someone truly special to pull you away from it."

Lena nodded, though her fingers still drummed an anxious rhythm against her thigh. She'd always imagined finding her mate as something magical and perfect, but that was when she was convinced he would be from Moonshadow. Now, the idea of leaving everything she knew—her pack, her friends, her home—made her nauseous.

"And if I don't meet him?" She wasn't entirely sure which answer she preferred.

Cian's gaze softened further. "If you don't, that's fine too. This summit isn't just about mates; it's about forging connections. You'll meet potential allies and learn where Moonshadow truly stands in the hierarchy. There's strategic value in that knowledge, whether you find your fated mate or not."

Ryker, who had been quietly listening, turned his head back toward her. "And if you don't meet him, we get to mate instead. Lucky me," he quipped, flashing her a teasing grin.

"Not this again," Lena groaned. "Also, Dad offered me three options: a warrior, Jace, or you. What makes you think you're the first pick?"

"Hey, I'm pure perfection in wolf form," Ryker shot back with a lazy grin. "Not my fault Selene's still scouring the earth for someone worthy of all this." He gestured to himself with a sweeping motion. "If it comes to that our pups would be legendary—your stubbornness, my charm. Perfect beta-heirs." He tapped his temple like he'd solved a complex equation, then winked. "Besides, despite how The Incident turned out, don't forget how badly *you* wanted this." His eyebrows waggled suggestively as he patted his lap.

Lena smacked Ryker upside the head, fighting the smile that tugged at her lips. His joking always eased the tension she felt, even if the thought of mating still made her uneasy.

Beta Aiden snorted from the driver's seat. "You two are impossible," he muttered, though his tone was fond. "Ryker, focus on your beta training and making connections at the summit. You might find your own mate too, and then Lena will be spared your so-called perfection."

Ryker leaned back in his seat with a sigh. "Fine. But I've been thinking it's not the worst backup plan. Especially if it will mean that Lena gets to stay, because I'll be the next Moonshadow Beta."

Lena smiled at her best friend's desire to keep her close to home. She turned her attention back to the road ahead, nerves settling slightly as the Jeep climbed higher into the mountains. The scent of pine and wildflowers filled the air, and for a moment, she let herself imagine what the Summit might hold. Perhaps she would meet her mate. Perhaps not. Either way, she knew this journey was the beginning of something bigger than herself.

Hours later, that sense of standing on the edge of something momentous returned tenfold as the Jeep pulled into the lodge parking area. The sun dipped behind the mountains, casting long shadows across the grounds as Lena stepped out, stretching her legs and taking in the breathtaking view. Both she and Elara were alert to the thickness of power in the air. Her wolf prowled anxiously beneath the surface, pushing closer to her skin as if trying to taste the concentrated presence of so many pack leaders and their heirs directly on her tongue.

The grounds were massive—more than she'd imagined. Pack banners fluttered proudly in the wind, their colors vibrant against the clear blue sky. Each banner told a story—some ancient and proud, others newer but no less determined. Lena found herself wondering which one might someday be hers. The thought sent a pang through her chest even as Elara's curiosity pushed forward.

The lodge was an expansive structure, its wooden beams and stone accents blending with the wilderness. Black SUVs and luxury vehicles lined the parking lot. The scent of alpha auras hung heavy in the air, each unmistakable in their power, making Elara pace restlessly beneath Lena's skin, muscles twitching with each new dominant note.

Ryker whistled low. "They really outdid themselves this year." He swept his arm toward the lodge. "Look at this place. Do you think they'll roll out a red carpet next?"

Cian chuckled, grabbing his bag from the back. "Every summit is a chess match. The moves you make here will echo long after we return home."

Ryker snorted quietly. "And a chance for alphas to flex their muscles while betas do the real work of making alliances."

Lena glanced around, stomach fluttering with nerves as she noticed the subtle shifts in body language from nearby wolves. As an unmated female from a well-known pack, she drew attention—some curious, some calculating. Groups of unmated females gathered throughout the lobby, their designer clothes and careful makeup a stark contrast to Lena's practical traveling outfit. Some moved with the fluid grace of trained fighters, while others carried themselves with the polished poise of those groomed for leadership roles.

A few shot appraising looks her way. Lena caught fragments of their conversations about eligible heirs and alliance possibilities, their ambitions as sharp as their perfectly manicured nails. Moonshadow was respected, but here, surrounded by the gathered might of so many packs, she felt the precariousness of her position more keenly than ever. She gathered her belongings and fell in stride with Ryker, following Cian and Aiden toward the entrance.

Inside, the lodge buzzed with activity. Alphas, betas, elite warriors, and their families mingled in the grand lobby. The competing auras pressed against Lena's skin like static electricity, making the fine hairs on her arms stand on end. The scent of wood and pine mingled with the markers of different packs—cedar, rain, stone, forest—each staking their claim in the shared space. Elara catalogued each wolf, alert for...something. Something Lena wasn't ready to name.

Beta Aiden's voice rang out from the front, pointing to various packs as they passed. "That's the Blackwater pack—their alpha is a master strategist. And over there, the Ironclaw Pack, led by Alpha Thorne. He's not to be underestimated."

Lena's gaze flitted from group to group, noting how the dynamics shifted with each introduction. The Blackwater wolves stood tall and imposing, while the Ironclaw delegation exuded raw power, scanning the room like hunters sizing up prey.

Unmated males tracked her movement through the crowd, their interest making Elara prickle beneath her skin. Each new masculine scent made her wolf pause, assess, then dismiss—none carrying that spark of recognition she both yearned for and feared. Her grip on her bag tightened as she fought the urge to expose her neck, to let their scents wash over her.

Aiden continued to scan the crowd before turning to Cian. "The alpha and beta from the Crescent Fang pack are attending this year. I think it would be smart for you and Ryker to get to know them. That connection could prove invaluable if they reintegrate. And with everything going on in the territory, it wouldn't be the worst thing to have an alliance with Selene's favored pack."

"Selene's favored?" Lena asked. The pack lore sparked excitement in her chest—reminders of stories her father and nan had shared of the first wolves, of bonds blessed by the Goddess Herself. Elara perked up at the mention of such ancient bloodlines.

Cian nodded. "Crescent Fang was the first pack ever blessed by Selene. Their alpha is said to be a direct descendant of Caelum, the first alpha." His voice dropped lower, respect clear in his tone. "Their history runs deeper than most packs dare to claim, though they've been isolated for decades." He exchanged a loaded look with Aiden. "If they're here, it means the rogues have everyone more rattled than we thought. I'll keep an eye out for them."

Elara pressed against the boundary between wolf and human with unexpected intensity, as if the mention of such ancient power called to something primal within her. Anxiety clawed at Lena's throat even as her wolf's interest burned like embers stoked by a sudden wind. The very idea of speaking to wolves who carried such ancient power made her mouth go dry. What could she possibly say to living legends?

Cian turned to her, nostrils flaring as he caught the stale scent of her unease. He leaned in, voice dropping to that authoritative murmur that had once chased away monsters hiding under her bed. "Stay close tonight. This will be overwhelming, but it's important. Observe, listen, and remember that you represent Moonshadow. You're stronger than you think, Lena."

She nodded, grateful for his understanding even as she gripped the strap of her bag tighter. Ryker's hand found her shoulder, his familiar touch centering her as he flashed his signature grin.

"Relax. You'll be fine. Just don't trip over your own feet—or mine, since we might end up mates and all." His teasing carried an undercurrent of protectiveness that made her wolf settle slightly.

She shot him a glare but couldn't help smiling. "Thanks for the vote of confidence, Ryker."

"Anytime," he said with a wink. "And if anyone gives you trouble, just point them out. I'll handle it."

Aiden shook his head, though affection colored his exasperation. "You'll handle it by making more trouble, no doubt."

Ryker shrugged, unbothered. "Trouble keeps life interesting. Besides"—his gaze swept the room with surprising shrewdness—"sometimes a little trouble is exactly what's needed to see where everyone really stands."

The group laughed, the sound easing some of Lena's tension. Elara remained alert, as they stepped deeper into the crowd, scanning faces and scents with an intensity that made Lena's skin prickle. Her wolf knew something was coming—something that would change everything. All Lena could do was hope they were ready for it.

CHAPTER NINE

KAI

The banquet hall buzzed with conversation, the low hum of leaders exchanging pleasantries, the clink of champagne glasses, and the scent of expensive perfumes and rich colognes filling the air.

Kai barely noticed. He stood slightly apart, just on the edge of his father's presence, where the older alpha's magnetic pull could do the talking. Years of watching Darius navigate these gatherings had taught Kai the value of the shadows—how to be seen without being noticed, how to observe without engaging.

But tonight? Tonight was different.

A scent hit him, cutting through the crowded space like a blade through silk—cranberries and rosemary. Earthy, crisp, and so intoxicating, it nearly knocked the air from his lungs. The purity of it sliced through everything—through the artificial perfumes, through the phantom traces of Ava on his skin, through seven years of carefully constructed certainty.

Kai froze, heart stuttering in his chest. The air hummed with tension as Orion's low, insistent growl resonated inside him. Unlike his usual steady presence, the wolf swelled within Kai's consciousness as if trying to break free from the confines of their shared body.

"Mate."

Kai's stomach twisted. He wanted to look away, to deny it, but the truth gnawed at him with the ferocity of an animal caught in a trap. The pull was undeniable—primal and ancient, everything the stories had warned him about. He resisted, body going rigid with the effort, muscles straining against Orion's unprecedented strength. There was no way he was ready for this. Not when he was still desperately holding on to the faint taste of Ava on his tongue. Not when their morning promises were so fresh in his memory.

He glanced around the room, trying and failing to maintain his composure as he searched for the source of that maddening scent. His breath came faster now, each inhale drowning him deeper in cranberries and rosemary until his head swam in it. His eyes darted across the room, landing on a group of women, and then—

"*There,*" Orion whispered through their connection.

Across the banquet hall, her presence cut through the noise, drawing all his attention like a magnet. She was here. Reddish-blonde hair cascaded down her back in soft, natural waves. The strands danced like firelight in the ambient glow of the chandeliers. Her strappy satin ivory dress molded to her curves, accentuating the swell of her breasts and the sensual lines of her hips and ass. The elegant neckline framed the slope of her neck where the pulse point at the base of her throat beckoned him.

His fangs ached with a sudden, primal yearning to sink into that tender flesh, to claim her as his own. Her full lips, painted a deep umber, shot a jolt of desire through him. His body responded to the subtle promise of her curves, to her scent that guaranteed a rich, heady aroma that would bloom when aroused.

She was everything that scent suggested—an energy that prickled against his skin like static electricity. A presence that commanded attention, demanding acknowledgment without a word spoken. Her power resonated with something deep in his core that always felt vacant.

Until now.

He wasn't prepared for this, for the storm that was about to hit him. The morning with Ava felt like a distant dream now, replaced by a reality he'd spent years trying to avoid.

Kai's muscles locked, body rebelling against itself as Orion pushed toward their mate while his human half retreated. He took a hesitant step back. He couldn't let fate win—not after fighting so hard against it.

"Father," Kai said, but the older alpha barely glanced at him, still engaged in conversation with another leader. "I'll be right back," Kai muttered, voice strained as he tried to hold back the growing panic.

Orion was frantic, clawing against the edges of his control, urging him to go to her. *"She's our mate, Kai. She's ours!"*

With a deep breath, Kai forced himself to move, but his legs betrayed him with a step towards her scent instead of the exit. His body was drawn to her—to his mate—even as his mind screamed to turn the other way, to escape before she might recognize him, might realize who he was.

Too late.

LENA

Lena stood at the entrance of the banquet hall, excitement thrumming through her veins. She'd been wavering between anxiety and anticipation for weeks, preparing herself for the politics, the alliances, the dance of power between packs. Tonight felt different. There was a palpable charge in the air, something more fundamental than pack politics.

And then she felt it.

That unmistakable pull, drawing her toward something she couldn't see but knew was there. Everything inside her stilled. She could smell him—her mate.

It was a familiar, intoxicating scent. Orange and nutmeg—warm with a touch of spice, like the smell of winter mornings and sweet treats baking in the oven. But it wasn't just a fragrance. It was the feeling that came with it. The way it made her body hum in anticipation, like a piece of her was waking up from a long sleep.

Elara thrashed beneath Lena's skin, claws scraping along the inside of her veins as she surged toward the surface. *"He's here."*

The instinct was immediate, urgent, and absolute. All her earlier fears about leaving Moonshadow, about losing her place, faded against the certainty of this moment.

Lena drew in a breath to speak to Cian, but he was already watching her with that intuitive awareness only twins possessed. "Go, Lena." His knowing smile matched his warm, understanding tone. "Find him."

Lena's pulse quickened as she nodded, barely able to contain the excitement bubbling up inside her. She stepped further into the banquet hall, each step drawing her closer to that tantalizing scent of orange and nutmeg. Her spine straightened, each vertebra stacking with a confidence that spread through her limbs like liquid fire—a surety more profound than any she'd found in training sessions, pack meetings, or even running wild beneath the moon.

As Lena moved through the crowd, her anticipation only grew. She could feel Elara's elation, raw energy pulsing in her chest like a second heartbeat. The primal knowing made her blood run hot. *This* is what she'd spent years waiting for. What the elders spoke of when they told stories of Selene's greatest gift to Her children.

Lena's pulse raced as she scanned the room, eyes darting from face to face.

And then she saw him.

He stood tall and imposing, broad shoulders radiating a quiet power that drew her in like a magnet. Her gaze locked onto his, and for a moment, the room melted away.

His piercing green eyes burned with an intensity that left her breathless. Fitted gray pants hugged powerful thighs, his tailored navy jacket highlighting the chiseled planes visible through his V-neck shirt.

Lena felt the heat of his brooding stare like a physical touch, sending shivers down her spine and a flood of warmth to her core. His presence dominated the room, even as he stood motionless, trying to fade into the shadows. The air around him vibrated with power, making her instincts scream to submit, to bare her throat and present herself to him in a deep, surrendering arch.

She sucked in a breath.

"Him."

The pull was instant, undeniable, but it wasn't just physical attraction. There was something else in the air—a power, a charge she hadn't expected. Selene Herself seemed present, Her divine energy woven into the very bond drawing Lena forward.

"Mate."

His energy rippled as though his wolf—his soul—was already beginning to recognize hers.

Elara gave a soft whine of approval. *"Hurry, Lena. He's waiting for us."*

Without thinking, Lena's feet moved of their own accord. Her heart pounded, the rhythm growing more insistent with every breath. The energy in the room vibrated with anticipation, her cells humming with the promise of connection.

She *needed* to touch him. Everything else—the summit, the politics, even her fears about leaving Moonshadow—was background noise against the symphony of their bond flaring to life.

KAI

Kai's heart thudded against his ribs as he tried to pull away from the crowd. He searched for an escape route, but his feet remained rooted. Conversation and laughter faded to background noise, leaving only the harsh sound of his own ragged breathing.

Just as he tried to turn towards the exit, she emerged from the sea of faces, her presence as sudden and jarring as a splash of cold water. Her scent hit him with full force now—wrapping around him like a physical touch, drowning out every other sight, every other sound, every other scent, until there was nothing but *her*.

She launched herself into his arms without warning, soft body colliding with his in a perfect, natural fit that made Orion howl in triumph.

"Mate!" she declared, voice ringing out, filled with a joy and certainty that screeched in his ear like feedback.

Kai's breath caught. For a moment, the world halted. His arms hovered stiffly around her perfect body, caught between Orion's desperate need to pull her closer and his own instinct to push her away.

Beneath his skin, Orion lurched forward with startling force, his presence no longer contained within Kai's mind but spilling outward like mist escaping through cracks in a stone wall—reaching for something beyond his physical form.

Her wolf.

The connection bypassed human thought entirely, pure and ancient—wolf to wolf, soul to soul. For that split second, Orion's joy coursed through Kai's veins like liquid fire, unfiltered by human doubt or resistance. The wolves recognized each other in a way that transcended words or reason—a recognition written in their very blood by the Goddess Herself.

A low growl built in Kai's chest. The sound grew louder, more forceful, until it became a deafening roar that shook his very foundations.

"Take her, claim her, mark her—she's ours!" Orion's primal cry echoed in Kai's head, leaving him breathless and bewildered.

His mind recoiled in horror—thoughts tangling in resistance as Ava's face flashed behind his eyes—yet his body betrayed him. The press of his mate made his pulse race, arms tightening around her despite himself. Where Ava's touch had always felt like a challenge, this—this felt like coming home.

"She's beautiful, Orion. Our mate is perfect." The admission slipped past his defenses—past seven years of denial. A vision took hold, and Kai felt his control slip. He saw himself capturing her lush mouth in a kiss, tongues tangling in a passionate dance. Her hands would slide down his back, fingers digging into his muscles. Her ivory dress would fall away like a river of moonlight. Her hardened nipples would press against his chest, sparking goosebumps across his flesh. He imagined taking her against the wall, sinking into her heat, her labored breaths and whispered pleas echoing in his mind.

But as the fantasy reached its peak, Kai's mind jerked back to reality, screaming in protest. He willed himself to pull back, to rein in the primal urges that threatened to consume him.

I'm not ready. This is too much.

LENA

The moment she collided with him, Elara howled in pure joy, the sound echoing through every fiber of Lena's being.

His body was hard against hers, fitting perfectly, as if Selene had carved them from the same stone. His scent enveloped her completely now, orange and nutmeg mixing with something darker, something that spoke of power and destiny.

Elara slipped beyond Lena's consciousness, reaching outward toward a presence Lena could feel but not quite touch. The connection was electric—wild, primal, and achingly familiar though she'd never felt it before. *His wolf.* A dark, powerful energy that caressed Elara's essence like an ancient greeting. For a heartbeat, the wolves communed without words or thoughts, recognizing each other as halves of the same soul, separated by time but joined by the Goddess's hand. The certainty in that wolf-to-wolf understanding was absolute, untainted by human fears or doubts.

"Ours." Elara's certainty blazed through their bond. *"Finally."* The wolf's joy was infectious, even as their mate's hesitation confused them both. Elara whined, pressing against Lena's ribs. His wolf called to them—she could feel it—so why did he fight?

Lena held tighter, refusing to let him pull away. Even through his panic, hope pulsed between them—undeniable in the heat radiating from his chest, in how perfectly their hips aligned as if crafted as matching pieces. Their bond flowed between them like an electric current, illuminating every cell with awareness.

"I'm Lena," she whispered, pulling back just enough to meet his gaze. His emerald-green eyes held secrets and pain she didn't yet understand. A muscle in his jaw flexed and his pupils dilated, the scent of orange and nutmeg intensifying with a honeyed warmth that hadn't been there before. "And you...you're my mate."

His breath hitched. His arms tightened around her, and for the briefest of moments, she felt him surrender—just a little—to the connection they shared.

Elara surged with hope. *"Yes, let us in."*

But it was fleeting. The tension returned just a moment later. Their connection was real, but he was fighting it with everything he had as if something held him back.

I need to help him see it, Lena resolved. *I won't run. I can't.*

CHAPTER TEN

LENA

A booming laugh shattered the haze of the mate connection. The banquet hall crashed back into focus—low hum of laughter, the clink of glasses, the competing scents of food and floral centerpieces. Everything overwhelmed her senses, harsh and intrusive, after the purity of his scent. Elara's presence curled protectively around the mate-bond memory, whimpering as the intrusion of voices and auras tried to wash away the perfect connection they'd just experienced.

Lena spotted a mountain of a male coming straight toward them. His gaze locked on her and her mate with an intensity that made her wolf cower. His presence filled the space around them, drawing every eye in the vicinity.

"Incredible!" The male stepped forward with a broad grin, wrapping his arm around her mate while placing his other hand on Lena's shoulder. "Selene has blessed us tonight!"

Lena blinked. Every head in the room swiveled toward them, the weight of countless eyes pressing against her skin until her cheeks burned and her breath came faster.

The male's presence was overwhelming, towering over most of the room, voice and energy impossible to ignore. His green eyes, so like her mate's, sparkled as they darted between them, cataloging reactions and measuring responses with the precision of a seasoned hunter.

"Alpha," Elara whispered within her, the wolf's presence shrinking instinctively as the raw power radiating from him pressed against their shared consciousness.

Cian materialized at her side, his shadow falling across her like a shield. His shoulders hung loose while his feet planted firmly in the stance their father had drilled into him since childhood—ready to move in any direction, ready to lead.

He nodded respectfully to both males standing before them. "Alpha Darius." Cian extended his hand, smile polite despite the guarded look in his eyes. "It's a pleasure to see you again. This is my sister, Lena."

Darius met Cian's hand with a firm shake, grin broadening. "It appears our families may have news to celebrate."

The words made Lena's head spin.

Cian offered his hand to her mate next. "And you must be Kai. We've never formally met. I'm Cian, alpha-heir to Moonshadow."

Kai hesitated for a fraction of a second before accepting the handshake, grip firm but not overly aggressive. "Cian."

Elara whined at the underlying strain in his voice.

A band of pressure squeezed around Lena's ribs as she watched the exchange, each breath becoming shallower than the last. It was happening so quickly—*too* quickly—but her thoughts stumbled over a new realization that made Elara's tail want to wag with pride.

My mate is Kai Bloodstone. Heir to the wealthiest, most powerful pack in the region.

The Bloodstone pack controlled vast lands, held alliances with fierce wolves, and were known for their unmatched strength. Lena was well versed in the stories of their lineage, of the power that ran in their blood.

Lena's pulse quickened, fingers tingling with an electric current that seemed to flow directly from the Goddess Herself.

"Look what Selene chose for us." Elara preened. *"Mate is strength, power, prestige."*

And yet, Kai's demeanor pulled her back to earth. He looked anything but proud to have found her, his rigid posture making Elara's earlier joy falter.

"It seems so," Cian replied evenly, gaze flicking between Kai and Lena, then back to Darius.

She recognized that careful tone—the one Cian used when weighing opportunity against threat.

A murmur rippled through the crowd, gossip spreading like wildfire through the gathered wolves.

"Fated mates? A Moonshadow and a Bloodstone?"

"Imagine the strength of that bond..."

"This could change everything..."

Each whispered speculation made the reality of the situation press harder against Lena's chest. This wasn't just about her and Kai anymore. This was about packs. About alliances. About *power*.

"But it should be about us," Elara protested. *"About our bond."*

Darius paid the murmurs no mind, though his excitement radiated outward like a kinetic force. His focus was squarely on Cian as he gestured toward a hallway leading out of the banquet hall. "Come. Let's discuss this properly."

Cian nodded, demeanor calm despite the magnitude of the moment. "Of course. Lena, Kai, with us."

As they moved toward the exit, Lena glanced over her shoulder, seeking something familiar in the chaos of the moment. She caught Ryker's eye near the buffet table. Unable to help herself, she mouthed, "OMG, so hot!" while fanning herself dramatically. Even with everything happening, even with the conversations swirling around them, she was still Lena—and her mate was *gorgeous*.

Ryker choked on his drink, eyes widening before he shot her that wolfish grin she knew so well. He mimed a lewd gesture, thrusting his tongue into his cheek.

Lena bit back a laugh, the moment of levity stabilizing her amidst the chaos.

She turned her attention back to Kai, who walked just ahead with a straight spine and measured steps that betrayed no awareness of her exchange with Ryker. Each stride deliberate, as if every step cost him something. Her eyes lingered on him, studying the tight set of his jaw. Despite his reluctance, she couldn't help but be drawn to him.

"Ours," Elara insisted, though her once-confident presence now prodded anxiously beneath Lena's skin, claws catching on uncertainty with each circuit.

That earlier confidence wavered with each step, replaced by a sense of foreboding that made both Lena and her wolf uneasy.

CHAPTER ELEVEN

KAI

The private room was a stark contrast to the lively banquet hall. Lamplight cast long shadows across the polished table. The thick walls muted the distant festivities into something ghostly. The air felt dense with unspoken words as Darius closed the door with a decisive click, his earlier joviality hardening into calculated focus.

"Well." Darius turned to Cian with a politician's smile. "This means big things for our packs!"

Kai stood stiffly at his father's side, limbs locked into place as he fought against the pull of his mate's presence. Even without looking at her, he felt Lena there—her scent, her energy. The air between them pulsed with possibility.

"Acknowledge her," Orion growled low in his mind. *"She is ours. She is home!"*

Kai gritted his teeth, shoving Orion down. The effort made his jaw ache. Now wasn't the time for weakness. Not with Ava's scent still clinging to his skin. Not with years of plans hanging by such a delicate thread.

Cian returned Darius's gaze with measured caution. "It does, but before we discuss alliances or politics, I should consult with my father, Alpha Raelen. And before that..." He turned, attention fixed on Kai with the precision of an alpha protecting his own. "I need to know where you stand in all of this."

The challenge in Cian's words unnerved Kai as all eyes landed on him. His throat tightened as the mate bond thrummed in the silence, demanding acknowledgment. Finally, he spoke.

"I didn't ask for this." His voice was steady despite the way Orion clawed at his control. "I... I don't know her. I won't make promises."

"Coward... Weak... She's ours."

Orion's accusation seared through his consciousness like a branding iron. The truth of the wolf's condemnation burned in Kai's blood, but he forced the thoughts away. Instead, he focused on a spot just past his father's shoulder, on anything but the pull of *her* presence.

Lena stepped forward, voice cutting through the tense air like a blade. "I didn't ask for this either." Her golden-brown eyes locked onto his with a mix of defiance and vulnerability that made Orion whine. "But we both have a duty—to our packs, to Selene. My wolf yearns for you. Can't you feel it?"

Her quiet plea struck Kai like a physical blow. The bond flared between them—raw and primal—tugging at the edges of his soul with a rightness that terrified him. The scent of cranberries and rosemary wrapped around him again, threatening to drown out every carefully constructed reason for resistance. He swallowed hard, forcing the wall between them back up.

Darius chuckled uncomfortably. "She's not wrong, Kai. The bond is a *gift*. One that will unlock your power and strengthen both packs beyond measure."

Cian's tone hardened, protective anger edging his words. "And what if your son doesn't honor the bond? What then?"

Darius's expression darkened, hand clamping down on Kai's shoulder like a vise. "Kai understands his responsibilities."

"Do I?" Kai snapped, voice rising as something in him finally broke. He turned to face his father, anger flashing in his eyes—anger at fate, at duty, at the way his body betrayed him with every breath of her scent. "You speak of duty and alliances as if that's all that matters. What about *choice?* What about..." He hesitated, tension cording his neck as he forced the words out, even as Orion howled in protest. "What about Ava?"

The room fell into a stunned silence.

Lena's breath hitched, chest rising once before freezing mid-inhale. A low growl, primal and wounded, rumbled through the air—not from her throat but from somewhere deeper. The mate bond twisted painfully, like a wire pulled too tight.

Kai forced himself to look at her, guilt twisting in his chest as he saw the confusion and betrayal etched across her face. Even Orion yowled at the pain they'd caused.

Cian stepped closer to Lena, shoulder angling just slightly in front of hers. The temperature in the room dropped as the alpha-heir's power expanded, creating an invisible barrier between his sister and the Bloodstones. "Lena will not be rushed or forced into anything. And she certainly will not fall second to whoever this Ava is." The timbre of his voice deepened, resonating with the same unmistakable cadence Darius used when delivering commands to the pack. "If this bond is meant to be, it will be. But my sister will not be treated as a pawn in some political game, nor will she endure the pain of a wandering mate."

Darius ground his teeth. His alpha aura rose to meet Cian's challenge, filling the room until the air crackled with tension. "This is no game, Cian. This is about the future of our packs. And like it or not, your sister and my son are part of that future."

"Enough." Lena's voice rang out, silencing both alpha males. Her shoulders were squared, chin lifted, but her eyes glistened with a sadness that made Orion howl in despair. "I understand the stakes, but it's obvious Kai and I need time. Time to understand our bond and what it means—not just for our packs, for *us*."

Kai's groin tightened at her strength and resolve.

Orion roared with approval. *"She is perfect. Proud. Strong. Our luna."*

The truth of it ached in his chest, making his resistance feel more like self-sabotage with each passing moment.

Kai pushed Orion further into the recesses of his mind, though the effort left him shaking. He focused instead on Lena's words, on how they embodied everything he should want, everything he knew he should accept. But thoughts of Ava lingered like a shadow he couldn't escape—a chain of his own making that now felt impossibly heavy.

Cian placed a steady hand on Lena's shoulder, pride evident in the small flicker of his expression. "Agreed. This conversation can continue with our father after the summit. It will give Lena and Kai a chance to figure things out."

Darius nodded curtly, though his displeasure was clear in every line of his body. "Very well. But we don't have the luxury of waiting forever. The state of our community is in no position to delay the inevitable."

Kai's ears filled with static, his father's warning slipping away as his focus shifted back to Lena like a plant turning toward sunlight.

She stood tall, her wolf's energy flashing around her like lightning before thunder. He felt the bond stir again—a pull he couldn't ignore, no matter how hard he tried. It whispered of possibility, of power, of *completion*. Everything his chosen path with Ava might never offer, no matter how much he wished otherwise.

CHAPTER TWELVE

LENA

Lena exhaled deeply as she watched Cian and Darius leave the room, voices fading into the distance as the door closed behind them with a soft click. No doubt they were already continuing discussions about alliances and partnerships—conversations that now centered on her and Kai. The room contracted in the absence of their alpha auras, the distance between her body and Kai's now measuring in heartbeats rather than feet.

Her pulse quickened as she faced him. He lingered by the door, fingers hovering above the knob as if he couldn't decide whether to stay or bolt. She could sense the storm raging beneath his surface as his wolf's power rolled off him in waves, making Elara whine with longing. His energy brushed against hers—tentative but electric—like a live wire testing its connection.

"Prove we are worthy." Elara urged with primal certainty. Lena didn't want to push Kai, but her wolf's compulsion thrummed through her blood like a war drum, propelling Lena forward.

Her first step wavered, ankle nearly buckling. The second came stronger. By the third, she was close enough for the heat of his skin to warm the air between them, his body a furnace she couldn't resist nearing. His scent intensified with each step, spicy warmth mingling with something deeper and animalistic that made her dizzy with need.

"Kai," she whispered. The name felt right on her tongue, like it been meant to fall from her lips forever.

His shoulders stiffened, and for a moment, she thought he might flee without a word. But then he turned, his green eyes locking onto hers. The intensity of his gaze stole her breath, the vibrant color shifting as his wolf fought for dominance. His nostrils flared as he scented the air, and Lena's cheeks burned as she realized what he smelled—her arousal, thick and unbidden, perfuming the space between them.

The air condensed until each breath required effort, her lungs straining against the pressure of their bond. Her pulse thudded against her eardrums, each beat a call seeking its answering rhythm. She couldn't tell if it was courage or desperation that drove her forward. She closed the final distance between them, fingers brushing against his arm. The simple touch sent tingles dancing across her skin.

She saw something flicker in his eyes—something unfettered and feral that made Elara howl in triumph. But it vanished in an instant, replaced by that tightly controlled mask she was beginning to hate.

Kai tensed, fingers tightening around the doorknob until his knuckles went white, but he didn't pull away. Instead, he stood frozen, as if caught between instinct and restraint.

Elara seized the moment, pushing Lena forward with a surge of energy that made her bold. She leaned in, lips brushing against the hollow of his throat as she inhaled deeply, letting his scent wrap around her like a warm embrace.

"Mine," she purred. Elara's voice resonated through her.

Lena nipped at his skin, tongue flicking against his pulse point. The room faded away, replaced by the sensation of his heartbeat pulsing against her lips—rapid and unsteady, betraying what his rigid posture tried to hide. The taste of him was enthralling—salt and power on her tongue.

She felt Kai's body tense beneath her touch, his wolf's presence amplifying in response. His breath came hot and quick against her face, each exhale raising goosebumps on her flesh. For one glorious, breathless moment, she believed he might give in.

She turned her head, baring her throat to him in submission, eyes drifting closed as she waited, for him to scent her, to taste the flesh where his mark would rest. To acknowledge what they both knew was true.

She felt the faintest brush of his nose against her neck, so light she might have imagined it, but the burning trail it left behind was undeniable.

Elara trembled with anticipation, already imagining his teeth against their throat. His claim made real. The connection fractured without warning. The warmth of him vanished, replaced by the cool emptiness of the room.

Lena's eyes snapped open just in time to see the door click shut. He was gone.

Her knees nearly buckled. She pressed her palm against the wall to steady herself, the space where he'd stood now achingly empty. Not rejection—she refused to call it that—but retreat. He'd run from what blazed between them, and that somehow hurt more than outright denial.

"Why?" Elara keened, retreating into the recesses of her subconsciousness. *"Why does he run from us?"*

Lena leaned her forehead against the cool wall, allowing herself three deep breaths—only three—to process the hollow ache spreading through her chest. Her mate might need time, but she wouldn't hide away while he sorted through his conflict. She straightened her spine. She wouldn't let herself break—not here, not now. Not when so many would be watching. Judging how the daughter of Moonshadow handled resistance from her fated.

By the time she re-entered the banquet hall, the reception's noise had swelled, washing over her like a wave. Laughter and conversation felt distant—like a song playing underwater. The scents of food and wine pressed in, but all she could smell was his lingering essence on her lips.

Ryker's familiar voice broke through the haze. "So?" He sidled up to her wearing his signature grin, one eyebrow arched as he handed her a drink she hadn't asked for but now realized she needed. "How's Prince Charming?"

She rolled her eyes, but she couldn't suppress the small, tired smile that tugged at her lips. Trust Ryker to still see her as just Lena, not some doomed fated or political pawn.

"Complicated," she said, her voice quieter than she intended.

Ryker snorted, grin widening as he clutched his chest and staggered back a half-step in theatrical dismay. "Complicated? After that entrance? Yeah, well, if you need me to punch him, just say the word." He flexed his arm with exaggerated pride, winking at a nearby wolf who happened to glance their way.

A soft laugh escaped her, and the pressure in her chest relaxed. She glanced at Ryker, grateful for his unrelenting joy and support. He'd always been her rock, the one person who could make her laugh no matter how dire things felt.

The laughter died in her throat as her gaze drifted back to the hallway where Kai had disappeared. Elara's nose pressed against the boundary between wolf and female, tracking their mate's fading scent. Their bond throbbed like a fresh wound, each pulse sparking pain through nerve endings that hadn't existed before today.

Complicated didn't even begin to cover it.

CHAPTER THIRTEEN

CALEB

T he lodge loomed ahead, an imposing structure of timber and stone nestled against the dramatic backdrop of snow-dusted peaks. Caleb stepped out of his truck, awestruck by the grandeur of the scene before him. The hum of power was palpable, a near-tangible current in the air as auras from dozens of alphas and betas mingled. The faint scent of dominance, ambition, and territorial energy lingered, a cocktail that made his wolf stir uneasily within him.

"This is what they call unity?" Fenrir huffed. *"Feels more like a battleground."*

Caleb brushed off the edge of Fenrir's sarcasm, though he couldn't entirely disagree. The energy surrounding the lodge wasn't just political—it was primal. He could almost taste it in the air, thick and heady with possibility and threat. Even the pack banners seemed to reflect the tension flapping restlessly in the crisp evening breeze.

Crescent Fang had no banner here. Not because they lacked what others valued—their territory housed Selene's first blessing, their bank account rivaled packs twice their size—but because Caleb refused to participate in this display of peacocking. These alphas would measure him by the acres of his land and the gold in his vaults, missing entirely what had sustained Crescent Fang through generations: unwavering devotion to their Goddess. Selene had rewarded that devotion with favor and blessing and power that no amount of political posturing could match. Let them underestimate him. Let them see only what *they* valued, while overlooking everything that truly mattered.

Asher stepped out of the truck behind him, bringing instant relief. The larger male adjusted his cuffs casually, but Caleb knew better. Asher's sharp gaze swept over their surroundings with the measured calm that had kept them both alive more than once.

"Well, this is...overwhelming," Asher murmured, in a tone meant only for Caleb's ears.

"It is," Caleb admitted, rolling his shoulders to release tension. "But this is why we came. To remind them who we are, right?"

Asher's lips twitched into a faint smirk. "Then you'd better make sure they remember."

Caleb chuckled, finding Asher's hand as they entered the lodge. The energy inside was even more intense—voices echoed against the high ceilings, laughter and the occasional territorial growl punctuated the space. The distant clink of glasses from the banquet hall hinted at the liveliness of the ongoing event, but Caleb's focus was on the check-in desk. They'd purposely arrived late to avoid being pulled into the social chaos, preferring to settle in and prepare for tomorrow.

The desk agent, a young wolf with wide eyes, greeted them nervously. Caleb could feel the ripple of his alpha aura brushing against the male, and he pulled it back to avoid overwhelming him. Even restrained, Fenrir's presence made the young wolf's scent spike with anxiety.

"Welcome, Alpha Crescent Fang," the agent stammered, glancing at the ledger. "You're...um, you're in room 412."

Caleb nodded, but the male hesitated, his gaze darting between the ledger and Caleb.

"Oh, there seems to be a mistake. We only have one room under the reservation...with, uh, one bed?"

Caleb arched a brow, aura unfurling like a shadow spreading across the room. The action wasn't meant to intimidate—just to make a point.

"There is no error. One room. One bed." To punctuate his words, Caleb placed a possessive hand on the back of Asher's neck.

The desk agent looked away, hands fumbling to pass over the room keys, but not before Caleb caught the flash of understanding in his eyes. "Of course, Alpha." The agent's cheeks reddened.

Asher leaned into the touch, body language effortlessly confident. Caleb's hand slid down to the small of Asher's back, palm resting on the curve of his ass as they walked toward the elevator. The gesture and their mingling scents were a silent message to any wolves nearby: *mine*.

The elevator doors closed with a ding, tension waxing in the small space. Asher leaned casually against the wall, lips quirking into that knowing smirk that always made Caleb and Fenrir stir in equal measure.

"You know," Asher said, "if you keep pushing your alpha aura out like that, you might end up topping me this week."

Caleb's breath caught as a vivid image seared through his mind—Asher face down, broad shoulders pressed into the mattress, submitting to him for once. Fenrir growled approvingly, a rumble of possessive hunger that made Caleb's blood heat.

"Careful," Caleb warned. "You're playing a dangerous game."

Asher's grin widened, scent thickening with arousal in the confined space. "Am I? Or am I just giving you ideas?"

The elevator chimed again, breaking the moment, though the tension lingered between them. Caleb let out a sharp breath, stepping out first. Asher followed behind, close enough that Caleb could feel the heat of him.

By the time they entered their suite, Caleb had regained control, though Fenrir still paced restlessly in the back of his mind. The room was warm and inviting, its large bed dominating the space—a sight that made both wolf and male take notice despite their attempts to focus on business.

Caleb set his bag down by the desk, attention shifting as they began unpacking. The Summit packet lay waiting, filled with schedules, maps, and details about the attending packs. He picked it up, flipping through the pages as Asher hung their clothes in the wardrobe, the domestic familiarity of the moment anchoring them.

"Darius Bloodstone is leading tomorrow's negotiations on the northern territory disputes," Caleb said, his tone thoughtful as he scanned the documents. "His son, Kai, will probably be involved. Their pack borders ours, but they've shown no interest in Crescent Fang."

Asher glanced over, his earlier playfulness replaced by the laser focus that made him such an effective beta. "Maybe this is the time to change that."

Caleb nodded, considering the implications.

"Look beyond alliances of convenience," Fenrir cautioned. *"Selene weaves threads we cannot always see. Some bonds transcend paper agreements."*

"It's worth considering, but the Bloodstones...they're a different world, Asher. Wealthy, powerful. Their pack is practically an empire. They've probably forgotten we even exist."

"She *remembers*," Fenrir encouraged. *"Being forgotten is our greatest strength. We move unseen where others stomp with heavy feet."*

Asher snorted, the sound carrying both amusement and challenge. "Then make them pay attention—remind them."

"Hmmm... Moonshadow," Caleb's tone was contemplative as he continued scanning the list. "Their alpha-heir, beta, beta-heir, and it looks like the alpha's daughter are attending. They're...intriguing."

"Why?" Asher paused his unpacking to give Caleb his full attention.

"Reputation," Caleb replied, tapping the page. "Erik said they're one of the few packs that seem to have avoided the greed and corruption plaguing the others. Strong, respected, but never overreaching. They've stayed small but built a legacy on loyalty and honor."

Asher nodded, moving to stand behind Caleb, close enough that his warmth seeped through his shirt. "Could be worth building a connection. If they're as principled as you say, they might align with us."

"Possibly," Caleb agreed, trying to focus on the papers despite Asher's distracting proximity. "Erik advised treading carefully. We don't know much about any of them or their true motivations."

"Erik is not alpha. He is not here. You are," Fenrir intoned.

Caleb let out a slow breath. These packs would only see the alpha of a forgotten pack when they looked at him, never the male beneath who questioned every decision, who relied on his council's wisdom and Asher's unwavering support. His public mask was refined now—smooth and seamless from years of practice—while the raw honesty he shared only in Asher's arms remained his true face.

They continued strategizing late into the night, conversation flowing easily as always. But when the clock struck midnight, Asher stood, stretching. He stepped closer, hands settling on Caleb's shoulders.

"That's enough for tonight," he said, his voice firm but laced with affection. His thumbs worked the tense muscles at the base of Caleb's neck as he tugged him away from the desk. "Time to wind down."

Caleb allowed himself to be pulled toward the bed, tracking Asher hungrily as he shed his shirt and pants with grace. The sight of his naked lover never failed to stir something deep within him—something primal and reverent all at once.

Asher climbed onto the bed on all fours, presenting himself to Caleb. His dark eyes smoldered with unrestrained desire as he glanced over his shoulder. "I'm yours, my alpha."

The sight of Asher offering himself so willingly ignited something deep within Caleb—adoration, hunger, the undeniable urge to claim what was his. A shiver ran through him as Fenrir surged forward. The wolf growled possessively, its presence a fierce reminder of the primal bond between alpha and beta.

Climbing onto the bed, he trailed his hands over the broad expanse of Asher's muscled back. His fingertips lingered at each dip and curve, mapping valleys and ridges with the veneration of an explorer on sacred ground. Caleb pressed his lips to the base of Asher's neck, breath hot against his beta's sensitive skin.

Fenrir growled in his mind again, urging him to bite, mark, and make Asher his in every way. But Caleb resisted. They weren't fated, and no matter how strong their connection was, he wouldn't dishonor Selene's will. He trusted Her plan—trusted that She would find a way to let them remain lovers and partners for life.

"Watch for her signs," Fenrir encouraged. "Our Goddess speaks through the unexpected."

The thought pierced through Caleb's haze of desire. They'd built this life together without Selene's blessed bond, finding depth and meaning through choice rather than fate. Yet he couldn't silence the whisper of doubt—the question of whether this summit might reveal why they'd been denied that sacred connection.

"Choice is its own blessing," Fenrir reminded him. "Selene honors those who forge their own paths with intention."

The possibility both terrified and intrigued him, but tonight, in this moment of connection, he would silence those doubts and celebrate what they'd created together.

Asher arched his back under Caleb's touch, a low growl of anticipation vibrating in the beta's throat. Caleb slid his hands around Asher's chest, feeling the rapid thrum of his heartbeat, before moving down past his waist to stroke the hard length of his weeping cock. The sensation of Asher's arousal in his palm heightening Caleb's own need. He leaned in, lips brushing Asher's skin as he whispered filthy promises, each word laced with a mix of dominance and worship.

He trailed his lips down Asher's spine, mapping the terrain of his beta's body, alternating between tender kisses and sharp nips. The glossy veil of sweat forming on Asher's skin tasted like devotion—salt and heat mingling on Caleb's tongue. Asher's skin prickled as his muscles responded to Caleb's unspoken commands, each subtle arch and twist honored the trust between them.

When Caleb pulled away, Asher whimpered at the loss of contact. Caleb stood, hands shaking as he stripped off his clothes. He caught Asher watching him, the beta's expression blazing with raw hunger. Caleb's gaze softened, a flicker of tenderness cutting through the primal intensity.

Caleb rummaged through his toiletry bag, retrieving a bottle of lube and tossing it onto the bed. His gaze lingered on Asher's waiting form as he steadied his breathing.

While Caleb typically surrendered to Asher's lead in the bedroom, tonight's rare offering of submission filled him with equal parts pride and responsibility.

Circling back behind Asher, Caleb let his hands roam over the firm curves of his beta's ass. He alternated between playful spanks and gentle kneading, the contrast eliciting soft groans from Asher. Kneeling, he spread Asher wide, mouth watering at the sight before him. He leaned in, warm breath ghosting over Asher's puckered entrance.

Asher sucked in a breath, fists clenching the sheets as Caleb's tongue flicked out to tease him. The first lick was slow and testing, before Caleb worshipped him in earnest. Each stroke of his tongue was a methodical exploration of the tantalizing haven Asher offered up for him.

"My beautiful beta," Caleb murmured between licks, voice thick with ardor.

Asher whimpered at the praise, body yielding under Caleb's attention, his submission absolute.

Fenrir's voice was a guttural whisper. *"Take him. Show him he is ours."* Each word rippled through Caleb's muscles, turning human movements into something wilder.

Gripping Asher's hips, Caleb buried his face deeper, tongue probing with relentless precision. Desperation radiated from the beta's taut muscles—his body responding to every caress, every deliberate sweep of Caleb's tongue—revealing his submission. Each soft cry seeped into Caleb's blood, making his own erection strain with maddening pressure against his stomach.

When Caleb finally pulled away with one last lingering taste, Asher let out a broken sound. Caleb stood, cock aching as he slicked it with lube. The sight of Asher—breathless, vulnerable, utterly open—made his chest tighten with an overwhelming tenderness that transcended mere desire.

He drizzled more lube onto Asher's entrance, fingers spreading it—probing, stretching his beta—with practiced ease. Asher gasped at the intrusion, hips bucking in response. When he reached for his own erection, Caleb caught the beta's wrist with a firm grip.

"No," Caleb growled. He leaned down, lips brushing Asher's ear as he pressed the slicked head of his cock against his beta's entrance. "Your pleasure is mine alone tonight."

The tight heat of Asher's body nearly undid Caleb as he pushed in. He groaned, fingers digging into Asher's hips as he stretched past each tight ring of muscle. Asher's sharp inhale turned into a deep, guttural moan as Caleb bottomed out. Their bodies perfectly aligned.

"Goddess, you feel amazing," Asher gasped, voice trembling with pleasure.

Caleb moved, strokes attentive and unhurried, each one brushing against Asher's prostate. Fenrir roared in approval, the wolf's presence bleeding into Caleb's movements, lending them an edge of primal intensity.

"Hold it," Caleb growled as he felt Asher's body tighten around him. His own control wavered, but Caleb held firm, pushing Asher to the edge again and again, only to pull him back. He wanted Asher to feel everything—to know, without a doubt, that he was cherished, worshipped, and wholly his.

Asher's moans bounced off the walls, body shuddering beneath Caleb's steady rhythm. Each thrust reaffirmed their bond—alpha and beta, lovers, partners bound by trust deeper than hierarchy.

"Caleb, *please*," Asher begged, desperation filling his voice.

"Not yet," Caleb commanded, voice brimming with alpha authority.

Fenrir howled in delight, reveling in the display of power and devotion.

Finally, when Asher was on the verge of breaking, Caleb growled, "Now!"

The word was a release. An alpha's order. A promise carrying all his love and affection.

Asher cried out, climax ripping through him as his body clenched around Caleb. The intensity of it was enough to pull Caleb over the edge, release spilling into his beta as Fenrir roared triumphantly in his mind.

Caleb collapsed onto the bed, pulling Asher into his arms. Their breaths mingled, their bodies slick with sweat, but the world felt quiet and whole.

Afterward, they showered together, movements slow and intimate. Asher pressed Caleb into the cool tile, making love to him in return. By the time they went to bed, tangled in each other's arms, Caleb felt a sense of peace—the first in weeks since the invitation arrived in the mail. He sent a silent prayer to Selene, thanking her for Asher.

Tomorrow would bring the chaos of the summit, the landmine of politics and pressure. But tonight, in this quiet space, he had everything he needed.

CHAPTER FOURTEEN

LENA

The party carried on, lively and buzzing with the hum of mingling auras, clinking glasses, and the occasional burst of laughter. Lena had done her best to stay present, throwing herself into the social chaos. With Cian and Aiden occupied in deep discussions with other pack leaders, Ryker had anchored her throughout the evening, his jokes and casual touches providing stable ground while her wolf continued to surge and retreat like a tide chasing the moon.

He dragged her from one cluster of wolves to another, introducing her to alphas, betas, and their heirs. Even the stern Redridge Beta's lips had twitched at Ryker's compliments, while Alpha Thorne Ironclaw's booming laugh had drawn stares when Ryker whispered something that made rivalry temporarily forgotten.

His charm and wit kept her from dwelling too long on the events of the evening. On the whisper of warmth where Kai's body had pressed against hers. On the phantom brush of his breath against her neck. On everything she couldn't have.

She learned more about the Night Walker and Silver Hollow packs' trading networks and Ironclaw's warrior training program. She'd laughed at Ryker's shameless attempts to flirt with Runa, Alpha Blackwater's daughter, who'd brushed him off with amused disinterest. Eventually, the Redridge Beta and Luna's daughter gave him an enticing smile and whispered something that turned his confident grin feral.

"I'll see you tomorrow," he said with a wink, vanishing from the crowd with his new companion.

Lena rolled her eyes but smiled despite herself. Ryker's absence left her feeling untethered though, his departure removing the last buffer between her and her thoughts of Kai. The banquet hall seemed to expand without Ryker's familiar comfort. Each laugh and conversation amplified. Each empty space between wolves was a reminder of her solitude. Still, the corners of her mouth lifted when she thought of her friend's antics. Without him, she would have spent the evening trapped in her own thoughts rather than mingling with her peers.

The sounds of the party had faded, and the heavy weight of the evening settled back onto Lena's shoulders by the time she returned to her suite. Elara's restlessness rippled through her muscles now that she was separated from the social distractions.

The room was quiet, the low hum of the lodge settling for the night as wolves retreated to their suites. Lena lay curled on her bed, staring at the ceiling. The soft glow of the moon, filtering through the sheer curtains, cast silver patterns on the walls that reminded her of Selene's blessing—of the mate bond she could still feel vibrating beneath her skin.

She exhaled deeply, willing herself to relax, but her mind wouldn't stop racing. Elara ran tight circles within their shared consciousness, each loop bringing flashes of green eyes and broad shoulders. With every circuit, the wolf's presence pushed closer to the surface, fur rippling just beneath Lena's skin as memories of his barely contained power triggered answering pulses of her own.

"Mate is strong. Handsome. Ours," Elara purred.

Lena groaned, burying her face in her pillow. The cotton pressed against her heated skin, muffling her breath but doing nothing to silence her wolf's insistence. Her skin prickled as if his power radiated across distance and time. She couldn't deny it. Deny *him*. Even in memory, his aura dominated her senses, commanding her attention as effortlessly as he had commanded the room.

She pulled the blanket off her body, but the cool air didn't quell the fire building beneath her skin. Images of Kai flashed in her mind—his broad shoulders, the sharp angles of his jaw, the way his voice had sent a shiver down her spine even as his words raked against her chest wall.

This wasn't like fleeting attractions or casual flirtations that burned out after brief intensity. This was bone-deep, soul-claiming. The mate bond reached into her very core, awakening something ancient that had always slumbered there. The stories described the physical pull but never captured this spiritual ache—this void that only he could fill.

Why does he fight it? The question burned, but she refused to accept defeat. They were fated—destined by Selene. She needed to find a way to bridge the gap between them.

As her thoughts spiraled, they kept circling back to their charged encounter in the private room. To the set of his shoulders when he'd been so close, the scorching intensity in his gaze when it had flicked to her, even for the briefest moment. She could still feel the magnetic pull of his presence, the raw energy of his wolf calling to hers.

Her breathing faltered as she imagined him unleashing that power. Not just in a room full of pack leaders, but with her. Alone.

The fantasy struck her like lightning—the image of Kai towering above her, eyes dark with primal need, body caging hers against the mattress as he prepared to claim her. She could almost feel his weight pinning her down, the savage tenderness in his calloused hands as they explored her skin.

Her cheeks burned, and a soft whimper escaped her lips. She pressed her thighs together, but it did nothing to ease the ache building between them.

Elara's voice was a sultry hum in Lena's mind. *"Call for him. He will come."*

"No," she whispered to her wolf, the words trembling despite her resolve. "He doesn't want me... Not yet."

But Elara didn't care. Her own body didn't care. The pulsing in her core was insistent, growing stronger with every passing moment. Without realizing it, Lena's hand drifted down her stomach, slipping beneath the waistband of her shorts and into her panties.

Her fingers slid through her slick folds, and she bit her lip to stifle a moan. She was soaked, already throbbing with need.

"Kai..." His name slipped from her lips in a breathless whisper as her fingers traced lazy circles around her clit. Her eyes fluttered closed, and she let the fantasy consume her.

She imagined him above her, muscles coiled with barely contained desire, grip both tender and merciless as he pinned her wrists above her head. His mouth would trace the hollow of her throat, burning a path of devotion against her skin as he growled one possessive word: *"Mine."*

She shivered, imagining the moment he'd enter her—the exquisite fullness as he pushed into her, giving her body time to welcome him completely. She pictured the way his eyes would darken, and jaw would tighten as he sank deeper. The satisfaction etched across his face as he filled her. Their mate bond would pulse between them, weaving their souls together strand by strand, transforming every touch into a ritual as ancient as the moon itself.

He would start slow, moving deep and deliberate. Each thrust a declaration of his devotion. His hands would guide her hips into their shared rhythm. His voice would be rough with passion as he murmured her name. *"Lena. My Lena."*

His emerald eyes would hold hers. Wild and desperate. The pressure would build as his pace quickened, her body arching beneath him. Each movement a testament to his surrender, pouring from his soul into hers with every thrust.

The thought of his knot—swelling inside her, locking them together—made her thighs clench around her fingers.

Could I take him fully?

"Yes," Elara whispered, her voice a soothing certainty. *"We were made for him, and he for us."*

Lena's breath grew shallow as she imagined the feel of him swelling with his pending release, the way his body would tense and shudder above her as he gave her everything. She could see the raw emotion in his gaze as he looked down at her, hand brushing a strand of hair from her face.

"I love you," he would say. *"You're mine. I'm yours."*

Her fingers quickened, tension coiling tighter in her body.

She pictured the moment his wolf would surge forward, fangs grazing her neck before sinking into her flesh. Her back bowed off the bed, as lightning coursed through her veins.

She imagined their bond blazing into life. The rush of his love and adoration flooding her through the connection. She saw herself writhing beneath him, surrendering completely as he spilled inside her, marking her as his in every way.

"My alpha." Her voice broke as she came. Her body shuddered as waves of ecstasy washed over her, slick coating her fingers. She pressed her face into the pillow, muffling the sounds of her release as her muscles spasmed, her breath hitching in the aftermath.

Even as the physical pleasure rippled through her, an emptiness remained that her climax couldn't fill—a spiritual vacancy where their bond should be completed. Their lovemaking would be merely a vessel for the sacred communion that would make them one entity in two bodies. Forever bound by Selene's design.

Lena lay there boneless as the high faded, her wolf purring in the back of her mind.

"He will come, Lena." Elara's voice resonated through her marrow, the wolf's certainty settling into her bones like an infallible truth. *"He is ours."*

Lena sighed, rolling onto her side and pulling the blanket back around her. She didn't know what the future held, didn't know if she and Kai could overcome the barriers between them, but as she drifted off to sleep, one thought lingered in her mind.

I will find a way to reach him. Whatever it takes.

CHAPTER FIFTEEN

KAI

K ai slammed the door to his hotel suite, the muffled noise of the reception fading into the distance. The tense confrontation in the private room had been suffocating, and he'd fled to escape Darius's gloating and machinations. Politics, alliances, and Bloodstone's future drove the alpha, never Kai's feelings.

Now, alone in his suite—skin still burning where Lena had touched him, her scent hovering like a stubborn echo—the party's vibrant energy might as well have been on another planet. He wouldn't risk returning. He didn't trust himself to maintain control around Lena, and he didn't want to endure another of his father's self-indulgent monologues about destiny and divine matches.

He'd been avoiding Ava's calls as well. What was he supposed to say to her? How could he possibly explain what had happened without lying—without admitting that Orion howled for their mate?

Instead, Kai drowned his turmoil in whiskey, the half-empty bottle dangling from his fingers. The smoky flavor scorched a familiar path down his throat, its warmth spreading through his chest. He leaned his head back, staring at the ceiling. While the alcohol dulled the edges, it couldn't silence the whirlwind in his head. The evening had been chaotic—worse than that, it had been an absolute disaster.

He'd come to the Summit expecting negotiations, politics, and his father's smug commentary. Not *her*.

Lena.

His fated mate.

The thought of her alone made his pulse race. Heat pooled low in his belly even as his stomach twisted with guilt. His muscles coiled with restless energy, caught between the desire to reach for Lena or punch a wall. Every moment spent with her replayed in vivid detail, each memory sharpening Orion's focus.

Her cranberry and rosemary scent had engulfed him, sweet and intoxicating enough to make his wolf howl. It clung to his senses, binding Lena to nearly every thought.

Her golden-brown eyes locking onto his, wide with wonder...

The perfect fit of her body against his...

Her fire, her strength, her affection—even as he'd dismissed her...

Kai huffed a frustrated breath. He refused to be forced, but Orion fought back against each denial.

Ava's face flashed in his mind, reminding him of his promises, but the bond's relentless pull chipped away at his resolve with every breath.

His phone buzzed on the coffee table, Ava's name lighting up the screen for the eighth time tonight. He stared at it as it rang, the sound grating against his frayed nerves.

She'd texted, too. The messages piled up, one after the other.

AVA

> Did you get to the Summit ok?

AVA

> I miss you.

AVA

> How's it going with your dad?

AVA

> Where are you?

AVA

> Why aren't you answering?

AVA

Magnus said your dad pulled you into a room with another alpha and some she-wolf. What's going on?

AVA

Kai, we need to talk.

AVA

STOP IGNORING ME!

Kai rubbed a hand over his face, shoulders sagging under crushing guilt. He hesitated to answer Ava, but ignoring her felt just as wrong.

He typed out a short reply, fingers heavy and dragging across the screen.

KAI

It's been a long day. My social battery is shot. I'll call you tomorrow after everything settles down.

He hit send and watched as the message status changed from "Sent" to "Read."

No response. Her silence was a condemnation.

Kai tossed the phone aside and poured himself another glass. The guilt twisted like a knife in his chest, carving deeper with each shallow breath.

And it wasn't just Ava.

Lena's crumpling expression when he mentioned Ava's name gnawed at him. The look of betrayal had branded itself into his brain, burning deeper with every second he'd stood there, frozen and unsure.

"Coward," Orion growled.

Kai flinched, gripping the glass tighter. *"I'm not a coward. I'm trying to do the right thing."*

"You hurt mate." Orion's voice pulsed with anger and anguish. *"She needs us. Go. Apologize. Claim her."*

Kai shook his head, temples throbbing, breath coming in short bursts as he pounded his fist against the table. *"It's not that simple!"* he argued slamming the glass down, the sound echoing in the silence. The walls pressed inward, the air thick with Orion's suffocating fury.

Grabbing the bottle, he left the room and wandered aimlessly through the dimly lit halls of the lodge. The whiskey burned with every swig, but the warmth never came. Orion's awareness sharpened with each step, as if he knew something Kai couldn't sense.

His feet carried him to the opposite wing without thought, the now empty bottle dangling loosely at his side. He jerked to a stop, breath catching as he found himself outside a door.

Lena's door.

Even if her scent hadn't been unmistakable, he would have known. There was something magnetic about the space. As if the bond itself was pulling him closer, demanding he acknowledge what he was trying so hard to deny.

"Knock." Orion surged, his presence a fiery, insistent force. *"Take what's ours. Give what's hers."*

Kai clenched his fists. He pressed his forehead against the doorframe as he fought for control. Alpha instincts roared in his blood, urging him to break it down, complete the bond, to claim what was his by divine decree.

Then he heard it—a soft, breathy moan filtering through the door.

He froze, pulse spiking.

The sound was unmistakable. Another followed it, even sweeter.

The scent of her arousal hit him like a punch to the gut, intoxicating and irresistible. Jealousy clawed at him, thoughts careening into chaos.

Is she with someone? The idea sent a wave of rage surging through him. *Is there another male in there, touching her, making her moan like that?*

He knew of the parties thrown by the Night Walker wolves. Ten years of attending summits had made him familiar with the hedonism that fueled them—the hormonal urges, the thrill of hooking up with wolves from other packs. Stunning didn't even begin to describe Lena. He'd be an idiot to assume there wasn't a line of males desperate to fuck her, to break her in during her first summit.

His teeth clenched as Orion howled in his mind, the wolf's fury and possessiveness threatening to overwhelm him.

Kai's hand reached for the doorknob, trembling with the effort it took to hold himself back. The image tormented him—another male pressing Lena into the mattress, hands roaming over her body, mouth tasting what should have only been his.

But then, her voice broke through the haze, soft and pleading.

"Kai..."

His name. She moaned *his* name.

The jealousy ebbed. Heat rushed through his veins as his breath quickened, something far more dangerous taking its place. Desire.

He pictured her on the other side of the door, body writhing in pleasure as she thought of him, her hands exploring where his should be.

Kai's cock hardened. He closed his eyes and drew in a deep breath, relishing in the way Lena's arousal thickened her already delectable scent.

Does she taste just as sweet? he thought, mouth watering with unrestrained hunger. *Would she be ready to be claimed? Ready for my knot?*

"Yes!" Orion's voice a guttural demand. *"Go. Now."*

"No," Kai refused, forcing himself to step back.

The thought of barging in, of taking her like this, revolted against the part of him still clinging to loyalty. It wouldn't be fair—to Ava, to Lena, or to himself.

He tore himself away, the sound of her pleasure echoing in his ears as he raced back down the corridor.

His hands were shaking by the time he reached his room, body burning with unspent need. He stepped into the shower, letting the icy water pound against his skin.

Afterward, he grabbed his phone and sent another message to Ava.

KAI

> Good night. I miss you. I love you.

Again, there was no response.

Kai lay back on the bed, staring at the ceiling. The whiskey created a haze over his thoughts, but didn't erase them entirely.

He closed his eyes, willing sleep to come, but the image of Lena—her scent, her voice, her moaning his name—haunted him.

And somewhere, deep in the recesses of his mind, Orion growled relentlessly. *"No more running. She's ours."*

CHAPTER SIXTEEN

CALEB

Morning light filtered through floor-to-ceiling windows, casting golden streaks across high-thread-count sheets. Caleb stirred, the warmth of Asher's body pressed against him a welcome reminder of their intimacy. His beta was already awake, fingers tracing lazy patterns across Caleb's chest.

"Morning, Alpha." Asher's voice was a deep, sleepy rumble.

"Morning." Caleb blinked with heavy lids, the word thick on his tongue.

Asher shifted, pressing a kiss to Caleb's collarbone. "You slept better than I thought you would."

Caleb huffed a quiet laugh. "You made sure I was too exhausted to overthink anything."

Asher grinned, lips brushing against Caleb's skin. "My pleasure." He paused, his tone turning playful. "Or rather, *our* pleasure."

Fenrir awakened within Caleb's mind, the wolf's presence unfurling like wisps of smoke from a sacred fire.

"Mine." Fenrir's purr vibrated through Caleb's chest, raw possessiveness blending with his own affection.

Caleb rolled them over in one swift movement, pinning Asher beneath him. "If I wasn't convinced we'd be late, I'd take you again right now," he growled, nipping at Asher's jaw.

Asher chuckled, hands sliding down Caleb's back. "Hold that thought for later."

Reluctantly, Caleb pulled away, the responsibilities of the day nudging at the edges of his consciousness.

The smell of freshly brewed coffee filled the room as Caleb and Asher settled into the small sitting area near the suite's windows. Their breakfast had arrived moments earlier, and while the spread of pastries and fruit remained mostly untouched, the coffee carafe was already half-empty. The easy intimacy of moments before shifted naturally into the focused partnership that made them such an effective team.

Caleb spread out the packet on the table, skimming through the agenda for the day. "The annual review kicks things off," he said, tapping the schedule.

Asher leaned forward, scanning the page with the careful attention he'd given every challenge they'd faced together. "It's a good opportunity to get a sense of the region's dynamics, but it also puts us under the microscope."

Caleb nodded. "They'll have questions. Crescent Fang's generations-long absence isn't something they'll overlook. We'll need to be prepared for curiosity, skepticism, and unsolicited advice."

Asher's lips curved into a smirk, that confident expression that always steadied Caleb's nerves. "Let them ask. They won't find us unprepared."

Fenrir rumbled in anticipation as they prepared for the challenges ahead. *"Remember our roots. Remember our purpose."*

"I just hope they're ready to listen as much as they're ready to talk," Caleb said, drawing strength from his wolf's certainty. "Reintegration isn't just about showing up. We need to stay true to who we are—what we stand for."

Asher reached across the table, hand brushing Caleb's wrist. "We'll remind them."

Those words again—a mantra for the journey they had embarked on.

The moment lingered between them in quiet understanding as Fenrir stretched beneath Caleb's skin, muscles rippling with contentment at their beta's reassurance.

The lodge's corridors were a flurry of activity as Caleb and Asher made their way toward the conference center. Designer fragrances and whispered conversations filled the air while curious glances followed them. Some speculative, others appraising—especially from the females. Questions about Crescent Fang's return hung unspoken in every look. Fenrir stood alert, attention snagging on each tilted chin and each lowered gaze.

Asher leaned in, voice low and teasing. "Seems you've caught a few eyes, Alpha."

Caleb shot him a sidelong glance. "They're not looking at me. They're looking at Crescent Fang. Wondering if we're serious about reintegration—or if we're just here for the show."

"Or," Asher drawled, a hint of protective possession in his tone, "they're wondering if you're looking for a mate."

A cold weight settled in Caleb's stomach. The thought of strategic marriages to solidify alliances dried his mouth and left a bitter taste.

Asher must have sensed his unease because he added softly, "We'll handle it. Together."

Caleb nodded, releasing a slow exhale as the muscles along his spine loosened one by one.

The conference room was mercifully quiet when they entered. A massive oval table of polished walnut dominated the center, surrounded by ergonomic leather chairs subtly embossed with each pack's logo. Smart glass windows lined one wall, currently adjusted to a slight opacity that softened the mountain view without obscuring it.

Only two others were present—a young alpha with a commanding presence and an older beta, both seated near the center of the table.

Fenrir's interest piqued, noting the natural authority the younger wolf carried.

Caleb strode confidently toward them, shoulders squared, Asher at his side. The alpha looked up as they approached, golden eyes assessing them with a predator's focus before crinkling at the corners.

"I'm Caleb, Alpha of Crescent Fang," he said, extending his hand. "And this is my beta, Asher."

The younger male stood, grip firm as he shook Caleb's hand. "Cian, Alpha-heir of Moonshadow. This is my father's beta, Aiden."

Asher exchanged a polite nod with Aiden before settling into the chair beside Caleb.

Cian perked up with interest. "It's nice to meet you. My nan used to tell my twin sister and me the story of Crescent Fang's creation. She loved that one."

Caleb raised a brow. "Did she now?"

"She did." Cian chuckled, warmth threading through his voice. "She always said Crescent Fang was proof of Selene's vision. A pack born to lead. To guide. I imagine she'd be thrilled to know you're here."

Caleb's eyebrows rose, lips parting. Moonshadow's reputation for loyalty and honor had preceded them, but Cian's genuine warmth caught him off guard. Fenrir perked up, awareness sharpening in a way Caleb had rarely experienced. The wolf focused intently on Cian's aura, detecting something Caleb's human senses couldn't fully grasp—an old energy, reminiscent of Crescent Fang's own sacred connection to Selene.

"Trust this one," Fenrir urged, the wolf's immediate acceptance surprising Caleb.

"We're glad to be here," Caleb said, his tone genuine.

Asher shifted beside him, a subtle signal of agreement.

Cian leaned forward, his interest clear. "How does it feel, coming back after so long?"

Footsteps echoed through the room as more leaders filtered in before Caleb could answer.

Cian leaned closer. "If you're free for lunch, we'd love to continue this conversation."

Caleb glanced at Asher, who nodded almost imperceptibly. "We'd like that."

The four exchanged small smiles before turning their attention to the elder seated at the head of the table. The room grew quiet as the meeting was called to order, the start of the Summit settling over them like a heavy cloak. Yet something about the exchange with Cian left both Caleb and his wolf feeling lighter.

As Caleb settled into his seat, a flicker of hope bloomed his chest. Asher's unwavering presence beside him, Fenrir's quiet approval, the unexpected respect in Cian's words—it all hinted at something deeper than politics.

For the first time since taking his oaths, Caleb glimpsed a future where Crescent Fang thrived within the larger community while honoring their sacred purpose. A new beginning where his choices could serve both his pack and his commitment to Asher.

CHAPTER SEVENTEEN

LENA

The dining hall buzzed with early morning activity, scents of freshly brewed coffee and sizzling bacon mingling with the low hum of chatter. Lena sat across from Ryker at a small table tucked in the corner, her scrambled eggs and toast largely untouched. Elara lurked beneath the surface of Lena's skin, nostrils flaring at phantom traces of orange and nutmeg in the air.

Ryker tore into his second helping of waffles with unrestrained enthusiasm. "I'm telling you, Lena"—he leaned in conspiratorially, fork waving between bites—"last night was *wild.*"

She glanced up from her coffee, visions from the night before clinging to her consciousness—Kai's piercing gaze, his breath against her neck, his dominating presence. Even now, his scent teased her senses, pulling a plaintive yearning from Elara that echoed through their bond.

"Earth to Lena!" Ryker waved a hand in front of her face. "Are you even listening to me?"

"Huh? Oh, yeah." Lena blinked rapidly, pulling herself back to reality. "You were saying something about...last night?"

Ryker smirked, clearly delighted to have her attention again. "Only the *greatest* night of my life! So, there I was, in the Redridge suite, right? Thurston's daughter is on her knees, and she's got me *all* worked up. It was so fucking hot. I had her pressed down, chin to balls, choking on my cock, and then—wait for it—out of *nowhere*, she shoves a finger in my ass!"

Lena choked on her coffee, sputtering as Ryker leaned back in his chair, howling with laughter. "Goddess, Ryker!" she shrieked, grabbing the toast from her plate and lobbing it at his head. "I did *not* need to know that!"

He caught the toast midair, unbothered by her outrage. "What? It's rude to kink shame, you know." He took a bite, winking at her. "I didn't even have time to freak out. I came so hard I thought Axel left my body."

Lena smacked his arm, face burning with both horror and amusement. His usual raunchy banter helped ground her, even as Elara continued her incessant hunt for traces of their mate. "I fully support you letting your freak flag fly, but for the love of Selene, can we *not* discuss this over breakfast?"

"Fine, fine." Ryker shrugged, grin never wavering. "But for the record, I'm still trying to figure out if I liked it."

Lena rolled her eyes, shaking her head as she tried to suppress a laugh. Ryker had a way of dragging her out of her own head, no matter how heavy her thoughts felt or how insistently Elara pined for their mate.

He leaned forward, expression sharpening. "So, what about you? What'd you do after I left? Have a super-secret rendezvous with Kai?"

Heat crept up Lena's neck as fragments from her fantasies surfaced. Her thighs pressed together beneath the table, body responding anew to phantom sensations of Kai's dominance.

She shook her head, hoping Ryker wouldn't notice the color rising in her cheeks. "Nothing nearly as exciting as your escapades." She kept her tone light despite the prickle of energy from her wolf dancing along her nerve endings. "Last night was...intense. I'm giving him some space for now, but I'm hoping to steal a moment with him later today."

Ryker's expression shifted, his usual mischief giving way to something sharper. "Oh, you're going to give *Kai Bloodstone*, the proverbial Prince of the Pacific Northwest packs, space?" He leaned in closer, his voice dropping. "Did you hear all the rumors flying around about him last night?"

Lena frowned, stomach twisting as a low rumble of unease vibrated through her connection with Elara. "What rumors?"

Ryker rubbed his hands together, clearly relishing the opportunity to share gossip. "Apparently, Kai and this she-wolf, Ava, have been inseparable since his dad brought her in with a group of survivors from a rogue attack when they were pups. They started dating not long after their first shifts—against Darius's wishes, I might add—and were convinced they'd be fated mates. Except, you know, they're *not*."

Lena's heart sank, but she forced herself to listen as Ryker continued. The sharp sting of her wolf's distress pulsed through their shared consciousness with each word.

"So, when she turned eighteen and realized they weren't fated, things got...tense. The only thing Kai and his dad ever fight about is Ava. Some people think Darius just doesn't like her. Others say Darius loves her but just doesn't think she's right for his son. Either way, it's a whole mess." Ryker leaned back in his chair, crossing his arms. "And now, enter *you*, the gorgeous, brilliant, *virginal* fated mate. The heirs are *salivating* over the drama. There are even bets on how this is all going to play out. You, Kai, and Ava? Love triangle doomed for heartbreak, or throuple of the century?"

Lena groaned, burying her face in her hands. "First, I don't share—"

Ryker interrupted her with a snort. "Yeah, unless it's cock. Or do I once again have to remind you of the Incident?"

Lena huffed, not daring to broach that subject again, before continuing. "Second, my life is not some Goddess-damned soap opera."

He shrugged, clearly unbothered by her exasperation. "Hey, I'm just the messenger. But for what it's worth, I don't think the competition is as fierce as you might think."

Lena peeked up at him, brow furrowed. She felt Elara's attention snap into sharp focus, ears pricking forward. "What do you mean?"

Ryker leaned closer conspiratorially. "Magnus, the Bloodstone beta-heir, spent most of last night trying to calm Ava down. She was blowing up *his* phone after Kai ignored all her calls and texts. If you ask me, Kai's just waiting to get back home to break things off with her face to face. Sounds like he's trying to do right by both of you."

A spark of hope ignited in Lena's chest, spreading through her veins like honey-warmed whiskey as her wolf's energy purred through their bond. She knew Kai felt the bond—knew it as surely as she knew her own heartbeat. Maybe his hesitation wasn't about rejection. Maybe it was about doing the honorable thing.

She straightened in her seat, confidence returning. "You really think so?"

Ryker grinned. "I do. And if he doesn't figure it out soon, you've got me and Cian. We'll knock some sense into him together."

Lena laughed, the sound light and genuine. Elara's energy softened with anticipation at the prospect of claiming their mate properly. For the first time since feeling the mate bond, she felt like she could breathe.

A mischievous grin spread across her face as she turned to Ryker. "So, does this mean you're going to need a finger up the ass to get it up from here on out?"

Ryker burst out laughing, pulling Lena into a tight side hug. "Goddess, I fucking love you, you little psycho! Now pick up your shit. I'm thirty seconds away from being late to the first meeting." He shot her a wink as he darted out of the dining hall, calling over his shoulder, "I'll keep an eye on your hubby and catch up with you at lunch. Unless you're busy spending your break on your back!"

Laughing, Lena gathered her things, excited for the rest of the summit. With renewed determination, she made her way to the morning session with the lunas, gait energized by Elara's infectious confidence.

CHAPTER EIGHTEEN

KAI

Too much whiskey and too little sleep had left Kai raw and irritable as he entered the conference room for the annual review. His temples throbbed from his hangover as he scanned the room, mapping alliances and rivalries, while Orion instinctively cataloged potential points for connection and influence. The Silver Hollow alpha caught his eye and smiled—too knowingly. Word about his fated mate had apparently spread fast.

Kai settled uncomfortably into his seat. The heavy scent of dominance—dozens of alphas posturing and positioning—filled the room. Beneath that thick layer of power, he caught a hint of a sweet, earthy fragrance.

His muscles tensed. *Lena?* No—just a phantom scent and his wolf's wishful thinking.

Orion stalked the confines of their shared mind, each step reverberating through Kai's skull like thunder. Whether the wolf's agitation stemmed from the hangover or the mating bond's constant pull, Kai couldn't tell.

Next to him, Darius was in his element, exuding confidence and charm as he greeted the other leaders. His deep, booming laughter rang out above the hum of voices, and Kai couldn't help but wince. Each sound felt like a hammer striking his skull.

"Alpha Darius!" a voice thundered from across the table. "Good to see Bloodstone's banner flying high as always."

Darius clasped the man's forearm in a firm shake. "Great to see you too, Garrick! Even better days ahead." His hand landed on Kai's back like an anvil. "Especially with Kai taking his oaths with his fated mate by his side."

Kai's stomach twisted. He hadn't been paying attention to the conversation, but those two words snapped him out of his haze. Beneath the alcohol-induced fog, Orion roused at the mention of their mate, sending nausea rolling through Kai's gut.

His gaze swept the table, landing on Cian Moonshadow. The alpha-heir's expression was neutral, but Kai caught the slight tick of his jaw before Cian schooled his features, replacing irritation with the polished mask of diplomacy. Something in that controlled reaction made Kai's shoulders press inward—this was a wolf who would fight for his sister's honor.

Cian nodded respectfully, voice calm and measured as he addressed the group, "Yes. Congratulations are certainly in order, Alpha Darius. My father is eager to discuss this exciting news. We'll certainly want to find time to strengthen the bonds between our packs."

Kai ground his molars as Cian's attention focused on him. Orion's hackles rose, muscles bunching beneath Kai's skin as the wolf sensed a challenge beneath the diplomatic words.

"Perhaps you'd consider joining us, Kai." Cian's fingers traced the rim of his water glass with deliberate precision, each movement a controlled contrast to the steel in his tone. "It might be valuable to spend time at Moonshadow after the summit. My father and I would welcome you to our packlands as we prepare for my alpha ceremony at the next equinox."

The alpha-heir's power rippled beneath his composed exterior, making the water tremble ever so slightly. "After all, proper introductions should be made...given the circumstances. It would allow our families to bond, and perhaps allow you and my sister to deepen your connection. I believe she deserves a proper courtship, befitting her rank."

The ultimatum in those words was clear: *prove yourself worthy or stay away.*

Kai tensed, sinking further into his seat. The last thing he wanted was to spend time at Moonshadow, surrounded by the constant reminder of the fated bond he was desperately trying to ignore. Just the thought of being near Lena, breathing in her intoxicating scent day after day, made both his body and his wolf ache with need.

He forced a polite smile, preparing to decline the offer, *privately*, once the meeting was over. Before he could open his mouth, Darius cut in, face lighting up as if the moon radiated from within him.

"Splendid!" Darius smacked the table with an open palm. Several heads turned in their direction, curious whispers rippling through the room. The scent of interest and speculation thickened the air until Kai felt like he was drowning in it. "A brilliant idea, Cian. I think that's exactly what our packs need—time to build trust and unity before the big day."

Kai's head snapped toward his father, a cold weight dropping through his chest and settling in his gut. *Big day?* Even Orion went silent, fur rising at the edge of their shared consciousness.

Darius continued, utterly oblivious to Kai's internal turmoil. "I'll send Kai back with you after to start forging relationships with his father-in-law and second family. I'll join you all for your alpha ceremony. It'll be the perfect opportunity to start planning for Lena and Kai's mating ceremony!"

The room went unnervingly quiet, Darius's insinuation that the mating was inevitable settling heavily over the table. Kai could feel the eyes of the nearby alphas, betas, and heirs boring into him, their curiosity and speculation thick in the air. The pressure of their attention intensified his discomfort, each heartbeat pounding in his skull.

Cian's lips tightened into a diplomatic smile. "That's very generous of you, Alpha Darius. I'll be sure to relay your enthusiasm to my father."

Kai's tongue stuck to the roof of his mouth as the oxygen vanished from the room. For the last year, he'd meticulously planned his mating ceremony: the handfasting, the vows, Selene's blessing, the claiming. Now the image of his bride had fractured. Two faces overlapped, each vying for dominance.

Ava's confident smile pledging herself to Bloodstone.

Lena's sincere smile pledging herself to him.

The images clashed, merging and separating: Ava riding him on the altar, wild and demanding; Lena shuddering beneath him, throat bared in submission.

Acid rose in his throat.

Kai barely registered the rest of the conversation as nausea churned in his gut. His gaze dropped to the table, mind racing. He needed to find a way out of this. There was no way he could endure a month at Moonshadow with Lena. Not with the bond pulling at him so intensely. Not when every breath might carry her scent. And certainly not with the specter of Ava looming over every decision he made.

"We must go," Orion growled, low and insistent. *"Complete the bond."*

"Not like this," Kai thought, fists clenching under the table.

The meeting progressed in a blur. Voices faded into background noise as Kai's thoughts spiraled. He gritted his teeth, gaze fixed on the polished table, the whispered discussions about trade agreements and alliances falling on deaf ears.

Until a new voice pulled his attention back to the room.

"...grateful for the opportunity to join you all here today. It has been many years since Crescent Fang has taken part in a summit like this, and we are honored to be among such distinguished leaders."

Kai glanced up, green eyes narrowing as he took in the speaker: a young alpha he didn't recognize. The male was tall and lean, with sharp, regal features and an undeniable air of confidence. Something about his presence made both Kai and Orion take notice as the alpha stood, addressing the table with a steady voice. His tone was measured and thoughtful as he detailed the accomplishments of his pack.

"Despite operating independently for the last two generations," the alpha continued, "Crescent Fang has remained steadfast in our traditions and our worship of Selene. We have worked tirelessly to preserve the values instilled in us by our ancestors, and we are committed to ensuring the safety and prosperity of our pack in the face of the rising threat posed by the rogues."

Kai inwardly scoffed, rolling his eyes at the impassioned speech. *What is this male trying to prove?* he thought, leaning back in his chair.

Orion growled in disagreement at his dismissal, but Kai ignored him. The alpha went on, voice growing more fervent as he spoke of Crescent Fang's long history and deep spiritual connection to Selene. The words were reverent, almost poetic, and Kai couldn't help but scoff at the sentimentality of it all.

Seriously, is this wolf auditioning for Selene's Number One Fan club? Kai snorted under his breath at his own joke. *"Maybe he's the alpha Lena should be fated to. Seeing as he's got such a hard-on for Selene's will,"* he muttered to Orion.

Orion's thunderous roar shook the walls of Kai's consciousness, the wolf surging forward with teeth bared. *"No! Mate is ours!"*

The wolf's possessive anger spiked the pain pounding in Kai's head, but it was more than just Orion's response that made his stomach twist. The idea of Lena belonging to someone else—even in a hypothetical scenario—sent a sharp, inexplicable ache through him. He swallowed hard, mind flashing back to the previous night. To the moment of rage he'd felt when he thought those soft moans had been for another lover. The memory of that jealousy burned through his veins, his jaw clenching until his teeth ached, fingers flexing with the phantom urge to tear any rival limb from limb.

Kai shook his head, forcing the memories away. Lena's labored breaths echoed in his ears, his name on her lips as she—

His body tensed, heat flooding his core. *Not here. Not now.*

Not in this room filled with the most powerful wolves in the region. He focused his attention back on the speaker, determined to bury the intrusive thoughts.

As the Crescent Fang Alpha continued, Kai observed the reactions around the room. The responses were mixed. Some of the leaders looked bored, gazes fixed on their notes or phones. Others feigned mild interest, nodding along politely without fully engaging. It was clear that Crescent Fang's reappearance in the regional fold was a curiosity at best, an afterthought at worst.

But one male at the table was utterly captivated by the speech. Seated to the alpha's right was a broad-shouldered beta who listened with rapt attention, dark eyes fixed on the speaker as though every word was a revelation. Kai had noticed the beta when he first entered—something about the way he held himself, confident but not aggressive, drew the eye. Now, watching him listen to his alpha's speech, Kai found himself studying the beta more closely, noting the sharp cut of his jaw, the slope of his nose, and the way his full lips pressed together in concentration.

The male's hair—a mess of dark curls—fell across his brow in a way that seemed effortlessly undone, and when his tongue darted out to wet his lips, Kai felt his stomach flip unexpectedly.

Whoa! Kai was startled by his own reaction. *Where the hell did that come from?*

"Irrelevant," Orion huffed. *"Focus."*

Kai straightened in his seat, forcing himself to look away. His gaze landed on his father, who was, predictably, hanging on every word the alpha spoke. Darius's expression was one of keen interest, but Kai knew his father well enough to recognize his strategic instincts engaging. Crescent Fang might be a relic of the past, but in Darius's mind, even relics could be useful if positioned correctly.

As the alpha finished speaking, Kai felt a subtle shift in the room's dynamics. The other pack leaders relaxed, postures easing as they offered polite applause. Kai's tension only spiked.

He replayed the alpha's words, wondering if he'd been too quick to dismiss the fervor in Caleb's voice. His father's interest and the beta's attentiveness now seemed like warning signs he'd ignored. A nagging sense of unease settled in his gut—had he missed a crucial thread in the alpha's speech? One that might weave together the intricate politics of the packs.

Kai's attention drifted again as the meeting rolled on, but the image of the Crescent Fang Alpha and Beta lingered in the back of his mind. Just as unshakable as the memory of Lena's moans, of her scent, of the way their bond pulled at him with every breath.

When the review finally adjourned, Kai was the first to leave the room, ignoring his father's attempts to pull him into another conversation. He needed air, needed space. The walls felt like they were closing in, thick with everyone's expectations and endless speculations about what his fated pairing meant for their packs.

He stormed down the corridor, barely registering the greetings of other pack leaders and their heirs as he passed. All he could think about was escaping.

Escaping his father.

Escaping the summit.

Escaping the bond that was tearing him apart.

Kai desperately hoped to avoid Lena through the rest of the event. The memory of her scent made it impossible to think straight. He couldn't stomach a run-in with her right now. Couldn't bear seeing her hope—or worse, her hurt—knowing that he planned on rejecting her as soon as possible.

The mountain air welcomed him as he stepped onto the balcony. His thoughts refused to settle even as he breathed in the sharp, clean air. Faces blurred together in his mind—Lena, Ava, Darius, the Crescent Fang Beta... Pressure rose in his chest, heart racing with a growing sense of helplessness. He needed to escape, to find some way to clear his head and take back control of his future.

It was all too much.

"You're running, Kai," Orion growled. The wolf's voice was a harsh whisper in the back of Kai's mind. *"Coward."*

Kai closed his eyes, the words cutting deep. Maybe Orion was right. Maybe he was a coward, but he didn't know how to be anything else right now.

CHAPTER NINETEEN

LENA

The pen lay idle in Lena's hand as Luna Eden Blackwater spoke of mating ceremonies. Each sacred detail should have filled her with excitement, but uncertainty twisted in her chest instead.

Will I ever stand before Selene with Kai?

The striking female's silver-streaked hair caught the sunlight as she spoke of the ancient rite with reverence. Elara pressed closer to the surface, ears pricked forward with keen attention to traditions that might soon be theirs.

"The mating ceremony"—Eden paused, fingers twisting her wedding ring. The golden band reflected the light as memories seemed to dance across her features—"is not merely a public declaration of the bond. It's a renewal of the pack's connection to Selene and a reaffirmation of the luna's role as the alpha's partner in leadership. The ceremony is a balance of love, power, and responsibility."

Warmth bloomed in Lena's chest at Eden's words, pulse quickening as she envisioned the ritual.

An image materialized: her and Kai bathed in moonlight as they stood hand in hand on Moonshadow's sacred grounds, golden wristbands pulsing with Selene's blessing. Lena's breath hitched, cheeks flushing as her thoughts veered toward what cemented the bond—the claiming.

She was thrust back into her fantasies again. Elara's energy coiled with hunger, sharpening each imagined sensation: Kai's hands exploring her body, his lips pressing against her neck, then the exquisite sting of his bite marking her as his own.

She envisioned Kai's alpha aura blazing to full brilliance after the marking, her bite the key that unlocked his true power. Her skin tingled at the thought of his wolf surging forward to claim her—not just as possession, but as equal.

"Yes," Elara purred. *"Ours. As we are his."*

"...and, of course, the luna helps to preside over all pack ceremonies, from the first shift to the crowning of a new alpha and his beta and gamma," Eden continued, her words jolting Lena back to reality.

Lena sat up straighter, mortified at her wandering thoughts, though Elara remained contentedly lost in their shared vision. Flipping her pen nervously between her fingers, she tried to catch up, but her focus remained scattered, the phantom sensation of Kai's imagined claiming still tingling on her skin.

Lena made her way to the dining hall once the morning sessions concluded. She saw her brother and Beta Aiden seated with an alpha and beta pair that she didn't recognize. Ryker didn't appear to be with them.

She scanned the rest of the room in search of her friend, secretly hoping to catch a glimpse of Kai as well. Neither one of them was there. Disappointment surged as she realized that she didn't know when she'd see Kai again—she didn't know where his room was, and she had zero interest in engaging Alpha Darius to find him.

Elara whined in the back of her mind as dejection chilled their bond and frosted the edges of Lena's thoughts.

Lena swallowed her disappointment, refusing to let it ruin her day. She spotted Luna Eden sitting at a small table near the windows, something about the older she-wolf's calm presence drawing her forward. Eden's inviting smile and attentive gaze promised the wisdom Lena craved, offering a welcome distraction from her spiraling thoughts.

"Luna Eden?" she tentatively asked. "Would you mind if I joined you for lunch?"

Eden's smile brightened. "Of course, dear. Please, sit."

Lena slid into the chair, tension easing from her shoulders as Luna Eden leaned forward with genuine interest.

"Tell me about your first summit experience," Eden prompted, questions flowing naturally, punctuated with knowing nods and comments about Moonshadow's history that made Lena sit taller with pack pride even as Elara remained increasingly aware of Kai's absence.

As their plates emptied, Lena hesitated before voicing the thoughts that had been gnawing at her all morning, thoughts that even quieted Elara with uncertainty.

As an alpha's daughter, Lena knew the expectations: tradition, patience, submission. Either let destiny chart her course and wait for her fated mate or marry well to strengthen pack alliances. But she'd always wanted more, and thankfully her father had encouraged her ambitions—allowing her to train alongside warriors and learn leadership beside Cian. A chance to prove herself beyond bloodlines and gender norms.

"Luna Eden," she began timidly, "can I ask you something...personal?"

Eden set down her teacup with a gentle clink. "Of course, Lena." She leaned forward slightly, clearly ready to listen. "What's on your mind?"

"I... I guess I'm struggling to find my place," Lena admitted, fingers twisting the edge of her napkin. "I know I'm the daughter of an alpha, but my future is tied to this bond—this fated connection I didn't choose. I've always wanted to be strong and independent, but...everything feels like it's out of my control. What if I'm not ready? Or...what if I'm not enough? There's a lot of pressure, considering the prestige of Bloodstone. I desperately want to be a great luna to Kai, to his pack."

Elara shifted uneasily at the admission of their fears, but Eden reached across the table, warm hand covering Lena's restless fingers.

"Oh, my dear. Let me tell you something I've learned in my years as Luna. The most important job we do—our truest purpose—is to support our alpha. But don't mistake that for subservience."

Lena looked up, brow furrowing in confusion, both she and Elara caught by the strength in Eden's words.

"The alpha may be the head of the pack," Eden continued, voice rich with experience, "but the luna is the neck that turns the head. We lend strength, not because we complete them, but because we amplify them. We keep them focused on a good path, remind them of their humanity when their wolf instincts threaten to take over, and help them make decisions that serve not just themselves but the pack and the region."

Lena felt something shift within her as Eden spoke, Elara rising closer to the surface, standing at attention.

Eden's smile softened. "It's not about being perfect, Lena. It's about being *present*. Your strength doesn't come from knowing all the answers—it comes from being willing to ask the right questions and standing beside your alpha as an equal partner, not a shadow."

Lena swallowed hard, understanding dawning as she nodded. Elara's purr vibrated through her bones, straightening her spine with growing confidence.

"Thank you," she whispered. "I needed to hear that."

Eden's eyes twinkled as she patted Lena's hand. "You'll do just fine, Lena. I can see it already."

Lena lingered for a moment after lunch ended, hoping Ryker would appear. She smiled to herself when he didn't, imagining he was off charming—or aggravating—other beta heirs.

She headed back to her room to change for her afternoon sessions, Elara's energy building with anticipation. Today, she'd chosen to attend the beta-female training, curious about how these strong she-wolves balanced their roles within their packs. While it might not directly apply to her future, their experiences could provide valuable insight.

She also planned to join the last warrior session of the day. And if she could find Ryker in the process—or better yet, take him down in a sparring match—then all the better.

Pulling on her training gear, Lena smirked at the thought of the Bloodstone beta-heir witnessing her in action. The idea of him relaying stories about her prowess to Kai—or even Ava—made her pulse quicken.

"Let them see what kind of luna they're getting," Elara growled with pride. *"Warrior. Leader. A force to be reckoned with."*

As she made her way to the conference rooms, determination straightened her spine with each step. Eden's wisdom and Ryker's encouragement had ignited something within her. Her future role as Bloodstone's Luna wasn't about submission—it was about partnership, strength, and the power of the bond she shared with Kai.

And no one—not even Ava—could take that from her.

CHAPTER TWENTY

CALEB

Late-morning sun streamed through the wide conference room windows, but the natural warmth did little to ease Caleb's simmering frustration. The summit's earlier sessions had gone well—Fenrir's presence a steady anchor as they'd shared Crescent Fang's accomplishments despite veiled skepticism from other alphas.

But all of that goodwill was obliterated the moment the northern border negotiations began.

Caleb leaned back in his chair, steepled fingers forming a tight cage. Before him, Thorne Ironclaw and Garrick Redridge bickered like pups over a bone. The disputed territory: a stretch of uninhabited land once belonging to the now-decimated Denali pack. The alphas' posturing over territorial claims made Fenrir recoil in distaste.

"This land has been adjacent to Ironclaw borders for over three decades!" Thorne barked, pounding his fist on the table. His icy blue eyes blazed with fury, sharp gaze sweeping the room as if daring anyone to contradict him. A lock of long, dark blond hair fell across his forehead, framing his chiseled features and emphasizing the determined set of his jaw.

Garrick leaned forward, his normally soft brown eyes now hard with anger. "And it's closer to our hunting grounds," he shot back at Thorne, face red with indignation. The wrinkles etched around the older alpha's mouth, usually a testament to his quick smile, now deepened into a scowl as his voiced dropped to a low, menacing growl. "You couldn't manage that territory if you tried, pup!"

Caleb's jaw locked, teeth sinking into the inside of his cheek until copper bloomed on his tongue, the urge to groan trapped at the base of his throat.

"This is absurd," Fenrir rumbled irritably. *"The Goddess didn't give them land to squabble over like scavengers."*

Caleb couldn't disagree.

His gaze shifted to the Bloodstone alpha-heir, seated two chairs down. Kai had been silent for most of the morning sessions—his stillness a stark contrast to the rustle of papers and murmured conversations in the room—but Caleb didn't miss the tightness in his jaw, the subtle rise and fall of his chest as he exhaled deeply, or the faint scent of whiskey, spiced with orange and nutmeg, that clung to him. Fenrir expanded within their shared consciousness, both wolf and male drawn to the controlled power radiating from the heir.

Kai surged to his feet, broad shoulders taut with restrained anger. Caleb studied him, noting the strong angles of his face, the lean strength of his frame, and the way his green eyes glinted like shards of jade beneath furrowed dark brows.

The Bloodstone heir reminded Caleb of that Night Walker Gamma from a particularly wild weekend last year—broader, leaner, but with the same intensity. He chuckled internally at the memory of how the little gamma melted between them and found himself sneaking a glance at Asher, wondering if he'd made the same connection.

Before he could share his thoughts, a sharp, resounding bang snapped his attention back to the room, the sound echoing off the polished wood paneling and making Caleb flinch.

Fenrir's attention sharpened, recognizing the surge of alpha power about to be unleashed.

"Enough!" Kai roared, the sheer force of his aura making the table tremble.

Thorne and Garrick fell silent, mouths clamping shut as if a spell had been cast.

Kai's glare swept over them, his voice like ice. "Your incessant sniveling is beneath you and beneath this summit. We're facing a rogue threat that has already destroyed countless lives, including those of the wolves who belonged to the land you're fighting over. And here you are, using this crisis to further your greed!"

Caleb's eyebrow arched as he leaned forward, breath catching at the alpha-heir's command. Even Fenrir rumbled a deep purr of approval, the wolf's respect pulsing between them like a second heartbeat. The entire room held its breath as Kai continued, tone sharp and uncompromising.

"Neither of you has a reasonable claim to the Denali lands," Kai declared. "And even if you did, your time would be better spent focusing on the safety of your existing territories. Not overextending yourselves." He turned his gaze to the rest of the room, addressing the gathered leaders and heirs. "I propose we keep the land neutral for the time being. Once the rogue threat has been addressed, we can revisit its potential uses as a collective."

There was a beat of silence before murmurs of agreement rippled through the room. Even Darius Bloodstone looked pleased, nodding approvingly at his son. Caleb found himself studying Kai's profile, admiring the way power flowed from him as Fenrir noted his leadership.

He leaned toward Asher, whispering through their telepathic connection, *"Impressive."*

Asher smirked, catching the undertone in his alpha's words. *"Not bad. He's got some bite to his bark, but I'd love to see if we could make him purr."*

After the session adjourned, Caleb and Asher made their way to the dining hall to meet Cian and Beta Aiden. The dining hall was bustling, but they spotted Aiden seated at a small table near the back. The Moonshadow Beta waved them over, his usual air of calm confidence evident.

"Gentlemen," Aiden greeted, rising to shake their hands. "Cian stepped away to grab my son, Ryker, who will be his beta. They should be here shortly."

Caleb settled into his seat, and Asher slid into the chair beside him, their shoulders brushing as they did. A steadying calm pulsed through their bond, centering Caleb as the group fell into easy conversation, recapping the morning's events and joking about the chaos of the negotiations.

"Poor Kai," Aiden remarked. "I thought he was going to burst a blood vessel by the end of that session. Not that I can blame him—dealing with Thorne and Garrick would test the patience of a saint."

"Or a pack of them," Asher quipped, earning a smirk from Caleb and a chuckle from Aiden.

Caleb grinned, Kai's commanding presence still fresh in his mind alongside the sinful fantasies Asher had whispered about capturing the heir between them. "He handled it well, though. I didn't expect him to take such a firm stance."

Aiden nodded. "Kai's got a lot on his plate right now. It's not easy being Darius's heir. The Bloodstone name carries a lot of prestige. Between the rogue threat, those northern alphas, his pending alpha ceremony, and—" He hesitated, eyes darting between Caleb and Asher. "Well, I suppose you've heard about the...developments last night."

Caleb raised a brow, Fenrir stirring with curiosity. "Developments?"

Aiden sighed, leaning back in his chair. "Kai found his fated mate last night. And it just so happens to be Cian's twin sister, Lena."

Caleb's hopes of seeing the Bloodstone heir unravel under his and Asher's hands and mouths were dashed upon learning that Selene had promised him to another. To the sister of the soon-to-be-alpha he'd hoped to forge an alliance and friendship with.

Asher let out a low whistle. "Interesting timing," he said, though Caleb didn't miss his beta's teasing pout.

"It gets better," Aiden added dryly. "Kai has a long-time girlfriend back home. They've been planning to pursue a chosen bond. It's a source of contention between Kai and Darius, who's been adamant Kai prioritizes finding his fated. So, as you can imagine, things are...complicated."

Ice water replaced his blood despite the dining hall's warmth. How many times had he and Asher danced around discussing this very scenario? What would happen when Selene decided it was time for one of them to meet their fated? His stomach knotted, acid rising in his throat at the thought of their connection being severed by divine decree, each breath becoming shallow as phantom loss constricted his chest.

"Trust in Her wisdom," Fenrir rumbled, warmth flowing through their bond. *"What Selene has joined, she does not easily break. Your path with Asher was never a mistake."*

Caleb gripped Asher's hand beneath the table, their fingers intertwining as the worry receded.

Before he could speak, Cian appeared at the table, complexion unusually pale. He slid into his seat, avoiding Aiden's gaze. Even from across the table, Caleb could scent his discomfort.

"Sorry I'm late," Cian muttered.

Aiden frowned, brows knitting in concern. "Are you alright? Did you find Ryker?"

Cian gulped, face flushed as he avoided eye contact. "Uh...yeah. I found him. He, um...he might not be joining us."

Aiden's frown deepened. "Why not?"

Cian hesitated, then blurted, "Because when I got to his room, he was...getting head. And she, uh...might have been...fingering his ass."

The table fell silent. For a moment, all Caleb could hear was the clink of silverware and the distant hum of conversation from the other tables. Fenrir's amusement rippled through him, matching his own.

Then, Asher snorted. "Well, good for him. Nothing beats a prostate orgasm!"

The tension shattered as the table erupted into laughter.

Aiden doubled over, tears streaming down his face as he shook his head. "That boy," he managed between gasps, "is going to be the death of me."

Cian groaned, burying his face in his hands. "I didn't need to see that."

Asher slapped him on the back, still chuckling. "Consider it a lesson in the diversity of claiming rituals."

Caleb shot Asher a look of mock exasperation. "You're impossible, you know that?"

Asher smirked, leaning closer to Caleb, his voice just loud enough for the table to hear. "And yet, you love me anyway."

The group fell into a more relaxed rhythm after that, their laughter dispelling the intensity of the morning. They spent the rest of lunch getting to know one another, sharing stories about their packs and histories. Fenrir stretched and curled within Caleb's mind, muscles relaxing as the wolf basked in the warmth of genuine connections forming.

When the conversation turned to Crescent Fang, Caleb spoke openly about their isolation, their deep connection to Selene's teachings, and the challenges of reintegration.

"Living outside the fold meant we had to be self-sufficient," Asher chimed in, dark eyes sweeping over the group. "But it also gave us perspective. We've thrived, built something strong and bountiful. Something worth protecting. That's why reintegration isn't just about Crescent Fang. It's about bringing that strength back to the region."

Cian leaned back in his chair, sharp gaze thoughtful as he posed his question. "Caleb, I have to ask. What's it like being descended from Caelum, the first alpha? I can't imagine what it must feel like to carry that kind of legacy."

Fenrir's presence surged at the mention of his original counterpart, ancestral memories flickering like shadows at the edges of Caleb's consciousness.

Caleb's expression was pensive as he weighed his response. "Honestly? I didn't feel much pressure growing up," he admitted. "When rogues killed my parents, I was just a pup. Too young to understand. What I remember is the aftermath. Feeling lost, adrift in a void where my world had been."

Asher squeezed his hand, their fingers interlocked.

Caleb offered a faint smile before continuing. "Asher's father, Garreth, was my dad's beta. He saved me. Stepped in as interim alpha and raised me not as some mythological heir, but as a pup who needed guidance and love. He taught me loyalty, tradition, resilience. Those years shaped me. And even after taking the mantle at eighteen, Crescent Fang's council has guided me every step."

Cian nodded, empathy evident in his features. "It sounds like you have incredible mentors."

"They are," Caleb agreed. "But the real turning point was when I met Fenrir."

"Your wolf?" Aiden asked, setting down his cup and bracing his forearms on the table.

Asher's lips curved into a small, smug smile. "Not just any wolf. Fenrir's the reincarnation of Caelum's wolf. The first blessing."

"I didn't fully understand what that meant at first," Caleb added. "Meeting him was like finding the missing piece of myself. Not just a counterpart—an anchor. My link to Selene and everything Crescent Fang stands for."

"You honor me." Fenrir's presence warmed like sunlight through Caleb's chest, the wolf's affection vibrating through their bond.

Cian's brows lifted. "That's...extraordinary."

"It is," Caleb said softly, gaze distant for a moment as he communed with Fenrir. "His wisdom is incredible, but he's always been more than a guide. He's a reminder of what's possible when you trust Selene's will. Even now, as I consider what reintegration means for Crescent Fang, Fenrir keeps me focused on the right path."

Fenrir rumbled again, his tone resolute. *"These wolves. This connection. It feels right. Keep going, Caleb. I will see you through."*

Caleb exhaled, the sincerity of his wolf's support grounding him. "Coming here has been eye-opening. It's not just about politics. It's about connection. Building something that will endure for all our packs."

Cian leaned forward. "That's a perspective not many alphas would have. You've embraced your role without letting heritage define you."

Caleb inclined his head with a faint smile. "What drives me is the future. The wolves I lead. The lives I'm responsible for and," he paused to kiss the back of Asher's hand, "the people I trust to walk beside me."

Asher smiled, his earlier humor giving way to something quieter and more intimate. "Always."

CHAPTER TWENTY-ONE

LENA

Lena smirked as she stretched her legs in the back seat, rolling her shoulders with exaggerated ease. "Ah, it feels good to be a champion," she teased, voice laced with mock superiority.

Ryker groaned dramatically, leaning his head against the window. "Don't start."

"Don't start?" Lena's smirk widened, savoring her victory. "I took you down three times during warrior training today, Ryker. *Three times*!"

He jabbed a finger at her defensively. "I let you win."

"Oh, please." Lena snorted, flicking her wrist dismissively. "The first time, maybe, but you were actually trying the second and I *still* wiped the floor with you."

"Let's not forget the Blackwater beta-heir," Aiden chimed in from the driver's seat, tone full of pride. "Lena annihilated him in her next match. That wasn't beginner's luck, it was skill. You should be proud, Cian."

Cian arched a brow, glancing at his sister through the rearview mirror. "I am. I always knew she could hold her own. The real question is whether Ryker's ego can survive this summit."

Lena laughed, leaning back in her seat. "You know, I was worried at first. I thought maybe Ryker was taking it easy on me, but after seeing him get knocked around a few times, I realized I'm just that good."

"Watch it," Ryker grumbled, tone more playful than irritated. "I'll remind you that I did take down the Bloodstone and Ironclaw betas after I got into my groove."

"*After*," Aiden emphasized, smirking as he caught Cian's eye. "It took you a few rounds of getting your ass handed to you first."

Cian snorted, a rare smirk tugging at his lips. "Maybe if Ryker hadn't had his soul sucked out through his dick while getting finger-fucked in the ass at lunch, he might've had a better showing."

Aiden barked out a laugh, and Lena's gasp filled the car. She smacked Ryker's arm, golden-brown eyes wide with mock horror. "Wait! *Again?* Goddess, Ryker, wasn't last night enough?"

"What do you mean, last night?" Aiden demanded, jerking the wheel. "What happened last night?"

Ryker raised his hands defensively, grin as unapologetic as ever. "First of all, we already talked about how it's rude to kink shame, *Mrs.* Bloodstone," he began, leaning toward Lena. "Second, I told you at breakfast that I wasn't sure if I liked it. So naturally, I had to verify the results."

Lena groaned, covering her face with her hands. "Goddess, give me strength."

Ryker leaned back with a dramatic sigh, placing a hand over his chest as if recalling a fond memory. "She lubed me up with her tongue this time, so I was ready for it. And guess what? I fucking *loved* it!"

Cian groaned, pinching the bridge of his nose. "Selene, spare me."

"I don't know what I did to deserve this," Aiden muttered, shaking his head despite his obvious amusement as he focused on the road.

"Don't act like you're not impressed," Ryker shot back, grin impossibly wide. He reached forward, wrapping his arms around Cian from behind the seat. "She's special, you know. Truly a gift."

"Why don't you tell them who this paragon of virtue that you've been letting defile you is?" Lena prodded dryly, though she couldn't suppress the laughter bubbling in her chest.

"Her name is Tessa," Ryker said, sighing dreamily. "Beta Thurston's and Luna Ylva's daughter. And honestly, I'm almost hoping I don't find my fated. I have half a mind to claim her as my chosen. Gah, that mouth. Those hands. The pups we'll have together!"

Aiden snorted, unable to contain his laughter. "You're hopeless, I swear." The humor in his voice faded as he continued. "Be careful where you talk about your escapades. Thurston is a serious male, and I doubt he'd take hearing about your dalliances with his unmated daughter too kindly."

Cian shook his head, voice filled with resigned exasperation. "I'm starting to think coming to this summit without Dad was a mistake."

"Stop lying to yourself," Ryker teased, settling back with a cocky grin. "You'd be bored out of your mind if Alpha was here to reel me in."

Lena couldn't help but laugh, shaking her head at the absurdity of it all. "Just...try not to embarrass the pack too much, okay? We're supposed to be impressing people here, not scandalizing them. Or do you want to explain to my father how news about your appetite for anal play was a prominent discussion of the summit?"

Ryker winked at her. "Don't worry, Lena. I'll keep the scandal confined to my bedroom."

Their laughter echoed in the confines of the Jeep, carrying them the rest of the drive. Elara's energy melded seamlessly with the invisible threads connecting them all.

Aiden pulled into the parking lot minutes later, the warm glow of the restaurant's lights spilling out onto the pavement. The sign above the door, *The Silver Fork Steakhouse,* promised hearty meals and good conversation. Exactly the kind of break they all needed from the intensity of the summit.

Rich scents of grilled meats and fresh bread hit them as they stepped inside. The cozy atmosphere contrasted the summit's stark formality.

A young hostess with a bright smile greeted them at the entrance. "Welcome to The Silver Fork. Do you have a reservation?"

"Moonshadow party, table for four," Aiden replied, glancing at his watch.

"Perfect." She made a note on her tablet. "Just a few minutes. Feel free to wait by the bar."

As they stepped aside, Lena scanned the lively restaurant. Conversation hummed beneath clinking glassware, the place surprisingly busy for Monday. She couldn't help but wonder if other summit attendees had the same idea about dining off-site.

Her gaze drifted over the tables of diners, curiosity piqued as she searched for familiar faces. She spotted a table of beta-heirs she vaguely recognized from the training grounds, another with older alphas deep in discussion. Then her gaze stopped, catching on something—or rather, someone.

His brilliant emerald eyes held her captive, piercing her even from across the room.

Kai.

Lena's breath hitched as her gaze locked with her mate's, their bond singing even at this distance. He sat near the back, tearing apart a dinner roll, surrounded by Darius, the Bloodstone beta, and his heir. Her pulse thundered in her ears as Elara's presence surged forward, a molten ripple of need coursing from her core to her fingertips.

Goddess, he's gorgeous, she thought, unable to tear her gaze from him despite the stiff set of his shoulders and tight line of his jaw. The restaurant's low amber light caught on the sharp edges of his cheekbones, casting shadows that only emphasized their perfect cut. His gaze alone sent invisible fingers trailing down her spine, each vertebra igniting one by one.

The spell lifted when she took in Kai's expression. There was no warmth or longing in his gaze.

Just anger.

He wasn't happy to see her. Not in the slightest.

Lena felt herself deflate, the initial spark of excitement snuffed out by the icy edge of his glare. Elara curled inward like a wounded animal, the wolf's vibrant energy dimming to a protective flicker.

"Lena?" Cian's voice pulled her back. "You okay?"

She blinked, tearing her gaze from Kai to find her brother's concerned frown. "Yeah," she managed, lips stretching into a forced smile. "Just taking in the place."

Before Cian could press further, the hostess returned. "Your table is ready."

Following her, Lena glanced back once more. Kai's gaze remained stoney, their bond thrumming dangerously tight like a guitar string, ready to snap.

Lena slid into her seat, trying to shake off the burn of his glare as she felt her wolf's agitation churning beneath her skin like stormy waters.

She'd barely started to settle when a large shadow fell across the table. She glanced up, anxiety spiking as the now-familiar figure of Alpha Darius stood confidently at the head.

"Well, well," Darius exclaimed, booming voice carrying above the lively chatter of the restaurant. "What a pleasant surprise! I insist we all dine together, seeing as we'll be family soon."

Lena's forced smile faltered, fingers clenching around the edge of the menu.

So much for a quiet reprieve.

CHAPTER TWENTY-TWO

KAI

K ai picked at the roll he'd grabbed from the breadbasket. The soft, crusty bread crumbled beneath his fingers as he pushed the crumbs into a pile on his plate. They'd just been seated for dinner, but his appetite had vanished. His father held court across the table, regaling Maxim and Magnus with summit stories. Kai's mind, meanwhile, tangled in a relentless loop of frustration and exhaustion.

He couldn't tell what had been more draining—pretending to care about the alphas boasting their successes, enduring the grueling border negotiations, or surviving the tense car ride to dinner where he'd clashed with his father yet again.

A muscle twitched along Kai's temple as the memory surfaced.

"If you dare to reject her"—Darius's glare had frosted over, each word striking like an icicle—*"you'll lose everything. Your title, your name, your pack. You'll fight in the coming war as a rogue before I let you disgrace Bloodstone."*

The force of his father's alpha aura had been oppressive, leaving no room for argument. The threat lingered in Kai's mind, a suffocating reminder of what was at stake.

And then there was Ava.

A vision of her tear-streaked face haunted him, sobs echoing as he imagined breaking her heart. She'd trusted him, planned a future in her mind—a future he'd promised her. Now, that promise felt like sand slipping through his fingers.

Kai clenched his fists under the table, anger simmering just below the surface. Darius had no right to force this on him, to use his legacy as leverage to bind him to a mating he didn't want.

Movement near the entrance caught his eye, pulling him from his thoughts. The Moonshadow group had just arrived, their arrival drawing attention as they stepped into the restaurant. His gaze landed on her instantly.

Lena.

She stood with her brother, Cian, and their packmates, golden-brown eyes scanning the room. She was radiant, her confidence and warmth filling the space like sunlight breaking through clouds. For a moment, Kai let himself take her in—the way her glossy hair framed her face, the strength in her posture, the quiet determination in her expression.

"Our mate is stunning." Orion's whisper carried longing that vibrated beneath Kai's skin.

He struggled for air, the bond's pull like a fist wrapped around his throat. This wasn't some fairy-tale meeting. Lena had upended his life, shattered everything he'd built. She wasn't a gift. She was a reminder of everything he stood to lose.

Her face lit up when she saw him. Kai froze, resolve wavering under her gaze. Then his anger surged forward like a tidal wave, drowning out the bond.

He glared at her, emerald eyes hardening to cold jade. Her joy faltered in stages: first confusion, then disbelief, finally hurt. Her smile collapsed as she followed the hostess, gaze dropping to the floor.

His stomach twisted with a flash of guilt as he watched her joy crumble, but he hardened himself against the feeling. She wasn't a victim in this. She was the complication that had destroyed everything he'd planned.

Good, Kai thought bitterly. *Let her feel the chaos she's brought into my life*. His gaze followed her, mouth pressed into a hard line, even as Orion whined in protest.

He was so fixated on Lena that he didn't notice his father rising until Darius's booming voice filled the restaurant, inviting the Moonshadow wolves to join them for dinner.

Acid churned in Kai's gut as servers rearranged the tables. He glared at his father, who gestured for more wine without acknowledging his son's silent fury.

"Whatever my Moonshadow family needs," Darius declared, "add it to my bill."

Once the tables were joined, Darius facilitated the introductions. "This is my beta, Maxim; our beta-heir, Magnus; and you already know my son, Kai."

Cian followed suit. "Aiden, my father's beta; Ryker, my future beta; and, of course, my sister, Lena."

The crumbs on Kai's plate blurred as he stared downward, jaw muscle pulsing, while Magnus leaned toward Lena with undisguised admiration.

"You were phenomenal in warrior training today," Magnus said. "The way you had the Blackwater beta-heir on his back wheezing...it was impressive."

Lena blushed. "Thank you. I'm grateful for the training my father provided." Her gaze flicked to Kai before returning to Magnus. "It's given me the confidence to support my future alpha in any way I can."

Kai's eye twitched at the insinuation of her claim on him. He forced himself to stay silent, teeth grinding together. Orion, however, was nearly purring with approval.

"Perfect," his wolf murmured. *"She will fight by our side. She will protect the pack, our family."*

Reluctant appreciation flickered through him at her tactful response. She'd managed to acknowledge their bond without making him seem weak or cornered. He also couldn't deny the appeal of having a fighting luna by his side. Ava might have a mind for strategy, but she wasn't interested in bruising her fists or getting blood and dirt under her claws.

If circumstances were different—Kai slammed a mental door on the thought, burying it beneath his resentment.

Darius beamed, his pride unmistakable. "What an impressive female," he said warmly. "I couldn't picture a better luna to usher in the next era of Bloodstone leadership."

Kai's expression hardened, the praise for Lena scraping against his raw nerves. Meanwhile, Orion stretched languidly within their shared consciousness, radiating with delight at their mate's acknowledged strength.

The meal progressed in a haze of forced smiles and polite conversation. Kai watched Cian's posture soften by Darius's enchantment with Lena. Watched Ryker's easy humor bridge both packs. Watched Lena include Magnus in their banter without hesitation, her natural charm drawing everyone closer.

Kai even felt jealousy flare as she laughed with Ryker, golden-brown eyes alight with affection. He hadn't felt such a genuine warmth since his mother passed and couldn't help but crave all of Lena's affection be directed at him, and him alone.

He found himself leaning forward, despite himself, drawn to the sound of her voice, hanging on to every word, completely dazzled by the way she interacted with everyone at the table. She was kind and captivating, and Goddess was she beautiful. He leaned closer, elbows braced on the table, as she and Ryker told Magnus a story in tandem, one effortlessly picking up where the other dropped off.

I want to know all your secrets. The thought came unbidden. *I want to know your memories, make new ones with you that we can tell our—*

He caught himself before he could finish the thought and jerked back, scowling at how easily his traitorous body and mind responded to her.

"She's everything." Orion's conviction radiated through Kai's bones with marrow-deep heat. *"Ours."*

Aiden's voice interrupted the wolf's musings. "Alpha Raelen is eager to host you after the summit, Kai. He's looking forward to your visit and seeing Darius at Cian's ceremony. He's sending the gamma-heir, Jace, with a car so you can ride back with Lena and Ryker."

Lena's gaze snapped to Kai, voice bright with hope. "You're coming home with me?"

Unwanted images flashed—walking Moonshadow's territory with Lena, seeing her home, sharing her bed. The speculation snuffed itself out before taking root, leaving him unsettled by his wayward curiosity.

Darius cut in before Kai could respond. "Yes, we're very excited, but no need to send a car. Our gamma-heir, Elias, will bring Kai's car down personally."

Kai's shoulders tensed, a flash of panic crossing his features as he glanced at his father. "That's not necessary," he said even as Orion snarled in protest. "I'd be happy to return to Bloodstone with you, pack some things, and address a few personal obligations. I can make the journey to Moonshadow the following day."

"Liar," Orion snapped. *"You're running."*

"No. I need *to see Ava."* Kai felt another wave of anger surge at the corner his father had backed him into. *"What am I supposed to do, disappear for a whole month then show up with Lena on my arm hoping Ava gets the message and doesn't lose her mind? I know you don't like her, but she deserves better than that."*

"I'll just need the day, Dad." Kai kept his tone steady, but his eyes pleaded with Darius for this small reprieve.

Darius's smile didn't falter, but his tone left no room for argument. "It's already arranged."

Kai's knuckles whitened as he swallowed his retort, Darius already turning the conversation back to Cian's upcoming ceremony.

When the meal ended, the groups moved toward the exit. Lena lingered outside the restaurant, waiting until the others had moved ahead, then approached Kai.

Before he could step away, she looped her pinky around his, golden-brown eyes soft and searching as she tilted her face toward his. The moment stretched as she rose on her toes, lips pressing softly against his cheek. The kiss lasted a few heartbeats, the warmth of her touch spreading through him like wildfire and softening the tension in his body. Orion's contented purr vibrated from his chest to his throat, the wolf surging forward as their mate's scent wrapped around them like a tangible caress.

She pulled back, voice barely a whisper. "I'm glad dinner happened. Being close to you makes my wolf, Elara, and me so happy. I can't wait to have more time with you. To share my home with you."

Kai's lungs refused to work as Lena turned and joined her packmates near the Jeep. She glanced back as she climbed in, smile gentle and sweet.

"Goodnight, mate," she called softly.

Kai stood rooted to the spot, the ghost of Lena's kiss still burning on his cheek. Orion preened in Kai's mind even as his chest ached with the futility of his fight. He exhaled shakily, thoughts spinning. "I'm fucked," he muttered as he made his way towards the limo.

CHAPTER TWENTY-THREE

LENA

The banquet hall blazed with energy. Warm lighting cast a golden glow over mingling leaders and heirs. Crystal clinked like wind chimes while laughter echoed off high ceilings as Lena's fingers tightened around Ryker's arm. They entered together, Elara stirring restlessly beneath her skin, scanning for one scent among the many.

The beta-heir looked unusually composed—for now—though mischief danced in his eyes as they reached the bar. Champagne fizzed in their glasses, tiny bubbles racing to the surface. Elara huffed with impatience, the wolf's excitement barely contained beneath Lena's polite veneer.

"To surviving your first summit." Ryker raised his glass with that trademark grin and wink that always preceded trouble.

Lena laughed, the sound genuine despite the constant ache in her chest—the hollow space that seemed to pulse whenever Kai wasn't near. She clinked her glass against his. "To surviving you."

They wove through the crowd, exchanging pleasantries that felt both diplomatic and sincere. Pride swelled in her chest at how well the Summit had unfolded for Moonshadow.

Her thoughts scattered as they approached a small group where a striking blonde female stood laughing. The sound was musical as she responded to something a tall, dark-haired male had said.

"Tessa!" Ryker's grin widened impossibly. The way his body gravitated toward her caught Lena's attention—there was something almost magnetic in his movement.

The female turned, sapphire-blue eyes lighting up at the sight of him. "Ryker," she breathed, her voice warm as honey dripping from a comb. Elara perked up at the scent of affection between them, a pleased rumble vibrating through Lena's chest.

"Miss me?" He slid an arm around her waist with practiced ease, but there was something different in his touch—a tenderness that made Lena's chest tighten. When he leaned into whisper in Tessa's ear, the shiver that ran through the female was visible. It was clear how lust had matured into something more over the last few days. How being in Tessa's orbit had smoothed the edges of Ryker's usually frantic aura.

Lena watched them with a mixture of delight and longing to know how it felt to have that kind of connection.

"Tessa, I don't know how you tolerate him," she said, extending a hand to the Redridge Beta's daughter. "I'm Lena."

Tessa took Lena's hand. "I've heard so much about you." She beamed. "Ryker hasn't stopped singing your praises all week."

"Hasn't stopped singing yours either," Lena quipped, lips curving into a knowing smirk. "Some of them not quite appropriate for the breakfast table."

Tessa laughed while giving Ryker a playful shove. His hand traced the slit of Tessa's dress, lips brushing her ear as he whispered promises that made her flush crimson.

"Ryker," she gasped, voice catching with both embarrassment and clear desire.

"You'll make a perfect beta-female." His grin turned wicked. "You have no idea the things I want to do to you—the ways I want to love and worship you, how I'll keep you filled with my pups."

Before Lena could decide between rolling her eyes or applauding his boldness, Aiden appeared, expression caught between amusement and exasperation.

"Ryker," he said, lips twitching despite his firm tone. "Cian's waiting. Rounds."

Ryker groaned dramatically and pressed a lingering kiss behind Tessa's ear before following. "Did you have to take lessons to become an epic cock-block, or does it just come naturally?"

Tessa covered her mouth, nose scrunching as she giggled. Lena couldn't help joining in, the levity of the moment a welcome distraction.

After Ryker disappeared with his father, Lena turned to Tessa. "So, is this just a Summit fling, or are you hoping for more?"

The smile slipped from Tessa's face, shadows of pain darkening her features. "I found my mate when I was eighteen," she said quietly, hands wringing together. "One of our warriors. We had so many plans..." Her voice cracked, and she swallowed hard. "He died in a rogue attack before we could complete our mating ceremony."

Something shriveled in Lena's chest, a physical ache spreading beneath her ribcage. Elara's whimper resonated through their bond, the wolf's grief vibrating through her marrow. She reached for Tessa's hands, feeling them tremble against her steadier ones.

"I'm so sorry," she whispered, throat tightening around words that felt inadequate against such profound loss. "That must have been unbearable."

Tessa nodded, tears glazing her eyes. "For years, I felt...empty. Like part of me died with him. My father pushed me to come here—not to find a chosen mate, necessarily, but to make connections. To heal." A bittersweet smile curved her lips. "Then I met Ryker."

"And?" Lena leaned closer.

"He's..." Tessa laughed softly, wiping a tear from her cheek. "He's everything I didn't know I needed. He's made me laugh again, awakened something inside me that has long felt dead." Her laugh died as she shook her head vigorously. "But I won't let him throw away his chance at a fated bond—not even for me. If Selene wills it, we'll find our way back to each other."

Before Lena could respond, Tessa's father called her away, leaving Lena alone with her thoughts.

She sank into a nearby chair, mind drifting to Kai. Elara brightened, sending warm pulses through their shared consciousness. The bond between them had grown stronger over the past few days, and both

Lena and her wolf had delighted in the dangerous game of testing Kai's resolve. Every touch, every whispered affirmation, every innocent kiss on the cheek—all designed to draw him closer, to help him understand the inevitability of their connection.

Yet, as much as she wanted him, he wasn't truly hers... Not yet. Not until he ended things with Ava.

Pressure clamped around Lena's ribcage at the thought. She rose, determined to find Kai. Winding through the banquet hall, she searched for his scent. Finally, she spotted him through the glass doors of the lobby, but he wasn't alone.

CHAPTER TWENTY-FOUR

CALEB

C aleb hadn't planned on attending the closing reception, but the past three days had shifted his perspective. He'd arrived at the Summit expecting thinly veiled judgments and banalities. Instead, he'd been greeted by unexpected warmth, finding deeper insights than anticipated.

He stood just inside the banquet hall's grand doors, surveying the space—warm wooden beams and soft chandeliers casting elegant light over the gathered wolves. Laughter and music intertwined with the delicate chime of glasses as the summit's final night reached its peak.

Even Fenrir, his ever-cautious wolf, settled into the evening's energy. *"You've done well, Caleb."* The wolf's approval resonated through their shared consciousness. *"Selene's will unfolds. Keep going."*

Caleb glanced to his left where Asher held court with a cluster of betas, his natural charm and quick wit drawing raucous laughter. Affection bloomed in Caleb's chest at the sight. Asher had woven himself seamlessly into their community, particularly bonding with Ryker, Moonshadow's future beta. A soft chuckle escaped as Caleb recalled overhearing their conversation during last night's Night Walker party—Ryker's eager questions about progressing from rimming and fingering to pegging, and Asher's delighted, and very detailed, responses.

"He's a marvel, isn't he?" Fenrir's affection colored the words.

"He is," Caleb agreed, pride swelling in his chest.

What struck deepest was the acceptance he and Asher received from the other leaders. No sideways glances or skepticism, only respect. One conversation with Blackwater's Alpha, Renford, kept replaying in his mind: *"You two seem to have a love that strengthens your leadership. Have you considered seeking a chosen mate who could bond with you both?"*

The possibility of a shared fated had taken root in Caleb's mind, sparking both curiosity and cautious hope.

Across the room, Asher caught his eye. His beta's smile turned devilish as he excused himself and crossed the floor. Without hesitation, he slid an arm around Caleb's waist and pulled him close for a kiss that tasted of wine and want.

"Don't look so serious." Asher's words vibrated against Caleb's lips. "This is supposed to be a celebration."

Caleb leaned into his touch, shoulders softening. "I suppose you're right."

"Good." Asher stepped back just enough to straighten Caleb's tie, fingers lingering on the knot. "Now go. Make the rounds." He nodded toward the Blackwater wolves. "Start with Renford. He's been watching you all night. Seems open to collaboration. Then Garrick from Redridge. He's prickly, but Fenrir's spiritual edge will resonate. And don't forget Moonshadow. Aiden's been raving about your historical insight during training all summit."

"How do you know all this?" Caleb's lips quirked.

"I'm me," Asher replied with a wink, stealing another quick kiss. "Now go. Work your magic."

Following Asher's guidance, Caleb chatted with Renford first. The Blackwater Alpha's warm greeting led to an easy discussion of trade possibilities and joint warrior training. Each exchange fueled Caleb's confidence, handshakes firm and smile genuine as he circulated through the gathering.

By the time he reached the bar for a refill, the pleasant buzz of conversation and music had settled into a comfortable rhythm around him. He wasn't usually one to linger at parties, but tonight, something in the air felt worth sinking into. The bartender refilled his bourbon, and as Caleb reached for the glass, he noticed a familiar figure down the bar—broad-shouldered, silver-flecked, and watching the room like he was cataloging every threat and opportunity it held.

Garrick Redridge.

Beside him stood a lanky teen with sharp cheekbones and soft brown eyes—clearly his son.

Caleb stepped closer, drink in hand. "Alpha Redridge."

The older wolf turned, offering a handshake. "Caleb Crescent Fang." He tilted his head toward the young male. "You've met my son, Niko?"

"Only in passing," Caleb said, extending a hand to the heir. "It's good to meet you properly, Niko."

The teen shook his hand with steady confidence, despite the slight edge of nerves in his scent. "You too, Alpha."

"Bonfire still going?" Garrick asked, tone casual but knowing.

Niko perked up. "Yeah. The younger heirs were headed that way. Can I...?"

Garrick raised a brow. "Don't light anything on fire. Or anyone."

With a grin and a muttered "Yes, sir," Niko vanished into the crowd.

Garrick watched him go, then took a slow sip of his whiskey. "His first summit. Was a little overwhelmed at first, but he's warmed up. Holding his own."

Caleb nodded, a smile tugging at the corner of his mouth. "I can relate. It's been...intense. But I'm glad we came."

Garrick's expression shifted, more reflective now. "Redridge has only been with the Collective a little over fifty years. My grandfather made the call. Ruffled feathers. Some said we were selling out. Didn't want to answer to anyone outside our borders. Still don't, really."

Caleb studied him, then asked, "Do you think it's worth it?"

The older alpha grunted. "Most days." He swirled his drink. "Of course, there's bureaucracy and posturing—especially at events like this. But the connections? The right ones? Those matter. You'll find that's what turns tides—not money, not power. *Wolves.* Trust."

Caleb absorbed the words in silence, Fenrir's consciousness rising closer to the surface, ears pricked forward in keen attention.

"And how do I make the right ones?" he asked quietly, the wolf's curiosity blending with his own.

Garrick's gaze sharpened. "By watching what matters to them. Not what they say in public. Where they send their sons. Who they ask to train their warriors. Who they toast when they think no one's watching." He set his glass down, facing Caleb fully. "Your territory's valuable. And your budget..." He let out a low whistle. "Damn near triple what other packs your size operate on. That'll attract attention, but that's not what I find most impressive."

His voice softened just enough to land the blow with grace. "The way you and Asher carry yourselves... It's changed how people talk about your pack. You lead like wolves with nothing to prove. That kind of clarity? It's hard to ignore."

Caleb didn't speak right away. Garrick's words resonated deep in his chest, pride building with each heartbeat. When the older alpha lifted his glass in casual toast, the simple gesture tightened Caleb's throat in unexpected recognition.

"You'll be hearing from Redridge soon," Garrick said. "We'd like to send a delegation."

Caleb blinked. "Selene willing, we'll be ready to receive them."

Garrick gave a nod of acknowledgment before making his way back into the fray.

Caleb lingered for just a moment longer, then glanced back toward the gathering. He let his eyes move intentionally—Moonshadow's Beta talking with Silver Hollow's Alpha, Renford deep in discussion with Darius, and Lucien Night Walker circling the edge of the room like a hawk. He didn't just see wolves anymore. He saw potential.

He squared his shoulders and stepped back into the crowd, newly attuned to subtle dynamics—shifts in posture, tracked gazes, unguarded smiles. When he reached the far side of the hall, Kai Bloodstone's approach surprised him.

"Alpha Caleb." His tone was polite but carried an undercurrent of hesitation. "Do you have a moment?"

"Of course." Caleb studied the Bloodstone heir with interest.

As they moved to a quieter corner, the rigid line of Kai's shoulders began to soften, fingers fidgeting with his cuff links. "I've been thinking about what you said about Crescent Fang's history," he admitted, voice dropping to barely above a whisper. "Your connection to Selene, your traditions—it's fascinating, but I also have...questions."

The tone of Kai's voice spoke of something deeper than mere curiosity. Caleb waited, letting silence draw out the real purpose behind this conversation.

"I heard that you and Asher have been together since you were fifteen," Kai continued. "But you're not fated."

"That's right." Caleb watched understanding dawn in those emerald eyes.

"What will you do when you find your mate?" Raw vulnerability bled through Kai's practiced restraint. "Will you...follow Selene's will? Or do you think She would allow you to choose Asher instead?"

"Selene's will is sacred," Caleb said quietly. "But so is what we build, day by day, with the ones we love. Asher and I weren't gifted a bond. We choose each other, every day. Our wolves accept each other, not just as partners in leading our pack, but as lovers. We've built a life—one rooted in trust and respect. In something that feels holy in its own right." He held Kai's gaze. "I believe Selene sees that. That She values love just as much as destiny. I trust that whatever comes, Asher and I will face it together."

Kai's jaw worked silently, brows furrowing as he opened his mouth—but Darius's shadow fell across them, the air heavier with dominant pheromones.

"Alpha Caleb." The Bloodstone Alpha nodded politely. "Apologies for interrupting. Kai, may I have a word, privately?"

Something shuttered in Kai's expression as he followed his father away. Caleb watched them go, a quiet ache rising beneath his calm. He didn't envy the crossroads the Bloodstone heir stood at—chosen or destined. The implications of such a question could crush even the strongest alpha.

He bowed his head, not in deference but in silent prayer. *May Selene grant him clarity and the strength to walk whatever path leaves him whole.*

The evening continued its flow, each interaction building bridges between once-segregated packs. The whispers of rogue movement along northern borders threading through conversations only confirmed what Caleb already knew—no pack could stand alone against such threats. What he once viewed as surrendering autonomy now seemed the only rational path.

Fenrir rumbled agreement.

From across the room, Caleb caught a glimpse of Asher standing with Cian and Aiden, both wolves hanging onto his every word. Pride swelled in Caleb's chest as he watched his beta shine, grateful for the male who had stood by him through everything.

Caleb slipped onto the balcony, mountain air cooling his skin as moonlight painted the landscape silver. Through the windows, he watched the mingling packs—a living model of what their territories needed to become: one cohesive landscape standing against rogue threats. The summit's theme—"In Defense of Our Future"—wasn't merely ceremonial. It was a sign. Crescent Fang could no longer afford isolation, not with what lurked beyond their lands.

Warm fingers threaded through his as Asher joined him. "You've done well, my alpha," he murmured, triumph rich in his voice.

Caleb turned, drinking in the sight of his beta silvered by moonlight. "I couldn't have done it without you."

Hunger sparked in Asher's eyes. "Damn right. And now, I think you owe me."

"Oh?" Caleb's eyebrow arched.

Asher pressed close, breath hot against Caleb's ear. "Come on, my alpha. I have a hankering to be on my knees worshiping that gorgeous cock of yours before you ride my ass hard."

Heat flooded Caleb's veins, pulse jumping at the images Asher's words painted. He grinned, already tugging him toward the lodge. "As you wish, my beta."

Their laughter echoed through empty hallways as they raced for the elevator, the promise of pleasure and connection drawing them to their shared sanctuary. The night wasn't over yet.

CHAPTER TWENTY-FIVE

KAI

Aged whiskey burned Kai's throat as he leaned against the bar, days of accumulated tension pushing down on his shoulders. Magnus stood beside him, his easy smile a stark contrast to the storm brewing behind Kai's eyes.

"Well," Magnus drawled, amber liquid swirling in his glass, "we've survived another one. Though I have to say, this is the first summit you haven't disappeared every five minutes to call Ava." His smile broadened, voice warming with genuine affection. "It's been nice to have this time with you, Kai. Feels like the old days."

"I don't need to call Ava." Kai snapped. "You've been her messenger well enough." He hadn't intended to be so brusque—to gloss over his friend's happiness at their time together—but irritation had been brewing steadily inside him since that first night. He felt like a powder keg bracing for combustion.

"Hey." Magnus lifted his hands, though concern and a hint of rejection flickered beneath his casual defense. "I only spoke to her that first night. Told her I didn't know what was happening with those private meetings your dad pulled you into. That she should wait to hear from you."

"And?"

Magnus sighed, pulling out his phone. "She's been blowing up my messages all week. Though..." His thumb scrolled through notifications. "Nothing today, though. Maybe she's finally giving you space."

Kai's grip whitened around his glass.

Magnus shifted closer, voice softening. "What are you going to do?"

"It's not like I have a choice, do I?" Kai said. "Almost a lifetime of history and years of love don't seem to matter to Selene. And my feelings or happiness definitely don't matter to Dad."

Magnus's gaze held steady. "Look, I love Ava like a sister—we were all thick as thieves when we were pups. I want her happy. You know that. And I've got your back, no matter what. But Kai...Lena's something else. If Selene blessed me with a mate like her, I'd count myself the luckiest wolf breathing."

The mention of Lena sent tension rippling through Kai's frame. He'd barely spent time with her since that dinner. She'd been consumed with luna sessions, sparring matches, and charming every wolf she encountered. She'd given him space, sticking close to Ryker or Cian during her down time, a mercy Kai couldn't voice his gratitude for.

In their rare encounters, she approached with a quiet certainty that left him reeling. The way she'd hook her pinky with his, golden-brown eyes warm with affection. How she'd lean close, breath ghosting his ear as she whispered, *"It's good to see you"* or *"I missed you."* Each time, she'd press a soft kiss to his cheek—though that morning, her lips had lingered dangerously near the corner of his mouth. *"Have a good day, my mate,"* she'd murmured, hope and sweetness threading through her voice before she'd slipped away.

The delicate web she wove around him—gentle but deliberate—was maddening. Every touch sparked something in him, threatening to ignite feelings and desires he wasn't sure he could trust, love that wasn't built on years of knowing and understanding.

"She's under your skin." Magnus smirked with satisfaction at hitting a nerve.

"Shut up." Kai drained his glass in one burning swallow.

Magnus's assessment had struck true, and Kai's mind drifted to watching Lena train from the lodge balcony yesterday. He'd been on the verge of leaving, but he was transfixed the moment she stepped into the ring. Her movements flowed with lethal grace, each strike precise and powerful. She commanded respect not just from beta-heirs but from the betas themselves. Orion had practically glowed with pride, going on about her brilliance, how perfectly she embodied everything they could want in a mate.

"She's extraordinary," Orion had breathed, admiration thick in his voice. *"Our Luna."*

Heat flooded Kai's face at the memory of the past two nights. How he'd found himself posted outside her suite, straining to catch the soft sounds of her pleasure, to hear his name fall from her lips again in climax. That sound haunted his dreams. He'd never admit how deeply she'd worked herself into his soul, filling cracks he hadn't known existed.

He hated it. Hated how effortlessly Lena affected parts of him never touched before. Not even by Ava.

Ava.

Her silence gnawed at him. Every call, text, and voicemail had gone unanswered. While he never mentioned Lena, he'd be an idiot to assume that Ava hadn't already found out, that she didn't know what *"Can we talk?"* meant or hadn't noticed that he'd stopped saying, *"I love you."*

He needed to speak to her—to explain—to make sure she knew how much this hurt him too, how much he wished things could be different. He didn't want to say it in a text or voicemail, but he was running out of options. Panic had continually clawed at his thoughts as each day passed without response.

The impending stay at Moonshadow loomed like a guillotine blade. He knew his extended absence would hurt Ava the most, but what choice remained? His legacy, his pack—everything hung in the balance. He prayed she wouldn't shut him out completely, that she'd at least still want to be friends when he returned.

He straightened, facing Magnus fully. "I'm sorry for being short. You're right. It has been good to spend more time together again. I need to be better about that when we get home."

Magnus smiled. "I'd like that. I know Elias would too. It's been so long since we've hung out. Just the three of us."

Kai nodded. The truth struck home. He'd drifted from his friends as he fell deeper with Ava, especially after his mom died. Magnus and Elias weren't just his beta and gamma or best friends—they were his brothers. Bonds he'd neglected for too long.

"Another?" Magnus asked, gesturing to his empty glass.

Kai shook his head. "I'm fine. Let's make the rounds."

They wove through the crowd with practiced diplomacy, Magnus's steady presence anchoring him as they greeted familiar faces. When they reached Cian and Ryker, the Moonshadow alpha-heir's usual frost had thawed.

"Kai." Cian nodded. "You've been impressive this week. Your handling of the Denali negotiations was sharp."

"Thanks," Kai said, genuine surprise coloring his voice. "Though your sister's been the real standout. She's made quite an impression."

Cian's lips curved, a flicker of pride crossing his face. "She has, but don't let her hear you say that. It'll go straight to her head."

Ryker laughed, clapping Kai's shoulder. "Not bad for the future Luna of Bloodstone, huh? Though sometimes she forgets to turn down her beast. If you need help taming the wolf, give me a call, and I'll come running, brother."

Kai snorted, shaking his head as they fell into easy banter. The camaraderie forming between their packs felt tentative but real—worlds away from their earlier tension.

As Magnus drifted to another conversation, Kai continued his rounds alone. Each handshake and exchange came easier. Orion's satisfaction vibrated through their shared consciousness as leaders praised Kai's deft handling of contentious moments.

"You're ready," his wolf praised. *"This is who you're meant to be."*

Across the room, Caleb Crescent Fang moved through the crowd with quiet confidence, pulling others into his orbit. Kai had learned the favored alpha was involved with his beta, a chosen pairing. If there was anyone who might meet him with empathy and understanding, it had to be Caleb. Before Kai realized it, his feet were carrying him forward.

"Alpha Caleb." He approached carefully. "Got a moment?"

Caleb smiled, inclining his head. "Of course."

In a quieter corner, Kai found himself voicing the questions that had plagued him since the summit review. He hadn't planned this conversation, but something about Caleb's calm demeanor compelled honesty. The words tumbled out—his curiosity about Crescent Fang's traditions, his desperate need to understand how someone could choose love over fate.

When he finally asked the question that had been burning in his chest—what would happen when Caleb found his fated—Caleb's answer wasn't the clear guidance Kai had hoped for. There was no confirmation that fate was the correct path or if it would be okay to blow up his life to have the love he'd chosen. Instead, the young alpha spoke of building something sacred through choice, of wolves accepting each other, of trusting Selene to value love as much as destiny.

The stark difference between Caleb's situation and his own felt insurmountable. Caleb and Asher's wolves encouraged their bond, supported their choice. Orion's vehement opposition to Ava and his yearning for Lena made everything infinitely more complicated.

"Kai." His father's deep voice cut through the moment.

Darius approached, nodding at Caleb with a firm smile, offering apologies for the intrusion and asking to speak to Kai alone

Kai shot Caleb a grateful look, though frustration gnawed at him. He'd been so close to understanding, to finding a path forward that didn't require destroying everything he held dear. Now, bracing for another contentious discussion with his father, he felt more lost than ever.

Caleb's words about facing the future together echoed in Kai's mind as he trailed his father to the lobby. Though laughter and conversation spilled from the banquet hall, it felt distant, muted by the charged silence stretching between him and Darius.

They came to a stop by the tall windows. Moonlight carved sharp angles across the alpha's face as he turned, but his expression softened in a way Kai hadn't witnessed in years.

"Kai," Darius's tone lacked its usual edge. "I want you to know how proud I am of you."

Kai's spine stiffened as his muscles locked in place, mouth opening but producing no sound. His father's approval—that perpetually dangling prize always yanked away at the last moment—now lay before him like an unexpected gift. His pulse thundered in his ears, mind struggling to process praise after years of criticism.

"Watching you at this summit..." Darius continued. "You've stepped into your alpha power in ways beyond my dreams. Your command during the Denali negotiations, your presence in every session—seeing you embrace your legacy brings me more joy than you can imagine."

Kai's throat constricted. The warmth and pride radiating from his father felt alien. Darius's aura reached out with comfort rather than the suffocating dominance Kai had come to expect, allowing him to breathe freely for perhaps the first time in years.

"I know I've been hard on you," Darius admitted, rare vulnerability threading through his tone. "Especially this past year. But I see your potential, Kai. You're *so close* to becoming the leader Bloodstone needs. And this is the most important lesson: being alpha means putting the pack first. *Always*. Even when it hurts. Even when it fights against everything you want."

Kai's breath caught as his father's words settled. He knew where this led.

"Dad..." His voice cracked. "What you said means everything. All I've wanted was to make you proud. I know I haven't made it easy, but this tension between us... It's been crushing."

Darius nodded, features softening further. "I know, son. I hate that it's been this way. I only wanted to guide you—protect you and the pack—not break your will. I've seen how this summit has changed you. I believe you're ready to make the right choices now."

"He's right." Orion's conviction pulsed through their bond like a second heartbeat. *"Time to move forward. Lena is our path."*

Darius exhaled. "I know sending you to Moonshadow without letting you return home first was underhanded. I feared you'd panic, act rashly. I hated forcing my will on you, but I had to. These past days proved I chose right." A wistful smile crossed his face. "Your future luna... She's remarkable. You feel it too, don't you? How she steadies you? How she sparks something in you?"

Kai couldn't deny how Lena had woven herself into his soul with terrifying ease, but his mind clung to Ava. To the seven years of whispered promises and shared dreams that he'd carved into his identity.

Darius's next words fractured his composure.

"I heard what you said about 'personal obligations.' I think I know what, or rather who, you meant. You'll still leave with Lena tomorrow, but...I asked Ava to come with Elias to deliver your car."

Kai's vision tunneled, blood draining from his face, lungs incapable of drawing air. "What?" The word escaped on a strangled breath. "She's here? Now?"

"Waiting in the parking lot with Elias," Darius confirmed gravely. "Talk to her, Kai. Tell her the truth. Do the honorable thing before three hearts break and two packs suffer."

Panic clawed at Kai's chest, each breath becoming shallow and insufficient. His legs turned leaden, stomach twisting into knots. He wasn't ready. How could he face Ava now with his world crumbling?

Darius gripped his shoulder, the touch meant to be assuring. "You're a good male, son. You'll be a good alpha. I know you'll choose right. It won't be easy, but clarity is kindness. And if you're not up to returning to the reception tonight, I'll understand."

He turned back toward the hall, leaving Kai alone in the quiet lobby.

Kai stood frozen, thoughts churning. His legs faltered as he moved toward the exit, each step heavier than the last. When he pushed through the doors, his stomach dropped at the scene before him.

Elias leaned against the Range Rover, expression stormy and posture rigid. Beside him, Ava paced frantically, gesturing wildly as she spoke in hushed tones. Her usual composure had vanished, replaced by raw, untamed energy Kai had never witnessed.

"She's unraveling." Orion's observation came with a retreat, the wolf curling into a tight ball of discomfort deep in Kai's core. *"Because of us."*

Kai drew a steadying breath before stepping forward. "Hey," he called, voice strained.

Ava's head snapped toward him, eyes wide and glassy. For one charged moment, they stared at each other. Then she raced toward him. She leaped into his arms, legs wrapping his waist as she sobbed into his neck.

"Kai," she choked out. "Oh, Goddess, Kai..."

Her body trembled, tears soaking his shirt. Even Orion fell silent, protests dying in the wake of her anguish.

Kai wrapped tentative arms around her, stroking her back. "It's okay," he whispered. "It'll be okay."

She pulled back, reddened eyes locking onto his with wild desperation that was devastating in its beauty. "Kai," she whimpered. "Please...please tell me it's not true."

Pain laced through him. Before he could speak, her lips crashed against his. The kiss was frantic, pleading. The world fell away, and old instincts took over. Her tongue sought his, body pressing tight as Kai's hands gripped her hips while she ground against him.

His restraint crumbled as she moaned into his mouth. Each kiss demanding more of him—*all* of him. He tightened his hold, deepening the kiss as his cock throbbed against the confining seam of his pants. Desperation clouded his mind as he wrestled one arm between them, clumsily working his fly and fumbling with her jeans.

Like a male possessed, he stumbled toward the SUV, mouth never leaving hers. His fingers finally found her panties, dipping beneath fabric to seek her wet pussy, needing to feel her readiness.

"Fuck waiting for a claiming ritual," he growled against her ear. Seven years of yearning burned in his veins, driving him to press her against the hood.

The air shifted violently as his fingers slipped inside her, a feral snarl splitting the night. In an instant, Ava was torn from his arms.

Kai staggered back, horror dawning as he saw Lena crouched over Ava, hand wrapped around her throat.

"Keep your filthy fucking paws off my *mate*!"

Kai's stomach twisted at the tableau—Lena's face contorted with rage, Ava whimpering, his own pants barely held up by his straining erection.

"Fix it!" Lena barked, voice sharp with barely contained rage. Her chest heaved as she fought to restrain her wolf, eyes flickering between golden-brown and molten gold.

Kai watched, stunned, as Lena wrestled for control. Her fists clenched and unclenched, claws extending and retracting with each labored breath. Her snarling lip faltered as rage gave way to vulnerability. As she steadied herself, pain twisted her features—pain Kai couldn't bear. Shame clawed his insides, shredding at the hollow confines of his chest.

"Lena," he choked out.

Her hand shot up, silencing him. "Don't." The grief-edged word came through clenched teeth. Her body trembled as she forced another steadying breath, claws inching back beneath her skin.

When she met his gaze again, fury had been replaced by gut-wrenching sorrow. Her lip quivered as she repeated, "Fix it." Her voice broke on a barely controlled sob. "I can't bear to see you again until you do."

The plea struck like an arrow, rooting him in place, robbing him of speech and movement.

Without another word, Lena strode back into the lodge. The soft click of the closing door echoed like thunder in the sudden silence, leaving Kai drowning in shame and regret.

CHAPTER TWENTY-SIX

LENA

The soft click of the lodge doors echoed through the silent lobby. Lena paced with sharp, angry strides, emotions churning like a storm—rage, betrayal, heartbreak—each one cutting deeper than the last.

The scene outside replayed in brutal detail. She'd known instantly that the leggy blonde wrapped around Kai had to be Ava. At first, she'd tried to rationalize what she was witnessing. Seeing the female's distraught expression and shaking shoulders, Lena had assumed Kai had ended things. She'd even felt a flicker of empathy.

Then Ava had kissed him.

And Kai—*her mate*—had kissed Ava back.

Lena's hands flexed and unflexed unconsciously remembered watching his restraint slip, hands moving with intimate familiarity, pressing Ava against the car hood...

No. She wouldn't let herself relive it.

What terrified Lena most was her own feral response. She'd attacked another she-wolf, drawn blood. She should feel remorse for that violence, but all she felt was Elara's ferocity echoing in her mind: *"How dare she touch mate! He's not hers to have!"*

She'd demanded Kai fix it before fleeing, but now, pacing the empty lobby—skin too tight, every nerve raw and exposed—she wondered if it was even possible. How did you repair a bond after watching your mate nearly give his body to someone else?

Then came a voice, warm and proud. "There's my beautiful daughter-in-law! You look—"

Lena whirled on Darius, golden-brown eyes blazing. A growl rumbled in her chest as she stalked toward him, primal rage bubbling to the surface. Her claws extended unconsciously, muscles coiled tight.

"I am *not* your daughter-in-law." She stepped into his space, teeth bared. The towering alpha loomed over her, but she didn't flinch. Her head tilted back, staring the arrogant male down. "And I may *never* be—especially considering that your son was just wrapped up in his girlfriend's arms, with his dick out, ready to fuck her on the hood of a car!"

Darius's sharp intake of breath cut through the lobby. His commanding presence faltered as his eyes darted between her face and the glass doors, shock and devastation warring in his expression.

He opened his mouth to speak, but Lena cut him off with a raised hand, stepping back. "Save it." Her voice dropped to a biting whisper. "I'm not in the mood, and I have a party to get back to." One clawed finger jabbed toward his chest. "I suggest you keep your idiot son away from me tonight unless you want a scene."

Not waiting for his response, Lena strode past the stunned alpha, head high despite the trembling in her limbs. Each step toward the banquet hall felt like lifting lead weights. She paused outside the doors, drawing deep breaths. Her hands shook as she smoothed her dress, mentally pressing against Elara's presence until the wolf reluctantly retreated, coiling tight in the darkest corner of her mind. The mask had to be perfect—she couldn't let them see her break.

Inside, she spotted her family. Cian, Aiden, Ryker, and Tessa huddled around a cocktail table. Ryker was speaking, gesturing animatedly. Whatever he said had Tessa blushing furiously, Aiden throwing his head back with a howl of laughter, and Cian doubled over, giggling uncontrollably.

The sight sent a bittersweet pang through her chest. These were her people. Her pack. Her anchors. Her posture softened, the fight draining from her body.

Lena counted each inhale and exhale, mentally pressing Elara's grief down. She grabbed a fresh flute of champagne from the bar, her fingers trembling as she plastered on her brightest smile and walked toward the group.

Ryker glanced up, his grin widening. "Well, if it isn't the future Luna of Bloodstone," he teased, lifting his glass in mock toast.

The title landed like the swing of an axe, stealing her breath for a moment, but her smile remained frozen in place.

Lena rolled her eyes. "Don't start, Ryker."

Aiden raised his drink. "To Moonshadow and the end of one of the most unpredictable and entertaining summits."

Lena lifted her glass, willing her hand not to shake. The crystal caught the light, throwing fractured rainbows across her face that helped hide the tears threatening to spill.

"To family," she managed, voice steady even as her throat closed around the words.

Her pack's laughter surrounded her like a shield, and for just a moment—enveloped by their warmth, their strength, their unwavering presence—Lena let herself believe that everything would be okay.

But beneath her smile, beneath the careful mask of composure, the bond in her chest throbbed with each heartbeat. Like an open wound exposed to salt air.

CHAPTER TWENTY-SEVEN

CALEB

C aleb's body was slick with sweat, muscles straining as he pressed Asher against the window. The glass fogged beneath his beta's flushed skin, each breath leaving clouds of condensation on the surface. Below, Summit attendees gathered in the courtyard, their voices a distant hum beneath the rush of blood in his ears.

He couldn't bring himself to care who might look up and glimpse Asher braced against the glass, forehead pressed to the cool surface as gasps tore from his throat. All that mattered was the way Asher's body yielded to him, that perfect heat gripping him tighter with each punishing thrust.

The air thickened with their mingled scents—the sharp tang of sweat, the heady musk of arousal, the distinctive notes of their wolves merging into something wild and untamed. Each stroke drew guttural groans that vibrated through the walls as the wet, obscene sounds of their joining echoed in the room in a primitive rhythm feeding Caleb's frenzy.

"Asher." Caleb's voice dropped to the alpha register that made his beta shiver. "Do you have any idea how good you look like this?" His hands tightened possessively on Asher's hips. "Spread out for me, every part of you mine to take."

A broken moan was his only answer. Asher exhaled in short gasps that left ghostly patterns on the window. His arms quivered with the effort of holding himself up, thighs already weakening from Caleb's relentless pace.

Caleb hadn't intended for things to spiral like this, but something fundamental had shifted this week. Respect replaced doubt as pack leaders deferred to him and the public acknowledgment had awakened something primal—a consuming need to claim Asher completely. The desire burning between them felt deeper than usual. Darker. More intense.

They should have been on the road back to Crescent Fang already, but seeing Asher bent over—the muscles in his back rippling as he tied his shoe—had ignited something feral in Caleb, obliterating all sense of control.

Maybe it was standing tall among alphas last night, no longer an imposter but an equal. Maybe it was pack leaders seeking his counsel. Or maybe it was simply Asher's beautiful submission, standing beside him as lover, anchor, *everything*.

Whatever the cause, Caleb's restraint had shattered altogether. He'd spent the night taking Asher over and over, throat raw from Asher's cock stretching him open, knees bruised from hardwood floors, muscles burning with exertion as he kept himself buried in his beta until language dissolved from their brains—leaving only groans, gasps, and desperate pleas.

They'd barely slept, yet Caleb had awakened with the same hunger clawing at him, that need burning fiercer than before.

"Goddess, Asher," Caleb growled, voice thick with authority and reverence. Heat coiled low in his abdomen, ready to snap. His grip tightened enough to bruise as he pulled Asher back against him. "You take me so well. So perfectly."

"YES!" Asher howled, voice raw and desperate. "Fuck! *Harder*, Caleb!"

Caleb obeyed, movements turning savage as he pounded into his beta with unrestrained force. The sharp slap of skin on skin filled the room, mixing with Asher's cries and the deep growls rumbling from Caleb's chest.

Just the sight of Asher was enough to push Caleb toward the edge—muscles rippling with each thrust, body arching to take him deeper, each pant leaving ephemeral trails down the glass. Caleb's hand slid up Asher's spine, tracing each vertebra before gripping the nape of his neck and pressing down, commanding complete surrender.

"You're mine," Caleb grunted, voice thick with claim. "All of you. *Completely*."

"Yes." Asher's sob broke around the word, body shuddering under Caleb's brutal pace. "Always yours. Always."

Caleb's knot caught without warning, stretching Asher wider than ever before. He rutted into his beta at lightning speed and roared as he came—no longer the carefully controlled alpha who second-guessed every decision, but a leader who claimed what was his without apology—the primal cry echoing through the suite. His knees buckled, vision darkening at the edges as pleasure crashed through him, washing away the last vestiges of the hesitant male he'd been before the Summit.

His climax saturated the air, rich and potent. Caleb's nostrils flared, pupils dilating as animal instinct took over. Asher's scent changed too, carrying the unmistakable markers of being thoroughly claimed. Their breathing fell into a harmonized rhythm, resembling their wolves' panting after a successful hunt—victorious, sated, and deeply connected to their essence.

Asher's body shuddered, release painting the glass as he bit down on his arm to muffle his screams. Caleb's heart stalled with realization—this was the first time he'd knotted Asher. Satisfaction surged again, settling deep in his bones.

Knotting was untested terrain, a line never crossed in their years together. Usually, their bedroom dynamic flowed like water, with Asher typically taking control. But the Summit had changed something in Caleb, unleashing the alpha dominance he rarely expressed. His knot swelling inside Asher felt like the culmination of this transformation. Physical proof of how the week had permanently altered not just how others saw him, but how he saw himself. It transcended physical pleasure—this was claiming, possessing in ways Caleb had never allowed himself before.

For a moment, the world stood perfectly still. The only sound was their labored breaths as Caleb's knot kept them locked together in this new, intimate way.

He pressed his lips to Asher's shoulder, tasting salt-slick skin as he whispered, "Goddess, I love you."

Asher turned his head, sweat-dampened hair clinging to his forehead as he managed a weak smile. "I know," he murmured, voice hoarse but warm. "I love you, too."

As his knot finally subsided, Caleb slipped out with a soft groan. His hands gripped Asher's shoulders, pressing him forward gently. "Show me."

Asher arched his back deeply, presenting himself as instructed. Caleb crouched behind him, breath catching at the sight. Asher's hole remained stretched, evidence of Caleb's knot still visible, his release trickling out in lazy rivulets. Fenrir's presence blazed beneath Caleb's skin, a fire that burned from his chest into his hands gripping Asher's flesh.

"Fuck," Caleb growled, running his hands over Asher's hips before grabbing his jeans and pulling them up. He stood, pressing a kiss to Asher's neck before moving to his ear, lips curving into a wicked smirk. "Keep me there," he purred. "I want you to feel me leak out of you all the way home."

Caleb punctuated the words with a sharp smack to Asher's ass, drawing out a startled gasp and soft chuckle from his beloved beta.

As Asher straightened, their eyes met in the reflection of the fogged window. Pupils dilated as understanding sparked between them—the magnitude of this threshold crossed visible in Asher's trembling lip and Caleb's wondering brow. Asher's expression softened as he turned, pressing his forehead against Caleb's.

"That was..." Asher's voice was still rough, trailing off as he searched for words.

"Different," Caleb finished for him, a hint of uncertainty creeping into his tone. The alpha dominance that had consumed him receded, leaving room for reflection.

Asher's lips curved into a smile as he brushed his thumb across Caleb's cheekbone. "Necessary," he corrected. "We've always had this balance, but sometimes..." He paused, eyes darkening with memory.

"Sometimes we need this too. Raw. Primal." His fingers traced the back of Caleb's neck. "I've never felt more connected to you than when you surrender to what you truly want."

Caleb let out a long breath, shoulders dropping as a tightness he hadn't realized was knotting his spine unraveled vertebra by vertebra. "The things I did to you," he stammered, "the things I still want to do to you—sometimes they scare me. I've spent so long afraid of what my power might make me become."

"They shouldn't," Asher replied simply, pressing a gentle kiss to Caleb's lips. "Your restrained control, your surrender, your alpha dominance—I want all of it. I want all of *you*."

The words flowed through Caleb's veins like warm honey, each pulse carrying them deeper until his breath expanded his chest fully for what felt like the first time in years. Something within his core released. That piece of himself he'd always kept leashed clicked into place with an almost audible sensation.

He adjusted his own clothes with smug satisfaction. The world outside could wait—right now, everything that mattered was right here in front of him, flushed, utterly spent, and perfectly his.

CHAPTER TWENTY-EIGHT

LENA

Lena tugged at the hem of her cropped black sweater, the soft material weak armor against the morning ahead. She paired it with high-waisted jeans and her favorite leather boots—the ones that gave her an extra inch of height, steadying her against what was to come. Her fingers trembled as she secured her hair into a low ponytail, leaving a few strands to frame her face, a habit born of nervousness. The simple gold hoops in her ears and her mother's pendant at her collarbone finished the look, though no amount of jewelry could disguise the strain in her golden-brown eyes.

The Summit's triumphs—her connections with the leaders, the respect she'd earned—felt hollow in the shadow of last night. Her stomach churned as unwanted images played like a horrific highlight reel in her mind: Kai's hands on Ava, their bodies pressed together, the moment she'd nearly lost everything that was meant to be hers. Each image scraped against her insides like broken glass. Acid scorched her esophagus, crawling up her throat with each breath, though she tried to tell herself it wasn't truly betrayal. He wasn't hers.

Not yet.

Maybe not ever.

Her hand steadied as she reached for her lipstick. The crimson shade was her final defense, painted carefully over lips that had demanded more from him: *"Fix it. I can't bear to see you again until you do."*

Questions echoed in her mind, sharp and heavy as she gathered her things to leave: *Will he show up? Do I even want him to?* Yet, a small, traitorous part of her hoped he would—that he'd make the effort, that he'd choose her.

Elara's presence singed like hot embers shifting beneath Lena's skin as she made her way down to the lodge's parking lot. *"He doesn't deserve us if he's too weak to fight."* The wolf's simmering fury was like steel scraping against bone, reverberating through Lena's ribcage.

The crisp morning air hit Lena's face as she stepped outside and joined her family near the Jeep. She forced her shoulders back, chin high—the picture of composure she needed them to see. No one needed to know how close she was to falling apart.

Ryker spotted her first, his grin cutting through the tension. "Well, well, look who finally decided to grace us with her presence." He swept into a mock bow. "Your Royal Highness, the future Luna Bloodstone herself."

A genuine smile tugged at her lips. "Someone has to keep you in line. Goddess knows you can't be trusted unsupervised."

"Wounded!" Ryker clutched his chest dramatically. "After all I've accomplished this summit—"

"Like what?" Aiden's eyebrow arched as he cut in. "Drinking all the champagne? Hitting on every female who made eye contact?"

"Hey, I made a genuine love connection!" Ryker shot back, earning a snort from Cian.

The easy rhythm of their banter loosened the tightness in Lena's shoulders—until Ryker's smile faltered, his usual bright eyes dimming as he glanced down at his boots.

"She told me about her mate." His voice was thread-thin, shoulders curving inward. "Tessa. She lost her fated in a rogue attack. Said their bond was stronger than anything, even without completing the ceremony or claiming rite." He scuffed a boot against the ground. "She's asked for space. Says she likes me—*really* likes me—but doesn't want to rob me of finding my fated."

"How do you feel about that?" Lena asked softly, hand resting on his arm.

Ryker's grin returned, though it was tinged with melancholy. "She's...different, you know? Feels like there's something real there." He paused, voice dropping. "No offense, Lena, but I can't imagine a fated bond feeling better than I've felt with Tessa these last few days."

His raw honesty squeezed Lena's chest, each breath requiring conscious effort. She knew that ache, that barbed-wire pull between desire and destiny.

"Maybe space isn't a bad thing," Aiden offered gently. "If she is the one for you, give it time. See what happens when you visit for the delegation."

Ryker's mood shifted. "Oh, I plan to make the most of that delegation visit," he said, a wicked grin spreading across his face. "Speaking of, did I tell you Asher bought me a butt plug training kit? When I visit Redridge, Tessa and I are going to cement her status as my beta-female with a proper pegging, and I need to be ready for her."

"Ryker!" Lena yelped, playfully swatting at his shoulder.

"It's game-changing," he continued, undeterred. "Cian, you're missing out. Anal play is the difference between feeling your orgasm in your balls and through your entire body."

Cian's brow furrowed with genuine curiosity. "Wait...is it really that good?"

Ryker dove into his bag, emerging triumphantly with a bottle of lube. "Lesson one: prep, prep, and more prep." He tossed the bottle into Cian's hands. "If you think you've got enough, add more. Practice on yourself to find what feels good. Personally, I'm a 'come hither' guy."

Lena buried her face in her hands, laughing despite herself. "Why am I friends with you?"

The laughter died in her throat as Kai's frame cut through the morning bustle.

He moved like a marionette with damaged strings—shoulders hunched as if bearing an invisible weight, feet dragging against gravel with each step forward, gaze darting to her face then away as if the sight burned him. A chink formed in the armor she'd erected around her heart as his ravaged expression registered—eyes sunken, skin pallid, shadows beneath his lashes betraying a sleepless night.

He came.

Relief and terror crashed through her in alternating waves as she realized this moment would either be their beginning or their end.

CHAPTER TWENTY-NINE

KAI

K ai sat slumped in the armchair by the window of his suite wearing last night's clothes, the scent of sweat and regret clinging to him like a second skin. A violent tremor ran through his body, muscles twitching with exhaustion as cold sweat beaded on his skin. Staring at the floor, he pressed his palms flat against his thighs to still them as the events of the night before replayed in his mind on an endless loop.

"You ruined everything!" Orion's roar had rattled through him before the wolf retreated completely.

Between Ava's sobbing and Elias's disgusted glare, Kai couldn't take it. He'd fled like a coward, desperate to find Lena. But Darius had been waiting—cold, unrelenting. The alpha's disapproval pressed down like a physical force. *"Just go."* His father's suffocating aura had left no choice but retreat.

And now, hours later, he sat there—sleepless, unwashed, stomach roiling with persistent nausea—unmoved from the chair since his collapse. Thoughts crashed through his mind like storm waves, threatening to drown him in the wreckage he'd created.

"You're better than this."

Orion's voice pierced through the haze like an ice-tipped arrow finding its mark. Kai winced as the wolf materialized in their shared consciousness—not the warm, comforting presence he knew, but a thorned entity that unfurled around his lungs. With each inhalation, spectral barbs drove deeper between his ribs, transforming breath into an act of self-mutilation. Each breath he drew scraped his insides like pulverized glass.

"I know," Kai thought miserably, hands shaking so badly he had to clench them into fists. *"I've messed everything up. But how do I fix it?"*

The vibration of his phone startled him so violently he nearly fell from the chair. Dread spiked as he pulled it from his pocket. He hesitated before picking it up, dread pooling like lead in his stomach as he read the texts.

DAD

> Ava is awake

DAD

> She's asking to speak with you

DAD

> Finish this and then go fix things with Lena

Kai exhaled shakily, running a hand through his disheveled hair, fingers catching on the tangles. His father's message felt like both a directive and a lifeline—a chance to take the first step toward repairing the damage he'd done. He forced himself to stand, muscles screaming in protest after hours of stillness, legs nearly giving out beneath him.

After a quick shower that did nothing to wash away the shame or the persistent ache in his chest, Kai packed his things. The mundane task centered him just enough to keep the rising panic at bay even though his coordination faltered, requiring multiple attempts to zip his bag. When he finally stepped out of his suite, his heart pounded with every step toward his father's room. Blood rushed in his ears, a roar that drowned everything else.

The tension in the room was suffocating, pressing against Kai's chest until he could barely breathe. Ava sat perched on the edge of the sofa, arms wrapped tightly around herself, tear-streaked face hardened with anger. Near the window, Elias stood with his back partially turned, one hand braced on the windowsill as he stared out at the distant forest. The gamma-heir's posture was stiff, his stormy blue eyes shadowed with unspoken emotion.

Kai stood just inside the doorway, pulse racing as he took in the scene. A cold sweat broke out across his skin as Ava's head snapped up the moment he set his bag down, red-rimmed eyes locking onto him with a fury that sent guilt barreling into him like a battering ram. The force of it nearly drove him to his knees.

She stood, movements sharp, posture defensive. "Well?" The word cracked like a whip across the room. "What the fuck is going on, Kai?"

He felt an invisible hand crushing his windpipe, acidic bile scorching the back of his tongue as she threw her hands up, pacing in jagged steps.

"I heard you found your mate. That you'd been spending time together—not that you had the balls to tell me yourself." Her voice rose with each word, pain pouring out unchecked. "In all your texts and calls, not once did you mention how our lives were about to change forever!"

She spun toward him, anger radiating off her in waves. "And after all the gossip, I expected bad news when your father summoned me here out of the blue...but last night?" Her voice broke. Tears welled in her eyes as she stopped pacing and charged at him.

Kai's stomach lurched.

"You held me." She pushed at his shoulders, movements jerky. Each touch burned like brands against his skin.

"You kissed me." Another shove, harder this time, making him stumble back.

"You fingered me." Her voice cracked, another shove that had him gasping for air.

"You were about to fuck me on the hood of your car, but then your psycho mate attacked me and you just fucking left me there! You went after *her!*"

Kai swallowed hard, overwhelmed by shame that made his body sway. Perspiration slid between his shoulder blades, chilling his spine as his hands flexed uselessly at his sides. His mouth opened and closed several times as he tried to find the words, tongue feeling thick and clumsy.

"Ava, I—" Words stuck in his throat. "I'm sorry. I wasn't prepared to see you—didn't even know Dad had sent for you. When you kissed me..." Another wave of nausea rolled through him. "I wasn't prepared for how it would feel. I—"

He broke off, voice shaking as he ran a trembling hand through his hair. "I got carried away. Giving in to your kiss, letting things escalate, touching you like that...almost—" He gulped, acid burning his throat. He couldn't bring himself to finish that sentence.

"It shouldn't have happened," he finished, voice barely a whisper.

Ava stepped back, arms dropping to her sides as she stared him down. Her voice was quieter now but no less furious. "So that's it? Seven years, Kai, and you were just going to break up with me and what, go play house with your new girlfriend?" Her lip curled in disgust. "Oh, I am sorry, not your girlfriend—your *fated*. Girlfriends don't matter."

"It's not that simple." Kai's voice broke. His fingers curled into his palms, nails breaking skin. "It's not just a choice between you and her. If I reject her, I'll lose everything—my title, my pack. My father will banish me."

Ava's eyes narrowed, and she resumed pacing, steps growing more frantic. Kai's head spun as he tried to track her movement. "So, what? You're going to pick *her* because of politics? Because it's easier?"

Kai shook his head, voice rising with each word. "No! I'm trying to do what's right for everyone—for the pack, for Lena, for you." He stumbled forward a step, the room tilting dangerously beneath his feet. "I've loved you for years, Ava. Do you honestly think I want to hurt you? My heart is breaking, too!"

She froze mid-step, breathing ragged as she faced him again. "Where does that leave us then? Are you going to throw me away? Just like that?"

Kai struggled to speak the truth he needed to tell her. "The bond, Ava... I can't describe it. How intense the pull is. How strongly I feel. I need to go to Moonshadow, to get to know her. I owe it to Lena, to you, and to myself to sort out my feelings. Otherwise, it won't matter what decision I make."

"No." She shook her head. "You're *mine*... You *promised* me a life, Kai," Ava declared, voice filled with indignation. "She has to share. She may have a piece of your soul, but *I'm* your heart. *I'm* your luna. Your forever."

The floor and ceiling traded places as black spots danced across Kai's vision. He gripped the arm of the chair, trying to anchor himself to something.

Ava's voice softened, growing desperate as she stepped closer. Her perfume overwhelmed him, making his stomach roll. "I don't think I can survive losing you." Tears streamed down her face. "What we have. What we've built. It's worth fighting for."

Her words collided with echoes of Caleb's advice. *"Selene's will is sacred, but I believe she values love just as much as destiny."*

Can I have both? Destiny and love? The question made his head spin.

"I'll talk to her." Kai's voice came out hoarse as if raw from screaming. "I'll try to explain. See if there's a way to make it work. To have my soul and my heart."

Hope brightened Ava's face, though a flicker of jealousy marred her expression at the way he referred to Lena. He winced as she threw her arms around him, whispering, "Thank you, Kai. Thank you."

When she tilted her head up to kiss him, Kai wrenched himself backward, nearly losing his balance, hands gripping her shoulders even though they shook. "No," he said gently, bile rising again in his throat. "We can't. Not until I figure this out. Until I know she wants that too."

Ava's hope crumbled, face twisting as anger surged to the surface. "Are you serious?"

"Yes." Kai's voice steadied despite the noose tightening around his neck. "I know it's hard, but I need you as my best friend again more than anything right now. I have to minimize the chance of everyone getting hurt."

Ava's expression darkened. Before Kai could react, she grabbed a lamp and hurled it at his head. He ducked, muscles screaming as ceramic shattered against the wall. Shards rained down, cutting into his skin.

The sharp noise was followed by a blur of movement that made his vision swim. Elias was there in an instant. Crossing the room in quick, long strides to Ava's side. His arms wrapped around her tightly, holding her back with a strength that was more protective than restraining. He didn't speak, but his gaze cut through the room like steel, locking onto Kai. His stormy blue eyes burned with disappointment—and something deeper. *Anguish?*

For a moment, the air felt electrified. As if unspoken words and emotions had seeped into the silence between the two males. Elias's stare said enough: *Fix this. Do better.* The intensity of his gaze made Kai sway on his feet.

Ava's voice yanked his attention away from his future gamma. "Minimize everyone getting hurt?" she spat. Her wolf, Eris's, presence was palpable in the air as Ava roared. "You fucking *destroyed* me, Kai!"

She thrashed in Elias's arms, fighting to break free. He tightened his grip, one hand sliding into her hair in a calming gesture. His lips brushed her temple in silent comfort, even as he glared at Kai, making tears burn behind his lids.

Kai's jaw worked silently, torn between guilt and the suffocating pressure of the bond he was trying to protect. He felt a pang of jealousy—jealousy for Elias's ability to offer Ava the comfort she needed. Comfort Kai couldn't give her without risking the fragile threads of his bond with Lena. His ribcage constricted as he straightened, legs trembling as he grabbed his bag.

"I'm sorry," he said softly, each word like sandpaper against his throat. "I'm sorry for hurting you. For breaking promises that were not mine to make." His lungs fought to expand, every breath shallow and inadequate. "I wish I could fix this without hurting anyone, but I don't know how. It's killing me too, Ava, but all I can do is try. I have to try to find a way through."

He hesitated at the door, grip fumbling on the handle. His voice dropped to a near whisper. "I hope this isn't the last time we talk. That you'll give me the chance to figure everything out. That somehow, we'll still be in each other's lives—no matter what happens."

Ava didn't respond. She was still in Elias's arms, breathing harsh and ragged as her tear-filled gaze burned into him. Her fury, her pain, hung in the air like an invisible undertow, threatening to drag him beneath the surface and drown him in its depths. Elias lowered his head, resting his cheek against Ava's as he whispered something too soft for Kai to hear. The sight of Ava finding solace in Elias's arms made nausea coil in his stomach.

Kai turned the handle and stepped out into the hallway. Ava's muffled sobs penetrated the closed door, haunting each step as he fled.

His head spun as he made his way to the lobby. His steps were slow, almost reluctant, feet dragging against the carpet, each step landing on what felt like broken glass.

Darius waited near the lobby's tall windows, phone in hand. The temperature in the room dropped several degrees. His features hardened to stone, all warmth from the previous evening gone, when he spotted Kai.

"Is it done?" Darius's clipped tone was devoid of any sympathy. Each word felt like ice in Kai's veins.

Kai nodded, barely able to speak around the knot in his throat. "Yes."

Darius straightened, his towering presence as intimidating as ever, disapproval radiating off him in waves that made Kai's legs unsteady. "Good," he said curtly, studying Kai for a beat before turning back to his phone. "I'll see you in a few weeks."

Dismissed. That was it. No acknowledgment of the turmoil raging inside him, no reassurance that this was the right thing. Just the icy formality of a leader who had no time for anything less than absolute obedience. The rejection made Kai heave.

He swallowed hard and left the lobby, Darius's indifference slicing between his ribs and finding the soft vulnerable places beneath. He deserved the repudiation, yet the knowledge did nothing to stop his insides from hemorrhaging.

Outside, the crisp morning air did nothing to clear the fog in his head. The murmur of activity from the departing summit attendees reached his ears—wolves saying their goodbyes, loading luggage, the mundane sounds of life moving forward while his world crumbled.

His breath caught when his gaze landed on the Moonshadow pack. They were gathered near their Jeep, their easy camaraderie contrasting the chaos of Kai's own emotions. Ryker was talking animatedly, hands gesturing wildly, and Lena's laugh rang out in response. The sound soothed Kai's frayed nerves, and he allowed himself to hope—just for a moment—that things might be okay.

But then Lena noticed him. Her laughter faltered, and a flicker of sadness crossed her face before she masked it with a bright, practiced smile. The spark of hope Kai had felt was replaced by a pang of guilt so sharp it twisted his gut and made his head spin. He hesitated as he approached—feet dragging as he worked up the courage to face her. She deserved so much better than this, better than him, but he had to try.

"Mate!" she called as he neared, her tone overly light, overly cheerful. The false brightness in her voice made him flinch. "Ready to see Moonshadow?"

Kai nodded, nearly dropping his bag as he placed it on the ground. He reached for Lena, fingers shaking as he wrapped his pinky around hers—a gesture she'd used so many times over the past few days to draw him closer. One that now felt like his only lifeline.

Leaning in, he kissed the corner of her mouth, trying to hide his anxious state. Her now familiar scent wrapped around him, grounding him for the briefest moment before the guilt threatened to drown him again. His voice dropped to a whisper meant only for her, cracking on each word.

"I'm so sorry. I hope we can talk."

Lena's golden-brown eyes searched his, walls firmly in place. He thought he saw the crack in her armor—the vulnerability she was fighting so hard to hide. She nodded imperceptibly, a silent acknowledgment of his words, though he couldn't tell if it was forgiveness or resignation.

"I'll grab my stuff and meet you at the car," she whispered back, her voice neutral. She turned to the group, her voice bright. "I'm riding with Kai. See you losers in a few hours!"

Her words earned a chorus of good-natured teasing from Ryker and the others.

Kai watched her walk around the Jeep, hope and dread warring in his chest. He made his way to his Range Rover on unsteady legs, tossing his bag in the backseat before leaning against the passenger door as he waited for her. The cold metal pressed into his back as he exhaled shakily, mind racing. Everything felt like it was teetering on the edge of collapse—his relationships, his future, his very sense of self.

He sent a silent prayer to Selene. He didn't ask for forgiveness or even for Lena to understand, but for strength. Strength to face what was coming. Strength to hold onto the bond he'd nearly destroyed. Strength to be the alpha, and mate, he needed to be.

He straightened as Lena neared, her figure a beacon against the backdrop of bustling wolves. Her head was high, strides confident, but Kai could see the tension in her shoulders. Sweat prickled his hairline, ice-cold droplets sliding down his temples as he opened the door for her. She murmured a quiet thank you, but the tremor in her voice betrayed her controlled expression.

As he settled into the driver's seat, silence swelled, pressing against his eardrums. He swiped his palms down his thighs trying to settle his nerves as he braced himself for the conversation they needed to have.

"Are you ready?" His voice barely carried over the engine starting.

Lena answered with a nod.

The distance between them in the car felt both too vast and not nearly vast enough. His grip tightened on the wheel. Tension locked his jaw as he mustered the strength to tear down every barrier and show her his truth

The engine roared, and they pulled away from the lodge. He watched her stare out the window from the corner of his eye, knuckles white as she interlaced her fingers in her lap, pinning them in place as if to prevent them from reaching for him.

The road stretched ahead, winding through territory that felt as uncertain as their future. Neither spoke, but Kai knew this silence wouldn't last. Soon, he'd have to find words for the unforgivable. Soon, she'd ask questions he wasn't sure he could answer. And depending on what he said—and how she heard it—they'd either find a way forward, or this car ride would be the last time he'd ever see her.

CHAPTER THIRTY

LENA

The drive felt like drowning in slow motion.

Silent.

Tension thick as mountain air.

Each passing mile marker a countdown to confrontation. To the reality of last night. To the uncertain space between her and Kai.

Lena braved a glance at him. His posture was rigid, breathing shallow as his gaze fixed on the red Jeep ahead. His hands gripped the steering wheel, knuckles stark white against sun-darkened skin. Sher returned her stare to the window, taking measured breaths while a storm raged inside her.

Elara prowled the borders of Lena's consciousness. The wolf's agitation manifesting as electric pulses behind her eyes. Each spectral paw-step sent concentric ripples of tension across their shared mind, like stones dropped in still water.

"He won't speak first," Elara snarled. *"Too much a coward to face what he's done."*

A heavy sigh escaped Lena before she could catch it. From the corner of her eye, she caught his glance, saw the tension ripple through his jaw. Her fingers drummed against her thigh, each tap matching another passing mile marker.

"So," she said, voice sharp enough to make him flinch, "did you have a specific time frame in mind when you said you 'hoped we could talk'? Or were you planning to let me stew the whole way back to Moonshadow?"

He shifted, fingers flexing on the wheel as if testing their grip. His jaw worked before he managed, "I'm sorry. I—" He swallowed hard and released a shaky breath. "I don't know where to start."

"Well, pick somewhere," Lena snapped, then forced herself to soften. "Tell me about Ava."

The name hung between them like smoke. Kai's shoulders loosened, as if talking about Ava was safer ground. Lena's ribs contracted around her lungs, each breath shallow. She schooled her features into smooth marble, jaw relaxed, eyes steady as she waited.

KAI

Ava.

The question he'd been dreading most. Kai's grip tightened on the wheel as memories flooded back—not just of last night's disaster, but of years of shared history with Ava. How could he possibly explain it all to Lena without sounding like he was making excuses?

"She was from my mother's birthpack, Raven's Crest. She came to us after rogues destroyed the pack," he began carefully. "My dad and Maxim led the rescue mission. She was eight. Just a terrified pup who'd lost everything." He could still remember the way she'd trembled that first night, how small she'd looked huddled between Magnus and Elias. "She latched onto us—Elias, Magnus, and me. We were always following our dads around, playing at being alpha, beta, and gamma. I think being near us made her feel safe again."

Orion pressed against the confines of their shared consciousness. *"Tell mate the truth. All of it."*

"We were friends first," Kai continued, a ghost of a smile touched his lips. "Best friends. The four of us—sometimes Elias's sister, Lyric, too—were inseparable. Making everything into an adventure, always causing trouble, and Ava was at the center of it all. She was like a little sister to us, to me..." His hands flexed on the wheel. "Until she wasn't."

LENA

Lena nodded, memories of her own childhood with Cian, Ryker, and Jace flashing through her mind. She understood the comfort of finding safety in your packmates, the love that could grow from such a close bond.

"What changed?" The question slipped out before she could stop it. Part of her didn't want to know, but she had to understand. Had to know what she was fighting against. If she should even fight at all.

Color crept up Kai's neck as he cleared his throat. "Her first shift. Magnus and I ran with her. I, uh...I accidentally saw her. Before she got dressed. She caught me staring, and..." His ears burned red. "It was the first time I'd ever...reacted...to a female that way."

"Reacted?" Lena arched an eyebrow, watching him squirm even as something cold settled in her stomach.

"You know what I mean," he muttered.

She hummed noncommittally, but her hands curled into fists in her lap. The image of a younger Kai discovering Ava that way made jealousy curl hot and sick in her chest. Elara's growl began as a low vibration at the base of her skull, spreading down her spine, each vertebra resonating with the wolf's territorial fury.

"Things changed after that," Kai continued. "We spent more time alone—shifting, running, wrestling as wolves. And when we first kissed, it felt..." His voice caught. "Inevitable." A pause. "We were in love." Another pause. "Or what I thought was love."

Elara's snarl vibrated through Lena's mind. *"That's not love. Not like what we share."*

Could the fated bond even be considered love? The question burned in her chest as she stared out at the passing landscape.

"But then she turned eighteen," Kai continued softly, "and we realized we weren't fated." His voice dropped so low she had to strain to hear him over the hum of the engine. "I stayed up to bake her a cake. I wanted to be the first to wish her happy birthday at midnight. I was...desperate to know for sure if she was mine." A bitter laugh escaped him. "The cake was terrible, but the moment was worse."

"What happened?"

"Orion, my wolf, completely dismissed her." His words came out rough, like they were being dragged from somewhere deep. "After two years of running with her, wrestling with her, he suddenly wanted nothing to do with her. She wasn't his mate."

Lena's breath caught, windpipe closing as though she'd been the one rejected. The taste of copper flooded her mouth—the flavor of devastation. "And you?"

"I didn't care," he continued, the words spilling freely now. "I was too deep in it. Told myself that what we had was stronger than fate, but Orion fought me every day after that. He hates how close I've stayed to her. The promises I've made. How I've given pieces of myself he says aren't hers to have. And my father..." He snorted, gripping the wheel tighter. "He's always raised issue with our relationship. He doesn't believe it's what's best for me or the pack. He doesn't think what Ava and I have is genuine. At least not on her side."

"Not genuine?" Lena's brow furrowed. "How?"

Kai released an exasperated sigh. "He worries that Ava wants to be luna more than she wants to be mine."

KAI

The words hung heavy between them. Kai could almost hear the pieces clicking into place as Lena processed.

"So, what did you do?" she asked finally.

"We tried cooling things off for a couple months. Kept ourselves open in case we found our fated mates. But as time passed, we fell deeper." His throat worked, Adam's apple bobbing. "Once we decided to pursue a chosen bond blessing, nothing else mattered. We made so many plans—for us, for Bloodstone. It felt perfect and being with her was consuming, especially after..." His words evaporated, gaze fixed on the road ahead.

"After?" Lena's voice was careful, controlled.

Blood rushed to his face, staining his neck and burning the tips of his ears. "With the chosen bond as our goal, it was easier not to hold back...physically," he managed, words sticking to his tongue like peanut butter.

Kai heard her sharp intake of breath—a sound like fabric tearing. Her fingers dug into her knees, knuckles blanching beneath taut skin.

"You fell deeper after sleeping together." Her voice flattened to ice as she turned to stare out the window, jaw so tight he could hear teeth grinding.

"No!" The word burst from him. "We've explored each other but agreed to wait for the claiming ritual for...that."

The rigid line of her shoulders eased slightly, but her voice stayed hard when she spoke again. "So, what the fuck was that last night then?"

Kai felt her question like a slap, the venom in her tone slicing through his fragile control. Shame burned through him as memory flooded back—Ava's mascara tracking down flushed cheeks in black rivers. The hiccupping sobs that had made her shoulders shake so violently he feared she'd break apart. Eyes so swollen, so red-rimmed they barely resembled the bright blue he'd known for years. She'd looked broken. Lost. Like the same frightened pup who'd first come to Bloodstone. No matter how he tried to justify it, shame burned deeper. It wasn't just Ava's pain that had driven his actions, it was his own weakness.

"I'm sorry," he whispered. "I don't even know how to explain it."

"Just tell me the truth." Her voice softened but remained insistent. "What happened last night? What were you thinking?"

LENA

Lena braced herself for Kai's truth, fingernails biting into her palms. Deep down, she already knew the answer. Had seen it in the desperate way he'd pressed Ava against that car. In how his hands had gripped her hips with such familiar possession. The memory made bile rise in her throat and the bond twist in her chest.

Elara's grief bled through their connection. *"He wanted to have her first,"* the wolf whimpered. *"Make her his before being bound to us forever."*

The thought felt like a punch to the gut. As if Ava was his choice, and Lena was just his sentence.

"I've *never* been out of control like that. I wasn't thinking." The confession fell from Kai's lips barely above a whisper, breaking through Lena's ruminations. "I know that's not an excuse, but it's the truth. I was overwhelmed—by the summit, the bond, my dad threatening to banish me. I felt like I was drowning, and then Ava was there, crying, broken..." His voice cracked. "She's been my everything for so long. We were months from our mating ceremony, starting the life we'd planned for years. Seeing her shattered because of me..." He drew a shaky breath. "When she kissed me, I didn't stop it. I should have, but everything just poured out—frustration, desire, guilt, need. I lost myself completely."

The silence stretched. Tears shimmered in her eyes though she fought to hold them back.

"And let me guess," she said, voice unnaturally steady. "You hate what happened? But what would you have done if I hadn't stopped you?" Her tone cracked with fury. "Would you have fucked her? Given her what was meant to be mine?"

Kai flinched hard. "You're right," he choked out. "It's not hers to have. If you hadn't stopped us... I don't know if I would have stopped myself. And I hate *that* more than anything. I'd always planned... I mean, I thought my first time would be special. Sacred. On my mating night with—" He stopped speaking, swallowing hard before continuing. "I never wanted it to be like that. Desperate and panicked against a car. That's not...that's not how it should be, and I don't think I could have lived with myself."

Lena's chest heaved as she fought to control her breathing. She turned to stare out the window, unwilling to let him see how deeply his words cut.

"What do you want, Kai?" Each word came out measured and precise. "What are you doing here with me if she means that much to you?"

She counted her own heartbeats while he wrestled with an answer. When he finally spoke, his voice was raw.

"Honestly...I don't know. My feelings are so tangled."

Lena felt the bond pulse between them, making her breath hitch as Elara paced restlessly beneath her skin.

"The bond pulls me toward you with this...*gravity* that feels impossible to fight. It stirs a want and need for you that I can't even begin to comprehend. Orion aches for yours, like there's this magnetic force trying to drag us together."

His raw confession vibrated through the invisible cord connecting them, setting off ripples of heat that traveled from her chest outward. The current raced through arteries and veins until her fingertips pulsed with tiny heartbeats of their own, each one urging her hand toward his. Her knuckles whitened as she dug her fingers deeper into her knees, anchoring her hands in place. His scent filled the car—orange and nutmeg tinged with confusion and need—making Elara whine in response.

"But then I think about Ava and see everything we built. Everything we dreamed of and..." He paused, almost stealing himself for the rest, while Lena fought to control her breathing, to ignore the way the bond constricted with each mention of Ava's name. "I think I want both of you, but I don't know if it's real. If it's just the bond pulling me to you. If it's the fear of losing Ava and knowing she would share me that pulls me in the other direction. I hate that I can't give you a real answer, Lena. I'm just so...lost."

His admission hit her chest like a hammer to glass, hairline fractures spreading outward with each breath, sending shards into her lungs with every inhale. She straightened, vertebrae aligning one by one as she turned toward him.

"I will not share you."

Each syllable hung suspended between them, unmistakable in their meaning. The bond squeezed around her ribs like a steel band until each breath became shallow and insufficient.

She pressed on, voice softening though her resolve never wavered.

"That doesn't mean I don't feel the bond strongly. That I don't want you—" Heat crawled up her spine as her wolf stretched toward his. "Goddess, Kai, I do. But after last night?" Her voice caught. "I know I couldn't bear it. As your fated, I would feel it—" Nausea rolled through her as phantom sensations flooded her mind. "Feel it when you were with her. When you touched her. When you—" The bond contorted, making her gasp as images of him pressed against Ava splintered her vision.

"We cannot survive that, Lena." Elara's voice trembled, a mourning howl compressed into their shared body. *"We are not made to share our mate."*

Tears spilled from her eyes as she continued. "Don't ask that of me. It might seem simple to her, but she'll never feel her soul being ripped apart because her fated gave himself to someone else."

KAI

Her words carved into him like claws. Silent tears tracked down his face as he pulled the car onto the shoulder of the road, no longer trusting himself to drive through the blur of emotion. The engine idled, its quiet rumble the only sound besides their uneven breathing.

He turned to face her fully, needing her to understand. "I feel like I'm being pulled apart," he whispered. "My heart one way, my soul another. The bond feels like a rope around my chest, tightening every time I resist. Sometimes I can't breathe, and I can't tell what's real anymore—what's me versus the bond versus Ava. It terrifies me, Lena."

Orion scraped against Kai's consciousness, each bristled hair a separate point of pressure beneath his skin.

"Tell her the rest." The wolf's demand manifested as a bass vibration that originated in Kai's marrow and resonated outward through bone, muscle, and skin. *"Tell mate why you fight us."*

Kai swallowed hard. "It's not just about Ava. It's about the *choice*. About feeling like I have no control over my destiny. Like the Moon Goddess, my dad, and even my wolf, are invalidating everything I feel. Telling me that Ava isn't enough. Telling me that what's in my heart is wrong." The words came with a decisive exhale, releasing a burden he'd been carrying for too long.

"I understand that better than you might think," Lena said quietly. "As the daughter of an alpha, my future was never really mine to decide. Everything hinged on who my mate would be—where he'd be from, what his pack needed."

Something shifted in the air between them as she spoke, her normally confident voice gone soft and vulnerable. She turned to face him then, tears making her golden-brown eyes shine in the afternoon light. The sight made his chest ache.

"Before I met you, I was seriously considering a chosen bond with someone in Moonshadow. Just so I wouldn't have to leave. So I could keep some small piece of control over my own life."

The confession knocked the breath from his lungs. The alpha's perfect daughter—fighting the same battle as him? Orion stirred beneath his skin, drawn to her honesty.

"Yeah," he breathed. "You do get it."

LENA

Their eyes met, something electric and fragile passing between them that made the air in the car feel charged, more vulnerable than if they'd been skin to skin. Longing coursed through Lena for everything they could have been, everything they still might be—if only he were ready to choose her.

Kai pulled back onto the road. The remaining miles stretching ahead like possibility. Lena turned back to the window, watching the forest thicken as they neared Moonshadow. After a long moment, his voice broke through again, softer now.

"I never considered you might have the same fears," Kai admitted. "It's easy to think of you as...untouchable. Like you've got everything figured out."

A small, bitter laugh escaped her. "Trust me, I'm far from untouchable. You've seen me cry, scream, and—" Heat flooded her cheeks at the memories of how she'd behaved last night. "Let's just say I'm a mess like anyone else."

"You don't seem like a mess to me."

"Don't let the lipstick fool you," she murmured. "It's just armor."

Something in his expression softened. "I guess we've both been wearing armor."

The silence that followed felt different—not comfortable, but less suffocating. Then his voice came again, barely above a whisper.

"You know," he said, tone carrying a hint of something lighter, almost nostalgic, "it wasn't my dad threatening banishment that made me show up this morning. I think I was done for the second you hit me with your pinky."

Lena blinked, turning to him fully now. "What?"

He chuckled under his breath, the sound self-deprecating but tinged with warmth. "That night outside the restaurant, when you wrapped

your pinky around mine. That was it. The way you call me 'my mate'...
Ava always calls me 'my future alpha,' but it's never felt like this." He
paused, rubbing at his chest. "Hearing you say 'mate'—it changed so
much."

His sincerity sent an unwelcome flutter through Lena's chest. She
gripped her knees tighter, fighting back the surge of emotion. After a
long moment, she spoke.

"What I will agree to is time," she said. "Time to get to know each
other. Not as fated mates or as the future Alpha and Luna of Bloodstone,
just as us. As Kai and Lena." She offered him a small, tentative smile.
"I'll talk to my dad and maybe sweet-talk yours into letting us move
slowly. Hopefully, in time, you'll figure out what you want—from her,
from me—and we'll go from there."

His shoulders dropped, the lines around his eyes easing as tension
drained from his face. "Thank you. You have no idea the peace that
gives me."

Lena's gaze fixed on him, her emotions a tempest she couldn't tame.
His gratitude felt genuine, but it didn't quiet the unease in her chest.
This wasn't a resolution, but it was a start. And maybe, it would be
enough.

"You're welcome, Kai," she said quietly.

Silence settled between them for the rest of the drive. When his pinky
brushed against hers—tentative, questioning—she didn't pull away. The
simple contact sent electricity racing up her arm, the bond flaring
bright and warm between them. Elara pressed close to the surface,
reaching for his wolf, and his scent transformed, notes of possibility
rising through the layers of doubt.

Something unfurled in the center of Lena's chest, radiating outward.
Her ribcage constricted with each heartbeat—half-pleasure, half-pain.
Her pulse drummed a familiar rhythm: want-fear-want-fear. Turning
back to the window, she sent a silent prayer, trying to ignore the way
her skin still tingled where they touched.

*Please, Selene. Guide us. Give me strength to fight for our bond if it's
meant to be, or to walk away if it's not. Help me protect what remains
of my heart.*

Because I fear that Kai Bloodstone might be my undoing.

CHAPTER THIRTY-ONE

CALEB

The cool mountain air wrapped around Caleb like a welcome embrace. The Crescent Fang packhouse came into view, its familiar stone facade rising against towering pines. Late afternoon sunlight caught the weathered granite, transforming it to molten silver. The scent of home—pine needles, wood smoke, and mingled pack markers—filled his lungs, grounding him after days away. Beneath his skin, Fenrir's presence swelled, equally eager to return to their territory.

The courtyard had been alive with activity—warriors sparring on the packed earth, younger wolves hauling supplies, others lounging on wooden benches sharing stories—but the moment the Silverado pulled into view, everything paused. A wave of excitement rippled through the gathered wolves, their scents shifting from routine contentment to sharp curiosity tinged with respect as they spotted Caleb.

Abandoning their tasks, they closed in with eager curiosity. Their questions came fast and overlapping, a chaotic hum of voices swirling around him as he stepped out of the truck. The gravel crunched beneath his boots as his feet hit home soil.

"Alpha, what was the Summit like?" The young warrior's sandy hair was still damp with sweat from training, chest puffed with pride, clearly starstruck standing so close to Caleb.

"Did anyone challenge you?" a female warrior called out, incredulous, as though she couldn't imagine anyone daring to cross him. Her hand rested on the knife at her hip, ready to defend her alpha's honor even in story.

"Is it true other packs might be visiting us soon?" another voice chimed in, this one belonging to a slight woman with silver-streaked hair, tone more hesitant but no less curious. The scent of herbs clung to her clothing—one of the pack's healers, Caleb noted.

The fervor in their voices overwhelmed him, their loyalty and trust heavier than any alpha crown. He raised his hand, the subtle gesture carrying the full weight of his authority, quieting even the most eager wolves. Resolve tightened in his chest as he scanned their faces, noting the mix of curiosity and pride in their expressions.

This—these faces, these lives—is why isolation is no longer an option.

"I'll address everyone at dinner tonight." His voice carried the firmness of command, yet warmth underscored his words, visibly relaxing several wolves' shoulders. "First, I need to meet with Varek and the council."

The tension eased as Asher climbed out from the passenger side, his natural charisma working its magic like sunshine breaking through clouds. Slinging his bag over his shoulder, he flashed the group his signature grin, the one that made his dark eyes crinkle at the corners. "I promise, we'll tell you everything," he said, voice light as mountain air. "But only if someone saves me a slice of blueberry pie at dinner."

Laughter rippled through the group, warm as the afternoon sun. Caleb felt the energy shift. This—Asher's ability to soften his alpha authority without diminishing it—was why he made such a perfect beta.

"That's a lot of confidence in your charm, Beta," one of the younger wolves quipped, a dark-haired female who couldn't be more than nineteen. Her tone was teasing, but Caleb caught the slight blush in her cheeks. "But I'll think about it."

"You heard him," Caleb added, voice teasing but firm. "Save the pie—and your questions—for tonight."

He watched as Asher exchanged jests with the younger wolves, their scents transforming around his beta—anxiety softening like butter in sun. Caleb's own shoulders lowered as he watched Asher work through the crowd, his easy laugh drawing smiles even from the most reserved elders. The pack needed Asher's sunshine as much as they needed Caleb's steady shade.

As the crowd began to disperse, Caleb turned toward the packhouse. Asher fell into step beside him, their shoulders brushing as they walked

"That wasn't so bad." Asher's tone remained light, though his eyes sharpened as they stepped back into their roles.

Caleb smirked, a glimmer of humor breaking through the gravity of the day. "Let's see if you're still saying that after dinner."

The council room was a space steeped in history, its atmosphere thick with decades of pack decisions. Afternoon light filtered through high windows, catching dust motes that danced like memories in the air. Thick beams of aged wood lined the ceiling like ancient guardians, their surfaces worn smooth by time and the residual energy of countless meetings. A long oak table dominated the center, its surface bearing the marks of passionate discussions—small nicks and scratches that told stories of fists pounded in emphasis, claws emerged in heated moments.

The air carried the faint scent of cedar and old parchment, mingled with the distinct markers of each council member, weaving a tapestry of scents that centered Caleb as he took his place at the head of the table. The heavy wooden chair, worn smooth by generations of alphas before him, welcomed his weight. To his right sat Asher, steady and confident as a mountain peak, and to his left, Varek, his gamma, whose quiet intensity had always reminded Caleb of a still pool hiding deep currents. Around the table, the elders watched intently including Erik, whose silver-streaked beard caught the fading light, and Garreth, Asher's father, whose gaze missed nothing beneath heavy brows.

Caleb's voice cut through the room like a blade. "Crescent Fang has thrived in isolation for decades, but the Summit made it clear—this can't continue. The world around us is changing, and not for the better."

The room held its breath as he leaned forward, broad shoulders taut with conviction. The wood creaked beneath his forearms, a sound as old as the pack itself.

"Seven packs in the region have been annihilated by rogues. *Seven.*" He let the number hang in the air like smoke. "That's not just a statistic; it's a warning. The overall death toll across the region is staggering, and the survivors... There are fewer of them each attack. The rogues seem to be targeting smaller packs in the north, but we'd be fools to think we're immune. Crescent Fang must adapt, or we risk everything."

A murmur rippled across the table, a mix of unease and agreement scenting the air. Garreth's expression tightened, the lines around his mouth deepening as he focused on Caleb as though trying to predict where this was leading.

"And it's not just the rogues," Caleb continued, voice gaining a hard edge that made several elders straighten in their seats. "There are alphas out there—greedy ones—who see the abandoned lands of these destroyed packs as opportunities. Territory is currency to them, and they're willing to take it by force." His palm flattened against the warm wood. "Crescent Fang will not be seen as vulnerable. We will protect what is ours."

The table fell silent, Caleb's words landing like a gavel. Every face reflected the gravity of the moment—from Erik, whose fingers drummed nervously against his thigh, to Garreth, whose expression shifted from sharp skepticism to solemn understanding.

"You're right to be cautious. But this isn't just about protection, is it? You actually *want* to reintegrate." Garreth's voice carried the wisdom of his years as Caleb's father's beta and the interim alpha before Caleb took his oaths.

Caleb nodded to Asher, a silent signal passing between them, intimate as a touch. Asher straightened, picking up the thread of the conversation. The subtle shift in his posture—from attentive beta to passionate advocate—made pride swell in Caleb's chest.

"We need to think beyond survival." Asher's tone was filled with a quiet urgency that commanded attention better than any shout. "Think about growth. There are survivors out there—wolves who have lost everything to the rogues." His hands moved as he spoke, painting pictures in the air above the long table. "We should follow the example of other packs who are welcoming them in. Not for strategy or territory, but to give those wolves a chance to rebuild their lives, to find safety and community again under the guidance of Selene."

The room shifted, unease settling as Asher's words struck a chord. The scent of anxiety began to fade, replaced by something warmer—hope, perhaps. Or determination. Garreth's gaze softened, pride crossing his features as he regarded his son. The resemblance between them was strongest in these moments, when passion lit their eyes the same way.

"You've thought this through." Approval threaded Garreth's voice.

Asher nodded, spine straightening, and chin lifting as his hands flattened against the table. "Crescent Fang must stand strong with our community to ensure that no wolf, no family, has to face the rogues alone."

Varek spoke up for the first time, voice calm but resolute, like deep water over stone. "Taking in new members isn't a small task. It will take planning—resources, housing, food. We'll need to prepare."

"We'll be ready." Caleb's tone brooked no argument. Fenrir's strength resonated in his voice, making it carry the strength of both the alpha male and wolf. "We have the space, the resources, and the community to support the effort. Our lands are vast, and there is room to build."

He leaned forward, aura filling the room like an incoming tide. "As part of our reintegration, we'll host visiting delegations over the coming months. Securing alliances will be critical. Not just for trade or diplomacy, but for ensuring that Crescent Fang remains a respected and formidable presence."

Another ripple of conversation broke out, the elders murmuring among themselves. Their scents mixed—concern, excitement, determination all weaving together. Caleb let it play out for a moment, watching the interplay of expressions and reactions around the table.

"Lastly," he said, voice commanding attention once more, the single word silencing the murmurs like a clap of thunder, "we've established a connection with the Moonshadow pack. Their alpha-heir, Cian, has extended an invitation for us to attend his alpha ceremony. It's an opportunity to formalize our relationship and send a message to those who might seek to take advantage of our novice status in the Collective: Crescent Fang is not isolated."

The elders exchanged glances, nodding as cautious optimism replaced their initial tension. The scent of approval began to rise from around the table, their collective pride in what their alpha had accomplished at the Summit evident in their warming expressions. The council filed out after the meeting concluded, footsteps echoing against the ancient floorboards. Caleb rose, movements fluid, but slowed by the significance of the discussion. The wooden chair scraped against the floor, marking the transition from formal council to what came next. He turned to Asher, shoulders loosened now that the formalities were over.

"I'm going for a run before dinner.".

"Need to burn off all that alpha energy?" Asher's eyebrow arched, a teasing smile playing on his lips.

Caleb smirked, warmth spreading beneath his sternum at their easy intimacy. "Something like that."

Asher stepped closer, reaching for Caleb's hip. The touch was searing even through the fabric of his shirt. The beta's scent wrapped around him—pine, cedar, summer rain and something uniquely Asher that always made Caleb's wolf settle.

"Want company?" he asked, thumb tracing small circles against Caleb's hip.

Caleb leaned into the touch. "I'll be okay. Just need to clear my head."

Asher nodded, leaning in to press a soft kiss to Caleb's lips. "Don't take too long," he murmured, breath warm against Caleb's skin. "I'll see you at the dining hall."

Caleb watched Asher leave, following the fluid grace of his movements and the copper highlights dancing through his hair. The corners of his mouth lifted. Asher had always known how to meet him exactly where he needed—whether with a firm hand or a quiet kiss, sometimes both.

Caleb headed toward the edge of the forest. His thoughts, previously tangled like briars, began to loosen their hold with each step toward the tree line. Fenrir's presence pulled at his muscles, a restless tingling beneath his skin that promised release. The forest called to them both, a siren song of freedom and wild spaces. It was time to let go and reconnect—with his land, his wolf, and himself.

The shift was seamless, Caleb's body flowing into Fenrir's form like water finding its natural course. Bones reformed, muscle stretched, and fur erupted across his skin in a wave of midnight-black. The massive wolf surged forward, paws striking the earth with a rhythm that matched

Caleb's heartbeat. The wind rushed past them, carrying the scents of home—the sharp tang of pine needles, the rich loam of damp earth, the faint musk of deer paths, and the enduring markers of pack that defined their territory.

The forest blurred around them as Fenrir raced deeper into the territory, branches whipping past as their shadows dappled the wolf's dark coat. Questions about the Summit and the pack's future fell away with each powerful stride until there was only the freedom on the run, the primal joy of movement, and the perfect harmony of wolf and male.

"You handled it well." Fenrir's voice rumbled like distant thunder. *"With every choice, you prove yourself worthy of Crescent Fang—worthy of Selene herself."*

Caleb flicked Fenrir's ears at the unexpected praise, strides slowing as they navigated a narrow trail winding between ancient trees. *"You think so?"*

"I know so." Fenrir's deep baritone resonated with unwavering confidence. *"You held your ground among the alphas, showed respect to the council, and inspired your pack. They look to you not out of obligation, but because they trust you."*

Warmth spread in Caleb's chest. *"I can't do it without Asher or Varek. Or you."*

Fenrir huffed, a sound that was both amused and indulgent, breath misting in the cooling air. *"Humility suits you, but don't forget you're the one who makes the final call. You carry Crescent Fang and Selene's blessing. And you do so with strength and grace."*

They pressed deeper into the forest, breaths more rhythmic than before. The familiar scents of the territory grew stronger, mingling with the faint, ancient energy that always lingered near the sanctum—a power as old as the mountains themselves.

Fenrir slowed when they reached Lunaris Sanctum, steps careful as they entered the sacred ground. The clearing glowed softly under the early evening light, the ancient stones rising from the earth like the bones of sleeping giants. Each stone bore centuries of prayers etched into their surface, symbols worn smooth by time and devotion. The air here felt different—thicker, charged with an energy that made Caleb's skin prickle even in wolf form.

He shifted back into his human form, the air cool against his bare skin. The packed earth remained warm beneath his feet, holding the day's heat. He knelt before the largest stone, its surface silvered by countless moonrises, head bowing as he let the sanctity of the place settle over him like a mantle.

"What will you pray for, Caleb?" Fenrir asked, voice quieter now, almost reverent in the sacred space.

Caleb closed his eyes, hands resting on his thighs as he let his thoughts flow freely. *"For strength, always. To protect my pack. To guide them through whatever challenges lie ahead."* He hesitated, throat tightening as his thoughts turned inward. *"And for clarity. For Selene's wisdom to guide me through these changes. For her blessing on Crescent Fang as we step into this new chapter."*

The sanctum's stillness soothed his restless spirit like a mother's embrace. The ancient stones pulsed with stored moonlight, their energy seeping into his bones. His breathing slowed, each inhale deeper than the last, until the boundary between his body and the sanctum blurred.

Fenrir's voice broke through the quiet, low and commanding. *"Caleb."*

His eyes snapped open, pulse quickening at the urgency in Fenrir's tone. "What is it?" he murmured aloud, voice barely more than a whisper on these hallowed lands.

"Prepare," Fenrir said, golden eyes glowing in Caleb's mind like twin moons. *"Mate will be with us soon."*

Adrenaline flooded Caleb's system. *"Why now?"* he wondered, thoughts scattered like leaves in a storm. *"Is it because of the summit? Because Crescent Fang is stepping out of isolation?"*

A pang of worry surfaced. *"What about Asher?"* The thought of disrupting what they had built, of losing their bond—their love—made his heart ache. Images flashed through his mind: Asher's smile in the morning light, his steady presence during council meetings, the way his touch could ground Caleb even in his darkest moments.

"Trust Selene's will," Fenrir said firmly, tone soothing yet resolute. *"You will find her soon, and the path will reveal itself."*

The stones of Lunaris Sanctum stood silent witness to his resolution, their shadows lengthening as the sun sank toward the horizon, painting the sky in shades of promise. Caleb exhaled with ritual care, hands pressing against the soft earth, the sanctum's ancient power thrumming beneath his palms. He shifted back into his wolf form, Fenrir's midnight fur rippling in the fading light. The wolf's steadfast confidence settled over him, quieting the storm of uncertainty in his chest. Whatever lay ahead, he would face it—with his wolf, his pack, and Selene's guidance.

CHAPTER THIRTY-TWO

KAI

The Range Rover rolled onto Moonshadow's packlands, its engine humming beneath Kai's drumming fingers. The packhouse rose before them, timber walls blending with ancient pines—nothing like Bloodstone's imposing stone and glass. Wolves milled about across the grounds, several pausing to scent the air as they spotted the vehicle. Kai's shoulders hunched, making himself smaller beneath their scrutiny.

Beside him, Lena sat poised, golden-brown eyes drinking in familiar sights. The private smile playing on her lips sent a wistful ache through him. This was her home, where she belonged. Here, she wasn't his fated mate—she was a daughter of Moonshadow. The realization left him feeling strangely untethered.

As he pulled to a stop, Kai spotted a group gathered around the Jeep. Cian stood tall and self-assured. Beside him was Ryker, whose sharp features softened with an amused grin as he exchanged words with a lean wolf whose rust-colored hair marked him as clearly as his mischievous grin. And next to them—Kai's spine stiffened—Alpha Raelen observed it all. Silver threaded the Moonshadow leader's temples, his presence undeniable even in stillness.

"You ready?" Lena's soft voice broke through his thoughts, her head tilting toward him with gentle encouragement.

Kai's fingers whitened around the door handle. Swallowing past the desert in his throat, he managed a nod.

"Yeah." The word emerged as sandpaper against stone.

He watched as Lena slipped from the vehicle with a natural grace, smoothing her hands over her jeans before drawing herself up with pride. Kai was frozen, drinking in the sight of her illuminated by her own certainty. The contrast between her ease and his tension made Orion stir anxiously.

He inhaled deeply and stepped out. Before he could reach Lena's side, a loud, exuberant voice shattered the stillness.

"Hey! Thing 1!" The rust-haired wolf bounded forward, smile rivaling the sun. "Took you guys forever. I've been dying of boredom here!"

Kai's muscles locked as the wolf scooped Lena up, spinning her in a circle. Her bright laugh pierced something primal in his chest as she braced against the wolf's shoulders.

"Goddess, Jace!" Her voice rang with delight. "I missed you so much."

Kai's gaze locked on Jace's hands at the small of Lena's back, fingers splayed on the strip of bare skin below her shirt, inches from territory that wasn't his to touch.

His pupils dilated until black nearly swallowed the emerald-green irises, nostrils flaring as his breaths came in short, harsh bursts. His fingertips split as claws emerged, drawing pinpricks of blood from his own palms. The growl that tore from his chest vibrated through the ground beneath them, silencing birds in trees and freezing every wolf in the vicinity in place.

All eyes snapped to Kai, who stood rigid, barely containing the violence thrumming beneath his skin.

Jace set Lena down carefully, his earlier excitement fading to a sheepish chuckle as he stepped back. "Guess it looks like we won't be having those smart, diplomatic, gorgeous pups after all, huh, Lena?"

Kai's vision narrowed. *Pups? Diplomatic? Gorgeous?* The pieces clicked together in a sickening rush. Was this who Lena had been talking about—the wolf she'd considered pursuing a chosen bond with? Possessive jealousy surged again, red-hot and uncompromising.

"Absolutely not." The words ripped from Kai's throat like gravel as Orion surged forward with territorial fury. He yanked Lena to him, his body a wall of dominance between her and Jace.

"Mine!"

The declaration resonated with raw power, claiming what belonged to him.

Silence descended, heavy with implication. The onlookers exchanged glances ranging from amused to wary, the tension crackling like lightning before a storm.

Jace recovered first, though unease edged his returning smile. "Whoa there, big guy." His hands lifted in surrender. "Didn't mean to step on any toes. It was just a joke."

Kai's glare held steady, chest heaving as he forced his claws to retract. Each breath carried Jace's scent mingled with Lena's. The combination made his wolf snarl.

"Hi." Jace cleared his throat, extending his hand. "I'm Jace. Gamma-heir of Moonshadow. Nice to meet you, Lena's mate."

The tendons in Kai's forearm stood out like steel cables. His molars ground against each other, pain shooting through his jaw. One by one, his fingers peeled away from Lena's wrist, each release reluctant. When he finally clasped Jace's hand, the bones shifted beneath his grip, the other wolf's knuckles whitening in silent protest.

"Kai, Alpha-heir to Bloodstone."

Jace met his grip equally, challenge flickering behind his easy smile. "Looking forward to getting to know you, Kai. Promise I'm a lot more civilized than Ryker over there."

Despite himself, Kai felt his lips twitch. A reluctant chuckle escaped as some of the tension bled away. His gaze found Lena, who watched him with careful attention, gratitude brightening her golden-brown eyes.

"Welcome, Kai." Alpha Raelen approached, genuine warmth in his smile as he embraced Lena, pressing a kiss to her forehead. "It's good to see you again."

"Alpha Raelen." Kai bowed his head, hyper-aware of how his earlier display of dominance might have appeared to Lena's father.

Raelen's smile widened. "Come." He gestured toward the packhouse. "Let's meet in my office. I want to hear more about how you two met and how things are going."

He turned to Cian, who had been observing with barely concealed amusement. "Cian, join us. Aiden, have some refreshments brought to the study. Ryker, Jace—get their bags to their suites."

"Yes, Alpha," the two wolves responded in unison, moving to unload the vehicles. Jace caught Kai's eye briefly, expression unreadable before he turned away.

"You're being tested." Orion's presence unfurled along Kai's spine, vibrating through bone and muscle as they followed Raelen. *"This is mate's territory, her family. Don't lose sight of what matters."*

The study breathed with accumulated wisdom—ancient texts lining the walls, a hearth fire casting warmth over dark wood furnishings. Unlike Bloodstone's cold authority, history lived here.

Raelen settled behind his desk, studying Kai with shrewd consideration. "I'll be honest," he began, "when Cian told me Lena had found her mate, I was shocked, but mostly, thrilled."

Lena's cheeks colored, a soft smile spreading across her face as she met her father's eyes. Their silent exchange—tender and effortless—sent a pang through Kai's chest, a painful reminder of the distance that had grown between him and Darius over the years.

"Every father dreams of this moment," Raelen continued, gaze moving between them. "To see their child find the one destined for them by Selene Herself. It's a gift. I couldn't be happier for you, Lena. And Kai." His focus sharpened. "The Bloodstone heir—it's not what I expected, but it feels...fitting."

Kai stiffened, unsure how to respond.

Nostalgia softened Raelen's tone as he pressed on. "I know your father well. Darius is an excellent male—driven, loyal, and selfless. He was brilliant even when we first crossed paths as heirs, causing our fair share of trouble at summits." Raelen chuckled, his expression softening. "He has the kind of spirit that could inspire a pack to follow him to the ends of the earth."

Kai flinched at the word "selfless." His throat bobbed. His hands trembled against his thighs. A flush crept up his neck, staining his cheeks as he squirmed in the chair. His eyes flickered up, making it only to Raelen's chin before finding refuge on the wall behind.

Raelen leaned back in his chair, a fond smile tugging at his lips. "I'm glad to have you here with us, Kai. I know the bond between fated mates is...intense." His gaze drifted to Lena, fond but knowing. "I'm sure the two of you are eager to proceed with your mating and claiming."

Lena choked on her breath, face turning bright red as Kai's head snapped up. His mouth opened and closed, the only noise escaping was a dry, startled rasp.

Raelen chuckled, clearly amused. "I may be old, but I'm not old-fashioned. I understand you may not want to wait for a mating ceremony before completing the bond. I won't stand in your way—"

"Dad!" Lena interrupted, voice high and strained. "It's not—" She faltered, eyes darting between her father and Kai as she tried to find the right words. "It's not that urgent. Things with me and Kai... They're...complicated."

The room fell silent for a beat before Cian stepped forward.

"What Lena's trying to say," Cian cut in smoothly, "is that Kai is in a long-term relationship with a packmate at Bloodstone. The fated bond was unexpected, and there's a lot for them to figure out before they even start thinking about mating ceremonies or claiming rituals."

Raelen's brows knit together. His gaze swept from Cian to Lena before landing on Kai with the weight of a sledgehammer. He unfolded from his chair, shoulders squaring as the air in the room thickened, pressing against Kai's skin from all sides.

Oxygen vanished and Kai's shoulders curved inward, eyes dropping to the floor as an invisible hand forced his head to bow.

"I... Alpha Raelen, I'm sorry." his voice wavered, nearly breaking. He reached for Lena, wrapping his pinky around hers.

She squeezed back, a gesture of silent support that steadied him. He returned his gaze to Raelen, forcing himself to hold the older alpha's piercing stare.

"Like Cian said, this... It was unexpected. It's been an intense rollercoaster. I... *We*...need time to decide how we're going to move forward."

Raelen's jaw tightened. "And what does Darius have to say about this?"

Cian's posture shifted, shoulders squaring as he fell under his father's scrutiny.

"Darius is enamored with Lena," he said with a faint chuckle. "It may have been love at first sight. He couldn't stop calling her his daughter-in-law after meeting her." His tone grew more serious. "But he's frustrated. He expected Kai to end things with his girlfriend, Ava. When I spoke with him this morning, it was clear emotions were still running high."

Raelen's attention whipped back to Kai with renewed fury. "So, you come to my packlands"—his aura surged through the room—"and stake a possessive claim on *my daughter* while still entwined with another she-wolf?"

Kai flinched, head hanging in shame as the familiar sting of tears pricked at his eyes. Before he could respond, Lena's voice cut through the tension.

"Dad, that's not fair." Her tone was both firm and exasperated. "Kai and Ava grew up together. They fell in love. It's not easy to turn your heart off to someone you've let into it."

Kai turned to her, overwhelmed by her defense. She shouldn't have to shield him from her father's rightful anger, yet here she was, standing up for him.

"And honestly," she continued, incredulity lacing her words, "the shoe could have easily been on the other foot. Or have you forgotten that I spent *years* thinking I'd be mated to Jace and Ryker?"

Her voice softened, imploring empathy from her father. "If that relationship had manifested, could you imagine how intense that love would be? How *I* might fight fate to keep them, even though they aren't destined to be mine?"

Cian snorted, unable to hold back his laughter. "You mean what would've happened if I hadn't walked in on the three of you, naked after a shift, arguing about whether both their—"

"*Not the point*, Cian!" Lena's face was bright red as she elbowed her brother in the gut, making him double over with a groan.

Kai's mind spun. *Did they touch her? Taste her?* Orion fumed, blood-soaked visions unfurling for the males who dared touch what was his.

Lena turned her scowl away from her brother, focusing back on her father.

"The point is that this is all new. To both of us. Finding each other upended a lot of things. Regardless of how strong our bond is, it's not easy to just walk away from feelings that are deeply rooted in our hearts."

She looked to Kai, nodding for him to speak.

Taking a steadying breath, he met Raelen's gaze. "We've agreed to take time to get to know each other," he said quietly. "Without the pressure of the bond or the expectations of our union. We don't know what will happen, but we promised to try to chart a path that is right for both of us—one that doesn't cause harm."

"We hope you'll help bring Alpha Darius to this understanding with us, Dad," Lena added, eyes still locked on Kai. "He threatened Kai with banishment if he chose Ava over me." She turned her gaze back to her father. "What I feel for Kai is strong, and I know he feels it too, but I don't want to start a life with him because of an ultimatum. I want him to choose me for me. Not because his hand is being forced. And not just because Selene wills it so."

Her words shrunk something in his chest, making each breath shorter than the last. A tremor started at the base of his skull, racing down each vertebra before settling like ice in his gut. As he watched her, he noticed a tear clinging to her eyelash, threatening to fall but holding steady. The sight sent a painful tremor through him, and before he could think better of it, he reached out, gently settling his other hand over hers.

She glanced at him, lips pressing together in a faint but grateful smile before facing her father.

"Please, Dad. Keep an open mind. Help us."

The room fell silent as her plea hung heavily in the air.

Raelen leaned back, expression unreadable. Seconds stretched, leeching air from the room. Finally, he exhaled deeply, shoulders relaxing.

"I'll help," he said, voice steady but conflicted. "I want you to be happy, Lena. To have a bond that's strong and beautiful, whether it's fated or chosen. There will be no undue pressure from me—or from Darius—on how or *if* you come together."

She let out a soft sigh, shoulders slumping in relief. "Thank you, Dad."

Kai straightened in his seat, nodding toward Raelen. "Thank you, Alpha." He hoped his gratitude conveyed how much Raelen's support meant—not just to Lena, but to him as well.

Raelen offered a brief nod before grabbing his phone from the desk and typing out a quick message. Once done, he turned his sharp gaze back to Kai.

"Kai, Ryker is on his way to take you to your room. Get settled and get some rest. You're welcome to join us for dinner, but I understand if you need some quiet after the past few days."

"I appreciate it." Kai rose to his feet, movements slow as he fought the deep-seated tension in his body. "I'll see how I'm feeling."

Raelen's focus shifted to his children, a small smile breaking through his stoic demeanor. "You two, stay. I want to hear more about the Summit."

Kai hesitated for a moment, gaze flicking to Lena.

She reached for his hand, clasping it tightly as he passed her. The warmth of her touch steadied him. She leaned in just enough to whisper, "I'll talk to you later."

He nodded, throat tightening as he released her hand and walked toward the door. Ryker was already waiting as he stepped into the hall. With one last glance back, Kai met Lena's gaze, her silent encouragement enough to push him forward.

As he followed Ryker to the guest suite, Kai couldn't shake the feeling of gratitude mixed with a persisting sense of uncertainty. Whatever lay ahead, he knew he wasn't walking this path alone. Not anymore.

Silence crackled between the males. Ryker's usual swagger had vanished as they climbed the stairs, replaced by measured steps that echoed against the floorboards.

Finally, Ryker stopped in front of a door, hand resting on the handle. He turned to Kai, expression uncharacteristically serious.

"Look," he began, voice low but firm. "I know this isn't easy for you. But Lena's my best friend, and I've been here through all of it—watching her dream about her fated mate for years, then seeing her heart sink when she didn't find them here at Moonshadow." He paused, lost in memory. "She was terrified going into the Summit. Not just because she might find her mate, but of what it would mean if she did—having to leave everything she's built here, everyone she loves."

His gaze sharpened as it met Kai's. "She's choosing to open her heart to you anyway. Giving you a real chance, even with everything happening with Ava." His voice dropped to a protective growl. *"Don't* make her regret defending you. Don't make her regret choosing hope over fear." His expression softened. "And don't make me regret calling you my brother."

He pushed open the door. "Get some rest. We can talk more when you're ready."

Kai stepped into the room, chest tight as Ryker's warning and Orion's earlier caution echoed in his mind. The space was simple but welcoming—a large bed with crisp sheets, a sturdy desk near the window, and a small sitting area. The view beyond the glass showed the sprawling Moonshadow territory, dense forest stretching toward distant mountains.

"Thank you," Kai said quietly, turning back to Ryker. "For everything."

Ryker nodded once, his usual grin sliding across his face. "That's what pack is for." He stepped back into the hall, pulling the door closed. "Dinner's at seven if you're up for it."

Left alone, Kai sank onto the bed. His hands trembled as he ran them through his hair, breaths coming slow and uneven in the silence. Ryker's words hammered at him: *"She's choosing to open her heart to you anyway."*

She's risking everything.

I'm clinging to ghosts.

The first sob caught him off guard, ripping free with enough force to double him over. He tried to swallow the next one and failed. Everything he'd been suppressing—Lena's burning bond, his father's expectations, Ava's imminent loss—poured out in violent, wracking sobs. His legs gave out as he slid to his knees, pressing his face into the mattress to muffle sounds he couldn't control. He stood to lose everything, no matter what he chose.

Orion's presence folded around him, a gravitational force compressing his limbs. Heat bloomed at pressure points—sternum, temples, wrists—his wolf's energy pulsing against the thin barrier of his skin and matching the erratic stutter of his heartbeat. Silent comfort radiated through their bond as Kai's tears soaked into the bedding.

"Let it out," his wolf murmured. *"We're where we need to be."*

Kai didn't know how long he kneeled there, letting years of suppressed emotion pour out of him. His sobs eventually quieted to hiccupping breaths, his body trembling with exhaustion. Somehow, he managed to pull himself onto the bed, his limbs heavy and uncoordinated.

The late-afternoon sun cast long shadows across the room, and somewhere in the distance, he could hear the faint sounds of pack life continuing—voices calling, laughter echoing, the steady rhythm of a place that might one day feel like a second home.

The sounds grew distant, muffled, as emotional exhaustion dragged him under. Kai's last conscious thought before darkness claimed him was of golden-brown eyes filled with hope he knew he didn't deserve, and a future he wasn't sure he was strong enough to choose.

CHAPTER THIRTY-THREE

LENA

Lena sat quietly, hands folded in her lap. Her father stood behind his desk with a thoughtful expression that softened his typically sharp features. Cian had claimed Kai's recently vacated seat, posture relaxed as he toyed absently with the armrest. The tension of their meeting lingered, though the atmosphere shifted with Kai's departure.

"Lena." Raelen's warm tone broke the silence. "I'm proud of your presence at the Summit."

Lena blinked, startled by the shift to praise. "Proud?"

"Very." Raelen moved closer to her chair, the familiar scent of cedar and leather that always clung to him seeming warmer somehow. "Several alphas reached out to me personally to speak about you. Alpha Renford was particularly impressed. He mentioned how astutely you identified patterns in the rogue attacks, specifically the vulnerabilities of the smaller northern packs. He said your insights were sharp, well-informed, and invaluable."

Raelen paused, expression growing wistful. "You remind me so much of your mother in moments like this." His voice dropped to a reverent hush. "She had the same gift for seeing patterns where others only saw chaos, for finding the threads that held everything together. She could walk into a room full of wolves at odds with one another and leave them united. It wasn't just her instincts—it was her heart." He reached across, fingers hovering over Lena's hand before settling there with gentle weight. "I see the same in you, Lena."

Tears threatened, demanding release. The ache of her mother's absence—that ever-present hollow—expanded with her father's words. She swallowed hard, feeling the gentle press of her mother's gold pendant against her chest. The responsibility of shouldering that mantle felt both precious and heavy.

"Thank you, Dad." The words barely escaped her lips as her fingers found the pendant.

Raelen perched on the edge of his desk, hands braced against the lip. "She would have been so proud of you, not just for what you've accomplished, but for the courage and clarity you will bring to your role. You're stepping into your own light, Lena, and it's a brilliant thing to witness."

Cian grinned from the seat next to her, pride evident in his voice. "Renford and Darius weren't the only ones impressed, either. A few heirs mentioned how brilliant you were. Some even said they wish they had someone as sharp as you to guide their own packs. You're making waves, Lena, and not because of Dad. You're being recognized as a leader in your own right. A *true* luna."

Warmth spread across Lena's cheeks. Her shoulders squared while her fingers fidgeted in her lap, caught between pride and the instinct to deflect. "I was just trying to contribute," she murmured.

"You did more than that," Raelen said firmly. "You showed them what Moonshadow is made of. More importantly, you demonstrated that you have what it takes to step into a leadership role, whether that's in Bloodstone, here, or elsewhere."

Lena's gaze fell to her hands. A simple nod was all she could offer as the clock on the wall marked three beats of silence.

Cian shifted in his seat, tone growing more serious. "This year's summit wasn't just about strategy, though. It was a wake-up call, Dad." His eyebrows knitted together. "Seven packs have been wiped out by rogues. Their hierarchies gone, lands abandoned. And like Lena pointed out, the northern packs—the smaller ones—are the primary targets. If Lena were to join Kai at Bloodstone, they'll be right on the border of where most of the attacks are happening. It won't be long until they're pulled into this conflict."

Raelen's brow furrowed. "And the land disputes? What's the situation there?"

Cian leaned forward, resting his elbows on his knees. "It's a mess. Packs are scrambling to claim the abandoned lands, but it's turning into a free-for-all. Ironclaw and Redridge were fighting over the Denali territory. This type of in-fighting amongst the alphas is escalating, and unless something changes, it could turn into an outright war. The last thing we want is to be dealing with territorial battles while we are facing the rogue threat."

Raelen frowned, expression darkening. "Ironclaw has been especially aggressive, hasn't it?"

Cian nodded. "They've taken over the lands of two smaller packs in the past year, either through negotiation or force. Thorne's not just opportunistic—he's strategic. If Ironclaw gets their claws into Denali, they'll have a significant foothold in the region. It's something we need to watch closely." Cian leaned back in his seat. "The good news is that Kai bought us some time on that front. He managed to build consensus around keeping the Denali lands neutral, for now, which was no small feat."

Raelen tapped his fingers on the desk, mind clearly working through the implications. "And Crescent Fang? I know they attended this year. Did you have a chance to connect with them? What are your insights? Do they have a position in all of this?"

"Crescent Fang was...unexpected." Cian said, fascination evident. "Most alphas didn't know what to make of them at first." He leaned forward. "But Caleb commands respect without demanding it. Not just because of his lineage—though being Caelum's descendant definitely turned heads."

Raelen's brow lifted. "Caelum's bloodline?"

Cian nodded. "And more than that—his wolf is believed to be the reincarnation of Fenrir, the first alpha wolf...Caelum's wolf. Caleb's connection to divination gives him insights that most of us can't even begin to understand. He spoke about the need for unity and strategy, and his ideas gained traction throughout the week. Darius, Renford, even Garrick—leaders who don't impress easily—took a keen interest.

He's not just a strong alpha, Dad. He projects the kind of aura that makes you wonder if he's destined for something greater—something we can't yet see."

Lena, who had been listening quietly, spoke up. "Caleb is...compelling. He's strong, but he listens. He cares about his pack, but he's also thinking about the bigger picture. He's someone worth watching—someone that might be able to pull more packs together. If we want to expand our alliances beyond Blackwater, especially into the Washington territories, Crescent Fang would be a good fit."

Raelen leaned back, clearly intrigued. "And what about Caleb's beta?"

"Asher," Cian supplied. "He's sharp, charismatic, and fiercely loyal. Together, they're a formidable pair. Crescent Fang has been out of the Collective for a long time, but I think they're ready to reengage. I invited Caleb and Asher to my alpha ceremony. I thought it would be a good opportunity for you to meet them and for us to solidify our ties."

Raelen nodded, a thoughtful look on his face. "That was a wise decision. I look forward to meeting them." His gaze shifted to Lena, holding her eyes with the gentle intensity she'd known since childhood. "And how are you feeling about all of this? About Kai? What's ahead?"

The question caught her off guard. "I feel...conflicted," she admitted after a pause. "The bond is strong, but so is his struggle. I've seen his anguish." She looked down. "I've been praying to Selene for guidance—strength to persevere or strength to let go. My answer changes with each heartbeat."

The room fell quiet, her vulnerability hanging in the air.

Cian reached out, resting a reassuring hand on her arm. "Whatever happens, Lena, we're here for you. You're not alone."

Raelen nodded, his expression solemn. "Your path isn't set in stone, Lena. You have time to figure this out. Whatever decision you make, you'll have my support."

A knot formed in Lena's throat. She managed only a nod, the pressure in her chest making words impossible.

Raelen exhaled deeply, leaning back. "For now, let's focus on what's next. Cian, your alpha ceremony is fast approaching. I want you to spend more time at the ritual grounds—meditating, communing with your wolf, and praying to Selene. This is a pivotal moment, and I want you to be fully prepared."

Cian nodded, his rare grin replaced with his usual seriousness. "Understood."

"And Lena," Raelen continued, turning to her. "I'd like you to assist Ryker's mother with planning the ceremony. It'll be a tremendous learning experience for you, whether or not you step into the luna role at Bloodstone. I think you're ready for this kind of responsibility."

Lena blinked, then nodded enthusiastically. "I'd be honored, Dad."

Raelen beamed, rubbing his hands together with the excitement of an alpha father ready to set his children's future in motion. "Good. Then let's get to work."

Lena rose, mind already spinning with the importance of the task ahead. She nodded to her father and brother before stepping toward the door. The study door closed behind her with a soft creak. Pine scent and kitchen voices drifted through the dimly lit corridor as Lena moved toward the staircase. Her shoulders bowed beneath invisible weight—her father's pride and Cian's revelations warring against Kai's unresolved feelings and the pressures of decisions she wasn't ready to make.

The bond ached with each step up the stairs. At the landing, her feet veered toward the guest suite without permission as though pulled by an invisible force. Each step felt both reluctant and inevitable, her body drawn to the male behind the door despite her hesitation.

Her hand hovered over the knob, fingers trembling in the space between approach or withdrawal. The polished brass reflected a distorted image of her face—uncertain, torn. She drew in a slow breath, the scent of pine and cedar from the hallway mingling with something else. Something raw and broken that seeped from beneath the door.

Then she heard it. A muffled sob crept through the cracks of the door like smoke, curling around her lungs until she couldn't breathe. Another followed, sharper—suppressed then released. It tore through her, resonating in the hollow beneath her ribs where their bond pulsed.

A vise tightened around her lungs, making each breath a struggle. The mating bond vibrated like a plucked wire, the frequency building until her teeth ached with it.

"Mate is hurting." Elara surged from dormancy, clawing through layers of Lena's restraint. The wolf's consciousness flooded her system with foreign chemicals—anxiety that tasted of copper, longing that

burned her sinews, protective fury that sharpened her vision at the edge.

"He needs us. He needs the bond." Elara's instincts coursed through Lena's veins, sharpening her senses until Kai's pain became almost tangible—tremors she could feel beneath her skin.

Her windpipe closed. Her vision swam, saltwater rising unbidden, scorching trails down her cheeks before she could blink them away. Her other hand moved to her chest, pressing against the ache that had taken root there. The door's cool grain imprinted itself on her palm, each whorl and line telegraphing what lay beyond as every cell in her body thrummed with conflicting impulses.

Go to him.

Run from him.

Heal or be healed.

Elara howled—not with her voice but with her essence. The wolf's anguish reverberated through Lena's bones, a primal call that needed no words.

"Mate's heart breaks," she finally managed. The wolf paced restlessly within Lena's consciousness, bristling at her hesitation. *"Our bond frays. We are stronger together. Please."*

Tear tracks cooled on her cheeks. *"And what happens if I go to him? When today's comfort becomes tomorrow's wound?"*

Her forehead met the door. Cool wood. Thin barrier. Vast divide. *"Some wounds need space to heal."*

Inside, Kai's breathing hitched. Another sob, followed by the soft thud of something—a fist against a wall, perhaps, or knees hitting the floor.

The sound fractured something in Lena. Fighting against her reluctance, she pulled her hand away from the door, each muscle protesting. The bond stretched like a tendon torn from bone. It was a physical agony that stole her breath, made her vision dim at the edges.

Lena turned. Each step demanded more will than the last, floorboards creaking in soft betrayal.

Elara's resistance faded, the wolf's rage dissolving into a mournful acceptance. *"He needs us,"* her wolf acknowledged, the words landing like stones in still water. Then, softer still: *"But we need ourselves first."*

Lena paused as she reached her own suite down the hall, hand resting on the doorknob. She glanced back, the shadowed corridor stretching between her and Kai. The phantom echo of his pain followed her still.

Tears slipped down her cheeks as she opened her door. "If I try to mend his heart while mine is breaking, neither of us will make it through," she whispered, the words meant for herself alone.

With a deep, shuddering breath, Lena stepped inside her room. The familiar scent of lavender and moonstone incense greeted her as she leaned against the door, sliding down until she sat on the floor, knees drawn to her chest. Her body trembled with quiet aftershocks. Elara retreated to the quiet spaces between Lena's heartbeats—a shadow with amber eyes watching, waiting. The wolf's grief tasted like iron on Lena's tongue, but beneath it ran a current of resilience as steady as a forest stream.

Lena's arms wrapped around her torso, holding fracturing pieces together. The bond pulsed—wounded but whole. In the waning sunlight that painted patterns across the floor, Lena made a silent promise: *I won't sacrifice myself to save him.*

CHAPTER THIRTY-FOUR

CALEB

The dining hall buzzed with activity—voices, clattering dishes, and the crackling fire echoing against the vaulted ceiling. Ancient wooden tables stretched across the space like fallen trees, each filled with wolves eager to hear from their alpha. The scent of roasted chicken and fresh bread perfumed the air, mingling with the distinct markers of pack—anticipation, curiosity, and that underlying note of family that made Fenrir stir beneath Caleb's skin, aware of every heartbeat in the room.

A hush fell over the crowd like snow settling on pine needles. Caleb stepped to the head of the room, flanked by Asher and Varek. Nearly seventy sets of eyes turned to him—filled with trust, curiosity, and a glimmer of hope that tightened his chest. He took a moment to let the silence settle, to meet their gazes—from the youngest pups fidgeting in their seats to the eldest warriors whose silver hair gleamed in the firelight.

"My family," he began, his deep voice resonating through the hall carrying the weight of his authority. "It's good to be home."

A ripple spread through the room—murmurs and nods signaling agreement.

Caleb's expression hardened, shoulders squared as he addressed the gathered wolves. "The Summit showed me just how much the world around us is changing. Packs are disappearing, their lands left desolate, their people scattered—or worse." His hands gripped the edge of the wooden podium. "Rogue attacks have increased, targeting smaller, more vulnerable packs. They don't just take lives; they destroy entire legacies. While Crescent Fang is strong, we cannot assume we're untouchable."

Silence blanketed the room, punctuated only by logs splitting in the fire and utensils being laid down. Even the youngest pups stilled. Fenrir's strength surged through Caleb as he let the moment linger.

What followed was a careful balance of honesty and reassurance. Caleb outlined the same vision he'd shared with the elders. Reintegration—the need for alliances, for opening their borders to survivors, for adaptation in an increasingly dangerous world. Unease rippled through the pack at first, their scents sharpening with anxiety. Asher stepped forward, his easy charm flowing through the room like sunlight breaking through clouds as he addressed the pack.

"It's not just about our survival—it's about our legacy," he said, voice warm but resolute. "This is our chance to show the region what Crescent Fang stands for, to help usher our neighbors back into Selene's fold. Yes, it means change, but it also means opportunity. Together, we'll build something stronger—something no rogue, no greedy alpha, could ever threaten."

Questions started to bubble up, and Caleb and Asher fielded them with ease. One of the older warriors, Maya, rose from her seat, silver streaking her dark hair like moonlight on water. Her scarred hands, evidence of decades defending the pack, rested on the table as she spoke.

"Alpha." Maya's voice cut through the chatter with steel-edged clarity. "How do we know these wolves we welcome won't bring trouble? Rogues, spies, dissenters?"

At Maya's challenge, Fenrir crashed through Caleb's restraint—liquid gold flooded his irises, canines pierced his gumline, and his throat produced frequencies that belonged to forest depths, not dining halls. For one breath, the alpha wolf commandeered their shared body before Caleb's consciousness reasserted the boundary between their wills.

Caleb nodded, his wolf settling reluctantly as he acknowledged the concern that made Maya's scent sharpen with protective instincts.

"Every wolf will be vetted thoroughly," he said, meeting her gaze. "They'll prove their loyalty before gaining a permanent place."

He scanned the room, including everyone in his next words. "These survivors aren't our enemies—they're victims of the same threats we face, but compassion doesn't mean compromising security."

Another voice chimed in, a younger wolf from the training ranks. "Alpha, what about the alliances? Will other packs visit us? Will we be visiting them?"

Asher grinned, his charisma lighting up the room. "Oh, we'll definitely be visiting. And yes, we'll host delegations, too. Starting with Moonshadow. Their heir, Cian, has invited us to his alpha ceremony. It's a chance to formalize an alliance and show the region that Crescent Fang isn't just strong—we're connected."

The mention of Moonshadow drew murmurs of interest, and Caleb noticed some of the younger wolves exchanging excited glances.

Another hand shot up, belonging to a young wolf barely into his teens. "Alpha," he asked earnestly, "is the Moonshadow heir as strong as you?"

"He's strong." Caleb chuckled, the male's wide-eyed curiosity cutting through the tension. "But strength isn't just about power. It's about leadership, integrity, and heart. Cian has all of that in spades. He's someone I'm proud to call an ally—and a friend."

The male beamed, chest puffing out with pride at having asked a good question.

As the meeting began to wind down, Caleb stepped forward again, voice carrying over the low hum of conversation. "Change is never easy," he said, tone steady and resolute. "But it is necessary. Crescent Fang has always been a pack that rises to the challenge, adapts, and overcomes. Together, we'll face whatever comes our way. Together, we'll thrive."

The room erupted—hands clapping or striking tables, voices rising, even howls sounding from the younger wolves. The cacophony vibrated through the wooden floors and rattled the ancient rafters, affirming with sound what Caleb had built with words.

As the pack dispersed to enjoy their meal, the dining hall filled with renewed chatter and the scrape of plates. Caleb felt Asher's hand on his arm, the touch as familiar as his own heartbeat.

"You did good." Asher leaned close, pride warming his voice.

Caleb glanced at him, a small smile tugging at his lips. "*We* did good," he corrected, gaze lingering on Asher for a moment longer than necessary.

Fenrir rumbled contentedly within, equally soothed by their beta's closeness.

The dining hall buzzed with laughter, the pack's energy vibrant and alive. Caleb felt measured peace settle over him. Whatever challenges lay ahead, he knew he wouldn't face them alone.

Later, as the packhouse quieted, Caleb and Asher retreated to their shared suite. The fire crackled, casting shadows across familiar comforts—worn leather armchairs, a heavy wooden chest carved with pack symbols, their bed marked by a decade of shared intimacy. They lay tangled together, scents mingling in the quiet space.

"How was your run?" Asher's fingers traced lazy patterns on Caleb's chest. Beneath the question, Caleb caught the subtle scent of worry masked with a hint of teasing. "Did you howl at the moon without me again?"

The gentle ribbing—their private joke about Caleb's tendency toward solemnity—eased something in his chest even as he prepared to share Fenrir's revelation.

"Good. I went to the sanctum. Fenrir spoke to me."

Asher shifted, propping himself up on one elbow, his full attention focused on Caleb. The beta's jaw tightened almost imperceptibly, a tell Caleb had learned to recognize years ago. Fear—not for himself, but for whatever discovery lay ahead.

"What did he say?" Asher's voice remained steady, but his fingers had stilled against Caleb's skin.

Caleb's hand found Asher's in the dim light. "He said...mate will be with us soon."

The words hung between them, frost forming on each syllable. Goosebumps prickled across Caleb's skin as his gaze snagged on shadows gathering in the corner.

"I don't know what it means—for the pack, for us." His voice emerged thin as spider silk. His hand clenched into a fist, then relaxed with deliberate effort. "It's just..." He swallowed as Fenrir paced their internal territory, each restless circuit pumping adrenaline into Caleb's bloodstream. His hairline dampened, and his pulse fluttered against his skin like a trapped bird. "So much is happening at once."

Asher reached for him. "Hey," he said softly, scent wrapping around Caleb like a familiar blanket. "Whatever happens, I'm here. Always. You don't have to figure it all out right now. Trust Fenrir to guide you when the time comes."

Caleb turned to meet Asher's gaze, his rising anxiety dissolving under the strength he saw there. "I don't know what I'd do without you." The admission scraped his throat raw.

"You won't have to," Asher murmured, leaning in to brush a soft kiss against Caleb's lips.

The kiss transformed, comfort dissolving into an ancient language spoken only between them, syllables of breath and pressure instead of words. Each press of lips carried a lifetime of history—arguments and reconciliations, triumphs and failures, all woven into the fabric of who they were together.

Caleb felt the shift within himself: control surrendering, freedom finding him as Asher guided him onto his back. The cool fabric of the sheets beneath him contrasted with the warmth radiating from Asher's body as he hovered over him.

Their wolves awoke with shared desire, adding a primal layer to each sensation. Their mingled scents changed like weather, trust and longing crystallizing into something sharper, more urgent.

Asher mapped Caleb's body like territory both conquered and cherished. As if his hands were cataloguing a decade's changes—the new scar below his ribs, the strengthened muscle along his flank, the sensitive hollow where neck met shoulder that still made him gasp. His touch was methodical, grounding Caleb in the present while igniting a fire that burned away his doubts and fears.

Caleb's chest rose and fell rapidly, breaths sharp and uneven as Asher's lips traveled from his mouth to his jaw, then down the column of his neck. Where Asher's mouth roamed, Caleb's skin remembered.

Fenrir's consciousness slunk forward—ancient instinct coiling around modern desire. Their boundaries dissolved like mist at sunrise, wolf hunger and human need becoming a single insatiable force that throbbed with each heartbeat. The alpha mantle fell away, wild certainty of belonging replacing it. Caleb's fingers found purchase on Asher's shoulders, anchoring him to this moment as wolf-sense heightened every touch to near-unbearable clarity.

When Asher reached for the bedside table and retrieved a bottle of lube, Caleb's breath hitched, recognizing, *craving*, what was to come. He hadn't realized how desperately he'd been needing this, the precious feeling of walls crumbling. Only here, only with Asher, could his body remember how to receive under his beta's careful touch.

Asher's gaze held sacred understanding as he leaned in, pressing a kiss to Caleb's lips that tasted of recognition. The electricity between them transformed from sharp lightning to deep ocean current. Caleb's pulse fluttered in his throat, exposed and trembling, yet anchored in absolute trust as Asher's weight settled over him.

"You're so beautiful like this," Asher murmured as he coated his fingers.

Caleb's body relaxed instinctively, and when Asher's hand slid between his thighs, he let out a shuddering breath that made the connection between them spark like kindling.

The first press of Asher's finger was gentle, circling the tight ring of muscle with a reverence that sent shivers up Caleb's spine. Their arousal perfumed the air differently now—Caleb's scent softening from its alpha dominance to something honeyed and open.

Asher nuzzled the base of Caleb's cock, tongue darting out to trace a slow, deliberate line along the underside. Caleb groaned, hips jerking involuntarily at the contact.

"You taste incredible." Asher's voice dripped with desire as he wrapped a hand around Caleb's base. "Salt. Cedar. A pinch of brooding on the back end."

The unexpected quip pulled a choked laugh from Caleb that transformed into a moan as Asher licked a slow circle around the sensitive head of his cock. Even now—especially now—Asher knew how to cut through his defenses, how to make him remember they were more than just alpha and beta.

Fenrir rumbled with pleasure, completely at ease submitting to their beta as Asher's tongue flicked over him, teasing, savoring.

When Asher took Caleb's cock into his mouth, the world contracted to a single point of heat and pressure. Caleb's hands clutched at the sheets, not in the practiced way of lovers, but with the desperation of a male encountering raw pleasure without filters. Each swirl of Asher's tongue scattered his thoughts, each hollow of his cheeks pulled him deeper into pure ecstasy.

Asher's hand moved deftly. He slid a single lubed finger inside Caleb, his movements in perfect rhythm with the slow bob of his head. Caleb's thighs tensed as Asher added a second finger, stretching him carefully while taking more of him into his mouth.

"Asher!" Caleb's voice trembled with a mix of pleasure and vulnerability.

Asher hummed around him, the vibration sending shocks of sensation through his groin and outward to his fingertips and toes. The beta's fingers continued their steady rhythm, breaching him more deeply with each careful thrust. Time fractured around them—seconds stretching into eternity, then collapsing into breathless instants. By the time Asher pressed a third finger inside, Caleb's thighs quivered uncontrollably, lungs seizing as Asher's mouth slid all the way down, taking him to the knot.

Pack hierarchy dissolved and reformed into something holy—the public alpha privately yielding, the supportive beta now leading. This reversal wasn't contradiction but completion, the missing piece that made their bond whole. The freedom of being commanded rather than commanding sent Caleb tumbling toward edges he couldn't access alone, his perpetual vigilance unraveling like frost under morning sun.

Fenrir's consciousness expanded within him rather than surging forward, a vulnerability no other creature would ever witness. This was their most precious secret: how the alpha who led a territory trembled under his beta's touch, finding liberation through submission.

A guttural groan tore from Caleb's lips as Asher swallowed around him then withdrew with tantalizing patience, tongue trailing along Caleb's length like a whispered promise. Asher's lips brushed against the inside of his thigh, making his cock twitch in excitement.

"You're perfect," Asher murmured, the words vibrating against Caleb's skin as he pressed another kiss to his hip.

Caleb's chest heaved, body caught in the paradox of complete relaxation and electric anticipation as Asher shifted back up. Their eyes locked, and something primitive passed between them—wordless understanding that transcended their pack roles. His beta's hand remained perfectly steady while coating himself, revealing a confidence that made liquid heat pool in Caleb's core as Asher guided his length to the waiting entrance.

When Asher pushed forward, nerve endings Caleb had forgotten existed ignited along his spine—territories that remained dormant except during such intimate encounters. The stretch stung and soothed simultaneously, a pressure against hidden places that made his own cock throb without being touched, a completed circuit that made him feel whole.

Caleb's legs wrapped around Asher's waist, pulling him closer as he adjusted to the fullness. It had been days since he'd taken Asher into his body, and the sensation was almost overwhelming—physically and emotionally. Caleb's hands clutched at Asher's shoulders, nails digging into the skin as his chest rose and fell in rapid breaths.

"You okay?" Asher asked, pushing the hair back from Caleb's face.

Caleb nodded, eyes fluttering shut as he exhaled shakily. "Yes," he whispered, voice trembling with a mix of vulnerability and need. "Just...don't stop."

Asher obeyed, sliding deeper with achingly slow precision, hands bracketing Caleb's hips to hold him steady. The sensation bordered on too much, but it was exactly what Caleb craved, the intensity that reminded him of everything Asher meant to him.

When Asher was fully seated, they both stilled, foreheads pressed together as they shared a quiet, shuddering breath.

"You feel perfect," Asher whispered, voice thick with awe.

"So do you." Caleb shifted, legs tightening around Asher's waist. The movement drew a groan from both of them, their bodies finding a rhythm that was purposeful yet tender, every stroke a testament to their bond.

Caleb's hands roamed over Asher's back, fingers tracing the curves of muscle and the dips of scars that told the story of the male he loved. The feeling of Asher sliding into him again and again—the friction of his own erection caught between their bodies—sent charges of pleasure coursing through Caleb, building steadily with each thrust.

When the barrier finally gave way, it wasn't an eruption but a complete dissolution. Caleb's release painted his skin as Asher's name tore from his throat. His body clutched rhythmically around the intrusion, muscles he couldn't consciously control expressing what words never could: a primal need to keep Asher locked within him even as his climax rendered him momentarily weightless.

Asher groaned, quickening his pace, each stroke deeper, more urgent as he chased his own orgasm. His thrusts grew more erratic, breath hitching before he buried himself deeply one final time. His cum flooded Caleb in warm, pulsing spurts. The intensity left Asher trembling, his forehead dropping to Caleb's shoulder as he shuddered through the last of his climax.

Caleb's legs relaxed around Asher's waist, but his arms remained wrapped tightly around him, anchoring them both in the aftermath. Being filled so completely, sharing something so profound, left Caleb feeling both raw and whole at once.

They stayed like that for a long moment, breaths mingling in the quiet intimacy of the room. Asher pressed soft kisses along Caleb's shoulder, hands tracing soothing patterns along his sides.

"You're my constant," Caleb whispered, voice drowsy but filled with conviction. The fire in their suite had burned low, casting everything in shadows that made confession easier. "When Fenrir speaks of mates—" He swallowed, the word heavy between them. "I don't know if I could bear it if that meant losing this. Promise me I'll always have you, no matter who else Selene brings to us."

The admission dried his mouth. His pulse stuttered, then galloped. A decade of unspoken fear coalesced into those few syllables. They'd never directly confronted the possibility of a mate changing everything, though it had haunted the edges of their relationship since Caleb's eighteenth birthday.

Asher pressed a kiss to Caleb's temple, arms tightening around him. "Always," he promised.

Caleb closed his eyes, imprinting this moment into muscle memory.

But Fenrir's message thrummed beneath his ribs: *"Mate will be with us soon."*

His wolf, normally wholly content with Asher, now stirred with anticipation.

Selene had already blessed him with Asher's love. What more could She give? What would She take?

For now, with Asher's warmth surrounding him, "always" would have to be enough—even as unseen currents began to shift the foundation beneath them.

CHAPTER THIRTY-FIVE

KAI

K ai woke to the afternoon sun streaming through the heavy curtains of his guest suite in the Moonshadow packhouse. A dull, insistent pain throbbed beneath his sternum with each heartbeat. He eased himself onto his back, groaning as his stiff muscles protested the movement. He ran a hand down his face, trying to rub away the fog of his restless, dreamless sleep.

Even now, as the sun moved closer to the horizon, the emptiness lingered. He felt like Sisyphus rolling a boulder uphill only to have it crush him beneath its weight, shoulders bowing in an endless cycle. He knew he needed to move, to do something, anything, to pull himself out of this spiral. But how could he take that first step when Lena's wounded eyes haunted his memories, his pack waited for an heir who was less certain with each passing day, and Ava's voice echoed endlessly with promises made and broken?

For now, he just needed to quiet the storm in his mind.

He swung his legs over the side of the bed, stretching sore muscles and grabbed a pair of sweats. He didn't bother with a shirt, letting the cool air hit his skin as he padded barefoot to the door.

Opening it cautiously, he peered into the hallway, muscles tensed for quick retreat. The last thing he wanted was to face Lena's disappointment. Or worse, Cian and Raelen's protective glares. He couldn't handle another confrontation—not yet.

The house was quiet as he made his way downstairs, each step echoing faintly in the stillness. Reaching the back door, he slipped outside, the crisp afternoon air soothing his frayed nerves. The tree line loomed ahead, a dark silhouette against the orange glow of the sky. Without hesitation, Kai crossed the yard, steps quickening as he neared the forest.

At the edge of the trees, he stripped out of his sweats, leaving them folded neatly on a low-hanging branch. Taking a deep breath, he shifted, the familiar rush of energy coursing through him as his body transformed. When he landed on four paws, Orion's presence surged to the forefront of his mind—not overwhelming but integrating, their separate awareness melding into something that felt like bedrock beneath shifting sands.

His wolf's massive form cast a long shadow, black fur rippling with hints of silver that caught the sunlight. Refined instinct held his raw power in check beneath his thick coat as Orion's emerald eyes, keen and alert, took in their surroundings with predatory grace.

The forest welcomed him, its earthy scents and soft sounds calming the chaos in his mind. The wind whispered through the trees, carrying the faint scent of pine and moss, and for the first time in what felt like weeks, Kai felt the tightness in his chest ease. He took his time, paws crunching against the underbrush as he allowed himself to simply be.

He surrendered to Orion's instincts, their shared body navigating between Moonshadow's towering pines with a certainty that transcended territory—wolf knowledge overriding human hesitation with each powerful leap. These weren't his lands, yet his wolf moved with unexpected familiarity. The boundaries that consumed human politics dissolved beneath paws that recognized the larger truth—all wolves descended from Selene's first children.

The world blurred. His muscles burned—purging, cleansing. Moonshadow patrol scents drifted on the wind, clear but unthreatening. For the first time, Kai didn't feel like an intruder here but a welcomed ally. Every leap and turn freed him from worry—borders, politics, and romantic entanglements dissolving beneath his paws.

He wasn't running from anything anymore; he was running toward something—toward understanding, toward connection. His father had often spoken of the responsibility that came with alliances. Only now did Kai begin to grasp what that truly meant: not just formal agreements between alphas, but the weaving together of pack destinies.

Eventually, he found himself in the Moonshadow ritual grounds. The sacred space pulsed with a soothing yet powerful energy, calling to him like a forgotten melody. He padded to the center and lay down, soft grass cooling his paws as the place's aura washed over him.

Emptying his mind of tomorrow's contingencies and yesterday's regrets, Kai's heartbeat slowed to match the ancient rhythm of the forest. Silence filled his ears like water, drowning out even the whisper of his own thoughts.

Minutes passed, or maybe an hour—he couldn't tell. Then, Orion's voice rippled across their shared consciousness like a pebble skipping water.

"Kai."

Kai closed his eyes, allowing the connection to deepen. *"I'm here."*

Orion's presence was strong, but not demanding—a marked difference from the tension that had characterized their bond for months. *"This place... It humbles me. The power here is a reminder of what we've forgotten. Of what Selene once adored in us."*

Kai swallowed hard, the verity of Orion's words resonating deep within him. *"Orion...I can't keep fighting this war within myself. Every time I reach for Lena, Ava's memory pulls me back. When I honor Ava, our bond with Lena strains. My heart's divided into territories neither side can fully claim, and I don't know how to find peace between them."*

Orion was silent for a long moment before replying, *"You fight because you don't have choice. I understand now. Ava was yours. Your choice."*

Something constricted in his windpipe, making each swallow an effort. Behind closed eyelids, Lena's face appeared—chin lifted as she faced her father, voice steady as she spoke Kai's truth when he couldn't find the words himself.

"The only person who seems to care about what I want, who listens to my heart, is Lena."

Orion's voice softened, carrying tenderness Kai hadn't felt from him in a long time. *"Lena is special. Our Goddess chose well. I won't push anymore, but know her, Kai. See her. Not just the bond."*

Warmth flooded Kai's chest, replacing the familiar hollow with unexpected fullness. For the first time since Ava's eighteenth birthday, he and Orion breathed as one.

"Thank you, Orion. For this. For everything."

Orion's voice faded, leaving Kai alone in the quiet of the ritual grounds. He stayed a while longer, letting the stillness settle him. When he finally rose, his movements were lighter, more purposeful. The coiled springs between his shoulder blades unwound one by one as his spine straightened with newfound resolve.

The run back to the pack house felt different—less like an escape and more like a return. Orion's paws struck the earth with renewed confidence, each stride carrying Kai closer to something that felt like clarity. As he neared the edge of the trees, waning sunlight caught his fur, turning the black to midnight blue and making the silver highlights shimmer like starlight.

He shifted back into his human form as he reached the tree line, pulling on his sweats before slipping through the packhouse's back door. He made it to his suite without encountering anyone, closing the door behind him with a relieved sigh.

Sitting on the edge of the bed, Kai grabbed his phone. His thumb hovered over his father's contact, each second stretching as memories flashed—Darius's proud smile at his first shift, the hardening of his expression when Kai mentioned Ava's name, the disappointment etched in the lines of his face when they left the Summit.

With a steadying breath, Kai opened the messaging app instead, still needing to say the words. Words he'd swallowed down at every family dinner, bitten back during every argument, choked on through every disappointed look from his father. Words that had grown heavier with each passing moon until they threatened to suffocate him from within.

He pressed the record button, voice quiet but steady as he began to speak. "Dad... I know I've disappointed you. And I know I've fought you every step of the way, but I need you to know that I'm trying. I feel the bond—it's unlike anything I could have expected. It's powerful, overwhelming, like it's been stitched into the very fabric of my soul." He rubbed his chest feeling the steady hum of the mating bond flare in acknowledgement. "But even with it...Ava holds my heart. She's still there, Dad."

His voice cracked, the sound raking his throat like gravel, but he swallowed the rising heat behind his eyes and pushed forward. "Everyone—Selene, you, even Orion—consistently dismisses my feelings, my love. Telling me that Ava isn't right for me, that loving her is wrong. The only person who hasn't, who's even tried to understand, is Lena."

Kai exhaled shakily, chest aching with the difficulty of his confession. "I don't know how this will all work out, but I need you to know that I love you. I've always loved you and I'm sorry."

He ended the recording and hit send, watching as the message was marked delivered. Minutes passed. Then a half hour. Nothing.

Each passing moment without response tightened the knot in his stomach. His father's silence still pressed against his chest like a physical weight, but the pressure felt different now—less suffocating. Darius was a proud male, their relationship a tangle of expectations and disappointments, but the words were out there now, hanging in the digital space between them—the first thread in a severed connection.

Kai rose, his resolve strengthened by the communion he'd shared with Orion. He felt the familiar heft of responsibility settling differently as he stood—not as a burden, but as something he might finally be ready to carry. The reflection in his mirror showed someone changed, even if subtly. His emerald eyes held a new steadiness, and the tension that had been etched into his features had softened into something more contemplative.

The sound of warriors training caught his attention as he stepped outside into the Moonshadow courtyard. Wolves from a pack not his own, yet somehow familiar in their movements and discipline. These were Lena's people—the ones she'd grown up with, trained with. Understanding them might be the first step to understanding her.

He made his way to the training field, watching as the warriors paired off in practiced formations. Their fighting style differed from Bloodstone's—more fluid, less direct—but the underlying principles remained the same. Pack strength. Unity. Protection.

A few warriors glanced his way, expressions a mixture of curiosity and wariness. He was, after all, an alpha-heir from another territory—a visitor whose presence carried significance beyond himself. Once, that recognition would have made him turn away. Now, it drew him forward.

"Need a sparring partner?" a sandy-haired warrior asked, shifting his weight forward, stance relaxed but ready. Kai recognized him as one of the wolves that had greeted them at the gate when they arrived in Moonshadow.

"I'd appreciate that," Kai rolled his shoulders and stepped into the ring. "I'm Kai. Lena's mate," he said, extending a hand. The title fell naturally from his lips. Orion's approval vibrated through his ribcage, a bass note of satisfaction rumbling beneath his human words.

"Holden," the male responded with a firm shake. "And I know who you are. Regional royalty staking claim on our alpha's daughter doesn't go unnoticed." Holden stepped back, quirking an assessing brow. "Let's see if the proverbial Prince of the Pacific Northwest deserves to fight at Lena's side."

Kai snorted at the nickname but delighted in the challenge of proving himself beyond his bloodline. The essence flowing through his muscles felt different now. Not desperate or angry. Focused. Clear.

A good fight might burn off residual energy from his run, but as he squared off against the Moonshadow warrior, he realized it meant more. This wasn't just about physical exertion—it was about engagement. About stepping into spaces that would one day bridge their two packs.

Every movement felt like progress toward the wolf he needed to become, the alpha his pack deserved.

And maybe, toward the mate Lena saw in him all along.

CHAPTER THIRTY-SIX

LENA

Lena stood in her walk-in closet, holding up her third outfit option, frowning at her reflection. She was going for casual but a little sexy. She wanted to have an effect on him without looking like she was trying too hard because this wasn't just another evening together. She had a date. A real one.

With her *mate*.

While ceremony planning had consumed her days this past week, her evenings had belonged to Kai. Late dinners after long hours of work had become their ritual. She smiled as she sifted through her clothes, remembering how they'd progressed from sitting across from each other to side by side, how she'd nearly stabbed him with a fork when he kept stealing food off her plate with an infuriating grin.

Tonight would be different. Lena was unable to suppress the flutter in her stomach as she thought about waking to find the note he'd slipped under her door:

Fire and beers tonight with the warriors. Be my date?

She'd scribbled back:

YES! Pick me up at 9.

and signed her name with a heart before slipping it under his door, pulse racing like a teenager with her first crush.

The day had felt like it took forever to pass. Now Kai would be here in thirty minutes, and she couldn't decide what to wear.

Behind her, Ryker sprawled across her bed with theatrical drama, one arm flung over his eyes. "This is so unfair," he groaned. "*I* should be invited to warrior bonfires. I'm practically one of them."

"You're a few weeks from being one of their bosses," Lena reminded him, pulling out another option and holding it up in front of the mirror. "Unless you want to start extending invitations to our dads whenever you have kickbacks, you're going to have to suffer through your FOMO."

"But why do *you* get to go? And with *him*? He's not even a pack member!"

Jace snorted from his spot in her reading chair. "Poor Ryker, having to deal with the reality of rank and not being the center of attention."

"Suck it, Jace." Ryker threw a pillow at him. "At least you get to hang out with the elites tomorrow while I'm stuck at some boring council meeting."

Jace threw the pillow back. "I'm not 'hanging out' with them. I'm observing patrols and assessing who might be a good fit for Cian's detail. You know, *training*. Just like you are for the jobs we're about to take on."

Lena stepped out of the closet, adjusting the buffalo-print flannel she'd left unbuttoned over her longline, tan, lace bralette and black leggings. She tugged on her fur-lined ankle boots and turned to face her friends.

"Enough about that." She did a little spin. "How do I look?"

Ryker's jaw dropped, his playful complaints forgotten. "Holy shit, Thing 1! You look absolutely biteable."

She giggled, heat creeping up her neck. "That good?"

"Damn." Jace adjusted himself. "Bloodstone should take a number and get in line."

Lena rolled her eyes. "We'll see about that." She moved to her vanity, fingers trembling as she started working her hair into a messy top knot, pulling tendrils out to frame her face.

"How have things been going?" Jace's voice turned more serious. "With him, I mean."

Lena met his eyes in the mirror. "Good. Really good." She picked out a tube of lipstick—the umber shade she'd worn the night of the opening reception. "Being with Kai, especially here, it's as easy as breathing."

"That's awesome. How it should be." Ryker perked up. "And Kai seems to be settling in well here too. Full sentences, less broody, smiles—sometimes even with teeth—it's like watching someone come alive."

"Yeah. He's been showing up to warrior training every day. Has gotten in good with the elites," Jace added.

Lena quirked a brow, lipstick pausing before it touched her mouth. "How does he measure up?" She'd always wanted a strong mate, someone she could fight alongside.

"He's brilliant actually. He'll definitely be a fighting alpha." Jace paused with a smirk. "Though he did lose his first sparring match yesterday."

Lena gaped. "Really? Who?"

"Holden. Kai was too busy staring at you across the courtyard with fucking hearts in his eyes when you were walking with Nerina," Jace snickered. "It was all the opening Holden needed."

She couldn't help the smile that formed on her face as she dabbed lipstick across her mouth.

"That's actually adorable," Ryker said. "So...do you think tonight's the night? Mating and marking?"

Lena's hand stilled. "Goddess, no. We're definitely not ready for marks. It's still new, and there's so much uncertainty. I need to know this isn't temporary. That *I'm* the one he wants—*forever*—before I could even think about bearing his mark or giving him mine." She set down the lipstick and turned to face them. "But the tension between us is..." She fanned herself dramatically, then stood up, unable to sit still. "Palpable. I *really* like him. Like, even if he wasn't my fated, I think I'd still be completely smitten."

She paced, words tumbling out faster as her excitement built. "Having dinner with him has become the *best* part of my day. I learn something new about him each time—how his mind works, what makes him laugh, the way his whole face changes when he talks about something he's passionate about." She paused, pressing a hand to her chest. "And he *listens* to me. Really listens. Not like he's waiting for his turn to talk, but like every word I say matters to him.

"He asks about my day, what I think about pack politics. And when I tell him about the frustrating parts—dealing with vendors or the pressure of being a female first-born—he doesn't try to fix it or dismiss it. He just...gets it." She spun to face them, eyes bright, body vibrating. "I find myself *craving* that closeness, that connection."

"We need to meet his wolf," Elara interjected, voice eager. *"Ask him to run with us."*

The thought sparked something wild in Lena's chest. She'd never seen Kai's wolf, had only felt Orion's presence when they were close. *What does he look like? Are those emerald eyes even more striking in wolf form?* The idea of running alongside him, of experiencing that primal connection, sent a thrill through her.

Ryker grinned. "Now look who has fucking hearts in their eyes."

"I know!" She flopped back down on the bed beside him. "It's terrifying and amazing. I've never felt anything like this before."

"And?" Jace prompted.

"I think he feels it too. The way he looks at me like I'm the most fascinating person in the room. How his scent changes when I'm around. How his wolf's presence grows when we get closer. But he hasn't made a move." She pounded her fists into the mattress. "And it's driving me *crazy*."

"Define 'crazy'?" Jace asked.

Lena groaned, covering her face with her hands. "I'm embarrassed to admit how much I've had to charge my vibrator this week."

"Lena!" Ryker gasped, clutching imaginary pearls. "Masturbation? How *unbecoming* of a future luna." He rolled on top of her, eyebrows waggling. "Tell me everything! Did you imagine his fingers? His mouth? Taking his alpha knot?"

"Shut up!" She sat up, throwing him off and smacking him with a pillow before falling back onto the bed in frustration. "I'm desperate to feel him inside me—to have a non-battery or manually operated orgasm—but right now I'd settle for a kiss. A real one that isn't on the cheek."

A knock at the door made all three of them freeze.

"That's him," she whispered, bolting upright and making her way to the door before pausing. "How's my hair? My lipstick?"

"Perfect," both males said in unison.

Lena took a deep breath and opened the door.

The sight of Kai standing there stole the breath from her lungs. When she'd first met him, there had been a coolness to him—like a filter that washed out the vibrancy of his aura, dimming his presence to something manageable. Since he'd come to Moonshadow though, it was like color was bleeding through. Now he stood at her door wearing brand new jeans and a forest-green henley that brought out his eyes, a plush blanket folded over one arm and a six pack of beer in the other hand. He was in full technicolor—like Dorothy opening the door when she landed in Oz.

"Hi," he said softly. She caught the nervous edge in his voice as his eyes roamed her from head to toe. "Ready?"

Jace chimed in before she had a chance to respond. "Look at them, Ryker. All spiffed up for their first group date."

"These pups just grow up too fast nowadays." Ryker mimed wiping away tears. "Next thing you know, they'll be having a litter of their own."

Kai blinked, looking between them. "Are you guys...coming too?"

Ryker responded with a grumpy snort. "*We* weren't invited. Just keeping Lena company while she got ready."

Jace stood, kissed Lena's head, and clapped Kai on the shoulder as he left. "Have a good time, you two."

As Ryker brushed past Kai on his way out, he leaned in close and whispered something too low for Lena to hear. Whatever he said sent a rush of crimson racing up Kai's neck to the tips of his ears.

"Uh-huh," was all Kai managed, eyes locking on Lena as he swallowed hard.

Shaking her head, Lena closed the door behind her and grabbed the blanket from him. "Let's go."

The walk to the bonfire was easy, comfortable. Their hands brushed as they walked, and when she hooked her pinky around his, he squeezed back in response.

The fire was already roaring when they arrived, casting dancing shadows across the faces of a dozen Moonshadow warriors. The scent of burning cedar and pine mingled with the crisp night air. Holden raised his beer in greeting, and several others called out welcomes.

Kai spread the blanket on the ground and settled beside her, close enough that she could feel the heat radiating from his body. When he handed her a beer, their fingers lingered together longer than necessary.

"Hey, Bloodstone," Holden called out, breaking the moment. "We were just talking about how the scales have finally tipped in my daily matches with you."

Kai chuckled, the sound vibrating through his chest in a way that made Lena's pulse quicken. She could feel the rumble of it where their bodies touched, almost synchronizing their heartbeats—like being tuned to the same frequency as someone else's joy.

"Don't get too cocky," Kai replied. "I was distracted."

"By what?" Holden pressed with a knowing grin.

"Something worth being distracted by."

Lena could feel Kai's eyes on her, heat pooling low in her belly at the roughness in his voice.

"Speaking of which," Holden continued, "Lena, when are you getting back in the ring? I hope all that time at the Summit and ceremony planning hasn't dulled your edge."

Lena squared her shoulders, competitive fire sparking. "Trust me, I didn't go soft."

"She wiped the floor with most of the heirs and betas at the Summit," Kai said, pride clear in his voice. "You should have seen her."

Lena turned to stare at him. "You heard about that?"

"I saw it." His voice dropped in register. "I spent my afternoon breaks on the balcony watching you train. You're a marvel in the ring, Lena."

The praise, the intimacy of his tone, sent heat flooding through her core. She knew he scented the spike in her arousal when he sucked in a breath. Embarrassment started to creep in until she felt his arm drape over her shoulders, pulling her closer. She leaned back, settling into the crook of his arm like she belonged there.

"I'd love to see you two square up," Holden remarked, earning a chorus of agreement from the other warriors.

Kai leaned down, his lips grazing her ear. "How about it, Lena? Want a shot at trying to put me on my back?"

She knew he was talking about sparring, but the timber in his voice conjured a completely different image: her straddling his naked body, hands braced against his chest as she rode his cock until he yielded beneath her.

He stared at her intently, waiting for her response, and it took every bit of willpower not to pounce on him right there.

"You're on," she managed.

"Show him our strength," Elara purred with satisfaction. *"Let him see what he gets to claim."*

"Can't wait." He pulled her back against him, tucking her head under his chin.

Conversation flowed around them, but Lena was lost in the sensation of being held by him. The way his thumb traced lazy circles on her shoulder. How every so often she'd feel his lips brush the top of her head as he nuzzled her.

Kiss me, she found herself thinking, almost like a prayer whispered through their bond. *Spend the night with me. I don't want this to end.*

She didn't know when she fell asleep, but she was vaguely aware of strong arms lifting her, of being settled gently on her bed. She felt him removing her boots, tucking the covers around her, pushing her hair back from her face with gentle fingers that carried his signature orange and nutmeg scent, now richened by the smoky essence of the bonfire.

"Goodnight, mate," he whispered, pressing a soft kiss to her forehead.

Just as sleep pulled her back under, she heard him lean close to her ear.

"Dream of me."

CHAPTER THIRTY-SEVEN

CALEB

C aleb's fingers drummed against the steering wheel as he pulled into the gravel parking lot of The Chrome Counter, the modest building sitting like a time capsule against the backdrop of Yakima's rolling hills. Over a week had passed since the Summit, and Alaric Voss hadn't wasted time following up about Crescent Fang's reintegration plans. The elder had been delighted when Caleb confirmed their commitment, wasting no time emailing articles of incorporation and calculating their first quarter dues before extending an invitation to this breakfast.

"An orientation of sorts," he'd called it.

Now, staring at the weathered building with its neon sign flickering intermittently, Caleb wished he'd brought Asher along. His beta's calming presence would have been welcome, but someone needed to oversee the projects back home.

Taking a deep breath, Caleb grabbed his laptop bag from the passenger seat and stepped out of his Silverado. The morning air carried the faint scent of sage from the surrounding hills, mixing with the rich aroma of bacon and coffee drifting from the diner's kitchen vents.

With each step toward the entrance, he straightened his spine, squared his shoulders, and let the confidence he'd gained at the Summit settle into place. Yes, Crescent Fang was new to the Collective again. Yes, there was still morbid curiosity surrounding their return, but he'd earned the respect of influential alphas. The rest would come with time and trust.

The diner's interior hit him with a wave of nostalgic Americana—red and black vinyl booths lined the windows, their surfaces cracked but clean, while a long stainless-steel counter stretched along one wall, punctuated by barstools facing the open kitchen. The air was thick with the symphony of a well-seasoned griddle: butter, salt, and that indefinable richness that only came from years of perfectly executed breakfasts.

Caleb spotted Alaric, tucked into a corner booth at the back, silver head bent over a laptop screen while steam curled from the coffee mug at his elbow. The elder's weathered hands moved across the keyboard with surprising agility for someone his age.

"Elder Voss," Caleb said, approaching the table.

Alaric looked up, removing wire-rimmed glasses from his nose, and his face broke into a genuine smile. "Ah, Caleb! Great to see you again." He gestured to the seat across from him. "Have a seat. And please, call me Alaric."

"Thank you." Caleb slid into the booth, the vinyl cool against his back, and set his bag beside him. He picked up the laminated menu, scanning the options while trying to settle his nerves.

"I hope you brought your appetite," Alaric said, patting his stomach with a chuckle. "Best breakfast in Yakima. And the portions..." He gave a wink. "Well, try to save room for pie."

Caleb managed a laugh just as their waitress appeared—a woman with brown hair pulled into a messy bun, wisps of gray framing her face. She wore a black bowling-style shirt with the diner's logo, dark jeans, and a black apron tied at her waist.

"You boys ready to order?" she asked, pulling a worn pad from her apron pocket.

"I'll have the Country Breakfast," Alaric said without hesitation. "Ham steak, four slices of bacon, two sausage patties, hashbrowns, and scrambled eggs with a short stack."

Caleb's eyebrows rose. "I'll have the country fried steak and eggs, sunny side up, with a short stack as well."

The waitress nodded, then looked at Caleb. "Coffee, hon, or something else?"

"Coffee's perfect."

"I'll get that order in and be right back with your mug." She tucked the pad away and disappeared toward the kitchen.

"First time in Yakima?" Alaric closed his laptop, focusing on their conversation.

"It is. Beautiful drive through the valley."

"Wait until you see it in the fall. The orchards are something else." Alaric leaned back as the waitress returned with a fresh mug and a carafe of coffee for the table. "Food should be up momentarily," she said before hurrying off to check on other customers.

Alaric poured coffee for both of them. "Any questions about the articles of incorporation?"

Caleb shook his head, reaching into his bag. "We went through everything with our council and attorney." He pulled out a manila folder and slid it across the table. "Signed and notarized. The first quarter's dues are in there too."

The memory of that council meeting still left a sour taste in his mouth. Erik had been particularly vocal about the cost—one hundred dollars per member when it had been twenty-five forty years ago. Caleb had to remind them that Collective dues helped fund grants that packs like theirs could apply for, especially for projects like the sanctuary. That argument had finally secured the votes he needed.

"Excellent." Alaric tucked the folder beside his laptop. "The bureaucratic part is always the least exciting, but it's necessary."

Their conversation paused as the waitress appeared with a tray carrying four enormous plates. Caleb's eyes widened at the spread before him—a country fried steak that had to be close to eight ounces, smothered in thick, peppery white gravy, alongside two sunny-side-up eggs with perfect golden yolks nestled atop a mountain of crispy hashbrowns. The short stack covered the entire diameter of a separate plate.

"Wow," Caleb said, mouth watering as he unwrapped his silverware. "You weren't lying about the portions. I probably didn't need the pancakes."

Alaric chuckled, attacking his own impressive spread. "Take a bite while they're fresh, then box up the rest for later."

They ate in comfortable silence for several minutes, the scrape of silverware against plates and appreciative hums filling the space between them. The steak was perfectly seasoned, the gravy rich and comforting, and Caleb found himself relaxing despite the importance of their meeting.

After putting a significant dent in his meal, Caleb set down his fork and regarded the elder across from him. "Alaric, I've been wondering something. Why was Crescent Fang invited to the Summit this year? After all this time?"

Alaric paused mid-chew, then carefully set down his fork and wiped his mouth with his napkin. "It might sound silly." A soft smile spread across his weathered features. "Well, maybe not for you." He met Caleb's eyes directly. "The Denali massacre was rough news. We knew things were getting worse with the rogues, but an entire pack..." He shook his head grimly. "I went to our ritual grounds to pray for their souls. To seek guidance."

Caleb leaned forward, anticipation brewing.

"I don't remember exactly how long I was out there," Alaric continued, gaze drifting toward the window overlooking the parking lot. "Just asking for help, for some sign of what we should do. And that's when I heard it." He turned back to Caleb. "The faintest female voice, like a whisper in the wind, telling me to 'seek my first children, bring them home.'"

Fenrir surged, alert and focused. *"This is Her design,"* his wolf murmured. *"We will follow."*

"It felt like a dream, but there was this certainty." Alaric emphasized his words with both hands. "It was a sign that to face this threat, we needed to be one community."

Caleb wouldn't deny their Goddess's call, but apprehension knotted in his stomach. "I agree completely. I want to help in any way we can, but what exactly are you expecting from us?"

Alaric's laugh made the vinyl bench creak as he shifted forward. "I heard a whisper, not a fully outlined plan." His expression grew pensive. "Has anyone ever told you about the day your grandfather announced Crescent Fang's departure from the Collective?"

Caleb shook his head, reaching for his mug.

"It was during the Summit Review meeting. Odin had started giving his usual progress update, everything normal. Then suddenly he just...stopped, and began weeping."

The coffee turned bitter in Caleb's mouth. "Weeping?"

"His entire demeanor shifted. He condemned nearly every alpha in that room. For their selfishness, their self-aggrandizing, their greed." Alaric's voice took on the force of memory as he pointed forcefully across the table. "'Your apathy!' he roared at my father at one point."

Caleb's eyebrows shot up. "You were there?"

"My fifth summit. Quite the show." Alaric paused, clearly still affected by the memory. "Odin's aura was incredible. Damn near pressed every wolf in that room into their seats, demanding they listen to every word. He told the alphas that their 'Goddess was moonlight, not land or money.' Reminded them their power wasn't limitless, and their will wasn't absolute. 'Only Hers,' he said."

Caleb's stomach churned as he pushed his plates away, appetite completely gone. The grandfather he remembered had been joyous, gentle—a male who never needed to raise his voice because his presence alone commanded respect.

"He stalked to the conference room door," Alaric continued, "and warned them that they'd 'destroy themselves from the inside out unless they humble themselves and found a way back to Her light.' Then he ripped open the door and left. No one saw a member of the Crescent Fang delegation for the rest of the week. Apparently, a formal letter of separation was already in the mail."

"I always assumed it was a quieter departure," Caleb said, voice barely above a whisper. "It's hard to picture the even-tempered male I knew taking such a strong stand."

Alaric shrugged, palms upturned. "I can only guess it was a long time coming. A decision that clearly hurt him to make."

Caleb nodded, trying to process this new understanding of his family's legacy. "I still don't understand what that has to do with us being asked back now."

Alaric inhaled deeply, refilling his coffee and stirring in two sugars. "I was too young then to really understand the enormity of it, but packs don't leave the Collective. For the most favored pack to do so, and in such a dramatic way..." He stared into his mug as if searching for answers in the dark liquid. "I'm not saying Odin was completely right in his assessment, but given everything since, I'm not sure he was wrong either."

"What do you mean?"

"It's not just the rogues plaguing our community," Alaric explained, voice growing more serious. "It's the decline in birthrates, especially in the legacy bloodlines. Have you noticed that most of the alphas, betas, gammas, and their heirs are only children? Our community is shrinking, even without the losses to rogue attacks."

The observation rooted itself in Caleb's chest like a splinter. He thought of the leaders he'd met—so many were indeed only children.

"And then there's the mating bonds," Alaric continued. "We're constantly filing chosen pair marriage certificates, but it's been over twenty years since a chosen mating received the Goddess's blessing. *Twenty years*, Caleb..."

The ambient sounds of the diner—food dropping into fryers, diners' soft chatter, the bell sounding in the pickup window—felt impossibly loud against the elder's silence. Caleb found himself bracing for the gravity of what was coming.

When Alaric finally spoke again, his voice was heavy. "I worry our people may have lost, or be on the brink of losing, Selene's favor. That our existence will fade without Her blessings. And worse, that most have gotten so comfortable with arranged marriages and heat inducers and constant rogue threats that they either don't notice or don't care."

Caleb's equilibrium faltered as he took in each revelation. "And you want me to make them care?" he asked, incredulous. "What makes you think anyone would listen to me?"

Alaric waved a dismissive hand. "If your grandfather's warnings did nothing to sway the alphas, especially when Crescent Fang was still revered, I doubt you taking that approach would move the needle."

"Then what do you want?"

"I want you to be here. *With* us. Help us remember—not through force or preaching, but through your actions. Be the example of Selene's favor in this modern world."

"I don't—"

"I'm not suggesting you do anything you haven't done already," Alaric interrupted gently. "Look at the impact you had at the Summit. At what you're already doing to open your lands to wolves in need."

"We will show them who we are." Fenrir's voice was certain, proud. *"Remind them we belong to Her."*

Their waitress appeared tableside. "You boys want anything boxed up?"

"Yes, please," they said in unison.

"And box up a slice of pie for my friend here as well," Alaric added with a grin.

As she collected their plates, Alaric shook his head. "My apologies. I didn't mean to get so far off track or dump all this responsibility on you." He pulled his laptop back in front of him. "Shall we get back to the practical matters?"

Caleb nodded, grateful for the reprieve, and retrieved his own laptop from his bag.

For the next thirty minutes, Alaric guided him through the Collective's database—the newsfeed, payment portal, document library, delegation visit calendar, and how to complete Crescent Fang's profile and upload their pack registries. The sheer volume of information must have shown on Caleb's face because Alaric placed a reassuring hand over his.

"It's a lot, but you have six weeks to get it all completed. After that, it's just maintenance. If you need more time, just let me know."

The waitress returned with their checks and to-go containers. "Here you go. I can close you out whenever you're ready."

Alaric grabbed his wallet and placed his card over both checks. "My treat."

"Thank you," Caleb said.

"Alright." Alaric clapped his hands. "Last order of business. Would you like to register any alliances? I assume you'll be formalizing your relationship with Night Walker?"

"We've signed the paperwork and returned it to Lucien. I expect it will be submitted shortly. There have been talks with Moonshadow as well, and we plan to participate in delegation visits. I should know more after those conclude."

"If I may make a suggestion?"

"Of course."

"Hold off on hosting for now. Accept the invitations you receive and visit those packs first. Think about who you'd like to spend more time with before inviting anyone to your lands." Alaric leaned forward earnestly. "I'd even suggest holding off on making formal agreements until you know what would be asked of you and your pack. You don't need alliances to be part of the community. And you may find the 'something for something' approach some alphas take to be less advantageous for Crescent Fang, given all you have to offer."

Caleb considered the advice. Based on what he'd observed at the Summit, he'd thought Moonshadow and maybe Blackwater might be the only connections his council would endorse. Given his pack's anxiety about outsiders visiting their territory, Alaric's recommendation was a relief.

"Sound advice," Caleb acknowledged. "Garrick said something similar at the closing reception."

"Ah, smart male!" He pointed at Caleb. "And a good contact for you as a newer pack to the Collective."

They gathered their belongings and slid out of the booth, grabbing the to-go bags. Outside in the parking lot, the morning air had warmed, carrying the promise of another beautiful early-spring day.

Caleb extended his hand to the elder. "Thank you for your time, insight, and advice, Alaric. This has been...enlightening."

Alaric gave him a firm handshake. "Reintegration will change things for you, Caleb, and there will be a spotlight on Crescent Fang for some time. But that doesn't mean you have to change who *you* are. In fact, I hope you don't."

Caleb dipped his head in acknowledgment and made his way to his Silverado. As he settled behind the wheel, Fenrir's presence filled his consciousness with quiet certainty.

"The path becomes clearer," his wolf observed. *"Odin saw darkness. We must be the light to guide them back."*

Starting the engine, Caleb had much to discuss with his council when he returned home, but that could wait for their scheduled meeting later in the week. Right now, he needed a run through the forests of home and the chance to lose himself in Asher's body. His grandfather's legacy and the expectations now resting on his shoulders felt manageable when he thought of his beta's warmth.

As he pulled out of the parking lot, pie box on his passenger seat filling the cab with the scent of apples and cinnamon, Caleb rolled down the windows and let the cool air wash over him. Alaric's revelations settled in his chest as the diner disappeared in his rearview mirror, and he couldn't shake the feeling that this breakfast had been more than just an orientation. It felt like the beginning of something much larger—something Odin had seen coming decades ago.

The drive home stretched ahead of him, giving him time to process. By the time he reached Crescent Fang's borders, he would need to be ready to pick up the torch his grandfather had surrendered all those years ago, even if it meant walking into an uncertain future.

But first, he thought with a small smile, he would enjoy every moment of peace he could steal with Asher before the real work began.

CHAPTER THIRTY-EIGHT

KAI

Kai sat hunched over his laptop at the small conference table. The late morning sunlight streamed through the tall windows of Raelen's study, casting golden rectangles across the polished wooden floor. The blue glow of the screen reflected in Kai's concentrated gaze as Cian and Alpha Raelen leaned in beside him. The now familiar scent of leather-bound books mingled with the rich aroma of Raelen's coffee, creating an atmosphere of comfortable authority.

"See. Right there." Kai's finger tapped against the screen where footage showed him and Elias sparring, just as Elias slammed him to the ground. The impact echoed through the laptop speakers. "Now look at this exact same sequence with me and Sven from yesterday." He clicked to split the screen, pointing to the opposite side where the video played out in mirror fashion—except this time, Kai pinned Sven with decisive efficiency.

"Yeah. Sven is about a half beat behind you," Cian observed, squinting at the footage. "But couldn't that be because he's bigger or slower than Elias?"

"That's what I thought at first, but check this out." Kai's fingers moved across the trackpad, bringing up another clip. The rhythmic sound of blows landing and being deflected filled the quiet study as the same sequence played out—but this time Sven emerged victorious.

"Why does it look like you're moving slower?" Raelen asked, hands folded as he studied the screen with keen interest.

"Because I am."

"On purpose?" Cian's eyebrows shot up.

"Yes and no. Here. Watch this." Kai restarted the footage of him and Elias, finger hovering over the speed control as he dropped the playback to twenty-five percent. He leaned back in his chair, the leather creaking softly beneath him, and watched their faces as they focused on the slowed footage. Kai chuckled at Cian's sharp intake of breath.

"You both keep partially shifting," Cian remarked.

"Exactly." Kai's voice carried a note of satisfaction. "Short bursts of letting our wolves take over to advance, deflect, or weaken the impact. A full shift mid-combat is risky because your opponent isn't going to pause until it's complete. Limiting the shift allows you to leverage your wolf's strength, physical awareness, and speed as needed."

Cian leaned forward, examining the frozen frame.

Kai gestured to the screen. "That second clip of me and Sven, I didn't shift at all, and you saw how quickly I got my ass handed to me. In human form, Moonshadow's warriors are unmatched, but in wolf form they're slower and less sure of themselves. Holden and I did a few rounds yesterday, both in wolf form and then with only him shifted. He's your best, and he went down each time." Kai stabbed at the table, emphasizing his words. "With everything happening with the rogues, it might not be a bad idea to start building more skills fighting as wolves."

The afternoon light shifted slightly, casting new shadows across Raelen's thoughtful expression. "Is this something you can work with our warriors on? Maybe starting with the elite?"

"I could try." Kai shrugged. "I'm a better student than teacher, though."

"Do you think your dad might be open to having a few of our elites spend time training with your warriors?" Cian drummed his fingers against the table, clearly thinking it through. "Then they could come back here and teach our ranks."

"That's actually what I wanted to put out there." Excitement bled into Kai's voice as he spoke. "The Washington packs have a long history of hosting wolves from other territories to teach different skills. Ironclaw used to run a warrior intensive every summer. That's where I learned."

"I remember hearing about that when I was younger," Raelen offered, coffee cup pausing halfway to his lips. "They don't do it anymore?"

Kai snorted, shaking his head. "That's because Alpha Thorne's a dick, and he'll do anything to make sure Ironclaw has an edge. He stopped running the intensive when his father stepped down a few years ago. The good thing for Bloodstone is that Gamma Talon attended every year since his first shift. Once our gamma-heir, Elias, shifted, he joined him. They've incorporated what they learned into our training curriculum." He paused, meeting Cian's gaze directly. "When my dad visits for your ceremony, I think you should consider putting the ask out there, but can I make a recommendation?"

"Sure."

"If my dad agrees, prioritize getting the newly shifted wolves just starting training into the program. It's easier to learn how to control the shift when you're still building the muscle memory for it." He leaned back, arms crossed over his chest. "I expect Lena and I will be back and forth between here and Bloodstone quite a bit until I take my oaths. I could see about having Elias join us on some visits to work with some of the older wolves and elites."

The offer hung in the air like a declaration. Cian and Raelen stared at him for a moment without speaking. Kai felt his anxiety bubbling, worried that he'd overstepped, but then he played back what he'd said. He'd spoken as if Lena would be coming back to Bloodstone after the alpha ceremony—like it was a given, a natural progression. It was something that he hadn't dared consider consciously, but now that the thought was out there, settling in the sun-warmed air of the study, he couldn't imagine going back home without her.

"She belongs with us," Orion rumbled in his chest, a warm certainty that resonated through Kai. *"We belong with her."*

Cian's voice broke through Kai's rumination, a pleased grin spreading across his face. "Dad? What do you think?" He addressed his father but never took his eyes off Kai.

"I think it's your call, son, but I recommend talking about it with Jace. If Darius agrees, it will be up to the two of you to make it happen."

"And in the unlikely event that my father says no, I'll be alpha come fall." Kai lifted his chin, surprised by the conviction in his voice. For the first time, owning his birthright didn't feel like accepting a prison sentence—it felt like claiming destiny. "I'd love for us to come to an arrangement that benefits both packs."

Raelen's features creased with genuine pleasure. He clapped Kai on the back. "I'm happy you decided to spend time in Moonshadow, Kai. It's been wonderful to get to know you better, and it's also been great to reconnect with Darius."

Curiosity piqued, Kai straightened in his chair. "Did you and my dad have a falling out?"

"No." Raelen's brows shot up. "Why would you think that, son?"

"It's just that you talked about him like you were old friends, but I've never been to Moonshadow before, and I don't remember him ever mentioning coming here. I was just wondering why because..." Kai wasn't sure how to finish that statement. How to ask his mate's father why he'd been cheated out of getting to meet her sooner, getting to have known her longer. He wondered what their life would look like now if he had.

Would we have mated right away? How many pups would we already have?

He'd developed the biggest crush on Lena in such a short amount of time. Despite keeping himself busy, every day felt like a countdown to when he'd get to see her again, find some way to hold or touch her. He was certain, deep in his gut, that if they'd met as pups, Moonshadow visits would have been the highlight of his year because she was—

"Everything," Orion finished the thought for him, the word resonating through his chest like a bell.

"Nothing like that," Raelen explained. "It's more about geography. Interstate alliances are rare. It's easier to cultivate relationships with packs closer to you."

His response made sense. The knowing glint in Raelen's eye, however, suggested he understood why Kai really asked.

Raelen looked between the two heirs, expression thoughtful. "You're both stepping into your birthrights this year. While there is a heavy burden of tradition to consider, the legacy of your reigns should be entirely your own. Kai, I think your mating is proof that maybe our community has grown too siloed. That there's cause to start thinking a bit differently about the connections we make."

Cian nodded enthusiastically. "I'm planning to schedule visits with any pack willing to extend the invitation. My future luna is out there, and I don't want to risk not finding her because I've kept too close to home. Having met Caleb, and now hearing what you've shared about the Washington packs, Kai, I think we need to get our people out into the region more. We function well for a pack of our size, but could we thrive if we had access to more skills and resources? What other connections are we missing because we've kept to our little corner of the region?"

Kai looked at Cian, realizing he'd missed out on more than just meeting Lena sooner—he'd missed the chance to know Cian too, to build the friendship that was forming between them now. That wasn't something he could blame on Collective norms or pack politics, though. He and Cian had been attending summits together for a decade, yet Kai had spent most of them hiding behind his phone instead of making connections.

"I couldn't agree more. I look forward to branching out with you, brother."

Their fist bump was solid, connecting with a satisfying thump that sealed something between them.

Kai's phone buzzed against the wooden table as he shut down his laptop. A glance showed Magnus calling. He shot off a quick text and turned to Cian, gathering his things. "Sorry. That's Magnus. I'll probably be late for lunch." His chair scraped as he stood, confirming he would meet the heirs at the dining hall when he was done.

He called Magnus back as he closed the door to Raelen's study, footsteps echoing in the hallway as he made his way toward the stairs.

"Hey, man. Sorry about that. I was wrapping up with Cian and Alpha Raelen."

"No worries! Everything cool with them now?" Magnus's voice came through clearly, familiar and reassuring.

Kai released a breath as he climbed, hand trailing along the smooth wooden banister. "I think so. It was a bit frosty that first day, but Lena helped smooth things over. They seem to understand. Or at least are trying to."

"That's good. So, what were you meeting about?"

Kai explained what he'd shown the alpha and heir as he made his way up to the third level, voice gaining momentum as he talked about the ideas they'd come up with. Words poured out faster by the second, echoing slightly in the stairwell. By the time he reached his guest suite and pushed open the door, he'd barely taken a breath.

"That sounds awesome!" Magnus said. "I think Elias would love that too. He hasn't gotten a chance to venture out, and he doesn't get an annual summit the way we do."

"One sec. I need to put you on speaker." Kai turned on the speakerphone setting and tossed the phone onto his bed, where it landed with a soft bounce on the navy comforter. "About that. Do you remember that idea I had a while ago about deltas and a gamma retreat?"

"Yeah."

Kai rummaged through the dresser for a pair of running shorts and a shirt, the wood drawers sliding smoothly under his hands. "The heirs are all deep in their training since they take over next month. It's been really hard on Jace, especially because of how wide the gamma's net is. He also has cross-training to prepare for when Cian and Ryker will be away. I told him about my idea and he got so excited. Said he's been telling everyone that gammas need more support and deserve a summit of their own."

"Are you thinking Jace's endorsement could help sway your dad?"

"Not exactly." Kai pulled a soft cotton shirt over his head, the fabric settling comfortably against his skin. The mattress sagged as he sat to lace his sneakers. "Raelen was just telling Cian and me that the legacy of our reigns should be our own. Setting up a training exchange for the warriors would be a start, but what if the seven of us worked together to really drive innovation in the pack structure?"

"Seven?"

"Well, the Moonshadow heirs, you, Elias, me, and Lena. Maybe I can check with Cian about adding you guys to the invite for his ceremony. Then you can come down with my dad and we can all talk about what the next year could look like?"

"Lena too?" Magnus's smile bled through his tone. "Sounds like things are still going well."

Kai flopped back onto the mattress, sunlight streaming through his windows, warming his face as he stared up at the ceiling. "I *really* like her, man. Borderline obsessed. She's funny, and smart, and kind, and so Goddess-damn sexy. I just want to be around her all the time and know everything there is to know about her."

He ran a hand through his hair, grinning at the empty room. "When we first met, I thought it was the bond pulling me towards Lena, but honestly, I think I would be into her even if she wasn't my fated. She's just so fucking magnetic. Did I mention that she's hot? *Goddess!* The way her mind works is incredible. And what we saw at the Summit? Doesn't even scratch the surface... The pack's going to love her. Her legacy is sure to surpass my grandpa's. Not because she's going to make us bigger or richer, but just because of how extraordinary she is."

"Tell him how her laugh makes our heart race," Orion interjected, voice warm with affection. *"How she smells like Thanksgiving."*

Magnus's laugh crackled through the speaker. "So, you'll be bringing her home with you?"

"I want to, but I don't know if she's ready, and I don't know if a month will be enough time. I think..." Kai paused, remembering how he'd felt earlier about not wanting to go back to Bloodstone without her. The certainty of it settled in his chest like a stone. "I think I want to stay here, even after Cian's ceremony, until she's ready to be mine."

"Do you think you'll get there with her?"

"I hope so. Ryker keeps dropping not-so-subtle hints about how it's a sure thing." Kai ran a hand over his face, remembering what the future beta had whispered in his ear before the bonfire: *"Her vibrator's been working overtime because of you. Maybe give the poor thing a break?"* He was embarrassed about how he'd sat vigil outside of her room the last two nights, desperate to know if what Ryker said was true, to hear his name fall from her lips in that breathy moan that had haunted him since that first night at the Summit. "There are times when I'm so confident she feels the same way about me. Our chemistry is electric. And the way she just melts into me. And how easy it is..."

"I sense a *'but'* in there," Magnus said.

"It also feels really fragile. Like if I try to take the next step and she's not there with me, it could all fall apart. I don't know if I could survive that, Magnus. Even with how little of her I've had."

Magnus was quiet for a moment. Kai could hear the distant sounds of Moonshadow life through his open window—voices carrying on the afternoon breeze, the rustle of leaves.

"And what if she's afraid of the same thing?" Magnus asked.

Kai didn't have an immediate answer. He understood Lena had learned to keep the most vulnerable pieces of herself tucked away—a lesson she'd learned because of the way he'd tried to resist her and their bond. "Then I definitely need to stay. Prove to her that I'm not just here because my dad orchestrated it. That I *want* to be here. For *her*."

"Choose her every day," Orion rumbled approvingly. *"Make sure she knows."*

"Okay, then." Magnus released a breath. "I don't know how your dad will react or..." He trailed off, seeming to search for his words. "If you need backup telling Darius, I'm here."

"Thanks, man. I appreciate it." Kai picked up his phone to check the time, turning off speakerphone. He'd been longer than expected. "Hey, I've gotta run. The guys have the afternoon off, and I was supposed to meet them for lunch and some sparring." He sat up, pushing off the bed with renewed energy. "See if Elias would be up to coming to Moonshadow and what he thinks about an arrangement with Cian and Jace. I'll see about adding you guys to the guest list for the ceremony."

"Alright. Tell Ryker I said hi."

The door clicked shut behind him as Kai left his suite. "Will do. Talk tomorrow?"

"Yeah, but if you keep calling me before sunrise, I'm blocking your number. Just because you like to run at dawn doesn't mean the rest of us want to start our day as well."

Kai laughed as he made his way down the stairs. "Right. So 6:45 a.m. then?" He was met with the call disconnect tone, shaking his head with amusement.

Pocketing his phone, he jogged across the courtyard to the dining hall, the afternoon air crisp against his skin. The building hummed with the low murmur of conversation and the clatter of silverware against plates. He spotted Cian, Ryker, and Jace at a corner table, their lunch clearly finished, empty plates pushed aside and glasses of water half-empty.

He stepped into line, grabbing an apple, protein bar, and a bottle of water before making his way over. "Hey, guys. Sorry I'm late. Got caught up with Magnus." He took a large bite out of his apple as he dropped into the seat beside Ryker.

"How's he doing?" Ryker asked.

Kai paused to finish chewing and swallow. "Good. He says hi by the way." He turned to Cian, unwrapping his protein bar. "Would it be okay to add two more guests from Bloodstone to the invite? I was telling Magnus about our meeting with your dad, and we thought it might be cool if he and Elias came down too. We could sit down and start talking about options."

"Yeah! That's a great idea." Cian pulled out his phone, fingers moving across the screen. "I think invitations were sent out today, but I'm letting Nerina know to add them to the list." He set his phone down, leaning in. "I was actually telling Ryker and Jace about it and—"

"Enough about work. *Please*!" Ryker interjected, throwing his hands up in exasperation. "Warrior training exchange. Great. Let's do it. Moving on to more important topics." He turned to Kai, trademark smirk spreading across his face. "I want to know about last night. What went down that warranted Alpha clearing out the entire packhouse so that you could surprise Lena?"

Kai smiled, warmth spreading through his chest at the memory. "I went into town and bought her flowers. Lit a bunch of candles. I made her dinner, my mom's favorite, and we watched a movie. Well, it was a concert and there was more dancing than watching—" He didn't share that he'd spent his morning listening to one particular song on repeat, or the note he'd slipped under Lena's door this morning with its lyrics:

I hope last night "was the very first page. Not where the storyline ends."

"There he goes again," Jace jumped in, grinning. "Fucking hearts in his eyes."

His comment drew chuckles from around the table.

"Yeah. Candlelit dinner. Movie." Ryker rolled his hands forward in an exaggerated gesture, signaling Kai to proceed. "So did you finally move past pinky promises and cheek kisses?"

Kai felt heat creep up his neck, fingers fidgeting with the water bottle cap. "Uh...does the corner of her mouth count?"

Ryker's palm smacked the table with a resounding crack that made nearby diners glance over. "C'mon! The tension is so thick the warriors are hurdling over it for morning warmups! What are you waiting for? Are you not ready to complete the bond?"

Kai was flustered, stomach knotting with a mixture of embarrassment and something deeper. He wasn't used to talking about sex so openly, and it didn't help that his mate's twin was sitting across from him, watching with interest.

He desperately wanted to mate and mark Lena—to hear her moan in his ear instead of on the other side of the door, to see if her pupils would dilate when he moved inside her the way they did when her arousal spiked. He wanted to know if the rest of her body was as soft as her hands, if she tasted just as sweet and tart as her scent promised. He wished she'd give him a sign that she wanted that too. Even if she did, there was still that fear he'd mess it up, that he wouldn't be good, that all the buildup would end in something really disappointing for her.

Ryker stared at him intently, features hardening as he leaned forward. "You do want to complete the bond, *right*?"

The question hung in the air like a challenge. Kai's gaze dropped to his lap, hands clenching and unclenching. "Um... I've never had sex." He forced the words out in a whisper, afraid to make eye contact.

An awkward stillness settled over the table, the ambient noise of the dining hall seeming to fade around them.

"There's no shame in waiting," Orion's voice rumbled reassuringly in his chest. *"Mate is worth it."*

Ryker broke the silence sheepishly, voice softer than usual. "Oh... I'm sorry. I thought—"

Kai met his gaze. "No. I've done...stuff. Just not *that*."

"That's okay. Not all of us are hornballs like Ryker over here," Jace assured him, earning a laugh from the rest of the group that helped ease some of the awkwardness.

"Dude! I've fooled around, but Tessa was my first." Ryker pointed at Jace, his defensive tone making them all chuckle. "Let's not forget that summer Stella and Ivar kept finding themselves in your bed. Or that you," he said, looking at Cian, "had that fling with the waitress a few summits ago."

"We didn't... We just made out, and it was all over-the-clothes stuff," Cian protested, cheeks reddening.

"Whatever." Ryker waved a dismissive hand, expression growing more serious. "Look, I'm sorry. I didn't mean to pressure you like that." He paused, then shrugged. "Honestly, Lena's on pins and needles waiting for you to make a move. You don't have to jump right in and sink your cock and fangs into her, but you could at least kiss her. On the mouth." A familiar glint returned to his eyes. "Hell, even Jace has kissed her. Both sets of lips. And he has the sex appeal of steamed vegetables."

Ryker laughed at his own joke, but his admission hit Kai like a physical blow. He looked between the future beta and gamma, remembering Cian's comment about the almost threesome they'd had with Lena. Something hot and possessive flared in his chest, and he burst out into an overexaggerated laugh.

"Hey, Ryker." Kai reached out, gripping him by the shoulder and meeting his gaze with deceptive calm. "*Run.*"

Ryker stopped laughing, face going pale. He gulped so loudly it was audible across the table. "Shit!" He stumbled up from his seat, the chair clattering behind him, and sprinted away.

While Kai gave Ryker a head start, he heard Jace cackle from across the table. The sound grated against his nerves, and he fixed Jace with a dead stare. "You too."

Jace's laughter died. He unseated himself, mumbling, "Fucking Ryker and his big mouth," and ran after his friend, footsteps pounding across the wooden floor.

Cian rubbed his hands together, delighted. "Let's go! I can't wait to see this."

They rose from their seats and Cian clapped him on the back as they chased after the two wolves. Anticipation crackled between them as they burst through the dining hall doors. Kai felt Orion's satisfaction rumble through him as they raced across the courtyard, diabolical plans forming for the males ahead.

CHAPTER THIRTY-NINE

LENA

A lpha Darius Bloodstone.

Lena's fingers trembled as she pressed the wax seal onto the final invitation. The name had haunted her all afternoon, even as she'd worked through the mountain of envelopes for Cian's ceremony. Now, the rich crimson stamp warmed beneath her touch, Moonshadow's crest glistening in the sunlight—its intricate lines a weight she felt in her bones. She set the envelope aside to dry, joining dozens of others arranged in neat rows across the table.

"That's the last of them. I'll have the runners drop them in the mail this evening." Across from her, Ryker's mother, Nerina, gave a satisfied sigh, brushing her hands off on her apron. "Excellent work today, Lena. You've got a good head for detail—must be Raelen's influence."

Lena smiled, though her thoughts had already returned to the Bloodstone invitation. The work had kept her hands busy, but her mind circled back to one question: *What will happen when Kai faces his father again?*

Lena's spine tensed as Elara's resonant whine vibrated through her consciousness. The wolf's memory of Kai's anxiety-soured scent remained sharp as a fresh wound, intensifying whenever Darius's name crossed their thoughts.

Then there were Darius's threats, revealed during their drive back to Moonshadow: banishment from Bloodstone if Kai didn't accept their bond.

How could he give his son that kind of ultimatum?

She let out a quiet breath, thanking Nerina as she gathered her things and prepared to leave the beta house. The courtyard stretched before her, late afternoon sun casting long shadows across well-worn paths. The scent of fresh ink and melted wax clung to her fingers as she started walking.

Her thoughts drifted back to Kai as she neared the packhouse, anticipation humming through her for whatever surprise he'd have in place.

Lena smiled to herself as she recalled last night.

She'd walked into the darkened packhouse, finding candles flickering across the kitchen and dining room, a stunning bouquet of white magnolias and camellias gracing the table. Kai had been pacing frantically, gaze fixed on his phone as he furiously typed, deleted, and typed again.

She couldn't help the gasp that escaped. "Kai?"

He'd looked up, face breaking into that smile reserved just for her as he raced over, pulling her into the tightest embrace. "Good, you're home. I was starting to worry."

Home. *The way he'd said it—like* she *was essential to making it complete—had left her breathless. She'd wanted to hear him say that word in every context imaginable, as long as it was directed at her.*

"What is all this?" she'd whispered, taking in the romantic scene. Tears had threatened as she'd realized he'd done all this just for her.

"Date night." His hands had trembled as he took her bag and jacket. "I figured it might be too late to go out, but I thought we could do dinner and a movie here."

"Where is everyone?" she'd asked, noticing the unusual quiet.

"Your dad made sure we'd have the house to ourselves tonight. He and Cian are staying at the cottage. Ryker and Jace are with their parents."

The realization had hit her then—he'd specifically arranged for them to be completely alone. Her pulse had quickened.

"He wants to claim us," Elara had purred, alert. "Give us his mark."

She'd tried to push the thought away, but heat had pooled low in her belly at the suggestion.

He'd led her to the table, pulling out her chair before pouring wine with nervous precision. She'd taken a generous sip, hoping the wine would calm her own nerves. The butter chicken he'd made had been cold but absolutely delicious, though the rice...

"Sorry," he'd said flushing. "I've never made rice on the stove before. I always use a rice cooker." How he'd managed to both scorch and undercook it was beyond her. But then he'd scooped the curry up with naan and fed it to her. "Here. It's best this way."

All thoughts of imperfect rice had vanished. Especially when their gazes locked as she'd sucked and licked sauce off his fingers, watching his pupils dilate.

As the memory played, she could still feel the rightness of him—his racing heart as they curled up on the couch to watch the "Eras Tour" movie, the heat of his body as they danced around the living room. The way he'd kept in constant contact with her—slinging his arm around her, holding hands through dinner, pulling her close as they danced... And *Goddess*, his smile...

She remembered how he'd fidgeted nervously as he walked her to her suite, how he'd stared at her mouth as he said goodnight. He still hadn't kissed her. Just a soft peck at the corner of her mouth. She'd been disappointed at first—until she'd heard him humming "Enchanted" as he went downstairs to clean up.

The memory lingered like a dream, a soft ache blooming in her chest. Lena couldn't wait to see how he'd entwine his soul even deeper with hers tonight. It wasn't just her he was weaving himself around, though. Kai was building a place for himself here—quietly, steadfastly, as if he already belonged.

Something molten and sweet uncurled beneath Lena's breastbone, sending heat to her cheeks and releasing the knots between her shoulder blades one by one. Maybe he needed this—the quiet, the structure, the reprieve from being the Alpha-heir of Bloodstone. Here, he wasn't weighed down by the expectations of his birthright or whispers of disapproval from his father.

He was just Kai.

"He's finding his way." Elara's consciousness seeped into her mind like sunlight penetrating deep water, warming Lena from the marrow of her bones outward. The wolf's approval twitched muscles Lena wasn't actively controlling, pulling her lips into an unbidden smile. *"Mate grows stronger here."*

Her steps slowed as she passed the training grounds. She spotted Kai immediately, standing with Cian, Ryker, and Jace near the edge of the sparring ring. The four of them were chatting, voices carrying easily through the cool afternoon air. The fading sunlight caught in his dark hair, highlighting the relaxed set of his shoulders, the easy way he leaned against the fence.

The sight stopped her in her tracks.

Kai was laughing—genuinely laughing. His head was tipped back, shoulders shaking as his rich, deep chuckle filled the space around him.

Her lungs forgot their purpose, mouth parted, pulse fluttering like a trapped bird beneath her skin.

This is who he is when he's at peace, she thought.

He seemed free. Unburdened. The shadows of responsibilities and heartbreak nowhere to be found. Their bond vibrated like a plucked string between her ribs, sending heat through vessels as if his joy fed directly into her bloodstream.

She might have felt a twinge of jealousy if she wasn't so grateful to her brother and friends for sparking that joy in him—for showing him he could belong here, independent of duty or destiny. A small voice whispered that she wanted to be the source of his ease, but Elara silenced it.

Their mate was happy.

Nothing else mattered.

She watched them for a moment longer. Their easy camaraderie tugged at her, drawing her forward. Decision made, she began walking toward the group, their laughter growing louder as she neared. She caught part of their conversation just as she stepped into earshot.

"Yeah, Mr. Prep, Prep, and More Prep over here"—Cian jabbed a thumb toward Ryker—"thought they were both just going to dive in raw, no lube."

The entire group erupted into laughter, even Kai.

Ryker's hands flew up defensively. "What did you expect? We were hormonal, newly shifted wolves. We had no idea what we were doing, and it never occurred to us that we didn't need to be in the same hole. That any of the other holes were an option!"

Kai choked on his laugh, smacking Ryker in the chest. "Hey now, that's enough. Or do you need me to kick both your asses again?"

"Oh, I'd *love* to see that again," Cian wheezed, tears of laughter streaming down his face. "You need to teach me that move where you had Ryker in a sleeper hold and choked Jace out with your thighs. I'd love to have something like that in my back pocket."

Even as her cheeks burned with mortification, Lena couldn't help but feel moved by the bond forming between the males who meant the most to her. She closed the distance, crossing her arms as she stepped into their circle.

"Hey, losers!" Lena called. They wheeled around, still chuckling. "Are we done making a mockery of my botched attempt to build a harem, or are all your faux pas on the table for ridicule as well?"

She gave Cian a playful shove, smirking as he staggered back. "Because we can definitely talk about how I found printed instructions for going down on a female in the bag you packed for the Summit after we turned eighteen."

Cian's laughter stuttered, face going crimson. "Wait, hold on—"

"And you!" Lena spun toward Jace, who was already trying to edge behind Ryker. "Let's not forget how you used that aromatherapy oil as lube when you were fucking around with Stella and Ivar. You didn't just lose your fuck buddies—your dick burned so bad for days you thought it was going to fall off."

Jace groaned, burying his face in his hands, but his shoulders shook with repressed laughter.

"And Ryker..." Lena trailed off, giving him a long, pointed look. "Actually, I don't think there's anything I can hold over your head because everyone already knows what you get up to." She made a stroking gesture with her pointer and middle fingers.

Cian, Ryker, and Jace's laughter faltered completely, their expressions ranging from wide-eyed shock to sheepish discomfort. Kai, however, was still chortling, his broad shoulders shaking with mirth. The sound wrapped around her like a warm blanket.

Lena huffed, crossing her arms. "Yeah, thought so."

Her gaze softened as she turned to Kai. The late afternoon light caught his eyes, turning them from emerald to jade. "Hey, fancy a run?"

Kai's chuckles faded into surprise, brow lifting. He recovered in an instant, a sweet, almost shy smile spreading across his face. "Yeah," he said softly. "A run sounds nice."

Without another word, they began walking toward the tree line together, leaving the others behind. Their bond hummed between them, quiet but steady, like a song finding its rhythm again. Elara's contentment vibrated through Lena's bones, shared muscles finding balance on steady ground. For the first time since meeting Kai, Lena felt a flicker of hope blossom in her chest. Whatever lay ahead, maybe they could face it together—one step, one run at a time.

They walked in silence, the unspoken words between them making the moment feel both electric and fragile. Sunlight filtered through the canopy, casting dappled shadows across their path. Even their footsteps seemed muted, as though the forest itself was holding its breath.

As they reached the edge of the forest, Kai stopped, turning to face her. The fading light caught the sharp angles of his face, softening them somehow.

"So...clothes off, right?" His lips quirked upward, but there was a flicker of nervousness in his tone that made Lena's skin tingle.

Lena nodded, heat flooding her cheeks. "Right."

She turned, giving him a semblance of privacy. Her fingers trembled as she unzipped her hoodie and hung it on a low branch. The fabric caught on the rough bark, a tangible anchor in this surreal moment. As she removed the rest of her clothes, her pulse quickened, and she felt the cool afternoon air prickle against her bare skin.

When she turned back, Kai was already standing nude, clothes folded with careful precision at the base of a nearby tree. Lena's breath hitched as her gaze dropped, starting at the muscled contours of his calves, the powerful lines of his thighs, and the undeniable presence hanging between his legs. She caught herself watching him stiffen under her gaze—his body responding to her attention with primal honesty.

Her eyes flicked up, cheeks burning, but it was too late. Kai's emerald eyes caught hers, dark with desire, and the air between them thickened.

His lips quirked into a slow, knowing smile that made her stomach flip, and she realized with a jolt that he'd caught her staring.

"You're going to make me blush, Lena." His voice dropped to a husky whisper, the teasing words sending a shiver down her spine that had nothing to do with the cool breeze.

She opened her mouth to retort, but the words died on her tongue as his gaze swept over her, slow and adoring. It wasn't just appreciation—it was awe, a quiet intensity that made something flutter low in her belly. The bond hummed stronger between them, electric and alive.

He shook his head and smirked. The sight sent heat straight to her core as Elara stretched within her, eager and anticipating.

"Ready to meet Orion?" His voice was soft, almost wistful, filled with vulnerability that made her swoon.

Lena nodded emphatically, heartbeat thundering in her ears. Her wolf's excitement buzzed beneath her skin like static electricity.

She watched, transfixed, as Kai closed his eyes.

First, his breathing slowed.

Then, his muscles tensed, rippling beneath his skin.

The space around him danced with magic, reality bending as his form began to change.

She had seen countless wolves shift before, but this—the air shimmering around his form, muscles reshaping beneath skin, human scent dissolving into wild musk—left her breathless as if witnessing the first moonrise of creation. Kai's wolf landed on his front paws with a soft thud, transformation seamless and commanding.

Orion towered before her, muscle and sinew assembled into living shadow, his presence commanding the very air around them to stand still.

Her breath caught as the sheer size of him sank in. He exuded strength, his massive frame radiating a quiet power that left her both awed and comforted. His thick coat gleamed like polished obsidian, streaks of silver glinting along broad shoulders and haunches. Long, muscular legs ended in large, silent paws that defied his impressive bulk.

It was his eyes that truly stole her breath—emerald-green, vibrant and piercing, like sunlight filtering through the densest canopy of leaves. They were Kai's eyes, but on Orion, they were even more luminous, as if charged with Selene's power. Ancient wisdom and wild instinct merged in that gaze, making her pulse quicken.

"Orion..." she whispered, stepping toward him. She hesitated only briefly before reaching out to touch him, her fingers threading through the thick, soft fur along his head. The texture was like silk and steel combined, a perfect reflection of his nature.

Orion exhaled a long sigh that rippled through his massive frame, muscled shoulders dropping as he leaned into her touch, the tension in his body melting away like snow in spring. His eyes fluttered closed for a moment, but when they opened again, their gazes locked with an intensity that made her breath catch.

Lena smiled softly. "You're beautiful," she murmured, meaning every syllable.

The wolf preened under her praise, tail swishing behind him in a display that was both regal and endearing. She rubbed behind his ears, eliciting a pleased rumble from deep in his chest that she could feel through her fingertips.

"There's someone who can't wait to meet you." She stepped back as Elara's presence surged forward, eager and insistent.

Lena let the familiar warmth of the shift wash over her, human form melting into the amber-coated wolf. Bones reshaped with barely a whisper of discomfort, skin yielding to fur in a cascade that felt more like slipping into water than the usual burn of change—her wolf's eagerness erasing the boundary between forms. She shook herself to full height, her sleek, glowing coat catching the faint light that filtered through the trees.

Orion's ears perked as Elara padded forward, amber fur glistening like firelight against his darker frame. The two wolves locked eyes, gazes searching, tentative, yet drawn to each other like lodestones finding true north. They inched toward one another, the forest quiet except for soft paw-steps and steady heartbeats.

Orion broke the distance first, nuzzling Elara's neck. His large frame lowered in submission—a gesture that spoke volumes from such a powerful wolf. Elara purred, golden eyes shining as she licked the underside of his muzzle. Orion nipped at her ear playfully, massive tail wagging.

A sweet pain radiated through Lena as she witnessed the affection in Orion's nuzzle and Elara's delighted purrs. The tender interaction between the wolves was immediate, instinctual, and beautiful. It felt like watching a prophecy unfold, a promise of what could be.

As Orion nuzzled Elara again, Lena felt a pang of longing. This perfect harmony between their wolves only highlighted what remained unresolved between their human selves. Until the claiming rite, their wolves would remain partly unreachable to each other—connected yet separate—just like her and Kai circling one another from opposite ends of their bond.

Elara yipped, as if sensing her melancholy and determined to chase it away. She stepped back and lowered her body in a playful crouch, muscles coiled with anticipation. Her tail wagged as she spun around and darted into the forest, movements light and teasing. She glanced back, letting out a sharp bark that clearly translated to *"Catch me if you can."*

Orion's emerald eyes lit with amusement and determination. He sprang after her. Powerful legs propelled him through the trees with ease.

The chase was on.

Elara darted ahead. Weaving. Dodging. Like liquid fire between ancient trunks.

Orion followed. Powerful. Determined. His deeper frame moving with surprising grace as he closed the distance.

Lena felt Elara's heart race with exhilaration, her wolf's joy infectious as they played their game of chase.

The wind rushed through their fur.

Pine needles.

Damp earth.

The wild freedom that belonged only to wolves.

She glanced back. Orion's eyes gleamed as he surged forward, closing the gap.

Together, they disappeared deeper into the trees, steps falling into a rhythm that felt like the first notes of a melody neither of them had dared to hope for. And for the first time since feeling the mate bond snap into place, Lena didn't fear what morning would bring. Whatever walls still stood between them, tonight had proven one truth: beneath the hurt and hesitation, something real was growing—something even stronger than destiny's pull. The night stretched ahead, and Lena surrendered to it, one pawprint at a time.

CHAPTER FORTY

KAI

The forest pulsed with ancient magic, every breath seeming to vibrate through the earth beneath Orion's paws. Energy flowed between their wolves as they wove through the trees, paws striking earth in perfect rhythm, as though following the memory of an ancient dance. Moonlight filtered through the canopy, painting the forest floor with silver patches that their fur captured and reflected like liquid starlight.

Kai's consciousness merged with Orion's, making it impossible to tell where the wolf ended and the male began. The weight of duty, of choices unmade and promises unkept, melted away with each stride. There was only this—paws against loamy earth, wind whispering through pine needles, and Elara's playful yips echoing like music.

The trees began to thin, branches giving way to reveal a lake that mirrored the moon above, its surface dancing with pale, ghostly light. Orion's massive frame parted the underbrush at the water's edge, muscles rippling beneath his silver-streaked coat as he lowered his muzzle to the glassy surface. The cool water lapped against his tongue, carrying the mineral-rich taste of deep springs and ancient stone.

Elara joined him, her amber coat bathed in celestial light, as though she'd captured fragments of stars in her fur, movements delicate yet sure beside Orion's commanding presence.

His chest expanded beyond its normal capacity, muscles tensing with the urge to howl his claim to the stars. His skin prickled with hyper-awareness of every movement near his mate, ready to place himself between her and any threat. Something ancient and possessive flowed through his veins, demanding that he mark, shield, cherish. These weren't just his wolf's instincts anymore—they were echoes of his own heart, stripped bare under the watching moon.

When Elara pressed closer, nudging her muzzle against Orion's thick ruff, the larger wolf responded by curling his body around her smaller frame. Kai felt the rightness of it settle into his bones as his mind began to drift, surrendering to the peace of the moment.

He let Orion take control completely, their shared consciousness fading into the simple pleasure of being. The night sounds grew distant—the soft splash of water against the shore, the rustle of nocturnal creatures, the whisper of wind through leaves—until all that remained was the steady thump of Orion's heart beating in time with Elara's quiet breaths. Kai drifted into dreamless sleep, his consciousness ebbing away.

Awareness returned gradually, brought on by a different kind of warmth. Not the sun's gentle touch or his wolf's protective heat, but something far more intimate—something that made Kai's lungs seize. His senses awakened one by one: the silken slide of skin against his chest, the tickle of soft hair beneath his chin, the faint trace of cranberry and rosemary that was uniquely *her*.

Kai's eyes fluttered open, and his heart stumbled over itself.

Lena.

She was curled against him, bare back flush to his chest, warmth seeping into every inch of him. His heart rattled in his ribcage at the realization—they must have shifted back in their sleep, human forms drawn together as naturally as their wolves.

He became acutely aware of her.

The gentle rise and fall of her ribs against his chest, each breath drawing his own lungs into synchrony. The impossible softness where his calloused fingers rested against the dip of her waist. Moonlight transformed her skin into shimmering gold, warm and yielding beneath his touch. His hand had found her hip in sleep, fingers splayed possessively. Want swept through him as he registered the press of his erection against the silk-smooth curve of her lower back.

A sharp exhale slipped through his lips.

Lena stirred, sighing as she shifted, her movement sending a jolt of pleasure sparking through him. His muscles tensed, pulse hammering as she stilled, body going rigid when she registered exactly what she was feeling. Kai held his breath, waiting for her reaction.

Like a drowsy cat, she turned over, golden-brown eyes blinking up at him, wide with surprise. Then, just as quickly, her lips curved, and a soft giggle escaped—light, airy, like the first notes of a song. "Looks like we fell asleep," she murmured, voice husky from sleep but laced with amusement.

Kai's shoulders relaxed, tension bleeding from his muscles as something warm and tender unfurled beneath his ribs. "Yeah, looks like it." He chuckled, the sound vibrating between them.

He reached for her without thought, fingertips tracing the soft terrain of her skin. The contact was a tether grounding him even as his body hummed with the sheer *rightness* of touching her. "I really enjoyed tonight." He mapped her form with reverent touch, eyes never leaving hers—ribs, shoulder, the elegant curve of her spine—before anchoring at her waist. "Orion's...content. Happier than I've felt him in years. This...this was good for us."

Lena's lips softened into a gentle smile, her warm exhale caressing his skin. "Elara feels the same. It's like...she's found something she didn't even know she was missing."

Kai's gaze traced her features—the corners of her eyes, the pink that bloomed across her cheekbones like sunrise, those parted lips that trembled with unspoken words. "I'd like to do this again," he offered. "Often." His thumb stroked slow circles against her skin.

The flush deepened across Lena's cheeks. Her smile widened, lashes lowering even as she held his gaze. "Me too."

The words wrapped around them like silk, pulling them closer. His hand never left her body, his touch becoming more exploratory as he traced her silhouette, mesmerized by the feel of her beneath his fingertips. She moaned, and the world tilted sideways. The soft, breathy sound traveled from his ears straight to his groin, igniting a fire that threatened to burn through him.

His gaze snapped to hers, pupils blown wide with desire. The air between them crystallized, dense with pheromones and intention. Though the forest stretched endlessly around them, their world had collapsed to the centimeters between their bodies—a space charged with static that raised the hairs on his skin with each breath they shared.

Lena leaned in first, lips brushing against his—tentative, hesitant, testing. That first whisper of contact sent a current racing from his mouth to his core, a single spark flaring beneath his skin. Deep within, Orion rumbled in approval, the wolf's satisfaction flooding his nervous system.

Kai answered her question with hunger—mouth molding to hers, tongue flicking against her bottom lip—asking in return. She granted him entrance, and the kiss transformed like a gentle rain becoming a summer storm. Hesitation washed away, leaving only a deep, unfettered connection that resonated through him like thunder.

His body reacted—not just human desire but wolf instinct surging through his muscles. He rolled her onto her back and settled his weight above her. The contact of skin against skin made his blood hum, Orion's presence lending primal intensity to every sensation, awareness sharpening to hunting focus on every gasp, every subtle shift beneath him.

She moaned into his mouth, fingers weaving through his hair. Her nails scratched his scalp, sending shivers racing down his spine. He pulled back to press kisses along her jaw, down the column of her throat. The scent of her arousal filled his lungs as she rocked against him. The friction of her rubbing against his body drew a sound from him that was more wolf than male—a feral call that vibrated against the hollow of her throat where his lips pressed.

His teeth scraped against her pulse point—the place where he'd mark her after their mating ceremony, their wrists blazing with the glow of

Selene's blessing. He sucked gently as she trembled beneath him, fingers tightening against his skin.

"I need you." Her voice trembled with want. "Please, Kai... I need to feel you."

He froze, holding her still, forehead pressed against hers, chest heaving as his fingertips pressed into her flesh. He was so close to losing control, to greedily taking everything she was offering him. Orion's presence surged forward, the wolf's desire a primal undercurrent that threatened to overwhelm his human restraint.

"Lena." His hands flexed against her hips. "I want you too, but..." He swallowed hard. "If we go too far—I don't know if I could stop. I don't know if Orion would."

She cupped his face, anchoring him. "I'm not ready for the claiming marks," she admitted, voice gentle but unwavering. "But I am ready for this. I want to share this with you, Kai. On *our* terms."

Orion spoke with quiet authority, a steadying heat at the base of his skull, radiating certainty through their shared consciousness. *"I will not mark mate without her consent."*

The conviction in his wolf's words settled something deep inside him. He exhaled, letting the tension seep from his body as he relayed Orion's promise to Lena.

Her smile was radiant, and when her mouth found his again, he let himself go.

Kai's lips moved over hers with purpose. Searching. Tasting the softness of her. Coaxing breathy moans from her throat. She melted beneath him, body shifting, arms wrapping around his neck, pulling him closer. Her hands sliding down his back ignited every nerve ending, his need tightening as control frayed at the edges.

He broke away to taste more of her, trailing wet kisses down her neck, across her shoulder, and over the elegant line of her collarbone before descending to the gentle swell of her breasts.

His tongue flicked against the tightened peak of her nipple, the texture a delicious contrast to the smoothness surrounding it. Lena's body responded—back arching like a bowstring, offering more of herself to his mouth. Her fingers twisted in his hair, the sweet-sharp pain at his scalp heightening his arousal. The taste of her skin—salt and honeyed warmth—pulled a sound from deep in his chest, half reverence, half possession, as he drew the sensitive flesh between his lips.

When he moved to worship its twin, her whimpers transformed to urgent, broken sounds that vibrated from her chest against his mouth. Her legs restlessly tangled with his, hips seeking pressure, friction, *completion.*

His kisses grew wetter, hotter as his mouth dragged over the smooth plane of her stomach. Down. Lower still. His lips, tongue, and hands roamed every inch of her body. He pressed a kiss just above her navel, hands gliding down, parting her thighs.

He lifted his gaze to her, taking in the warm flush covering her skin, her chest rising and falling in quick, shallow breaths, her heavy-lidded eyes, their honey-colored irises darkening with desire.

Goddess, she's breathtaking.

"Can I taste you?" The question rasped from his throat, hanging between them like a prayer. His hands rested on her thighs, thumbs tracing teasing circles so close to where he ached to put his mouth. His emerald eyes held hers—patient, waiting, pleading—as his thumbs continued their deliberate path, each pass bringing him closer before retreating.

Lena propped herself up on her elbows, breath coming in short puffs as she watched his hands move against her skin. Her bottom lip caught between her teeth, hips shifting restlessly under his touch.

"Please," she whispered, the word barely audible.

His thumbs stilled, positioned just at the crease where her thigh met her pussy. "Tell me," he murmured. "Tell me you want my mouth on you."

"I want—" Her voice broke as his thumb brushed the very edge of her lips, feather-light. "I want your mouth on me, Kai."

The shy confession paired with the deeper flush spreading across her cheeks sent a surge of heat through him, and his entire body tightened in response. A feral sound rumbled from within him, vibrating between them as he lowered his head, nose brushing against her soft, slick-soaked sex.

Her scent overwhelmed him, awakening something ancient—a hunger that had waited lifetimes to taste what was his. His nostrils flared, drawing her essence deep into his lungs where it settled like a drug in his bloodstream. Then he pressed a soft kiss to her clit.

Lena's hips lifted as a tremor raced visibly from her core to her fingertips. The sound that escaped her—half plea, half surrender—echoed in the air between them.

Something inside him broke free.

Without breaking eye contact, Kai slid his arms around her thighs and tasted her for the first time, stroking with slow, teasing laps. Her flavor hit him like wildfire—sweet, intoxicating, uniquely hers—making his head spin as though he'd been drinking starlight. A sound of pure, untamed possession tore from his throat as he lost himself between her legs, that exquisite taste flooding his senses until nothing else existed.

Lena gasped, thighs trembling against his shoulders as she writhed beneath him. She fell back with a breathless cry, fingers digging into the earth. The sight of her—so open, so undone—was maddening.

He lifted his head. "Show me." He nipped at her sensitive flesh. "Show me how to love you."

A deep, needy groan escaped Lena's lips. Her hands fisted in his hair, guiding him closer, and he surrendered to her lead. His tongue moved with purpose, alternating between circling her clit and flicking over her entrance. Her thighs tightened around his head as she cried out, the sound growing louder when he growled against her.

His tongue slid lower, teasing the sensitive ring of muscle at her puckered hole, before dragging back up, licking a slow, languid path from her ass to her clit. She shuddered violently, hands fisting almost painfully in his hair.

Kai grinned against her, loving how utterly uninhibited she was under his touch. He pressed a finger inside her, feeling her slick, hot, and tight around him. She gasped, clenching at the intrusion.

He curled his finger, stroking in time with his tongue, searching—then finding—the spot that made her hips jerk against him. He focused there. Tapping, stroking, curling. His mouth sealed over her clit, sucking gently as his tongue flicked in perfect rhythm.

Lena's cries grew louder, body arching off the ground, pulling him more firmly against her as her walls fluttered around his finger.

"Kai," she gasped, voice broken. "Oh, Goddess, Kai—"

He didn't stop. He pushed her higher, faster, stroking, licking, *devouring*, until—

She exploded around him, her soaked pussy spasmed wildly, scream ripping through the night.

Kai groaned as he licked her through it. Drawing out every wave, savoring every pulse of her pleasure. He pressed soft kisses to her thighs. Then her stomach. Until her body finally relaxed beneath him—soft, boneless, utterly spent.

He crawled back up her body, capturing her lips in a searing, possessive kiss. Letting her taste herself on his tongue. Lena moaned into his mouth, hands clutching his shoulders, nails digging in as she settled from her climax.

Kai pulled back, breath uneven. His emerald eyes blazed as he took her in—flushed cheeks, swollen lips, golden-brown eyes glistening with aftershocks of pleasure.

"Are you sure you're ready?" he asked, voice rough but steady. "We can stop now, and I'd die happy just knowing what you taste like."

Her hand cupped his cheek, thumb brushing over his skin. "I'm ready," she whispered, voice filled with certainty. "I want *all* of you, Kai."

His breath hitched as her legs opened wider. He captured her lips again—deeper, slower this time, pouring everything into the moment.

Positioning himself at her entrance, he teased her with the tip of his cock, muscles shaking with restraint. With a gentle push, he began to enter her, resistance giving way to impossible heat that welcomed him inch by torturous inch. The sensation pulled a primal sound—part groan, part growl—from deep in his chest as her body yielded to his intrusion. His thoughts scattered completely as her impossibly tight warmth engulfed him.

She sucked in a breath, fingernails carving crescent moons into his shoulders. Her inner walls quivered around him—adjusting, resisting, *accepting*.

He froze, every muscle taut with the effort of stillness. His forehead dropped to hers, their breath mingling in off-beat synchrony, sweat beading where skin met skin. His thumbs painted soothing circles along the jut of her hipbones.

"Breathe, Lena," he whispered. "I've got you."

Her lashes fluttered, grip easing as she exhaled, a soft moan slipping from her lips. He felt her soften beneath him, hips tilting in silent invitation. When she nodded, he eased forward with gentle care until he was fully seated inside her.

Nothing had ever felt more right.

"Goddess, Lena," he groaned. "You feel... Your... It's everything."

Her head fell back, hands braced against his chest, hips rocking against him as she adjusted to his size. An unbridled sound—somewhere between pleasure and claim—escaped him as she pulsed around him. Her walls drawing him deeper, holding him there.

His fingers trembled as he tucked a wayward tendril behind her ear. *Beautiful. My mate. My first.*

A gift saved, perhaps by instinct—Orion knowing what Kai had denied—for her alone.

His vision narrowed to this single point in time: their bodies joined beneath the moon's witness. Not just physical connection, but the surrender of something protected without understanding why. This belonged to them alone—beyond even Selene's design.

Lena's eyes opened. Her golden-brown irises caught the moonlight, locking onto his, wide with awe, vulnerability, and something deeper—something he wasn't ready to name.

"So good," she whispered, voice thick with emotion.

An ache bloomed in Kai's chest, pulse jumping erratically.

She was perfect.

For Orion.

For *him*.

For every part of his soul that had been waiting for this moment, *this* connection.

Kai kissed her again softly, almost worshipfully. He drank in her taste, her aura, the very shape of her against him. Rocking his hips forward, he set a slow, steady rhythm, hands gripping her waist as he guided her through the sensation of him stretching her, filling her.

Lena moaned, pressing her chest into his, legs wrapping around his hips as if to anchor him there.

His head dropped to the crook of her neck, instincts screaming to mark her, to claim her fully like he should have done the night they met.

But Lena's words rang clear in his mind: *"I'm not ready for the claiming marks..."*

Nails raking down his back pulled Kai from his daze. She pressed against the base of his spine, pulling him closer, deeper. Her breaths came shaky and fast, moans sweet, and raspy. And Goddess help him, he wanted to make her feel everything. He wanted her to know that this was hers.

That *he* was hers.

Kai rolled onto his back, bringing her with him. "Take your pleasure from me." He guided her hips as he pushed inside of her. "Use me however you need... show me what feels good for you. I want to watch you fall apart on me."

She rolled her hips experimentally, finding her rhythm, movements growing bolder, more confident as she stroked just the right spot. The sight of her above him stole the air from his lungs.

"Goddess, Lena," he whispered, awe threading through his voice. "You're a dream..." His hands stilled on her hips, drinking in the sight of her. Her dewy skin glowed in the moonlight, giving her an almost otherworldly luminescence. A flush spread from her neck up to her cheeks, lips swollen from their kisses. Her breathy moans intoxicated him, each sound more beautiful than any song he'd ever heard. "You're perfect. So fucking perfect."

Lena's pace quickened as she chased her pleasure, back bowing until she collapsed forward, arms bracing against his shoulders. Their gazes locked—emerald meeting gold—the heat between them threatening to consume them both. Kai felt his orgasm building but held on, desperate to feel her shatter around him first.

He lifted his head, capturing one of her nipples in his mouth, rolling it gently between his lips before biting down, then soothing the sting with his tongue. Lena gasped, nails biting into his shoulders, muscles tensing, so close, so close—

Her walls clenched around him. A choked cry tore from her throat as the tight, soaked grip of her pussy sent him over the edge. With one final, claiming thrust, white-hot pleasure erupted at the base of his spine and radiated outward. His vision shattered into starbursts, the forest spinning around them as every sensation condensed to this single, overwhelming moment.

He came in pulses of liquid heat, each wave punctuated by the involuntary jerk of his hips and the fractured sound—part her name, part howl—that rumbled up from his chest. Lena melted against him, her weight a perfect anchor as aftershocks rippled through them both. He folded her in arms that still trembled with residual pleasure, their skin fused by sweat and satisfaction, hearts thundering against each other's ribs in chaotic harmony as they gasped the forest air.

His kisses slowed against her hair, fingers hesitating against her skin. He swallowed hard and swept an errant lock from Lena's flushed cheek. "Was that...what you wanted?" he whispered, searching her face. "I just... I wanted to be good for you. This was... It meant the world to me, Lena. I wanted to give you what you needed. What you deserve."

Her smile was soft and radiant as she lifted her chin to rest on his chest, golden-brown eyes meeting his. Her cheeks were still flushed, hair a wild halo around her face, and there was a blissful, almost dreamy quality in her gaze. "Kai," she whispered, cupping his face. "it was better than I could've imagined." Her voice was soft with wonder. "It was perfect. *You* were perfect."

He pulled her closer. "Thank you," he whispered against her hair. "For trusting me. For giving me this part of you. I didn't think I'd be ready for this." Orion's presence settled like warm honey in his chest, the wolf's usual post-intimacy pacing and restlessness nowhere to be found. "I thought..." His fingers lingered at the small of her back. "I'd wait until the marks, but now...now I can't imagine it being any other way."

Lena hummed, resting her cheek against his chest, fingers drawing idle patterns across his abs. He smiled faintly at the warmth of her breath against his skin. "Me neither," she whispered. "This was *ours*, Kai. Not the bond, or Selene, or anything else. Just *us*."

Her words quelled his insecurities. He closed his eyes, letting his hand continue its gentle path along her spine, feeling the steady rhythm of her heartbeat against his. Everything had shifted in a single night—Lena's trust, his surrender, something precious neither would take for granted.

They shifted back to their wolves and ran home side by side. The rhythm of their paws and the cool wind created a serenity Kai wasn't eager to leave. The night felt different, charged with an intimacy that hadn't existed between them before.

When they reached the forest's edge near the packhouse, they shifted again, catching their breath from the run. They dressed in silence, movements easy and unhurried. Kai glanced over at Lena as she pulled on her hoodie, moonlight catching on her hair and casting a soft glow across her face. A smile tugged at his lips. She was beautiful—hair tousled, skin still flushed, completely his.

They entered the house, footsteps light against the creaking wooden floor, careful not to disturb anyone. As they ascended the stairs, Lena reached for his hand, pinkies intertwining. A reassuring heat spread through Kai's chest at the touch.

He walked Lena to her door, pausing for a moment as she turned to face him. Her eyes held a gentle warmth, reflecting a mix of contentment and abiding awe.

"Thank you for tonight," she whispered, and the earnestness in her voice made something warm unfurl in his stomach.

He cupped her cheek, thumb brushing along her jawline. Leaning in, he captured her lips in a slow, tender kiss. The kiss lingered, blood singing in his veins as their lips moved together. He pulled back, nuzzling into her neck, and inhaled the scent of her skin mixed with the forest still clinging to her.

"Sweet dreams, mate," he murmured into her ear, pressing a soft kiss to her cheek, relishing the way she leaned into his touch.

Stepping back, he let his eyes linger on her for a moment longer. She smiled at him, cheeks flushed, before slipping into her room and closing the door behind her.

Kai moved toward his own room, walking backward a few steps as he watched her door. With a small smile, he turned and entered his suite, closing the door softly behind him. The quiet enveloped him, but for once, it didn't feel heavy.

He sat on the edge of his bed, running a hand through his hair as the events of the night replayed in his mind. Echoes of their run lingered in his muscles—the freedom, the weightlessness, Orion's presence seamlessly integrated rather than a separate force pushing against his human mind. It felt good to be in sync with his wolf again, their thoughts and desires aligned in a way that felt effortless.

Stretching out on the bed, he stared up at the ceiling as a faint smile tugged at his lips. His time at Moonshadow had brought unexpected gifts—peace without the pressure of birthright, genuine friendships with Cian, Ryker, and Jace built on trust rather than duty.

Then there was Lena.

Their bond hummed as he thought about her strength, her trust. He'd always planned to wait for the claiming ritual, for the certainty of Selene's blessing of his chosen bond, but tonight he'd accepted Lena and their bond freely. A quiet chuckle escaped him. He was falling for his fated mate—a thought that should terrify him but instead filled him with unexpected joy.

And yet the joy cracked, splintered by a familiar ache.

Ava.

Guilt settled like a stone in his chest. He'd given himself to Lena tonight—breaking another promise kept sacred through years of temptation. Worse, he hadn't thought of Ava once since he'd arrived in Moonshadow. The knowledge twisted in his gut.

What kind of person forgets someone they claimed to love so completely?

The tally of broken promises between him and Ava kept growing. Each one revealing that perhaps their connection had always been weaker than they'd believed. Kai exhaled, hands clenching into fists.

"She helped us become who we are," Orion offered, his presence a steady warmth in Kai's chest. *"But our path leads elsewhere now."*

After sharing so many quiet moments with Lena, after tonight, he'd finally understood what his parents had tried to tell him all along: there was a difference between loving someone and being right for them. Between promises made in youthful defiance and commitments that could withstand a lifetime.

He knew what he *should* do. He couldn't keep delaying the inevitable. They all deserved resolution—Lena, Ava, himself. But the thought of hurting Ava—the person who had been his constant for so much of his life—pierced his heart in a way that made his breath hitch and eyes sting.

"Endings are part of growth," Orion murmured, his usual impatience absent. *"Honor her friendship by being honest."*

Not tonight. This wasn't a problem he could face tonight.

Kai turned onto his side and pulled the blanket over himself. Closing his eyes, he let the scent of Lena clinging to his skin calm his restless thoughts. Tonight, he would hold onto memories of his mate. The way she felt against him. The way her love had never been a burden—never been a promise he felt obliged to keep. Tonight, he would let himself be happy.

Tomorrow...he would figure out the rest.

CHAPTER FORTY-ONE

CALEB

Progress hummed in the air as Caleb walked the courtyard—hammers striking wood, patrol boots moving in rhythm, wolves chattering as they coordinated. The past two weeks had been a whirlwind of activity for Crescent Fang, but he couldn't have been prouder seeing the pack surge forward with purpose, alive with shared vision.

"Alpha!" called a young wolf as he jogged up, beaming with pride. "The eastern garden beds are coming along great. We've already started planting those medicinal herbs you suggested."

Caleb clasped the youth's shoulder, feeling the eager energy thrumming beneath his palm. "Good work, Nate. Those herbs will serve us well come winter."

The young wolf beamed before darting back to his post, renewed purpose in his stride.

Caleb continued toward the construction site where Asher directed the action. The sanctuary project's foundation was already set, wolves moving in synchronized effort at his beta's calm instructions. When their eyes met across the site, Asher's smile sent a flutter beneath Caleb's ribs, heartbeat quickening as he returned the gesture. His beta raised a hand in greeting, and Caleb nodded back.

Farther out, Varek's patrol teams rotated in from the borders. Caleb intercepted his gamma. "How are the warriors holding up with the new schedule?" he asked as they fell into step.

"Better than expected, Alpha." Varek wiped sweat from his brow. "Injuries are down thirty percent, and alertness has improved significantly." He gestured to the returning patrol. "They're tired, but not exhausted. That's the difference."

Caleb nodded, squeezing his gamma's shoulder. "Well done."

The warriors had embraced Varek's revamped patrol system—the balance between readiness and rest impressive in its effectiveness. It wasn't just about preparing for an attack; it was about sustaining the warriors for the long haul. And the new alarm systems installed along the borders added an extra sense of security.

As he moved towards the forest edge of the pack grounds, Caleb's thoughts drifted to the Summit, to the new relationships he formed and the quiet ripples of change spreading across the region. Correspondence with Renford had reaffirmed a commitment to exploring an alliance between Crescent Fang and Blackwater, while Garrick had proven generous with advice and guidance on navigating regional politics. It was progress—slow but steady—and Caleb could feel the momentum building across his pack.

He thought of the invitation to Cian's alpha ceremony that sat on his desk. He looked forward to seeing his new friend take his place as Moonshadow's leader and reconnecting with some of the other alphas he'd met at the Summit.

But first, there was today—and the unexpected request from Darius.

Caleb shed his clothes as he reached the tree line and shifted. Fenrir's powerful form emerged, paws pounding earth, wind whipping through black fur. As he raced toward Lunaris Sanctum, the Bloodstone Alpha's call lingered in his mind.

As he reached the sanctum, Caleb shifted back into his human form. The ancient site pulsed with quiet energy, a tangible reminder of Crescent Fang's connection to Selene. He sank to his knees at the center of the grounds, bowing his head as he let the sanctum's peace settle over him. With his eyes closed, Caleb let his thoughts drift, seeking guidance from the Moon Goddess and ancestors that came before him.

Fenrir's presence coiled at the base of his skull, a low vibration that sent ripples of awareness down his spine. *"A meeting with Darius Bloodstone. Curious, isn't it?"*

Caleb released a measured breath, considering the alpha who had requested his consult. Darius's reputation as a domineering male preceded him, but the request for a private meeting had caught Caleb off guard. What could drive such a powerful figure in the region to seek counsel from someone like him, a younger alpha leading a smaller pack?

Fenrir's voice nudged him. *"You're right to consider what this meeting might bring, but remember—Darius isn't Crescent Fang. Approach him with curiosity, not expectation. Don't assume alliance or enmity. Keep your ears open and guard what you offer."*

The warning wasn't suspicious but measured. Caleb hummed in acknowledgment, taking his wolf's advice to heart.

The sound of tires crunching gravel announced Darius's arrival. Caleb straightened from where he stood on the packhouse porch, gaze sharpening as the Bloodstone Alpha pulled to a stop.

Darius unfolded from the vehicle, imposing frame blocking the afternoon sun. His critical gaze swept over the packhouse grounds with the automatic assessment of an alpha accustomed to command. Yet his usual fluid stride had shortened, shoulders hunched forward against some invisible weight. Gravity had carved trenches around his mouth since Caleb had last seen him. Shadows collected beneath his eyes like bruises never given time to heal. His jaw worked side to side, teeth audibly grinding against invisible resistance—chewing words that refused to be spoken.

"Darius," Caleb greeted with a respectful nod. "Welcome to Crescent Fang."

"Caleb," Darius replied gruffly, though lacking his usual sharp edge as he extended a hand. "Thank you for meeting with me."

Caleb clasped his hand firmly. "Please, come inside."

The two alphas moved into the packhouse, settling in Caleb's private office. Darius's gaze swept over the room, taking in the understated warmth and simplicity. Caleb poured them both a drink, the amber liquid catching the afternoon light filtering through the windows. He waited patiently, sensing that the older alpha needed a moment to gather his thoughts.

Finally, Darius spoke. "You've built something remarkable here, Caleb," he said, voice heavy with an emotion Caleb couldn't quite place. "Your pack... It feels strong. Balanced."

Caleb inclined his head, accepting the compliment even as he wondered at the alpha's true purpose. "Thank you. It's taken many hands to get us here."

Darius's lips twitched into a faint smile before fading. He leaned forward, elbows resting on his knees as he cradled his glass. For a long moment, he said nothing, gaze fixed on the liquid as though it held the answers he sought. When he looked up, his eyes were haunted.

"I don't want to waste your time with pleasantries." Darius's voice dropped, vulnerability seeping through his usual commanding tone. "I need your counsel."

Caleb nodded, keeping his expression neutral. "I'll help however I can."

Darius exhaled heavily, shoulders sagging. "It's about my son, Kai."

Over the next several minutes, Darius laid bare the story of Kai and Ava. He spoke of their childhood friendship and how it had morphed into a romantic relationship, one that had grown increasingly obsessive and codependent over the years.

Darius's jaw worked between sentences, muscles bunching beneath the skin. "I had my doubts early on in their romantic relationship. Ava's influence over Kai was...troubling. When Althea, his mother, passed, Ava isolated him, made him believe that she was all he needed. I tried to guide him, to help him see what Selene wanted for him—a fated mate, a true partner—but Kai resisted. And the more I pushed, the more he clung to her."

Darius's voice softened as he recounted the events of the Summit, though his tone still carried the depth of his burden. "When Kai found Lena, I thought it was the answer. Selene's will, clear as day, but he...he planned to reject her. For Ava." His hands tightened around the glass.

"I couldn't let that happen. I...I threatened him. Told him if he rejected Lena, he'd have no place in Bloodstone."

The older alpha admitted to bringing Ava to the closing reception to force an end to their relationship, agreeing to send Kai to Moonshadow to keep them separated so he could focus on growing his bond with Lena, and how it had all unraveled in a disastrous confrontation.

He looked up at Caleb, eyes heavy with pain. "Lena was enraged. Ava was devastated. And Kai... Kai was shattered. Afterward, I was distant. I thought I was sparing him my anger, giving us both time to calm down, but..." Darius's voice broke. He reached into his pocket and pulled out his phone. "He sent me this."

Darius played a voice memo, and Kai's voice filled the room, raw and broken. The alpha-heir's anguish was palpable. Caleb listened intently, compassion stirring for both father and son.

Fenrir's voice hummed in the back of his mind. *"Speak carefully, Caleb. A father's strength lies in knowing when to guide and when to let go."*

When the recording ended, Darius's frame vibrated with a barely contained tremor. His knuckles bleached white around the phone until the tendons in his wrist protruded like steel cables beneath paper-thin skin.

"I don't know what to do anymore." His voice broke as his hand raked through his hair. "Every instinct tells me to push him, to force him down the right path, but all I've done is drive him away."

Caleb let the silence stretch for a moment before speaking. "Darius," he began, tone measured, "it's clear how much you care for Kai. That care has driven you to fight for what you believe is best for him. But you're not just an alpha, you're his father." Caleb leaned forward. "Strength isn't always in control. Sometimes it lies in stepping back, in trusting those you love to find their own path."

Darius nodded, expression thoughtful. "Trust," he murmured. "It's not something that comes easily to me—especially since Althea passed."

"No," Caleb agreed. "But it's something we all have to learn."

Darius leaned back, eyes meeting Caleb's. "I reached out because of you and Asher. You're not fated, yet your bond strengthens your pack. I thought you might understand Kai's position, help me see what I'm missing."

Caleb's lungs seized mid-breath, heat flooding his neck as he forced his spine straight. "What Asher and I share is everything," he said softly, gaze fixed on a point beyond Darius. "When we realized we weren't fated, we were afraid of what might happen when our mates appeared. That fear still lingers." His fingers spread against his thigh. "But we trust in Selene's plan."

He returned his gaze to Darius. "My wolf has never discouraged me from sharing my life with Asher. I trust that whatever the future holds, he will always have a place in it. Selene's will is bigger than us, Darius. It's bigger than just fated or chosen bonds."

Darius fell silent, the gentle afternoon light catching the tension in his expression. When he finally looked up, the tightness around his eyes had softened, shoulders lowering a fraction from their previously rigid set. "Thank you, Caleb. For your honesty. For your perspective. I have a lot to think about."

Before Caleb could respond, Darius's phone buzzed in his hand. The alpha frowned, glancing down at the screen. His expression hardened as he answered the call, posture straightening as he settled into the authority of his role.

"What is it?"

The voice on the other end was tinny and frantic, the words spilling out in a rush. "Alpha, Bloodstone is under attack. Rogues. It's bad. We need you back. *Now!*"

Darius shot to his feet, weariness vanishing from his face as though it had never been there. "I'm on my way," he said, ending the call. He turned to Caleb, urgency etched into every line of his body. "I have to go."

Caleb stood, meeting the alpha's gaze. "I'm coming with you."

Darius paused—regarding the young alpha with a mixture of surprise and gratitude—then bounded down the steps of the packhouse, shifting on the fly, and racing towards the woods in the direction of Bloodstone territory.

Caleb followed, Fenrir's consciousness pushing against the membrane between forms like water against a failing dam. The wolf's hunger seeped through muscle fiber and sinew, saliva pooling beneath Caleb's tongue as primal instincts overrode human restraint—the urge to hunt, to fight, to run igniting each cell from within.

There was no time to waste. Caleb's telepathic call to Asher and Varek carried clear, concise orders. Minutes later, he stood at Crescent Fang's border, a dozen elite warriors assembled at his back. He turned to address them, voice ringing out with alpha authority.

"We go to aid Bloodstone," he said, gaze sweeping over the assembled wolves. "Our mission is to defend and protect. Do not attack unless provoked. Stay together, stay focused, and trust each other." He paused, meeting each warrior's eyes in turn. "I want you safe. I want you coming home to your families when this is done."

A chorus of "Yes, Alpha!" rose from the group, their resolve clear in the set of their shoulders and strength of their response.

The shift began at Caleb's core—his human form dissolving like salt in water as Fenrir's ancient power claimed dominance. Bones crackled like kindling as they realigned, muscles stretched and thickened beneath skin that prickled with emerging black fur. The transformation completed with a rush of heightened senses—scents becoming landscapes, sounds transforming into visible vibrations.

Where Caleb had stood, Fenrir now loomed, massive and electric with purpose, coat a tapestry of gradient shadow in the dying sun. He threw back his head, letting loose a howl that echoed through the trees—a rallying cry, a promise of aid to their neighbor. Then, with a final nod to his warriors, he bounded forward, leading the charge toward Bloodstone and the battle ahead.

The air crackled with tension as they ran. His heart pounded with Fenrir's strides, urgency thrumming through his veins. They didn't know what awaited them at Bloodstone, but one thing was certain—Crescent Fang would stand with their neighbors, no matter the cost. For the first time in generations, they were part of something bigger than themselves, and they wouldn't let the Bloodstone pack down.

CHAPTER FORTY-TWO

CALEB

The air grew heavier as Crescent Fang moved in coordinated silence through the woods. Even as the wolves crossed the forest expanse between the two territories, the acrid stench of smoke and blood reached Fenrir's nose, carried on the wind like a warning. Fenrir's powerful form navigated the uneven terrain with predatory grace, Caleb's consciousness riding the current of his wolf's heightened senses. Their shared awareness sharpened as they breached the tree line, their combined gaze sweeping over the Bloodstone courtyard.

The scene below was chaos.

Fires licked hungrily at homes and buildings, crackling flames sending up columns of bitter smoke that stung Caleb's nostrils. The air vibrated with a cacophony of sounds—snarls, yelps of pain, the wet tearing of flesh, and the hollow thud of bodies hitting the ground. The metallic tang of blood overwhelmed his senses, layered with the acrid scent of fear and the charred smell of burning fur.

Blood pooled in the dirt, soaking into the earth beneath the lifeless bodies of wolves—both defenders and rogues. Others writhed, their pained whimpers carrying clearly through the night as they fought to rise.

The flickering orange glow cast grotesque, dancing shadows across the battlefield, turning familiar packlands into an alien landscape.

Crescent Fang came to a halt at the ridge, eyes fixed on the carnage below, the heat from the fires palpable even from this distance.

It's happening again.

Caleb's lungs seized, each breath catching on invisible thorns. The world tilted sideways as buried memories clawed their way up from the grave he'd dug at sixteen. The mangled bodies of packmates, the wails of mourning wolves, the heavy silence of their loss—came rushing back with brutal clarity. He stood frozen, vision narrowing to pinpoints.

I've brought them here to die.

The thought lashed through him, sharp and unrelenting. His warriors trusted him, and he'd led them into this chaos, into this slaughter.

Fenrir's growl surged through his mind, a commanding force that cut through the spiral. *"This is not then. You are* not *helpless now. Trust them. Trust me."*

Caleb blinked, forcing the memories back. Asher's wolf, Leif, and the Crescent Fang warriors stood behind him, golden eyes glowing with readiness, awaiting his command. Caleb drew strength from their steady presence, mind sharpening with purpose. He gave a sharp bark, his telepathic bond humming to life as he issued orders.

"Defend the Bloodstone pack. Protect their wolves. Do not attack unnecessarily—focus on driving the rogues back."

With coordinated precision, Crescent Fang surged forward, their formation spreading like a wave of purpose as they descended into the melee.

The battle was unlike anything Caleb had faced before. Bloodstone wolves fought valiantly yet faltered against the rogues' relentless ferocity. Crescent Fang wolves surged into the fray—intercepting attacks, shielding the vulnerable, trying to turn the tide one skirmish at a time.

The enemy was a twisted mix of madness and precision. Some rogues fought in wolf form, feral and wild, their attacks reckless but brutal. Others were partially shifted, using their claws with eerie precision as they engaged Bloodstone defenders in hand-to-hand combat. Then there were those in tactical gear—rogues Caleb almost mistook for human if not for the sour, pungent scent that clung to them. They wielded weapons: knives and crossbows glinting in the firelight.

"This is no ordinary attack." Fenrir's growl rippled through the pack mind. *"There's a mind behind this chaos."*

Fenrir and Leif surged toward the center of the packhouse courtyard, where the fighting was thickest. The massive wolves carved a path through the chaos, Fenrir's muscular form a whirlwind of power as he tore through rogue ranks with devastating efficiency. Leif moved in perfect sync, covering his alpha's flank and dispatching any rogues who attempted to circle behind.

Twenty yards ahead, near the entrance to the main packhouse, Fenrir's golden eyes caught a flash of silver fur. Darius's wolf, Ronan, broad and commanding, fought with ferocious precision as he shielded a trio of pups scrambling toward the stone steps of the building. His teeth sank into the neck of a feral rogue, shaking the lifeless body free before whirling to meet another rogue charging from the direction of the burning stables.

Caleb spotted another rogue circling wide, its eyes locked on Ronan's flank. Fenrir pounced, intercepting the rogue mid-leap. His jaws closed around its throat, snapping it with a sickening crunch. The lifeless body dropped to the ground, and Fenrir turned toward Ronan, meeting the Bloodstone alpha's wolf gaze.

Ronan bowed his head in brief acknowledgment before turning to engage another rogue. Fenrir growled low, focus already shifting back to the chaos around him.

A rogue leapt from behind an overturned cart, matted fur hanging in clumps as its claws raked across Fenrir's flank with a sound like fabric tearing.

Caleb hissed as liquid fire bloomed along his side, the pain sharp and immediate, pulsing in time with his heartbeat. The rogue's fetid breath—a mixture of sour and rot—washed over him in hot waves.

Fenrir twisted in a fluid counterattack, muscles bunching beneath midnight fur slick with sweat and blood. His massive jaws locked onto the rogue's shoulder with a bone-jarring impact that Caleb felt through his entire body. Fangs punctured through muscle and sinew with a sickening tear, the resistance giving way with a sensation like biting through tough meat.

Warm blood sprayed in an arc across the dirt, spattering against Fenrir's muzzle with a coppery taste that flooded Caleb's mouth.

The rogue collapsed, its frantic snarls snuffed out, replaced by the hollow rattle of its final breath.

Fenrir's ears pricked at movement near the eastern fence—two wolves cornered against wooden posts as five rogues advanced in a coordinated half-circle. The tawny-colored male snarled viciously, placing himself between the attackers and the iridescent white she-wolf. Caleb's blood ran cold as the rogues tightened their circle.

The male lunged at the nearest attacker, teeth bared, but as he committed to the attack, a second rogue sprang from behind a burning storage shed. The ambusher caught the male mid-leap, jaws clamping around his exposed throat and ripping through flesh with a savage efficiency that sent arterial spray across the fence posts.

The she-wolf's anguished howl pierced the night—raw grief that vibrated through Caleb's chest. The unmistakable cry of a mate severed from her other half. She pawed desperately at the fallen male, claws scraping against his cooling fur with frantic urgency. She nudged him with her nose, leaving smears of blood across her muzzle, breath coming in staccato bursts that created small clouds in the cold evening air. The scent of her desperation—sharp and acrid—cut through even the overwhelming smells of death and fire.

Even as Caleb witnessed her grief, Fenrir's awareness shifted elsewhere.

"She doesn't see it." Fenrir's growl carried both urgency and dread.

A rogue in tactical gear raised its crossbow, aiming at the grieving she-wolf. Fenrir bounded toward her, muscles coiling with explosive power as he closed the distance. He was too late. The crossbow bolt struck her in the side, driving deep into her chest. The she-wolf collapsed beside the male, movements weak and sluggish as blood seeped from her wound. Caleb didn't know these wolves, but the tragedy of their loss overwhelmed him.

The rogues pushed harder, their coordination unsettling as they began to target Crescent Fang's warriors. Caleb caught sight of Leif battling two partially shifted rogues—one wielding a knife. The rogue slashed Leif's side, the blade cutting deep as he had intercepted Leif mid-leap.

Leif yelped in pain, collapsing to the ground as the rogue loomed over him.

Fenrir roared, his fury igniting a primal haze as Caleb's vision blurred with red and his wolf took complete control. They tore into the rogue ranks with vicious precision, Fenrir's claws slashing through flesh and bone. He pounced on the knife-wielding rogue, weight driving the feral wolf to the ground before his jaws snapped its neck in a clean, brutal motion.

Urgency tempered Fenrir's rage. He darted through the battlefield, golden eyes slicing through chaos until they locked on his fallen beta.

The brown wolf lay on his side, breathing shallow and labored. Blood matted his fur where the rogue's knife had slashed his flank. Fenrir nudged him gently, a low whine rumbling in his throat as Caleb's thoughts screamed with worry.

Leif. Hold on.

Leif's golden eyes flickered open. The wolf shifted back to Asher's human form, gaze meeting Fenrir's before his eyes closed again. Something cracked in Caleb's chest at the sight, a physical pain that threatened to buckle his knees.

But Fenrir's instincts surged forward, filling the hollow space. The massive wolf lifted his head, his howl tearing through the battlefield—a rallying cry that surged through the Crescent Fang warriors. Caleb felt their responses through the telepathic bond: renewed strength and unyielding determination. The Crescent Fang wolves redoubled their efforts, their attacks growing more coordinated and severe as they drove the rogues back.

The tide turned incrementally. First, the feral rogues broke ranks, their wild offensive crumbling against the combined might of Bloodstone and Crescent Fang. Then the partially shifted fighters retreated, overwhelmed by coordinated strikes. Last to withdraw were the tactical rogues, their retreat as calculated as their assault. Caleb's mind raced as he watched them disappear into the woods.

No random violence followed such precise choreography. Someone stood in the shadows, directing this bloody performance with unseen hands.

The battlefield fell into an eerie quiet.

The distant pop and hiss of collapsing timbers consumed by flame. Whimpers of injured wolves creating a grim melody. Soft padding of paws as survivors navigated the bodies strewn across blood-soaked earth.

The Crescent Fang wolves began to regroup, their telepathic bond buzzing like static at the base of Caleb's skull—sharp, urgent thoughts overlapping in a mental cacophony.

Caleb shifted back into his human form, bones cracking and body reshaping. The night air felt ice-cold against his sweat-slick skin, raising goosebumps across his flesh. His body was a map of pain—muscles screaming from exertion, cuts stinging from exposure to air, bruises throbbing in dull, persistent aches.

The taste of battle lingered in his mouth—blood, dirt, and adrenaline forming a bitter cocktail that coated his tongue. He stood tall despite the exhaustion that weighed on him like stone, surveying the carnage through eyes that stung from smoke and unshed tears.

Bloodstone pack members moved through the wreckage, tending to the wounded and extinguishing flames. Caleb's gaze lingered on the she-wolf, now being carried away by Bloodstone wolves as they fought to stabilize her. He noticed the lifeless body of her mate nearby, a sharp reminder of the battle's cost.

"Alpha Caleb." A Bloodstone warrior handed him a pair of sweats.

Caleb nodded in gratitude, pulling them on as he addressed his warriors through the bond. *"Return to Crescent Fang. Inform Garreth about Asher's condition and bring him to the Bloodstone hospital."*

The Crescent Fang wolves acknowledged his command, their forms slipping back into the forest as they began their journey home.

At the hospital, Caleb stood beside Asher's bed, his beta's pale face etched with pain. The wound on his side, where the silver-tainted knife had cut deep, was stitched and bandaged tightly. The Bloodstone pack doctor explained that silver poisoning prevented Asher's wolf from healing the wound naturally, leaving him pale and weak.

"It will likely take the night to purge the silver from your system," the doctor continued. "If the wound begins to heal by morning, the stitches can be removed, and you can be cleared to return to Crescent Fang."

"Another scar for the tally," Asher rasped, voice tinged with humor, despite his pain.

Caleb managed a faint smile. "You'll wear it well."

The doctor checked Asher's dressing one last time. "I advise against shifting for a few days. Your wolf will need to rest to allow your body to heal naturally."

Asher nodded, thanking the doctor again for his aid.

Caleb waited for the doctor to exit before turning his attention back to his beta.

Asher's grin faded as he met Caleb's gaze. "That felt wrong, didn't it? Those rogues... They weren't feral—not all of them. And the weapons?"

Caleb shook his head, his expression grim. "No. This was something else. Whoever's behind it... They're not finished."

Before they could continue, Garreth burst into the room, face pale. "Asher!" he cried. Relief washed over his face as he saw his son awake and conscious.

Caleb stepped back, expression soft. "He's wounded and suffering from silver poisoning, but the doctor expects him to be better by morning."

Garreth's shoulders dropped several inches. His fingers dug into Caleb's shoulder, conveying wordless gratitude before he crossed to Asher's bedside in three quick strides. Caleb excused himself, stepping into the waiting area to give them privacy.

He stood by the large window in the hospital's waiting room, looking out over the scarred packlands. Fires still smoldered in the distance, the faint cries of mourning wolves echoing in the night. His fingers pressed against the cool glass, trembling with a rage he hadn't allowed himself to feel during the battle.

This wasn't just an attack on neighbors anymore. Asher's pale face flashed through his mind, the image burning into his retinas. The she-wolf's anguished howl echoed in his ears, vibrating through his bones. Caleb's throat constricted, chest shrinking until each breath became a focused effort. This was personal now. These rogues—whoever was commanding them—had shed Crescent Fang blood. Had nearly taken someone he loved.

His reflection stared back at him, eyes harder than he'd ever seen them. The diplomatic and untested alpha was gone. In his place stood a protector with blood on his hands and retribution in his heart.

"This was only the beginning," Fenrir murmured low in his head. *"We need to be ready. We* all *need to be ready."*

CHAPTER FORTY-THREE

LENA

The scent of orange and nutmeg wrapped around Lena like a quiet embrace as she sat against her headboard, Kai's oversized shirt draped loosely over her frame. Dawn light filtered through the curtains in soft hues of gold and rose, but she barely noticed. Her attention was fixed on the ritual planning binder in her lap, pen idle in her hand as she toyed absently with the corner of a page.

Her gaze drifted downward to Kai sprawled beside her, his head resting on her thigh with one arm draped loosely over her legs. Dark hair fell haphazardly across his forehead, and his long lashes cast delicate shadows over his cheeks as soft, rhythmic snores escaped his parted lips. His fingers twitched faintly in sleep, his broad shoulders rising and falling with each unhurried breath—his entire body completely at ease.

Lena reached out, fingers moving gently through his hair, smoothing the wayward strands. She was in awe of the sight of him so unguarded, so trusting in his unconscious state—nothing like the alpha-heir she'd met at the Summit almost a month ago. That Kai had been hard-edged, rigid with duty and expectation, words clipped, presence commanding. This Kai was softer, quieter. The cracks in his armor had widened, allowing her glimpses of the male beneath.

Her fingers stilled in his hair, and she smiled softly before returning her attention to the binder in her lap.

Lena had been up for hours, reviewing the final details for Cian's alpha ceremony. Each page was packed with meticulous notes and lists, the result of weeks of planning with Nerina. Everything was coming together now, and Lena couldn't help but feel a swell of pride as she reviewed the plans.

The ceremony would be perfect. She was certain of it. From Cian's oaths beneath the full moon to the pack run that would mark his first as alpha, the night promised to be unforgettable. She pictured her twin's wolf, Zephyr, strong and commanding as he led the run, his presence uniting the pack in a shared rhythm.

Her thoughts turned to the reception that would follow—a night of dancing, laughter, and celebration. She couldn't decide what excited her more: watching Cian take his place as leader and swearing in Ryker and Jace as his beta and gamma, the run, or the chance to share the joy of the evening with Kai.

Her smile softened as she imagined the two of them slipping away from the crowd, finding a quiet moment for themselves amid the celebration. Or maybe they'd just stay until the last song played, her hand tucked in his, their laughter mingling with the music.

She resumed stroking Kai's hair absently as the thought lingered, glancing down at him again. Last night had been the first time he'd stayed over in her suite. She hoped it wouldn't be the last.

The past two weeks had been nothing short of extraordinary. Lena closed her eyes, letting the kaleidoscope of memories flash vividly behind her eyelids. They weren't just moments—they were pieces of something bigger, something that felt like it was slowly, steadily, becoming hers.

Their morning runs—sacred rituals before dawn—where Orion and Elara moved as one through the forest. The wolves expressing what they themselves couldn't yet name. The way Orion would press against Elara, nipping playfully before mounting her with a possessiveness that left both wolves—and their humans—trembling with satisfaction. These weren't mere animal instincts, but the physical manifestation of the bond Selene had blessed them with.

Two halves finding wholeness.

It wasn't the divine bond that made her pulse quicken. It was Kai himself—the way his emerald eyes darkened when he looked at her after a run, hunger and tenderness impossibly mingled. The way he challenged her during afternoon sparring sessions, movements fluid and precise, never condescending even as he pinned her with frustrating regularity.

"You're getting closer," he'd tease, that infuriating grin making her simultaneously want to punch and kiss him.

And then there was the sex. *Goddess*, the sex.

Heat pooled low in her belly as highlight reels played in her mind—Kai waking her with his mouth, tongue tracing paths that left her gasping... His whispered filth as he took her hard against the pantry shelves, the thrill of staying silent while her brother and friends sat feet away... His hands mapping her body as if memorizing sacred text...

Lena bit her lip, thighs clenching involuntarily. The chemistry between them was undeniable, but what she cherished most weren't the physical moments. It was the quieter ones.

The sweet notes they'd slipped under each other's door that hinted at emotions neither one of them were ready to voice out loud. The long walks to the ritual grounds, where they talked for hours under the soft light of the moon. Beneath the stars, she'd come to know Kai in ways that made her heart swell. He wasn't the proverbial Prince of the Pacific Northwest packs. He was a young wolf who'd grown up too fast, burdened with expectations too heavy to carry alone.

Somewhere along the way, in those quiet moments, she'd fallen completely. She loved him. Every messy, imperfect, beautiful part of him.

And that...that terrified her.

Lena opened her eyes, fingers still threaded in her sleeping mate's hair. The joy of these past weeks shifted beneath uncertainty. She and Kai existed in a beautiful bubble at Moonshadow. But bubbles always burst. They hadn't discussed what would happen when he returned home—to his pack, to his responsibilities.

To Ava.

The thought pierced like barbed wire wrapped around her chest, each breath catching on its sharp edges. Ava's name lingered in her mind like an uninvited guest who refused to leave. Lena wanted to believe their connection—the laughter, stolen moments, quiet conversations under stars—was enough to build something lasting, but Ava was part of his history, his pack. Possibly still his heart.

Was it selfish to want him to stake his claim? To make it undeniable that he was hers. That he felt the rightness of them too, the way they fit together beyond even Selene's design. She wasn't imagining the way his face softened when he looked at her. Or how his shoulders eased when she was near. If he could just make it clear, maybe then she'd find the courage to bear his mark. To give him hers. Lena wanted that. She wanted him.

But *wanting* wasn't the same as *having*.

As this reality settled over her, a warm current of certainty flowed through her chest—not her own emotions, but Elara's. *"He needs time, but he will choose us,"* the wolf murmured in her mind, steady and sure.

Lena closed her eyes, breath slowing to match the calm rhythm emanating from her wolf. The frantic edges of her doubt softened under Elara's quiet confidence, like jagged ice melting under gentle heat.

"Trust me," Elara urged. *"I've felt it since the first run. I feel it even now as he sleeps. He is* ours.*"*

But it wasn't that simple. Lena wanted to be chosen for herself, not because Selene had deemed it so. As much as she wanted to believe in Elara's certainty, the practical side of her knew that Kai's heart was a battlefield. She was fighting against years of history, of promises and memories that didn't include her.

Her chest tightened as she thought of what would happen when Kai returned to Bloodstone. *Will the expectations of his birthright overwhelm him again, force him to retreat into the guarded, stoic alpha-heir I met at the summit? Will he fall back into old patterns, drawn to the comfort of Ava's familiarity?*

Lena had no intention of sharing him—she'd drawn that line clearly—but what if, after everything, he still couldn't let Ava go?

Her fingers slipped from Kai's hair, and she stared down at him, overwhelmed by unspoken fears. He looked so peaceful, face untroubled by the storm she felt was coming. For now, they were safe. Together. That didn't mean the future wouldn't demand answers they weren't ready to give.

A knock at the door broke through Lena's thoughts, jolting her back to the present. She glanced down at Kai, his soft snores undisturbed, and carefully untangled herself from him. Padding across the room, she cracked the door open to find Cian standing in the hallway.

"Hey," she whispered, pulling the door closer to her body to block the view inside. "What's up?"

"Have you seen Kai?" Cian's jaw was tight, shoulders rigid with tension. "Darius has been trying to reach him all night, but he's not answering. He's not in his suite, and we can't—" His eyes flicked over her shoulder, landing on the naked figure sprawled in her bed. Then back to hers and down to her throat. His brows shot up, but he smoothed his features with practiced ease, swallowing whatever comment was forming. "Wake him up. Dad needs to talk to him. It's important."

"What's going on?" Lena's hand clutched the doorframe, knuckles whitening as her chest constricted at the seriousness in his tone.

Cian shook his head, already backing away. "Just get him to Dad's office. *Quickly.*" Without another word, he turned and headed down the hall. His hurried footsteps echoed in the quiet corridor.

Lena stood frozen for a moment, staring at the spot Cian had just left, the urgency in his voice replaying in her mind. She breathed deep, steeling herself as she returned to her mate's side.

"Kai," she murmured, fingers tracing gentle circles on his back. "Wake up."

He stirred, a low, groggy hum escaping him as his lashes fluttered open. His emerald eyes, heavy with sleep, blinked up at her, and a slow, lazy smile curved his lips.

"Man," he murmured, voice husky with sleep as he threaded his fingers through hers, "seeing your face first thing in the morning is something I could get used to."

Something fluttered behind Lena's ribs at the warmth in his voice and heat blossomed across her cheeks. He reached for her, pulling her down beside him and wrapping his arms around her waist in a gentle yet firm embrace.

"Can we postpone our run until tonight?" he whispered into her skin, breath warm against her collarbone. "I'm interested in a different kind of morning exercise."

A quiet laugh escaped her, tinged with regret. She wanted to stay in this moment, with his affection drowning out the unease creeping into her chest, but reality already clawed at its edges.

"I wish," she whispered, fingers brushing against his cheek. "But you've been summoned to my dad's office. It seems important."

Kai frowned, sitting up abruptly, the warmth vanishing from his expression as confusion flickered across his features. "Do you know what it's about?"

She shook her head, reluctant to mention Cian's discovery. "Your dad's been trying to reach you all night. He called mine when he couldn't get ahold of you."

Kai's frown deepened, brows drawing together as he processed her words.

Lena gave his thigh a reassuring pat as she slipped off the bed. "Come on, let's get dressed. I'll meet you outside your room," she said, voice soft but steady.

He sat up, movements deliberate, as though bracing himself for whatever was coming. "Alright," he said finally, running a hand through his disheveled hair. "Let's get this over with." He gave her a chaste kiss before slipping out of the room.

Lena rushed to dress, pulling on jeans and a hoodie, but her hands trembled as she tugged the fabric into place. Her unease had grown sharper, gnawing at the edges of her mind. Something was wrong. She didn't know what, but the tone of Cian's voice, the urgency of his words, was enough to leave her anxious.

When she stepped into the hallway, Kai was waiting for her, expression unreadable. As she reached for his hand, pinkies intertwining, a flicker of calm settled over her. Whatever was coming, they would face it together.

Lena hesitated before knocking when they reached the alpha's study.

Her father's voice came from within, calm but firm. "Come in."

The air in the room felt heavy. Unspoken tension pressed against Lena's chest as she followed Kai into the office. His hand slipped from hers the moment they crossed the threshold. The loss of contact sent a small pang through her. She paused near the doorway, but her father's voice stopped her before she could step back.

"Stay, Lena," Raelen said, tone measured but somber. He gestured to the empty chair beside Kai, eyes carrying a sadness that made her stomach clench.

Her insides knotted as she moved to sit beside Kai, the taste of copper blooming on her tongue. He lowered himself into one of the chairs facing Raelen's desk, movements precise, controlled. She glanced at her twin, seated on the sofa to the side, head bowed, hands clasped between his knees. The sight of Cian—usually so confident and unshakable—looking so subdued only deepened her unease.

Raelen stood by the corner of his desk, arms crossed over his chest. His face was grave, sorrow evident in the deep furrow of his brow. The silence stretched for a moment too long, growing unbearable, before he finally spoke. "Kai," Raelen began. "Son...I'm so sorry to tell you this..."

Cold fear washed over Lena as she leaned forward, bracing herself.

"Yesterday afternoon," Raelen continued, each word falling like a stone, "rogues attacked Bloodstone."

Lena gasped, hand flying to her mouth as tears sprang to her eyes. She struggled to process her father's words. *Rogues. Bloodstone.* Her thoughts scrambled, chaotic and disjointed, as she tried to piece together what it all meant.

Kai didn't move. He sat stone-still beside her, posture tense, fists clenched on his thighs. She reached out, her pinky brushing his in a silent offer of support, but he didn't respond. His gaze was locked on Raelen, face an inscrutable mask.

Raelen exhaled heavily, weariness evident in his sagging shoulders. "Your father received aid from Crescent Fang, but it was a dire battle. Much of the pack's central land has been scarred—several dwellings destroyed, and the damage to the primary packhouse was extensive. There were also...significant losses."

Lena couldn't hold back the silent tears that slid down her cheeks as her father detailed the destruction. The homes lost. The lives taken. Every word carved fresh wounds into her chest. She glanced at Cian, who remained silent on the sofa, head still bowed. He looked up briefly, meeting her gaze with an expression that mirrored her own heartbreak before shifting his attention to Kai.

Raelen hesitated, sorrow deepening as he prepared to deliver the final blow. "Darius asked me to tell you that he needs you home...to help lay your pack members to rest."

Kai's silence was deafening. He didn't flinch, didn't blink, but Lena could see the tension in his shoulders, the way his entire body coiled tighter with each passing second.

"I'm sorry, son." Her father's voice cracked as he continued, gaze fixed firmly on Kai. "But among the casualties was the Gamma-heir, Elias."

The sharp intake of breath from Kai ricocheted through the room. His head dropped forward, shoulders trembling as the first wave of grief broke through his composure. He covered his face with his hands, breaths coming in short, shuddering gasps. The sound of his pain—so raw, so unrestrained—broke something in Lena. Her own tears fell faster, vision blurring as she reached for his hand again, desperate to offer him some fragment of comfort.

Cian rose from the sofa, crossing the room in two quick strides. He placed a firm hand on Kai's shoulder, squeezing in reassurance. The sight of her twin offering that quiet strength made Lena's chest tighten further, and she bit her lip to keep from sobbing aloud.

Raelen cleared his throat, but his voice was no steadier when he continued. "Elias was killed protecting..." He paused, jaw working visibly as though the words physically hurt to say. "Protecting Ava."

Kai's head shot up, his wide, tear-filled eyes locking onto Raelen. "What?" he rasped, voice trembling.

"Ava was wounded," Raelen said, voice apologetic. "She's in critical condition...unresponsive."

Kai's reaction was immediate. He shot to his feet, the chair scraping loudly against the floor as his hands flew to his head, gripping his hair. "No," he muttered, voice cracking. "No, no, no..."

He began pacing in tight, frantic circles, movements erratic and charged with barely contained panic. "I can't be here," he said, voice rising with every word. "I can't—I have to go. I have to—"

"Kai, wait," Lena said, voice wavering as she stood. She took a cautious step toward him, hand outstretched. "Please, just—"

"*I have to go!*"

She flinched, recoiling as if struck, the intensity of his panic shoving her back. Her heart pounded as she struggled to steady herself, to push past the sting of his words.

Elara surged within her, not with fear but with understanding. The wolf's emotions flowed through her—not alarm at Kai's outburst, but a deep, primal recognition of his pain. Where Lena felt the sting of rejection, Elara sensed only the raw desperation of a mate in anguish.

"He runs toward his wound, not away from us," her wolf communicated. The insight offered Lena little comfort.

Kai's pacing stopped, head snapping toward the door. Without another word, he bolted from the office, footsteps echoing down the hall.

Lena turned to her father and brother, stammering. "I... I don't...."

"Go," Raelen encouraged. "He needs you now."

Lena found Kai in his suite, the door ajar, the sounds of frantic shuffling spilling into the hallway. She stepped inside cautiously, heart twisting at the sight of him. He was pacing between the bed and the closet, yanking clothes from drawers and tossing them into a duffel bag. His movements were erratic, his hands trembling.

"Kai," she said softly, voice barely audible over the rustle of fabric.

He didn't respond, his focus entirely consumed by the act of packing—as if the task was the only thing keeping him contained.

She stepped closer, his anguish pressing against her chest like a physical force. "Kai, please."

"I'm leaving," he said, voice sharp and strained. He shoved another shirt into the bag without meeting her eyes. "I'm sorry, Lena. I... I can't stay here. I have to go home. I have to—"

His words broke off as he struggled to zip the bag, his trembling hands failing to catch the zipper. Frustration flared, and he let out a low growl, yanking the bag roughly. It toppled sideways, spilling half its contents onto the floor.

"Kai." She reached out tentatively, brushing against his shoulder in a gesture meant to steady him.

He spun on her. Eyes wild and unfocused, the sharp edge of his panic rolling off him in waves. "*I don't have time!*"

Lena took a half-step backward. "It's okay," she whispered, palms raised in a placating gesture as she tried to cut through the haze of his panic. "It's going to be okay. I understand..."

Her words rang hollow. The grief etched into his features, the frantic energy radiating from him—these belonged to a landscape she'd never traversed, a pain she could name but never truly comprehend. All she could do was stand there, helpless, as he unraveled before her.

Kai turned back to his duffel bag, shoving the spilled clothes inside with movements that were growing more frenzied by the second.

"Let me come with you," she said. "Please. You shouldn't be alone right now."

He froze mid-motion, breathing ragged as his gaze flicked toward her. His eyes were glassy, jaw clenched so tightly it looked painful. For a moment, she thought he might refuse her, but then he nodded stiffly.

"Hurry." His voice cut like glass. "I'm leaving in five minutes...with or without you."

Lena's stomach dropped as a new fear emerged. *He's leaving me.*

She could feel it—not just in his words, but in the cold, distant tone of his voice.

He brushed past her without waiting for a response, footsteps heavy as he disappeared down the hall.

Lena stood frozen. *Can I really help him? Or am I setting myself up to be shut out completely?*

Shoving the thoughts aside, Lena took a shaky breath and snapped into action. She returned to her suite and packed her bags, throwing in clothes and toiletries at random. Her fingers hesitated over the ritual binder still open on her bed before sliding it into her bag as well. She might not be here, but she'd make sure everything was perfect for Cian—somehow.

With one last glance around the room that had sheltered her most vulnerable moments with Kai, she closed the door and raced downstairs.

Kai was already in his car, the engine idling. His hands gripped the steering wheel so tightly she thought the leather might tear. She climbed into the passenger seat, barely managing to buckle her seatbelt before he sped out of the packhouse driveway, gravel kicking up in his wake.

The silence in the car stretched taut between them, broken only by the low hum of the engine and the steady rumble of tires against asphalt. Lena sat rigid, stealing glances at Kai's profile. His emerald eyes fixed unblinkingly on the road ahead. He didn't speak. Didn't move. Just drove.

The needle on the speedometer climbed steadily as the car barreled down the highway, the trees outside blurring into streaks of green and brown. Lena's stomach twisted, the pressure of the vehicle's momentum throwing her back against the seat as Kai pushed the accelerator harder.

"Kai," she said softly.

He didn't respond, didn't even glance in her direction. Her heart clenched as she braced against the door and console.

"Kai, please," she said again, voice trembling. "You need to slow down."

Still, nothing. His grip on the wheel tightened, the muscles in his forearms strained. The car surged forward, the engine growling as the road narrowed ahead.

"Kai," Lena tried once more, tone firmer this time. "You're scaring me!"

The words broke through the haze. His foot eased off the gas and the car slowed, though the tension in his body didn't lessen. He still didn't look at her, but his white-knuckled grip on the wheel loosened—just barely.

"Thank you," she murmured, voice shaky. She turned to the window, focusing on the blurring landscape rather than Kai's rigid profile.

As the miles stretched between them and Moonshadow, Lena's thoughts raced, Kai's silence cutting deeper than any words could. With each passing minute, the territory that had sheltered their growing intimacy receded behind them.

Will he let me in when we reach Bloodstone? Or will Ava's pull be stronger than anything we've built?

Her fingers twisted anxiously until a gentle pressure built at the base of her skull. Elara stepped forward with a steadying presence that flowed down her spine like cool water.

"We will be here for mate," Elara whispered. *"Whatever way he will let us. Nothing more, nothing less."*

Where Lena's thoughts spiraled in chaos, Elara's instincts cut through with primal clarity. She unclenched and placed her palms flat against her thighs, drawing strength from her wolf's certainty.

She prayed silently to Selene—not for Kai, but for herself. For strength to withstand his distance. For patience to wait. For wisdom to understand what he needed.

Even if it wasn't her.

The car hit a bump. Lena glanced at Kai again—something raw and hollow flickered across his face, breaking her heart. She longed to reach for him, to wrap her pinky with his, but the wall between them felt insurmountable.

The road stretched endlessly before them, trees casting long shadows in the morning light. Their silence grew heavier with every mile, pressing against the windows and leeching the air from the confined space. Closing her eyes, Lena clasped her hands in her lap and sent one final prayer into the void between them.

Please, Goddess. Help me be enough.

CHAPTER FORTY-FOUR

CALEB

V ital sign monitors hummed softly, punctuated by distant beeps and the squeak of a nurse's shoes in the hallway—the sterile rhythm a stark contrast to yesterday's chaos. Antiseptic couldn't quite mask the metallic tang of blood that still lingered in the corridors and suites of the Bloodstone hospital.

Caleb had refused to leave Asher's side, even after Garreth's arrival, even after the doctors assured him his beta would recover. The stiff-backed plastic chair creaked as he shifted his weight, watching Asher sleep soundly beneath thin hospital sheets. His gaze shifted to Garreth snoring quietly in the recliner, head tipped back, exhaustion etching deep lines into his face even in sleep. Despite the calm in the room, Caleb's mind was far from quiet.

Fenrir stirred in the back of his consciousness, his presence a tangible warmth spreading across Caleb's shoulders like a protective cloak. Asher's scent—pine and earth after rain—briefly overpowered the antiseptic hospital smell as a low hum of comfort threaded through Caleb's thoughts.

"He's strong," Fenrir assured. *"He'll recover. So will we."*

The rogue attack on Bloodstone opened wounds Caleb thought he'd buried, but Fenrir had been a steadying force throughout the night, anchoring him even as memories of Crescent Fang's own devastations tried to resurface.

"Good morning, Alpha."

Caleb turned at the sound of the doctor's voice. The older male stepped into the room, expression kind and focused. He moved to Asher's bedside, checking the bandage that stretched across his beta's side.

"The wound is healing well," the doctor said after a moment. "It's a good sign that the silver has worked its way out of his system. I'll send a nurse in shortly to remove the stitches and redress the wound. He should be ready to leave in a few hours."

Caleb exhaled with relief, worry lifting from his shoulders. "Thank you."

The doctor gave them a reassuring nod before stepping out.

Caleb glanced at Garreth, still slumped in the recliner. Rising from his chair, he moved across the room and placed a hand on the former beta's shoulder. "Garreth." He nudged him awake. "He's doing well. The doctor says we'll be able to head home soon."

Garreth's eyes drifted opened. He sat up with a groan, rubbing his neck as the words sank in. Relief softened his features as he studied Asher, searching face for confirmation.

"Thank Selene," Garreth said softly. He moved to his son's bedside, his hand resting on Asher's shoulder. Garreth didn't say much else, but the way his hand lingered on his son's shoulder, thumb brushing against the edge of the bandage, spoke volumes.

Asher roused at the sound of their voices, eyes opening slowly. Still groggy, he managed a faint smile as he met his father's gaze. "I'm okay, Dad. You can stop worrying."

Garreth huffed. "You say that now. We'll see how you feel when I've got you chopping firewood again." The faint quirk of his mouth betrayed his firm tone.

Caleb watched the tender exchange before stepping in. He bent down to press a kiss to Asher's forehead. "I'll be back soon."

The nurse arrived just as Caleb slipped out the suite. He walked through the hospital corridors and stepped outside to the cool morning air. The fresh breeze was a welcome relief after hours in the sterile room as he made his way toward the dining hall.

The dining hall's high ceiling amplified every scrape of chair against tiled floor as Caleb entered the cavernous space. The scent of coffee blended with something hearty—oatmeal, perhaps—from the serving stations along one wall, where staff worked in hushed efficiency. Morning light slanted through tall windows, illuminating the haggard expressions of the few Bloodstone wolves scattered at tables, their conversations reduced to murmurs in the half-empty room.

Caleb's gaze landed on Darius, seated alone at a metal table near the back, where shadows still clung to the corners. A neglected cup of coffee sat in front of him, the liquid black and still, steam long since dissipated. The Bloodstone alpha's shoulders hunched, head bowed, tracing the rim of the ceramic mug.

Fenrir's voice came again. *"We are needed, but tread carefully. He carries more than he shows."*

Caleb grabbed two fresh cups of coffee and walked toward the table. He placed one in front of Darius before sliding into the seat across from him.

Darius glanced up, his green eyes bloodshot and heavy-lidded. "Caleb." Darius's voice was gruff but genuine. "I'm glad you're here."

Caleb nodded. "How are your wolves holding up?"

Darius sighed, running a hand through his hair. "It's...not good," he admitted. "The losses were worse than I feared. And the damage—" He shook his head, steeling himself. "We'll recover, but it'll take time."

Caleb let the silence stretch for a moment, studying the older alpha. Weariness aged his face, and a muscle twitched along his jawline as he clenched his teeth.

"Lead him. He'll follow if you offer him steady ground." Fenrir nudged.

"The rogues," Caleb began. "They weren't acting alone. The coordination, the weapons, the tactical gear... This wasn't a random attack."

Darius's eyes darkened, and he nodded grimly. "I agree. I received a call from Garrick this morning. Redridge was hit at the same time we were. Same MO—large-scale attack, weapons, precision, but no casualties." He paused, his jaw tightening further. "This wasn't feral madness. It was strategy. Someone is pulling the strings."

The two alphas exchanged a look. Understanding passed between them without words.

"Have you considered hunters?" Caleb asked.

Darius frowned, fingers drumming against the table. "Hunters targeting multiple packs simultaneously, with rogues as their foot soldiers? It doesn't make sense that they'd use feral wolves to take out peaceful packs when they're supposed to protect the humans from violent rogues."

Caleb leaned forward, voice dropping further. "Both Bloodstone and Redridge are powerful packs with established territories. Both survived. That can't be coincidence." His brow furrowed. "Were there survivors among the rogues? Anyone who might be questioned?"

Darius shook his head. "None that were captured alive. And the bodies..." He hesitated. "Some were scarred and matted as would be expected, but others were in pretty good shape for rogues." He rubbed a hand across his jaw. "I've sent word to the other regional alphas to increase patrols and report any unusual activity near their borders. If this is the beginning of something larger, we need to be prepared."

Fenrir's growl reverberated through Caleb's mind. *"These are not random targets. There is purpose here we don't yet see."*

Darius's expression shifted, his voice softening as his gaze dropped to his untouched coffee. "I can't stop thinking about Elias," he murmured. "He fought so hard. I knew he was strong, but the way he threw himself into the battle... It's like he was protecting something precious." He paused. "I found his wolf, Kael, in the aftermath, throat torn out." His gaze met Caleb's once more. "He was so young. He would've been Kai's gamma. Elias should be standing beside Kai when he takes his oaths this year."

An ache spread beneath Caleb's ribs as Darius spoke, throat constricting until each breath burned. The image of the male wolf's final moments flashed vividly in his mind. Fenrir lunged forward from the depths of his consciousness. Electricity crackled down Caleb's spine, snapping it straight. The hair at his nape rose, pupils dilating as Fenrir's certainty flooded his senses. The unmistakable scent of mating pheromones mixed with blood and grief flared in Caleb's nostrils as if he were standing on the battlefield again.

He hesitated for a moment before speaking. "Have you had any updates on his mate? The she-wolf who was shot with the crossbow?"

Darius's brow furrowed in confusion. "You mean Ava? No... Elias wasn't mated. And Ava—she's been Kai's girlfriend for years. That's who I was speaking to you about before the attack."

Caleb's gaze sharpened, mind racing. "I'm certain they were mates. Fenrir too," he said carefully. "I saw it happen. She cried out for him—her mating cry desperate as she tried to rouse him."

Darius stared at Caleb, disbelief and turmoil warring in his expression. "But Kai..." he whispered, color draining from his face. "That can't be right."

Silence stretched between them like a chasm, each second heavier than the last, neither willing to bridge the gap the words had created.

Fenrir rumbled in Caleb's mind, his tone heavy with meaning. *"This will fracture before it mends."*

Darius remained seated as Caleb rose, the second mug of untouched coffee cooling in front of him. The Bloodstone alpha stared into the cup as though searching for answers within its dark depths.

Caleb stepped closer, resting a hand on his shoulder. Darius stilled at the touch, as though bracing against an unseen force, exhaling with visible restraint as Caleb's hand stayed steady. The faintest tremor ran through him before the tension in his posture eased, shoulders dropping a fraction. He looked up, remaining silent, expression soft, though still laden with grief.

"I'll pray to Selene for the safe passage of your fallen," Caleb said quietly. "May they find peace in her light."

Darius's hand came up to cover Caleb's, squeezing once before releasing. A single tear slipped down his cheek, catching in the stubble along his jaw.

"Thank you," he whispered, voice raw. "For everything. Crescent Fang's aid made all the difference."

Caleb nodded. "We're stronger together."

Darius's lips twitched in what might have been a smile. "I'll be in touch. We'll need to strategize soon—about the rogues, about everything."

"We will," Caleb promised. "Rest when you can. Your pack needs you strong."

Darius nodded, hands curling loosely around the cooled mug of coffee, gaze returning to the table. Caleb hesitated, then offered a small nod of understanding before stepping away.

From the corner of his eye, he saw Darius shift in his seat, sorrow curling the male in on himself. The sight followed him as he made his way out of the dining hall and across the scarred courtyard.

Each step across the blackened earth drove the same thought deeper into his mind: He'd risked everything bringing his wolves to Bloodstone's aid. If they'd lost anyone, if Asher's wound had been worse...what would have become of Crescent Fang?

Is this leadership? Gambling with lives I've sworn to protect.

Fenrir clawed his way to the surface, golden eyes flashing behind Caleb's vision. *"You acted as She demands. As I was supposed to guide you from the beginning."*

Caleb faltered mid-step, surprised by his wolf's admission. *"What do you mean?"*

"I've held you back," Fenrir rumbled, voice tinged with something like regret. *"Let you defer too much to the council."* A ripple of remorse passed through their bond. *"My fear of risking the bloodline has kept you from claiming your full power. That ends now."* Fenrir vowed. *"This is your purpose, Caleb. This is why you carry Her blessing."*

Fenrir's admission pressed against his ribs, reshaping something fundamental in his understanding of himself. He'd spent years deferring, compromising, playing it safe. No more.

As the hospital came into view, Caleb felt the shift solidify within him. Whatever challenges lay ahead—the rogues, the coordinated attacks, the fractured alliances—he would meet them as the alpha Selene had intended him to be.

The nurse had already finished removing Asher's stitches by the time Caleb reached the room. His beta sat propped against the pillows, looking more alert than he had that morning. Garreth stood nearby, arms crossed over his chest as he watched his son.

"You're cleared to go," Caleb said as he stepped inside, voice lightening as he took in the sight of Asher's improved state. "How are you feeling?"

"Like I've been mauled by rogues and stitched back together by a particularly irritable healer," Asher quipped, though his grin took the sting out of his words. "But I'll live."

Garreth snorted, the sound a mix of exasperation and affection. "You could show a little gratitude. The doctor and nurses saved your hide."

"And your sense of humor," Caleb added with a faint smile as he leaned against the wall. His gaze softened as it shifted to Garreth. "Thank you for being here."

Garreth waved a hand dismissively. "He's my son. Where else would I be?"

The nurse returned with discharge paperwork. Caleb watched as Garreth and Asher exchanged quiet words while signing the forms, the small, familial moment grounding him amid everything.

The short drive back to Crescent Fang was quiet, though worry still lingered in the air. Garreth drove, steady hands guiding the vehicle along winding forest roads. In the back, Caleb sat beside Asher, whose head rested against the window as he dozed. The soft sound of his breathing was a comforting rhythm, a reminder that they had made it through another battle, another storm.

Caleb understood he was right to act, but his stomach churned at the thought of throwing Crescent Fang into others' battles. A cold sweat gathered at the base of his spine, and his hands trembled as he imagined what they stood to lose if they drew the rogues' attention.

"Your instinct to protect is not a weakness," Fenrir said, as if reading his thoughts. *"It's the fire that burns in your blood. This is the path Selene marked for us long before your birth."*

Fenrir's words carried ancient echoes, raising goosebumps across Caleb's skin. The wolf contained depths he'd never fathomed—prophecies beyond understanding that somehow resonated as truth in his very marrow.

Caleb's gaze shifted back to Asher, watching his chest rise and fall. Garreth glanced at his son through the rearview mirror, lips pressed into a thin, worried line. Caleb was grateful for Garreth's presence, for the fatherly support he provided not just to Asher but to him.

As the forest gave way to Crescent Fang's familiar territory, Caleb straightened in his seat. The pack would be waiting—eager for news, for reassurance. He would need to address them, share what he'd learned, and prepare them for challenges ahead. He allowed himself a moment of stillness, bracing for what came next as the car rolled to a stop outside the packhouse.

He placed a hand on Asher's shoulder, squeezing as the beta stirred. "We're home," Caleb said softly.

Asher blinked, a faint smile tugging at his lips. "Good," he murmured, voice thick with exhaustion. "Let's keep it that way."

Caleb's lips quirked in a small, tired smile of his own as he helped Asher out of the car. The beta house loomed ahead, familiar warmth and childhood memories beckoning them inside.

They were greeted by a flurry of activity as they entered the cottage, Crescent Fang's strength evident in every familiar face. Asher's mother, Carys, stood at the end of the hallway, coordinating healers as they arranged Asher's old room. The former beta-female's composure cracked once she spotted them.

"Asher!" She rushed forward, hands fluttering over him as though confirming he was real. "Look at you—pale as winter and trying to walk around like nothing happened."

"I'm fine, Mom," Asher protested weakly. "Just need a few days of rest, that's all."

Carys's sharp gaze shifted to Caleb, one eyebrow arching in a way that made him feel like a pup caught sneaking treats. "I hope you're not planning on staying here too, Alpha."

Caleb blinked, heat creeping up his neck. "I—"

"Years of you two under my roof," she continued, gesturing between them. "I know very little actual resting gets done when you're together." She crossed her arms. "You can have him back when he's at full strength."

"Mom!" Asher groaned, though his cheeks flushed pink. "Pretty sure getting our dicks wet is the last thing on either of our minds right now."

Carys flicked his nose. "Language! Now hush and get your hide in that bed."

For the first time since he'd seen Leif fall during the attack, Caleb laughed—a real, genuine sound that broke through the fog hanging over him. He and Garreth helped Asher to his room, Carys right on their heels, fussing and muttering about "stubborn males" and "no sense of self-preservation."

Caleb settled Asher into bed, tucking the blankets around him with gentle hands. "I need to meet with the council, but I'll check on you after." He pressed a soft kiss to Asher's forehead.

As Asher's eyes drifted shut, Caleb turned to Carys, pressing a kiss to her cheek. "I'm so sorry I didn't get to him faster," he whispered.

She blinked through tears, shaking her head firmly. "No. This is not your fault." Her gaze moved to Asher, already asleep. "He's home. He's going to be okay."

Caleb nodded, giving her hand a gentle squeeze. He stole one last look at Asher's peaceful face before slipping from the room.

"Stand tall, Alpha. This is only the beginning," Fenrir murmured as he left the beta house.

Caleb breathed deep, shoulders squaring as he nodded to his wolf's words. This was only the beginning, but they would be ready to face whatever lay ahead—together.

CHAPTER FORTY-FIVE

KAI

K ai skidded to a stop in front of the Bloodstone hospital, tires screeching against pavement. He didn't bother turning off the engine or putting the car in park. His only thought was Ava. Wrenching the door open, he stumbled out and sprinted toward the entrance.

The hospital doors slid open with a mechanical hiss. Antiseptic assaulted his senses, failing to mask the scent of blood and smoke that followed him in. Every breath tasted bitter, making Orion bristle beneath his skin, a low growl rumbling in Kai's chest that he couldn't suppress. His canines lengthened, pricking his bottom lip as his wolf pushed forward, demanding action.

"Kai."

The voice cut through the haze, sharp and commanding. He turned to find Darius standing near the reception desk, broad shoulders hunched with exhaustion. His father's green eyes softened as they met Kai's, and he took a hesitant step forward, arms lifting as though to pull him into an embrace.

Kai recoiled, shaking his head violently. "Where is she?" he demanded, voice breaking. "I need to see her."

Darius frowned, lips pressing into a tight line. "Kai, listen—"

"Where is she?" Kai shouted, fists clenching at his sides. The raw edge of his voice drew the attention of the nurses and other wolves gathered in the waiting room. He barely noticed.

Darius exhaled heavily, raising a hand in a placating gesture. "She's in Room 12, but—"

Kai didn't let him finish. Shoving past his father, he bolted down the hallway, footsteps echoing off the sterile walls. The numbers on the doors blurred together until he reached the one he was looking for. Without hesitation, he shoved the door open and barreled inside.

The sight froze him. Ava lay dwarfed by machines, skin ashen except where purple-black bruises bloomed like violent flowers. The monitors' rhythmic beeping hammered against his eardrums, each tone marking another second she remained broken. Her chest was wrapped in bandages and the small gash on her temple was just beginning to heal, its edges red and angry.

Her swollen eyes turned toward him as the door slammed against the wall. A piercing wail escaped her lips, body shuddering with the force of her sobs. Tears streamed down her face, unchecked and unrelenting, as she clutched at the blanket covering her.

"Ava," Kai whispered, voice cracking. He crossed the room in two long strides, collapsing onto the edge of the bed. He didn't care about the cramped space or the tangle of wires. He gathered her into his arms, pulling her trembling body into his lap.

"I'm here," he murmured. "I'm so sorry... I should've been here. I should've protected you."

Ava clutched at his shirt, sobs muffled against his chest. Kai buried his face in her hair. Tears spilled freely down his cheeks, mingling with hers as he pressed frantic kisses to her crown.

"I should've been here," he whispered again. "I'm sorry. I shouldn't have left..."

The words tumbled from his lips, raw and unfiltered, as he rocked her gently. He didn't know how long they stayed like that—her body shaking against his, his hands stroking her back in soothing circles. The clock on the wall ticked, minutes bleeding into hours as his breathing synced with Ava's, tears drying on his cheeks while fresh ones replaced them.

Kai was vaguely aware of his father stopping by the room multiple times, his shadow hanging in the doorway before retreating. At one point, he thought he caught the faintest trace of Lena's scent in the hallway, but he couldn't be sure. The extended exposure to the antiseptic air had dulled his senses, leaving him foggy and adrift.

When Ava's sobs finally gave way to quiet snores, Kai gently eased her back onto the bed. He tucked the blanket around her, brushing a strand of hair from her damp cheek before pressing a soft kiss to her forehead.

"Rest," he whispered. "I'm back. I won't let anyone else hurt you."

He struggled to his feet, legs stiff and unsteady, and stepped into the hallway. The quiet of the hospital was jarring after the chaos of his arrival. The sinking sun painted the sky in bleeding oranges and reds as he pushed through the exit. His car wasn't where he'd left it. He assumed his father had moved it back to the packhouse—only to remember that the primary packhouse was gone.

Pressure built beneath his sternum as he navigated the scorched pack courtyard, the devastation spread before him like a horrific canvas.

The ground was torn and bloodstained, scarred with boot prints and claw. Burned buildings loomed like blackened skeletons, timber creaking in the evening breeze. With each inhale, ash and the reek of death coated his throat—char, copper, fear—a bitter cocktail that no amount of swallowing could clear.

Kai's gaze fell on his Range Rover parked outside one of the dormitories. He moved toward it mechanically, retrieving his bag from the back seat. He knew he needed to speak to his father, to get his marching orders for the work ahead, but he also desperately needed a shower. The tang of the hospital's antiseptic clashed with Ava's floral scent and the remnants of Lena and their lovemaking. His stomach churned at the competing scents, each one an accusation.

The dormitory lobby was quiet when Kai entered. He grabbed a key from the desk clerk and climbed to the third floor, the creak of his boots on the stairs the only sound in the stillness.

Inside the room, he left a trail of clothes behind him as he made his way to the bathroom. He turned the shower to its hottest setting and stepped into the steaming stall without hesitation.

The water seared his skin crimson, steam filled his lungs, and pain bloomed across his shoulders and down his back. Welcome punishment. Each droplet hissed against his flesh, the sound mingling with the echo of water hitting tile, drowning out everything but his heartbeat hammering in his ears. Memories of the past day assaulted him in disjointed fragments—

Waking up in Lena's bed after making love to her deep into the night. How seeing her face when he opened his eyes made him desperate to spend the morning buried inside her...

The concern etched on her face as she told him he'd been summoned to her father's study...

Raelen's words and sorrowful expression as he delivered the devastating news...

Cian's hand pressed to his shoulder, his new friend offering him a small comfort...

Lena's sadness for him, her attempts to soothe his pain. How her tentativeness morphed into fear as he escalated...

Ava's bruised and broken body...

The shattered packhouse...

The bloodstained courtyard...

The guilt, the rage, the helplessness—all of it slammed into him like breaking tides during a hurricane battering his body as sobs ripped from his chest.

He lost track of time as the water burned his body, scrubbing away his choices like grime coating his skin. When he finally stepped out, his eyes were red and swollen and his chest heaved with the remnants of his grief. The fresh clothes felt stiff against his damp skin, the fabric catching on patches where he'd scrubbed too hard. He stood before the mirror, avoiding his own reflection, and tried to summon the strength to face what came next.

Grieving whispers, soft sobs, and the scrape of chairs against floor tiles greeted Kai as he entered the dining hall. The air hung thick with salt—tears shed and unshed—mingling with the earthy scent of wolves in mourning, their normally bright notes dulled by grief. Each breath tasted of collective sorrow, a bitter reminder that his private pain was just one drop in Bloodstone's ocean of suffering.

Kai spotted his father seated with Maxim and Magnus at a table near the back. He started toward them but stopped short when his gaze caught on her.

Lena.

She moved through the hall, steaming mugs balanced in steady hands, golden-brown eyes cataloging needs before they were voiced, a focal point amid the room's subdued turmoil. She approached the table where Darius sat, setting the mugs down with care. Her touch lingered on Magnus's shoulder, then Maxim's, offering a gentle squeeze of reassurance.

Darius reached for her hand, capturing it between his own. His typically stern expression softened, though the depth of his grief was imprinted on his face.

"Thank you," he said, voice so quiet that Kai barely caught the words.

Lena responded with a faint nod, leaning down to press a light kiss to Darius's temple. The older alpha closed his eyes at the gesture, shoulders sagging as though a burden had been lifted.

Kai's stomach twisted, a strange mix of emotions bubbling to the surface—jealousy, longing, guilt. He forced his gaze away from Lena, focusing instead on his father. The affection in Darius's expression when he looked at her was foreign, so at odds with the hardened alpha Kai had faced off with over the years.

He watched as Lena moved on, attention turning to a crying pup nearby. She crouched to meet the little wolf's gaze, voice soft and soothing as she wiped his tears. The pup fell into her arms, small frame trembling as she hugged him. Her presence was a quiet comfort amid the grief that filled the room.

"She's everything we need. Everything we could be." Orion's voice vibrated through Kai's bones, resonating with a truth he couldn't deny.

His nails bit into his palm until tiny crescents of blood formed beneath the pressure. His lungs compressed, making each breath shallow as he watched Lena circle the room like sunlight he couldn't bear to face. A physical ache spread beneath his ribs, cutting off the sensation as though his body refused him even that small comfort. He didn't deserve her light, not when he'd brought so much darkness to his pack. He focused on the table where his father sat and continued toward them, movements stiff and guarded.

Magnus was the first to rise when Kai reached the table, pulling him into a crushing embrace. The larger wolf's shoulders trembled, head dropping onto Kai's shoulder.

"He should be here." Magnus's voice cracked. "It's not fair. He was supposed to be here."

Kai stiffened, throat tightening at the suffering radiating from his future beta. Magnus smelled of smoke and sweat, of dried blood that wasn't his own. He'd been clearing bodies, Kai realized with a jolt. The future beta's hands bore fresh cuts and burns, badges of honor from the fight and recovery efforts while Kai had been absent.

Orion responded instinctively, a low rumbling comfort vibrating between them—pack wolves consoling each other. The sound emerged from deep in Kai's chest, too low for human ears to fully register but felt by Magnus's wolf, Ranulf.

He slipped into memory—three young pups standing in the moonlight by the eastern ridge, their small hands stacked atop one another. *"Blood and bone, fang and claw,"* they'd whispered, the ancient pack vow transformed into their private oath. *"We three will guard Bloodstone together."*

Elias had been the one to insist on it, after they'd coaxed a sobbing Ava—rescued from the rogue attack at Raven's Crest—to sleep her first night in Bloodstone.

"I know," Kai murmured, each syllable scraping his throat raw. "Elias was..." But he couldn't finish. What right did he have to speak of Elias when he hadn't been there to fight alongside him? When it was Magnus who had stood by their friend's side while Kai had been safe in another territory?

When they pulled apart, Magnus's shoulders slumped, and he swiped at his eyes before taking his seat. A flash of the old Magnus surfaced as he squared his shoulders, a silent testament to how they would all need to be stronger now. Kai turned to Darius, who rose and pulled his son into a brief but firm embrace.

"I'm glad you're home, son," Darius murmured. "I've missed you."

Kai couldn't bring himself to respond, only offering a tight nod before sitting down. He sank into his seat, shoulders curved inward, spine bowing. His voice was barely above a whisper as he finally asked, "What...happened?"

Darius recounted the events of the attack, tone laced with sorrow. The coordinated rogue assault. The destruction. The casualties. The loss of Elias, who had died protecting Ava. Alpha Caleb's arrival with the Crescent Fang warriors helping to turn the tide in Bloodstone's favor. Kai listened in silence, fists clenching beneath the table.

Each word felt like a knife slicing deeper into his chest. Elias—his future gamma and childhood friend. *Gone.* The guilt was suffocating, gnawing at his insides. He'd been away, indulging in his own happiness—indulging in his mate's body—while his pack bled and burned.

Cranberries and rosemary cut through the dining hall's heaviness—bright, sharp, alive—reaching Kai before he saw her. Orion alerted instantly, nostrils flaring to capture more of their mate's scent.

Lena returned to the table, the steady rhythm of her heartbeat as familiar to him as his own. She sat beside him, body angled toward him, but he couldn't bring himself to look at her.

"Do you need anything, Kai?" she asked softly.

He shook his head, the movement slow and almost imperceptible. "No," he muttered.

She nodded once, voice steady but faint. "Okay..."

Her lips parted as though she wanted to say more. Instead, she leaned in, mouth brushing against his cheek, her exhale unsteady against his skin. The touch was fleeting, but it was enough to make Kai stiffen, body going rigid against her.

She pulled back gracefully, expression blank, though her scent spiked with something sharp—hurt, perhaps, or fear. Kai noticed the slight tension in her shoulders as she stood, the way her fingers curled into her palm before relaxing. She didn't look back as she moved away, though she paused at the door, head tilting as if fighting the urge to turn around before her attention was consumed by comforting the other wolves scattered throughout the hall.

Orion's grief erupted in a mournful howl that pulsed through Kai's marrow, their shared consciousness bleeding sorrow until Kai couldn't separate his anguish from his wolf's. *"She is strength. We are fools to push her away."*

Kai's canines lengthened in response, a physical manifestation of his wolf's displeasure. His stomach churned as shame and dread warred within him. He forced his focus back to the table, avoiding his father's gaze as he studied him closely.

Maxim broke the silence, deep voice steady but somber. "We need to finalize the funeral rites for the fallen."

The air around the table grew heavier as the conversation shifted to the grim task ahead. They discussed the ritual—burning the bodies on the pack's sacred pyre and spreading their ashes on the ritual grounds.

"The pyre flames will carry them to Selene," Maxim said. "It's the way we honor the fallen—returning them to Her light, where their spirits can find peace."

Kai's gaze dropped to the table, images of the flames flickering in his mind. He could almost hear the crackle of the fire, feel the heat on his skin, smell the faint tang of smoke mingled with the earthy scent of ash. A creeping pain bloomed behind his sternum as the solemn duty of the ritual settled heavily on his shoulders.

He sat silently for most of the discussion, despair simmering beneath the surface. He nodded when necessary, throat too tight to form words.

Darius's voice cut through his spiraling thoughts. "Magnus, you'll oversee the preparation of the ritual grounds. Maxim and I will handle the pyre. Kai—"

"I'll do whatever needs to be done," Kai interrupted, words hollow and mechanical. "Just tell me where you need me."

Darius hesitated, gaze softening as he studied his son. "For now, focus on yourself. Rest tonight. We'll regroup in the morning."

Kai didn't argue. He lacked the energy to push back, and he knew his father was right.

The meeting ended. Magnus and Maxim excused themselves, shoulders heavy with the yoke of their assigned tasks. Kai began to rise, but Darius's voice stopped him.

"Kai." The plea was evident in his father's tone.

Kai shook his head, cutting him off. "I can't right now, Dad. I don't have anything else left in me today. Can we do this tomorrow?"

Darius hesitated, a muscle ticked in his jaw before he nodded. "Tomorrow, then," he mumbled. "But Kai...remember, you're not alone in this." His gaze darted across the room. Kai didn't need to follow his father's eyes to know they rested on his mate.

A flicker of something unnamable urged him to open up, to take hold of this fading lifeline. His jaw worked—searching for the words—but the day's trauma clouded his thoughts. Instead, he offered his father a tight, almost mechanical nod and turned away.

The walk back to the dormitory was a blur. Exhaustion weighed down his limbs by the time he reached his room, each step a monumental effort. He collapsed onto the bed fully clothed, the mattress creaking under his weight, but sleep eluded him despite his bone-deep weariness.

His mind became a maelstrom of conflicting thoughts and memories. Joy twisting into horror—Orion and Elara's playful chase morphing into pups fleeing rogues, Orion's triumphant howl as he mounted Elara warping to the anguish cries of wolves torn apart by merciless attackers. Lena's laughter became screams; the quiver of her pleasure corrupted by Ava's sobs. His lungs burned as guilt dragged him under, no surface in sight.

His pack had bled while he'd found joy in Moonshadow. The faces of the fallen flashed before him, their silent accusations clogging in his throat while memories of Lena's touch lingered on his skin—comfort unearned, sanctuary unjustified while Bloodstone lay in ruins.

He vowed to rebuild Bloodstone with his father. To help the pack heal and move forward. He would be the rock they needed, the alpha-heir they deserved. And when the time was right, he'd forge a new path. One that balanced his duty to Bloodstone with his desire and growing bond with Lena. She was his future, his forever—but right now, his pack needed him more than she did.

The distance between us will be temporary, he told himself. *A necessary sacrifice for now*.

"Don't run," Orion growled within him. *"We need her."*

Kai pushed the thought aside, but his wolf's agitation manifested in a sudden itch beneath his skin, muscles twitching with restless energy. Through his window, moonlight painted silver edges around the distant hospital helipad lights. Before conscious thought could form, he was already moving, keys in hand, drawn back to the one place he might find momentary peace.

Fluorescent lights buzzed overhead, casting long shadows across the empty hospital corridors. Orion's heightened hearing picked up the night nurses' whispered conversations as Kai slipped past their station. He pushed open Ava's door without hesitation, the now familiar antiseptic scent welcoming him once more.

Ava was still asleep, chest rising and falling in a steady rhythm. The machines monitoring her vitals beeped softly, the sound a faint backdrop to the hospital's stillness. Kai removed his shoes and sweatshirt, movements slow and careful as he climbed into the narrow bed beside her.

He pulled her onto his chest, arms wrapping around her slender frame. She murmured something unintelligible in her sleep, head nuzzling against his shoulder. As he focused on the velvety hum of her soft snores, Kai made a silent vow to be there for Ava, to support her through the dark days ahead.

He knew it wouldn't be easy. The road to healing would be long and arduous, but he would coax her into this new reality where their relationship had shifted. He would still be her rock, her confidant, but only her friend. The familiarity of their past providing a comforting foundation as they navigated the uncertain future.

With a deep breath, Kai let his eyes drift closed, and for the first time that day, a sliver of comfort crept into his chest, though it was fleeting and hollow.

Cranberries and rosemary—faint but unmistakable—pulled Kai from the depths of dreamless sleep. Orion responded before consciousness fully returned, pupils dilating behind closed lids, heart rate quickening, skin warming. The subtle rustle of movement drew his attention. His eyes blinked open to the morning light streaming through the window and drifted toward the source of the sound.

Lena.

She stood by the nightstand, fingers tracing the petals of flowers as she carefully set down a vase beside Ava's bed. There was a quiet sadness about her, a sense of empathy that only deepened his turmoil. His hands fisted the sheets as conflicting instincts warred beneath his skin—reach for her, push her away.

The vibrant flowers stood defiant against the backdrop of destruction visible through the window. Beauty mocking devastation—yet offering a reminder of what remained worth fighting for. Kai watched as Lena's fingers lingered on the edge of the vase as though ensuring it was perfectly placed.

She straightened and turned to leave, footsteps faltering when she caught him watching her. She startled, irises darkening like honey in shadow, and a soft gasp escaped her lips.

"Goddess, Kai..." The words came out in a breath. "I didn't realize you were awake."

He said nothing, gaze darting from the flowers back to her face, taking in the softness of her expression. Something flickered there—empathy? Concern, perhaps—in the way her brows knitted. He felt like he was drowning in the depths of his own silence, unspoken words and unresolved emotions pulling him under.

Lena broke the silence first, voice tentative but steady. "I... I was ordering the floral arrangements for the funerals," she explained, gesturing toward the vase. "I saw these and thought Ava might like them. Something beautiful to wake up to instead of..." She trailed off, eyes darting to the window and the fractured, scorched packlands beyond.

Muscles bunched along Kai's jawline, words lodging in his throat as renewed guilt flooded him. He was still failing everyone—Lena, Ava, himself. He glanced toward the window, the devastation outside as raw and jarring as the night before.

His attention drifted back to the flowers, their delicate petals swaying in the draft from the vent. They truly were breathtaking, and Ava would love them. Yet, they felt out of place—like a mockery of everything his pack had endured.

Lena's eyes traced his features, seeming to search for a glimmer of connection, a hint of the intimacy they once shared, but his silence stretched, cold and unyielding—a brittle shield protecting him from the vulnerability he couldn't afford to show.

Not now, when everything felt so fragile and uncertain.

Her gaze shifted lower, stilling as she took in the full scene—his arms wrapped around Ava's bandaged form as she slept soundly on his chest. Lena's composed façade cracked for a moment, revealing a glimpse of hurt and concern. The subtle shift in her posture made him want to disappear into the bed.

It's not what it looks like, he willed himself to say, but the words died in his throat.

She recovered, composure slipping back into place as she moved toward the door. "Do you need anything, Kai?" she asked softly, voice laced with that same quiet longing marked so many of their first interactions. She stared at him intently, waiting for acknowledgement, as if pleading for a hint that he still needed her.

He blinked, the recognition of his name on her lips cutting through the haze in his mind.

"Kai," not *"mate."*

The absence of that word carved something vital out of him.

When did she stop claiming me?

He shook his head. "No."

"Kai..." she breathed. "You don't have to do this alone."

She doesn't understand. How could she?

His expression remained stone, silence his only answer.

She nodded once, chin lifting—that subtle gesture of pride he'd come to recognize when she was holding herself together.

"Alright," she murmured, voice steady despite the slight catch in her breath.

She held his gaze as though waiting for something. *An apology, an explanation perhaps?* The tip of her tongue darted out to wet her lips, a nervous habit she only displayed when truly uncertain. A faint sheen of moisture lingered on her lashes as she gripped the doorknob tighter. If she found anything in his expression, she didn't show it.

Will I be able to fix this? Or has this tragedy that shattered our bliss damaged us beyond repair?

Without another word, Lena turned and left the room. The click of the door closing echoed in his ears, amplified by the sudden absence of her heartbeat, leaving only the mechanical beep of monitors and the rasp of his own shallow breaths.

Kai's gaze returned to the flowers, their delicate petals taunting him. He looked down at Ava's sleeping form curled against him, her face peaceful despite the bandages and bruises marring her delicate features. His fingers tightened around the edge of the blanket covering her, and he shifted, pulling her closer as though holding her tighter, making her better, might make everything else fade away.

But the ghost of Lena's presence lingered in the room, a haunting reminder of what he risked losing if he couldn't piece his fractured world back together. *I don't deserve her.* His teeth ground together as the emotions he'd fought to suppress spilled over. Tears fell as guilt twisted in his chest, sharp and suffocating—for the pain in Lena's eyes, for the quiet tension in her voice, for the truths he was too cowardly to speak.

Kai closed his eyes, willing himself back to sleep, but the emptiness in his chest only grew.

CHAPTER FORTY-SIX

CALEB

The energy in the Crescent Fang council chamber felt heavier than usual. Competing pheromones hung thick in the air—traces of aggression, subtle dominance markers, anxiety laced with determination. Caleb's nostrils flared, cataloging their scents from his position at the head of the table. Despite his composed face and straight posture, apprehension gnawed at him like physical teeth.

To his left sat Varek, arms crossed, his usual easy demeanor replaced by quiet observation. Erik, the eldest of Crescent Fang's council, sat near the center, his weathered face lined with displeasure. Across from Erik, Garreth sat with his hands folded, his expression unreadable. At the far end, two of the warriors who had joined Caleb in Bloodstone—Adolphus and Skol—remained silent but alert.

Caleb's eye twitched as the muscles in his jaw worked around the agitation brewing inside him. The empty chair beside him grew larger with each passing moment, Asher's absence creating a void behind his ribs. Fenrir paced restlessly, the wolf's concern for their injured beta bleeding into Caleb's own anxiety. He'd come to this meeting knowing the council wouldn't pull their punches.

"You had no right to act on your own!" Erik's voice detonated the silence as he faced Caleb, spine straight, chin lifted. "No plan. No consultation. You took warriors into unknown territory, into a fight that wasn't ours!"

"I made the call as your alpha." Caleb's voice remained level despite the challenge in the elder's posture. Without breaking eye contact, he allowed his aura to expand, filling the chamber—a quiet reminder of his position. He kept his gaze fixed on Erik until the elder averted his eyes. "I acted on instinct because there wasn't time to convene a meeting. Lives were at stake."

"Lives were also at stake here," Erik shot back, expression hardening. "What if you hadn't come back? What if Asher hadn't survived? Crescent Fang is small, Caleb. Every loss cuts deeper for us than for packs like Bloodstone."

Fenrir surged forward at the mention of Asher. Caleb's canines sharpened as a subtle flash of gold brightened his eyes.

Elder Norvik leaned forward. "You're young, Caleb. That fire in your chest is admirable, but dangerous." Each word selected deliberately, a reminder of the past costs of Caleb's impulsivity. "You're not just a wolf anymore—you're our alpha. Your decisions affect us all."

Something cold settled in Caleb's gut as he felt the leash tighten, pulling him back from the edge of action as it had done for over a decade.

Fenrir's voice hummed in the back of his mind, steady and encouraging. *"Lead, Caleb. Show them the alpha you are."*

Caleb's hands rested on the table, fingers splaying wide as he leaned forward. "I hear your concerns." He spoke through clenched teeth. "But let me be clear—I am not the same wolf who stood before you at sixteen, shaking in fear after we were attacked again." He straightened, aura sharpening, touching every wolf in the room. "*I* am the Alpha of Crescent Fang. Selene's favored. *I* carry the reincarnation of the first wolf." He paused, eyes flaring gold, Fenrir fully present. "I respect your wisdom, but the final say will always be *mine*!"

The room erupted.

Erik's hand slammed against the table as he leaned forward. "Respect isn't enough when your choices endanger our pack!"

Caleb's voice rose. "Endanger? If anything, what happened at Bloodstone saved lives!"

The shouting grew louder, voices overlapping as council members shifted in their seats—some leaning forward aggressively, others subtly angling their bodies toward Caleb in unconscious alignment with their alpha. A low-frequency growl, too deep for human ears but felt by every wolf in the room, rumbled from Caleb's chest.

Frustration boiled over.

Claws extended.

Wood splintered beneath his palms.

He was seconds from losing control when Adolphus stood abruptly.

"*Enough*!" Adolphus thundered, silencing the room, fist slamming onto the table. His chair toppled back as he shoved to his feet. The elite warrior's chest heaved, voice rising with unrestrained frustration. "The arguing is pointless!" Adolphus jabbed a finger toward the table. "We are not talking about what actually matters—what happened on the Bloodstone lands yesterday!"

Adolphus's gaze swept the room, daring anyone to interrupt. "They are our *neighbors*! That could have easily been our lands the rogues targeted. Yes, we're battered, and Asher was injured, but we came back *alive*. And we saved the lives of wolves who are part of our community, aligned or not!"

The room fell silent. Adolphus's words hung between them, undeniable. Norvik, who had been leaning forward in challenge only moments before, nodded his grizzled head.

Caleb's shoulders lowered incrementally, claws retracting from the gouges they'd carved in the wooden table. His breath came easier as the council's attention pivoted to the greater threat.

"What happened out there?" Erik asked finally, tone less accusatory.

Caleb gestured for Adolphus and Skol to take over, and they walked the group through the attack—the organized formations, the silver weapons, the calculated retreat that signaled outside coordination.

Garreth frowned. "That doesn't sound like rogues at all."

"They had the scent," Caleb confirmed. "That sour tang you can't mistake for anything else. But their behavior? It's unprecedented."

The council exchanged uneasy glances. Erik rubbed his temples. "Then this threat extends beyond Bloodstone. Their escalation demands our preparation."

The conversation shifted into strategy. Garreth suggested focusing on Crescent Fang's connections, trying to build more interest to rally the Collective. Erik emphasized the need for more information, urging Caleb to establish communication lines with other pack leaders.

"We need to notify as many packs as possible," Erik said, hands steepled as he spoke. "But we can't stretch ourselves too thin."

"I agree," Caleb replied. "We'll start with our closest connection, Moonshadow. Bloodstone, Redridge—they've already been hit. They may know how best to spread the word. We can take our lead from them."

As the discussion continued, Caleb shared details about Bloodstone's casualties—over twenty dead, with more injured. "The silver poisoning means the death toll may rise in the coming days," he said grimly. "I expect the funeral rites will be held within the week. I intend to go."

Erik's brow arched. "And what do you expect from this? A formal alliance?"

Caleb straightened in his chair, hands resting on the table as he met Erik's gaze. He hesitated momentarily, lips pressing into a thin line as he gathered his thoughts. When he spoke, his voice carried a quiet intensity that commanded the room.

"I saw wolves fall, Erik. Wolves whose lives we couldn't save." His hands fisted against the wood, knuckles paling as battle memories replayed in his mind. The chaos, blood, and scent of death lingered like a shadow. "We were fortunate. We came back with our lives intact, but they weren't so lucky. Attending their funeral rites isn't about alliances or politics."

Caleb's hazel eyes swept across the table, meeting the elders' wary stares. "It's about honoring the souls that fought, the lives that Selene has welcomed back into her embrace." He paused, lungs burning as he forced each breath to remain controlled. "It's what you do for neighbors, for the wolves who share our community. It's what's right."

As the meeting adjourned, Erik lingered, studying Caleb for a long moment, something shifting in his weathered features. The hard lines around the elder's mouth smoothed away, eyes no longer narrowed in judgment as he approached.

"I owe you an apology," he began, voice carrying a note of humility. "You're not that scared pup anymore. You've grown into a strong, capable alpha. What happened then wasn't your fault, and Asher's injury isn't either."

Caleb swallowed hard, Erik's apology and absolution landing harder than he'd expected. For twelve years, he'd carried guilt, adhered to the council's careful guidance, their protective boundaries, the unspoken question of whether he was truly ready to lead without catastrophe following in his wake. He'd told himself their caution was just politics, just tradition, but Erik's words peeled away that pretense, revealing a truth he hadn't dared hope to ever hear.

Erik exhaled, shoulders sagging. "I've watched you grow, Caleb. From a young wolf who needed guidance to an alpha who leads with conviction. I still see that pup who came to us after losing everything, but it's time for us to let go." He paused, studying Caleb's face intently. "You've learned all we can teach you. Now it's time for us to trust you."

Erik's words settled over Caleb like a benediction, a quiet moment of passing the torch. Before he could speak, the elder continued.

"Maybe I was wrong." Erik chuckled, the tension breaking. "Perhaps you really are the light."

Caleb allowed himself a small smile as Erik's faith bolstered him. His shoulders set into a new certainty, spine straightened by true acceptance. Fenrir uncoiled within him, stretching through his limbs with languid satisfaction.

"You are ready, Caleb." The wolf's approval manifested as a pleasant shiver down his spine, his skin warming with shared pride. *"You have always been."*

CHAPTER FORTY-SEVEN

LENA

T he wind at the Bloodstone ritual grounds carried the faint scent of ash, mingling with the earthiness of red cedar trees. Twelve torches lined the perimeter like solemn sentinels, marking the passage of time, of life, of loss. Their light flickered against the shadows of the forest, catching on the jagged edges of broken branches and patches of blackened grass. The sacred circle, once a sanctuary, now bore the scars of the rogue attack like fresh wounds.

Twenty-seven lives reduced to ash. Twenty-seven wolves who'd fought for their pack and paid the ultimate price.

Lena stood at the edge of the clearing, arms crossed over her chest. Her shoulders curved inward, lungs struggling against an invisible pressure as the night ahead weighed heavy on her chest. Her gaze lingered on the ceremonial altar at the center, its bloodstone surface gleaming under the full moon. *How beautiful this place must have been before the attack*, she thought, wishing she could have seen it in its prime, known these wolves, before loss and grief took hold.

A faint hum vibrated in the back of her mind, Elara's presence like a shadow at dusk—visible but fading. Her wolf's usual warmth had cooled, retreating into the recesses of Lena's consciousness, leaving a hollow space where their connection should be strongest. When Lena reached along their bond, she felt only echoes returning. It was as though Elara questioned her strength to weather the storms ahead. It mirrored how

Lena felt about everything in Bloodstone—Kai, the grieving wolves, the irreparable losses.

She glanced around the circle, eyes on the urns that lined the altar. For the past week, she'd poured herself into preparation—organizing meals for the injured, planning the rites with Darius, spending hours with Elias's family. Anything to keep herself busy, to keep her mind from straying to Kai's silence.

Well, that wasn't entirely true.

Lena knew she shared responsibility for the growing rift. Kai tried to speak with her, multiple times, but the image of him cradling Ava burned in her mind each time she saw him. She'd invented reasons to disappear, avoiding the heartbreak she was certain awaited. The frozen expanse between them gaped like a chasm, a wound that refused to heal. It stung more than she could admit.

Lena sighed, shoulders slumping as the stress of the week bore down on her. She sought Elara's strength, that familiar surge of resilience that had always steadied her, but her wolf remained distant, offering only the faintest flicker of acknowledgement.

Tomorrow, she would return to Moonshadow. The thought brought a mix of relief and sadness, a bittersweet ache she couldn't quite name. Bloodstone wasn't her home, but she had grown to care for the wolves here—for their resilience, their quiet strength. She was fated to be their luna, to lead them alongside Kai and be a guiding presence in their darkest moments. Yet, she didn't know if she could come back. Not when every glance at Kai reminded her of the ground they'd lost, of what they might never have again.

The faint sound of footsteps in the grass pulled Lena from her thoughts. A familiar scent weaved through the night air—cedar, sun-warmed leather, and home. Lena's heart lifted as she turned to see her father striding toward her, with Cian, Ryker, and Jace trailing close behind.

Raelen reached her first, arms wrapping around her with the kind of strength that had anchored her through every storm as a pup. Lena hadn't known how badly she needed this—the comfort of family to remind her of who she was beneath the ache and uncertainty.

"You've been strong, Lena." Raelen's voice rumbled against her hair as his hand cradled the back of her head. "We're here now."

She blinked rapidly, swallowing hard against the lump rising in her throat. She hadn't expected her father's words to hit so deeply, to soothe a loneliness she hadn't let herself name.

Cian pulled her into a tight hug next. Concern creased his features as he leaned back just enough to search her face. "How are you holding up?"

"I'm okay," Lena answered, though the words felt thin. The way Cian's hand lingered on her shoulder told her he didn't believe her entirely—and he didn't need to. Her twin's steady presence was enough.

Ryker wasted no time sweeping her up in a bear hug that lifted her off the ground, making her breath catch in a startled laugh. "Don't scare us like that again, Thing 1." Gruff affection roughened his voice. "You had us thinking we'd need to storm Bloodstone and drag you out ourselves. You're not married. You're not theirs, or his, yet."

Lena managed a small, grateful smile, ignoring Ryker's insinuation about her bond with Kai. "I'll try not to."

There was something achingly tender in Jace's expression as he wrapped an arm around her shoulder. "We've missed you," he said simply pressing a kiss to her temple.

"I've missed you all too," Lena replied as she looked between them.

Cian stepped back in, expression bright, pride unmistakable. "Darius said you've been helping plan the rite. That's no small thing, Lena. You should be proud."

Lena looked toward the altar. "It's not about me. It's about them—this pack, this place."

Jace rested an assured hand on her back. "They're lucky to have you. So are we."

For the first time in a week, Lena allowed herself to lean into the moment, to feel the solid presence of her family. The tightness around her ribcage loosened just enough to allow deeper breaths, her pulse steadying to a manageable rhythm despite the ache of every beat. For now, that would have to be enough.

The ritual grounds filled as the Bloodstone wolves and guests arrived, their movements solemn and subdued under the glow of the torches. Families clung together, their grief evident in every bowed head, in every whispered word of comfort. The air pulsed with shared suffering, a collective mourning that wrapped around the clearing like a shroud.

Tears threatened as Lena watched the gathered wolves, noting how they moved to support one another—hands resting on shoulders, arms interlocked in gestures of solidarity. Despite everything they'd endured, the pack's strength remained unbroken in its unity.

A figure stood slightly apart among the crowd, his tall frame casting a long shadow in the flickering torchlight. Alpha Caleb. He held himself with quiet dignity, hazel eyes scanning the ritual grounds as though committing every detail to memory. He didn't draw attention to himself, nor did he seem to expect recognition for being there. Yet his respect was apparent in the way he nodded solemnly to those who caught his eye, a silent acknowledgment of their loss.

Lena found herself observing him longer than she intended. Caleb's head dipped to an elderly she-wolf who passed him, her shoulders shaking with sobs. He murmured something low, his voice lost in the swell of the crowd, but whatever he said eased her pain. She reached for his hand, squeezing it before moving on.

Gratitude swelled in Lena's throat at the sight. Alpha Caleb stood as one of them tonight—a living embodiment of the invisible bonds between packs, of the implicit responsibility that all leaders shared to honor and protect all wolves.

A murmur of voices beside her drew Lena's attention back to her family. Her father stood in quiet conversation with Cian as they watched the pack gather. The air in the clearing seemed to grow denser, charged with the significance of what was to come.

Lena straightened her shoulders, hands brushing over the edges of her jacket. As the gravity of the evening descended upon her, she readied herself for the ceremony that would honor the fallen and bring a flicker of peace to a grieving pack.

A hush settled over the gathered wolves as Alpha Darius stepped into the circle, leading the procession of the grieving families. The flickering torchlight painted his broad shoulders in shadow and flame, a solemn figure carrying the burden of the fallen and the pack's hopes for healing.

The air thickened with collective grief making each breath labored. The soft crunch of feet on the sacred ground was the only sound breaking the stillness. Her gaze followed the procession, pausing on each family, cataloging their grief—their bowed heads and trembling hands as they walked toward the altar where the urns, lined carefully on the bloodstone surface, gleamed in the torchlight.

Heal their hearts, Lena prayed silently, fingers tightening into fists at her sides. *Grant them strength.*

Guilt crept into Lena's chest as she watched the mourners. She had poured herself into their pain this past week, but couldn't deny the sharp edge of her own.

I'm not sure what hurts most—Kai's distance, or the sheer weight of standing here among lives forever altered?

The two seemed inseparable now—her fracturing mating bond and the pack's grief twining together until she couldn't distinguish where one ended and the other began.

She focused on Elias's family approaching the altar. Lyric walked between her parents, hands clasped as though holding herself together. Talon's broad frame shadowed her on one side, while Maris, her auburn hair showing the first kisses of silver, rested a gentle hand on Lyric's arm.

Over the past week, Lena had grown close to the Gamma family, their quiet strength offering solace she hadn't anticipated. A memory of Lyric's trembling voice surfaced.

"It's like he's still here." The young she-wolf's whisper quivered with wonder. "Guiding me toward something...like he knows there's still something I need to find." Lena had squeezed her hand, her own voice steady despite the emotions building in her chest. "He'll always be with you, Lyric. In your heart, in your memories. In everything you do."

She blinked back the memory, exhaling through the pressure building in her throat as she watched Lyric and her parents step into place near the altar. Elias's spirit endured here, in this sacred place, in the hearts of his family, and in the whispers of the pack. Lena closed her eyes as she sent another silent prayer to Selene: *may they find peace in his memory.*

As Lena opened her eyes, her gaze stilled on the last two figures entering the circle.

Kai.

And Ava.

The sight of them together sent her heart plummeting to the bottom of her stomach. Kai's hand was braced low on Ava's back as she leaned heavily into his arms, her tentative steps faltering. The sight burned into Lena's mind, vivid and inescapable, as though the torches lining the circle cast an unrelenting spotlight on them.

Kai's expression was a mask of calm as he supported Ava—intimately, protectively. Their contact felt personal, as though their connection had deepened in Lena's absence.

Elara shifted in the back of her mind—the first strong movement from her wolf in days. A gentle pressure nudged against Lena's thoughts, urging her to look closer.

"See his burden, not just his touch."

Lena pushed her wolf's insight away. The image of Kai in that hospital bed flashed before her—Ava's bare form, save for her bandaged chest, draped over him, his arms wrapped protectively around her. She'd seen enough.

Did Kai use the tenderness we shared in Moonshadow to heal Ava with his touch?

The ruminations clawed at her heart. What she'd once believed sacred between them now twisted into something unrecognizable—their intimacy borrowed and given to another.

Lena's gaze dropped to the ground, nails biting into her palms as she willed herself to focus elsewhere, but she couldn't help watching Kai's every step, even as it tore her apart. She followed them as they crossed the circle, unable to look away despite the pain tearing through her chest. Kai ushered Ava toward a seat near Beta Maxim and Magnus, movements slow and careful, ensuring she was comfortable. Then, as though to seal whatever connection persisted between them, he bent and pressed a soft kiss to the crown of her head.

Heat rushed up Lena's neck, jaw locking as her canines sharpened. The rage formed and crumbled in the same breath, throat closing until her lungs burned, pressure building behind her eyes even as she forced the tears back. She fought to keep her expression neutral, to breathe through the storm raging inside her.

Kai straightened and moved toward his father. He looked unburdened—the proverbial Prince of the Pacific Northwest once more—as if the events of the week hadn't touched him at all. The torchlight caught on his hair and shoulders, casting him in a warm glow that felt at odds with the cold filter of his alpha-heir façade. She took a deep breath, steadying herself, even as her heart screamed at the injustice of it.

Don't let your emotions consume you, Lena reminded herself. She might have come here for Kai, but she'd stayed for the wolves of Bloodstone—to honor the lives lost and help guide the pack toward healing. Lena returned her focus to the altar, where the urns glinted softly beneath the moon's gaze, their presence reminding her of the task at hand.

Whatever turmoil swirled within her would have to wait. Tonight was not about her pain, nor was it about Kai's choices. It was about the twenty-seven wolves who had given everything for this pack, whose sacrifice had paved the way for Bloodstone's survival. And it was about the wolf she needed to become—the luna she was destined to be. She owed it to them—and to herself—to stand strong.

CHAPTER FORTY-EIGHT

CALEB

Caleb stood at the edge of the gathering on the Bloodstone ritual grounds, watching wolves arrive in somber clusters. They moved together like a tide, heads bowed, movements slow, yet their unity remained unshaken.

"This is strength—grief borne as one." Fenrir's voice resonated through Caleb's bones. *"They bleed together, heal together."*

Caleb looked toward the she-wolf he had comforted earlier. Her shoulders had been trembling, hands wringing a woven shawl as though it alone could hold her together. He'd murmured quiet words, nothing profound, but she'd gripped his hand with surprising strength, her gaze fierce through her tears.

"Thank you," she said with trembling sincerity. *"For standing with us. Then, and tonight."*

That moment lingered in his mind, a poignant reminder of the connections that transcended pack borders. Crescent Fang had been an island for too long. Tonight, more than ever, he knew that isolation wasn't the answer.

Caleb's attention turned toward the center as the murmurs of the gathered wolves hushed. Alpha Darius stepped forward, his imposing frame illuminated by torchlight.

"My pack," Darius began. His voice was steady, but Caleb noticed the telltale signs of strain in the way his fingers curled into fists, in the pauses between sentences, in how his throat worked before difficult words. "Tonight, we gather to honor the twenty-seven brave wolves who gave their lives to protect Bloodstone. The sacrifice of those we mourn ensured our survival. Their courage, their loyalty, their love for this pack will forever be a part of us."

Darius scanned the crowd. "Of all the rites an alpha must perform, none are more difficult than this. Saying goodbye to my packmates, my family, is a burden I will carry for the rest of my days. It has been three years since I laid to rest my beloved luna, Althea. I never imagined I would face such a loss again."

Around him, wolves lowered their heads. An older warrior placed a weathered hand over his heart. A mother pulled her pup closer against her side. Soft whispers of "May Selene guide her" drifted through the gathering like the flutter of fallen leaves caught in a gentle breeze.

Something constricted behind Caleb's ribcage as Darius's alpha persona cracked, revealing the raw grief beneath. His words unguarded in a way that made several wolves drop their gazes, unable to witness such naked vulnerability from their alpha. Caleb felt their deep respect for Darius, a respect that had been earned through years of steadfast leadership.

The hard lines around Darius's mouth smoothed as his eyes found a figure standing near the front of the gathered wolves. "Tonight, I am reminded that even in our darkest moments, Selene provides us with light. Lena, daughter of Alpha Raelen, daughter of Moonshadow, and future Luna of Bloodstone, has carried this pack with a strength and grace that honors both her lineage and her heart. It is in that spirit that I invite her to deliver the Invictus."

Caleb watched as Lena stepped forward. Fenrir rumbled within him, noticing what Caleb did—the momentary tightening of Lena's jaw, the deep breath she drew through flared nostrils before squaring her shoulders, straightening her spine as if growing into the mantle of responsibility before their eyes.

She stopped beside Darius, gaze sweeping over the crowd before settling on the altar. Her voice, clear and unwavering, carried through the circle.

"Tonight, we gather to honor twenty-seven brave Bloodstone hearts. From untamed freedom to eternal rest, their stories now silenced. In death, their legacy unites us. The moon, a witness to their lives, watches over their remains. Its gentle light reminding us that life is fleeting, but loyalty endures." Lena paused, body angling toward the altar. "These urns hold a universe of memories—of laughter, of battles fought and won—but their spirits will soar free as their essence transcends mortal bounds." She faced the gathering again. "May their sacrifice fortify our hearts. May their memory inspire our unwavering loyalty."

The crowd seemed to hold its breath, the power of her words resonating deeply. Caleb found himself transfixed by her grace.

"She speaks with the voice of a luna," Fenrir murmured. *"Bloodstone is fortunate to have her."*

Lena stepped back and moved to the left side of the altar. Kai, standing stoically on Darius's right, crossed the space to take his place opposite her. Together, in perfect synchronization, they lit the ceremonial censers. The blend of sage, bloodroot, and red clover filled the air, its earthy sweetness mingling with the crisp night breeze. Caleb inhaled deeply, the scents grounding him in the moment's significance.

"Life, death, and rebirth," Fenrir whispered. *"The cycle continues, as it must."*

Darius stepped forward once more to deliver the Blessing, his voice strong and reverent. "Selene, we humbly return these souls to your light. In their strength, they forged our unity. In their legacy, they guide us forward. May their essence merge with the wild, their spirits weaving into our hearts and our pack's strength. Grant them safe passage, Great Mother, and welcome them into your eternal embrace."

One by one, the families stepped forward to scatter the remains of their loved ones. Caleb watched as the ashes swirled in the cool night wind, carried through the forest as if guided by the Goddess Herself. He closed his eyes, offering his own silent prayer.

May they find peace, and may their families find the strength to carry on.

Heavy silence fell as the last ashes scattered. Darius broke it with quiet authority.

"Join me in the dining hall," he said, voice carrying over the crowd. "Tonight, we celebrate the lives of those we have lost as they make their journey back to Selene."

Caleb lingered at the altar as the pack moved around him, shoulders that had been hunched now relaxing, hands reaching out to clasp forearms or brush against backs. Cedar incense clung to his clothes as tear-stained faces turned toward the dining hall—not with joy, but with the determination that came from knowing that life, however altered, continued.

Scents of roasted meats, spiced vegetables, and fresh bread filled the air, intertwining with faint traces of incense that followed everyone from the ritual grounds. Long tables stretched the length of the dining hall, adorned with simple greenery and flickering candles that cast soft shadows across the room.

Caleb entered the hall at a measured pace, gaze sweeping over the gathered wolves. Though grief saturated the air, determination had begun seeping through the cracks—a collective will to honor lost lives through shared memories and warmth. Gentle hums of conversation filled the space, punctuated by the occasional scrape of a chair or the clink of a serving tray. It was subdued, but it was life—a testament to the resilience of the Bloodstone pack.

"They grieve, but they do not crumble." Fenrir's voice was low but resolute. *"This is the strength of a pack, Caleb. Bloodstone will endure."*

Lena's graceful movement through the crowd drew Caleb's focus. Sorrow-stricken wolves gravitated to her, drawn by her gentle warmth as she steadied them with whispered reassurances and soft touches. Her presence anchored the pack—a healing balm over the wound of their shared sorrow and marveled at the effortless way she held them together.

Fenrir hummed with a note of proud approval. *"The daughter of Moonshadow is a daughter of Bloodstone tonight."*

"Alpha Caleb," a familiar voice interrupted his thoughts.

Caleb turned to see Darius approaching, gratitude sparking in his green eyes.

"Alpha Darius," Caleb greeted, inclining his head respectfully.

Darius clasped Caleb's forearm in a firm grip. His touch held the steady assurance of a wolf who had weathered countless storms.

"It means a great deal that you stood with us tonight," Darius said. "Your presence, your warriors—it's a reminder of the bonds that hold *all* wolves together, even in the darkest times."

Caleb watched over the room, finding himself looking at Lena again as the significance of Darius's words settled in his chest. "It was an honor, Darius. Bloodstone's strength deserves to be seen and upheld. Crescent Fang will always answer your call."

Darius nodded, expression softening as he followed Caleb's gaze to where Lena stood. "You've seen the strength of our wolves tonight. It's wolves like her—like all of them—that make leading worth every trial."

Caleb continued watching her, noting the subtle shifts in her expression before returning to Darius. "Bloodstone's heart is strong. Your future will be bright."

Darius's lips curved in a faint smile, but the weariness on his face didn't fade entirely. "It's leaders like you, Caleb, who remind me why we rebuild after every loss. If you can stay a little longer, I'd like more of my pack to meet the alpha who stood with us when it mattered most."

Caleb relaxed his posture in agreement, expression thoughtful. "I'll stay a little longer. Thank you, Darius."

Darius lingered for a moment before he gave a curt nod, attention shifting back to the room. "Excuse me. There are others I need to speak with."

The ripple of Darius's aura withdrawing as he moved away left space for the gathering's energy to flow around Caleb. He moved through the room like water, nodding respectfully and pausing for those who acknowledged him. Each interaction created small eddies of connection, carrying him naturally toward the far side of the hall where familiar faces brought a smile to his lips. There, a group of wolves huddled together in easy camaraderie. Cian noticed Caleb's approach, brightening with recognition, as Caleb tuned into the group's dynamic energy.

Cian stood with a relaxed confidence that Caleb admired—a wolf comfortable in his skin and ready to take on the mantle of leadership. Beside him, an older male with dark hair streaked with gray exuded a commanding aura, tempered by a warmth that hinted at an approachable nature. Alpha Raelen, Caleb assumed, the male's presence sending subtle ripples of authority through the air that raised the hair on Caleb's nape. Beside him, Ryker's playful grin and relaxed stance contrasted with the quiet confidence of the russet-colored wolf standing next to him. Their bond a clear, balanced partnership.

Fenrir's voice rose again, laced with quiet respect. *"Their leaders' harmony flows into the pack. A unity of light and shadow. There is much to be learned here, Alpha."*

Fenrir's insight settled beneath Caleb's skin, the ancient wolf's wisdom integrating into his muscles and bones as he stepped into the group's orbit.

"Caleb, my friend," Cian greeted warmly, stepping forward to clasp his forearm. "It feels like it's been longer than a month."

"Agreed. The Summit feels like a lifetime ago," Caleb replied with a faint grin, hazel eyes lighting with genuine warmth. "It's good to see you, Cian. All of you."

Cian's expression sobered, speaking more quietly, "You've been busy. Bloodstone owes you. I've heard Crescent Fang's strength turned the tide."

"Bloodstone stood its ground," Caleb deflected. "We only helped where we could."

Cian's smile widened, gesturing to the older wolf beside him. "I'd like you to meet my father, Alpha Raelen."

Caleb offered a measured bow of respect. "Alpha Raelen, it's an honor. Moonshadow's reputation precedes you."

"The honor is mine, Caleb." Raelen's expression warmed, his commanding presence tempered by respect as he clasped Caleb's forearm. "I've heard much about you. You've done a great service for Bloodstone, and I look forward to getting to know you better."

Before Caleb could respond, Ryker leaned in, his typical playfulness replaced by quiet concern. "Speaking of Crescent Fang...how's Asher? We heard he was wounded."

"He's healing well, though the silver slowed him down." Caleb's composure cracked, revealing the fear he'd carried. "I thank Selene every day that his wolf is strong. He's eager to be back at my side, and he's looking forward to the alpha ceremony in Moonshadow."

Caleb's focus shifted to Lena, who had remained quietly attentive. His expression gentled as he addressed her. "Lena, congratulations on tonight's ceremony," he said. "Your words were powerful, and your presence was commanding. Bloodstone is fortunate to have you."

Lena's cheeks flushed as she dipped her head graciously. "Thank you, Alpha Caleb." The slight tremor in her words betrayed a weariness she couldn't fully conceal. "That means a lot."

Her quiet determination reminded Caleb of what true leadership looked like—not always loud or imposing, but resolute and unyielding, even in the face of unimaginable grief. She bore her burdens with an elegance that made it hard to look away, her strength anchoring those around her even as it left her raw.

In that moment, she reminded him of his mother. A female who'd carried wisdom and fire in equal measure. Who'd stood beside his father as a queen in her own right. Lena possessed that same power. The same grace under immense pressure that had made his mother so beloved throughout Crescent Fang.

Fenrir stirred with interest, presence vibrating with rare intensity. *"I think she carries the Goddess's spirit, though her flame burns with a different light. I wonder what fire lives within her wolf."* Fenrir paused, as if considering something profound. *"When her burden lifts, that fire will burn brighter than ever before."*

"Lena's been planning Cian's alpha ceremony too," Jace broke in with a teasing grin. "Though Ryker and I had to pick up the slack when she raced off to Bloodstone to play super-luna."

Lena rolled her eyes, though her smile lingered. "Thanks for the support, Jace."

Caleb's lips quirked into a faint smile. "I'm looking forward to witnessing Moonshadow's traditions. I suspect your ceremonies are as rooted in strength as they are in unity."

"Cian has arranged a suite for you and your beta at the dormitories." Raelen's smile was welcoming. "I know it's a tenuous time to be away from your pack, but Moonshadow values the ties we're building with Crescent Fang. I hope you'll stay so we can speak more formally about the future we might shape together."

Before Caleb could respond, Cian's posture stiffened. His nostrils flared, and a faint rumble vibrated in his chest as his head snapped toward a point across the room. The future alpha's demeanor transformed—focused, intense, as if drawn by an unseen force.

The group froze, watching as Cian stepped away without a word, moving through the crowd like a hunter who'd locked onto his target.

"Fate moves swiftly tonight," Fenrir murmured

Cian stopped before a young she-wolf with wavy brown hair, flanked by an older couple. She looked up at him, stormy blue eyes wide.

The hall held its breath.

Cian cupped her cheek, his touch impossibly tender. "Mate." The word resonated through the dining hall like the clatter of a bell.

"Yours," she responded, breath hitching as happy tears glinted in her eyes.

Cian pulled her into a protective embrace, pressing a kiss to her temple. The atmosphere lightened, grief momentarily lifted by the beauty of this moment.

A delighted gasp pulled Caleb's focus away from the fated pair. Lena's hands flew to her mouth, golden-brown eyes widening as the anguish that had haunted her all evening dissolved into the brightest smile he'd yet witnessed from her.

"Oh, my Goddess!" she exclaimed. "That's Lyric! Cian's mate is Elias's sister." Lena turned toward her father, voice tinged with awe and joy. "Dad! She's wonderful. Lyric has been one of the brightest spots for me this week, and I know that her light will shine brightly as Moonshadow's future Luna." Lena pointed to the older couple standing beside Lyric. "Her parents, Talon and Maris, have been so kind and strong. This is perfect."

Raelen watched his son intently, pride and joy etched into every line of his face. He clasped Caleb's shoulder briefly. "Excuse me. I am going to go meet my daughter-in-law and her parents."

The group watched as Raelen made his way through the crowd, his towering stature commanding acknowledgement without effort. A smile ghosted Caleb's face as Cian introduced his father to Lyric's family. The sorrow that had permeated the dining hall shifted, replaced by a collective sense of hope and renewal.

"A union forged in grief, strengthened by love," Fenrir murmured. *"A blessing for both packs."*

Caleb returned his attention to the group around him. Ryker's grin was as wide as Caleb had ever seen it, mischief dancing wickedly in his brown eyes.

"Well," Ryker drawled, leaning toward Jace, "looks like our boy is about to have the best night of his life. Think we should crash at Lena's tonight? Cian probably doesn't want an audience while he fumbles his way through his first time."

Lena let out an indignant snort, shoving Ryker in the chest. "Don't be rude," she scolded, though the laughter in her tone softened the reprimand. "But..." Her smile turned thoughtful. "A sleepover sounds amazing. It's been way too long, and I'm sure Cian would love to have time alone with Lyric."

"Sounds like a plan." Ryker smirked as he turned back to Jace. "We'll have to make sure he knows how to find the clit before we leave, though."

"*Stop*!" Lena's cheeks flushed as she swatted his arm. "Cian doesn't need your tips. He'll figure it out."

Jace turned to Lena, brow raised with curiosity. "Do you think this will change the alpha ceremony? Will Lyric take her oaths alongside Cian?"

Lena hesitated, mouth pulled to once side as she considered. "I'm not sure. I'll check with Nerina, but I don't know what the protocol is in a situation like this. I don't think it happens often."

"Looks like someone needs to brush up on their ceremony knowledge. You're slipping, Thing 1," Ryker teased.

Lena rolled her eyes, but her grin gave away her amusement. "Thanks for the vote of confidence, guys. I'll figure it out."

Caleb chuckled softly, shaking his head. "You might want to check with Cian first," he interjected. "Some newly mated pairs take time to grow their bond or complete the claiming rite before officially recognizing their mating. Lyric may also want time to bond with the pack before taking her oaths. They may likely wait until their mating ceremony."

Life returned to Lena's complexion, excitement undeterred. "That makes sense. It'll give them time to adjust and prepare. I've really enjoyed helping with rituals, and I'd love to be part of Lyric's transition when the time comes."

The conversation was interrupted by a light tap on Caleb's shoulder.

"Alpha Caleb," came a familiar voice.

Caleb spun around, straightening as Bloodstone's heir stood before him. Kai's expression was controlled but taut with something unspoken.

"Alpha Caleb," Kai repeated. His attention darted toward Lena before steadying on Caleb. "Thank you for coming to Bloodstone's aid. We are in your debt."

Caleb held the younger wolf's gaze, offering a small nod. "There's no debt between neighbors, Kai. Helping Bloodstone was an honor."

Caleb could sense the gratitude in Kai's posture, the way his shoulders eased just slightly. Yet beneath it all, there was still tension, a crack in the heir's composure, that spoke volumes.

Ryker stepped forward, breaking the formality with his gentle, playful smile. "We miss you at Moonshadow, brother." He pulled Kai into a hug. "Things aren't the same without you."

Jace nodded in agreement, clapping Kai on the back as he added, "Our condolences for Elias. We've heard that he was an exceptional wolf and would have been a phenomenal gamma."

Kai's lips pressed into a thin, bloodless line. His eyes clouded momentarily, focusing on some middle distance as grief surfaced. "Thank you. He was—" Kai's words faltered, overcome by his loss. "He was the best of us."

Shared sorrow thickened the air before it was interrupted by a shift. A tall blond appeared at Kai's side, her arrival as abrupt as her presence was invasive. She slipped her hand into his, fingers intertwining in a gesture that felt both possessive and performative. Pressing close to Kai's side, she offered a sweet but pointed smile to the group.

"Hello," she said with practiced brightness. "I'm Ava, Kai's *girlfriend*."

The words sliced through the tentative warmth. Lena's shoulders drew back, golden-brown eyes shuttering as they fixed on a distant point. Ryker and Jace flanked her in an instant, fingers interlocking with hers. A silent display of solidarity that tensed the air between both groups.

Muscles worked in Kai's jaw and tension coiled in his shoulders as his eyes darted between the three of them. His grip on Ava's hand spasmed, a jerk that might have been an attempt to pull free or silence her. Caleb couldn't tell.

Ava's smile brightened. "Alpha Caleb." Her voice took on a musical quality, smoothing over the earlier sharpness in her tone with sugary warmth. "Your bravery and the bravery of your warriors...it's inspiring. You saved my life."

Her words were deliberately crafted, landing with the obvious intent. She wrestled her hand from Kai's stern grip, sliding it up to rest over his chest. She traced idle circles with her fingers as she continued, voice softening to a near-coo. "If the battle hadn't turned when it did...who knows what might have happened. My future alpha wouldn't have been able to endure losing me."

Ava tilted her face up toward Kai, expression painted with adoration, but the faintest smirk tugged at her lips. "Right, my *love*?" Her hand dropped, gripping his again until her nails left marks.

A shudder of resistance passed through Kai's frame, the tension in his shoulders rippling down the length of his body. Something passed across his face—reluctance? Maybe regret? It burned for a heartbeat, before Ava's nails pressed deeper, smothering it completely. She continued to squeeze until a single word fell from his lips, flat and almost mechanical.

"Right."

Only then did Ava's hand relax, fingers slipping from his with a delicate finality as though she hadn't just forced his response. "See?" She faced Caleb again, saccharine smile firmly in place. Satisfaction flickered beneath her expression—a silent victory over the male standing beside her. Not love—control wearing affection's mask.

"Two-faced," Fenrir warned. *"See how he diminishes in her presence? Darius has failed to see the danger she represents."*

Caleb dipped his chin in acknowledgment, hazel eyes assessing Ava before returning to Kai. "Bloodstone has strong allies in Crescent Fang. I hope you know you'll always have them."

Kai's shoulders dropped a fraction, before the mask slipped back into place. The charged atmosphere between the group remained, unspoken hostility weaving through the air like an invisible tether. Caleb watched the interplay between all of them, the subtle way Ryker's thumb traced soothing circles against the back of Lena's hand, the icy glare Jace directed at Kai—a stark contrast to the warmth and affection the males had shared just moments prior.

The warmth vanished from Kai's expression, his features hardening like cooling wax as his gaze fixed on Ryker's, Jace's, and Lena's intertwined fingers. Ava appeared oblivious—or perhaps uncaring—as her smile remained unshaken.

"Bloodstone's future is fraught with uncertainty," Fenrir murmured. *"But that is not your burden to carry."*

Caleb breathed deep, allowing Fenrir's words to settle him. For now, he would observe and learn, but his focus would remain on the connections that strengthened his own pack and those he called allies.

Ava studied the group, eyes narrowing as if assessing the unspoken tension simmering between Kai, Lena, Ryker, and Jace. Her hand rose to Kai's chest again, and she turned to him with a polished smile. "My future alpha, we should go stand with your father." Her voice dripped with saccharine deference. "The grieving families need our support, and he'll want *us* at his side."

Kai hesitated. His eyes sought Lena's—a flicker of longing extinguished.

Ava yanked his focus back to her. "Come."

With a sharp breath, Kai nodded. The ease drained from his posture, replaced by a rigid formality as he allowed Ava to lead him away.

The discomfort Ava left in her wake lingered like a heavy fog. Caleb rolled his shoulders back, allowing the unease to dissipate as he turned back to the group. "I'm afraid I must also leave," he said. "I need to get back to Crescent Fang before dawn. Please tell Cian congratulations for me."

Lena looked up at him, golden-brown eyes softening. "Will do," she said, voice quiet but sincere. "It was good to see you again, Caleb."

Caleb leaned in, speaking quietly so only she could hear. "You were exceptional tonight. Fenrir and I...we were in awe of your grace. You will be a transcendent luna."

Lena's lips parted, eyes widening with surprise before she acknowledged the compliment with a gentle tilt of her head. "Thank you," she whispered. She offered him a small smile, though something guarded remained in her expression. Her response settled uncomfortably in Caleb's chest, a challenge he hadn't expected but found himself willing to meet.

Fenrir pressed against Caleb's mind. *"Her light will shine again."*

He turned to the two males. "Enjoy your sleepover," he said with a grin. "Take care of Lena—she deserves a little pampering after everything she's done for Bloodstone this week." He fixed Ryker with a knowing look. "And don't give Cian too much grief about his mating. He's heading into a huge transition, your role is to anchor him as he steps into leadership. He'll need both of you."

Ryker's usual smirk softened into something more genuine as he nodded. "We've got him," he said firmly. "And we've got Lena too."

Jace clasped Caleb's forearm, ice-blue gaze earnest. "Safe travels, Alpha."

Caleb's attention returned to Lena for a moment before he bid farewell to the group. "I'll see you all in a few days."

The cool night air brushed Caleb's face as he stepped outside, leaving the din of the dining hall. Fenrir clawed at him from within, hungry for earth beneath paws and moonlight on fur. Caleb paused, pupils dilating to capture every detail as his gaze lifted to the moon, its pale light spilling across the Bloodstone lands.

Fenrir's approval flooded their shared consciousness like sunlight breaking through clouds, warming Caleb from marrow to skin. *"You're no longer on the outside. You'll be the bridge between faith and the future. But remember—challenges still lie ahead for all of us, Alpha."*

The events of the evening settled in Caleb's chest as he crossed into the shadows of the forest. Lena's quiet determination, Cian's joy, and even Bloodstone's simmering tensions replayed in his mind. His thoughts inevitably turned to Crescent Fang. Asher would be waiting, no doubt eager for an update on the ceremony—and perhaps far too curious about the Moonshadow wolves. Caleb's lips curved faintly. They'd have much to discuss.

CHAPTER FORTY-NINE

LENA

The cold night air stabbed at Lena's skin as she stepped out of the dining hall. She dragged in a breath, but it did nothing to ease the suffocating pressure in her chest. Behind her, the energy of the wolves gathered in the hall faded as she pressed a hand against the doorframe, steadying herself against the first wave of emotion threatening to break free.

She'd told Ryker and Jace she just needed air. Her smile—though strained and brittle—had been enough to stop their protests, but their concern lingered in the way Ryker hesitated, fingers twitching as if he wanted to grab her wrist.

"I'll be right back," she'd promised, forcing confidence into her voice. *"Go find Cian and grab your stuff for the sleepover. I'll meet you soon."*

The promise was empty. A lie she couldn't even convince herself to believe.

Her legs moved on instinct—heavy and mechanical—each step disconnected from conscious thought as the path stretched before her, lined with faint patches of torchlight. She barely registered the crunch of dirt beneath her boots or the distant rustle of wind through the trees. The mask she'd worn all evening began to crack as she drifted closer to the tree line. The strain of pretending weighed heavier with every breath, a dull ache spreading from her chest to her limbs.

"Lena." Darius's voice broke through her thoughts, halting her mid-step.

He emerged from the shadows, broad frame bathed in the dim glow of torchlight. His eyes, green and weary, searched hers, and for a fleeting moment, she thought he could see everything—the cracks in her composure, the exhaustion carved deep into her bones.

"Alpha Darius," she managed, the words trembling despite her best efforts.

He stepped closer, aura commanding but gentle. "I wanted to thank you again for today. For everything you've done for Bloodstone. You've carried more than I could have asked."

The words hit like a blow. "It's...it's been an honor," she replied, voice barely above a whisper. Her hand tightened around her jacket until her knuckles whitened. "Bloodstone is..." The words tangled in her throat. "It's remarkable."

Darius studied her for a long moment before placing a firm hand on her shoulder. His touch centered her, but it also felt impossibly heavy. "Before you leave tomorrow, come see me. Please."

She nodded, unable to trust her voice.

His hand lingered, then fell away as he turned back toward the hall. "Get some rest, Lena," he said over his shoulder, disappearing into the glow of the gathering.

Rest. Her lips twitched with bitter amusement, muscles too tight to form an actual laugh. Her body twitched with nervous energy that wouldn't allow for rest—not yet.

Lena's feet moved again, carrying her further into the night. Her thoughts were a tempest, swirling with memories she couldn't control:

Her and Kai under the stars at the Moonshadow ritual grounds, his lips brushing hers as he'd whispered, *"You're my peace, Lena."* His touch had been reverent, as though she were something sacred. But the stars at Moonshadow weren't the same as the shadows that haunted her in Bloodstone

A tremor started in her hands, spreading up her arms as the memory shifted, jagged and sharp:

Ava's laugh, syrupy sweet and loud enough to draw every eye. The way she had leaned into Kai, her hands roaming his chest like she had a right to him. Worse, the way he'd *let* her.

Her breaths came in sharp, painful gasps as memories struck like individual blows, breaking down her walls:

"Do you trust me?" he'd asked her, hand cradling her cheek as his thumb brushed away a tear she hadn't realized she'd shed. She nodded then, without hesitation, because she had.

But now? What was there left to trust? Her vision blurred as the first tears pressed hot against her eyelids. She forced them back, clenching her jaw until her teeth throbbed.

The ritual grounds loomed ahead, shrouded in shadows cast by dying torches. The air was thick, damp with the scent of charred wood and earth. Lena stepped into the circle, breath hitching as she walked toward the altar. The acrid scent of burnt incense clung to the air like a memory similar to how Kai's scent still clung to her skin despite everything that had changed between them.

Her steps faltered. Once. Twice. The third time, her legs simply gave out, knees hitting the earth with a muted thud. Her hands trembled as she clutched the cold altar stone. She pressed her forehead to its surface, the chill burning into her skin as the first crack in her composure split wide open. "Selene." Her voice broke on the Goddess's name. "If you're there...if you can hear me...please."

The silence that followed was deafening. No flicker of warmth, no comforting glow. Just the cold, uncompromising stone beneath her hands and the shadows pressing in from all sides.

A hollow ache spread in her chest. Her ribcage felt too small, too fragile to contain what was building within. Each heartbeat sent fractures through the chest wall like glass struck with a hammer. "You made this bond." She drew a shaky breath. "It was supposed to be beautiful... It was supposed to make us stronger." Her fists clenched. "But it's broken. It's killing me." Her body curled forward as crushing sorrow pressed her into the earth, a strangled sob escaping her lips. "Why would you do this? Why would you bind me to someone who doesn't—" Her voice splintered into raw, guttural sobs. "Who *can't* choose me?"

The dam inside her broke, her cries ripping through the stillness of the sacred space. She clawed at the stone as she shook with the force of her grief. Every suppressed tear, every buried ache poured out in a torrent, her body buckling under its weight. Memories continued to assault her like waves crashing against the bluffs—

Kai making love to her under the stars at Moonshadow. *"Goddess, Lena,"* he'd groaned, his voice rough with passion. *"You feel... Your... It's everything."*

His touch that had once made her feel invincible. *"Show me,"* he'd said. *"Show me how to love you."*

The way he'd looked at her the morning everything changed. *"Man,"* he'd said sleepily. *"Seeing your face first thing in the morning is something I could get used to."*

And the way he looked at Ava now. The way he'd let her words hang in the air like a declaration of war. *"I'm Ava, Kai's girlfriend."* His hands on the small of her back. The comforting kisses he left on her temple, the crown of her head...

I gave him everything, Lena thought as she gasped for air. *And he gave it to someone else.*

A faint whimper resonated in her mind.

Elara.

Her wolf's voice surfaced weakly, primal and instinctive, tied to the mating bond rather than memory. *"I feel him, Lena. Orion's grief... It mirrors mine."* Elara's tone held the ancient wisdom of her kind, even as it fractured with Lena's anguish. *"But your pain... It's breaking me."*

Lena pressed her forehead to the altar, tears soaking into the stone. "I can't do this," she choked. "I can't survive him, Elara. I can't."

Elara's response came like a broken melody trying to find its rhythm, yet with the wolf's unwavering certainty. *"Then we go home. He will fight to bring us back."*

But for every tender memory of Kai's touch, there was now Ava's claim on him. For every whispered promise, now his deafening silence. Lena couldn't live in the spaces between what was promised and what was taken away.

She sniffled, fingers curling tighter against the altar. "It wasn't supposed to be this way," she whispered. "It wasn't supposed to hurt this much."

"You are more than the mate bond," Elara murmured, voice soft yet resolute. *"You are more than his struggles. He will learn."*

The bond in her chest pulsed faintly, a thread frayed beyond repair. Lena closed her eyes, sobs breaking into choked gasps as she forced herself to release the pain, the hope, the *love* she'd been clinging to. "I have to let him go," she said, vocal cords shredded. "I don't want to, but it will destroy me if I don't."

"We go home. Then maybe, he will heal. He will be ours again." Elara whimpered, tone filled with waning hope that Lena couldn't allow herself to feel.

The torches lining the grounds flickered one final time before extinguishing completely, leaving the ritual circle cloaked in darkness. Only the faint glow of the moon remained, casting silver shadows over the sacred space.

Her sobs echoed against the stone altar and the now-shadowed trees. The darkness pressed against her, smothering, as though the extinguished flames had stolen what little light and warmth she had left.

Lena didn't know how long she lay there, body crumpled against the altar, cold earth pressing against her skin, dirt clinging to her hands and knees. Tears leaked from eyes she no longer had the energy to close, each breath a battle she barely had strength to fight. Her body had become a husk, emptied of everything but pain.

She hadn't realized she wasn't alone until Ryker's warm arms enveloped her, lifting her from the forest floor and into his lap. Jace knelt beside them, hands brushing dirt from her face with quiet care. Neither of them spoke, their silence more comforting than any words could have been.

Ryker's breath was warm against her chilled skin as he pressed his forehead to hers. Jace's hold on her shoulders was protective, sheltering. The vise grip of pain in her chest loosened as they surrounded her, just enough to let her draw a full breath for the first time in a week.

Together, they carried her from the ritual grounds, their tears mixing with her own as they shielded her from the cold. The sacred circle remained shrouded in shadow, the darkness a quiet reflection of Lena's shattered spirit.

CHAPTER FIFTY

KAI

The ruins of the packhouse loomed around Kai. Its charred wood and twisted metal creaking in the wind, each sound echoing the fractures of his resolve. The sharp tang of ash clung to the air, mingling with the faint, metallic scent of blood that no amount of scrubbing could erase. His boots crunched against the uneven ground—littered with shattered glass and splintered wood—as he wandered through the skeletal remains.

He'd left the dining hall without a word. The oppressive weight of the somber celebration pressed against his chest until it felt like he might shatter. The soft murmurs of gratitude, the laughter breaking through grief, felt like a foreign language. He couldn't breathe. Couldn't think. Couldn't face Lena's golden-brown eyes, which now refused to meet his for even a fleeting second.

His fingers had trailed the wooden doorframe as he slipped out, the rough grain catching on his calluses. Outside, he'd gulped in the night air, each breath a desperate attempt to clear the suffocating sense of wrongness that had settled in his lungs.

Panic and guilt had consumed him when he'd arrived at Bloodstone after the attack. He'd seen the devastation—the scorched lands, the burned homes, the *bodies*—chest compressing as the extent of the damage sank in, but nothing had prepared him for the sight of Ava lying motionless in the infirmary. Her skin had been pale, breathing shallow.

The faint scent of blood and silver clinging to her a haunting reminder of what they'd lost.

Elias.

His stomach twisted as the image of his future gamma's lifeless wolf seared itself into his mind. The memory of the pyre burned even brighter—Darius's jaw clenched to breaking as the flames consumed Kael's—Elias's—remains, grief carving new lines into the alpha's face with each passing second.

Kai's boot connected with a charred support beam, sending it crashing into a pile of debris. The sound reverberated through the empty ruins but did nothing to drown out the accusation pounding in his head: *I wasn't here. I didn't protect them.*

He reached out, pressing a palm against the nearest wall. The soot was dry and crumbly beneath his touch as intrusive thoughts raked like claws against his ribs with each heartbeat.

In Moonshadow, Lena's warmth had surrounded him with something he barely recognized—her smile like dawn breaking after endless night, her laughter unlocking chambers in his heart he'd forgotten existed. For the first time in years, he'd felt the burden of his birthright lift. And while he'd been discovering what freedom tasted like and slowly falling for his mate, his pack had been drowning in blood and ash.

Guilt had flooded his system like a slow-spreading poison the moment he'd stepped back onto Bloodstone soil. It had churned and twisted inside him, mutating from regret to something darker. Something that tore at his insides with razor-sharp claws: *anger.*

Anger at himself for failing his pack.

Anger at how right it had felt to escape his responsibilities.

Anger at Lena for showing him a version of himself he could never truly be.

And he'd taken it out on her.

He'd let distance grow between them. Let his guilt and fear fester into something that pushed her away. By the time he'd started thinking more clearly, Lena had already shifted her focus to the pack. She'd thrown herself into caring for his people, planning the funeral rites, and easing Darius's grief.

Kai swallowed hard against the knot in his throat as he thought of how she avoided him now. He picked up a shard of glass, turning it over in his fingers as memories flashed across its surface like reflections. The way her eyes would slide past his, gaze focusing on anyone else—Darius, the mourning pack members, Ryker, Jace—never him.

The glass bit into his thumb. A drop of blood welled up, and he watched it with morbid fascination, the sharp sting a welcome distraction.

He used to feel like he could see pieces of her soul in her eyes, like the bond had opened a door between them that no one else could enter. Now, all he saw was a wall. Those beautiful, golden-brown eyes, once warm and inviting, were now distant and guarded.

He wiped the blood on his jeans and tossed the glass aside, listening to it clink against the stone floor.

She didn't stiffen or flinch when he entered a room, but her body language spoke volumes. Her shoulders were always squared, arms crossed, or her hands clasped in front of her as though bracing herself. When he'd tried to approach her, her voice became politely detached, like they were little more than acquaintances rather than lovers who knew the recesses of each other's hearts.

The physical distance stung almost as much. When they'd brushed past each other, fingers accidentally grazing, he'd felt a jolt of lightning. But then she'd pull away, leaving him aching in the void where their bond used to sing.

He'd tried to reach her. Once, after a long day of preparing for the funeral rites, he'd waited for her outside the dining hall, hoping to catch her alone. He was desperate to wrap her pinky in his. To thank her. To close the gap any way he could. She'd nodded at him, expression neutral. Before he could say anything, she'd murmured something about needing to speak with Lyric and disappeared into the crowd.

She was there. *Always* there. But he couldn't feel her anymore.

And it was all his fault.

"What did you expect?" Orion's voice was like stone grinding against stone. *"She'd wait patiently while you sulked and kept Ava's claws in your skin? Your silence was your choice."*

"I didn't choose *this*." The words scraped Kai's throat raw, ringing hollow in his ears even as they left his lips.

"No?" Orion's presence surged forward, wild instinct crashing against human hesitation. *"Then explain why you stand in ashes while mate slips away. Wolves don't hesitate, Kai. They* act.*"*

Kai's fists clenched at his sides, the dull ache in his chest growing sharper as the bond with Lena twisted inside him. He didn't need Orion to remind him of all the ways he failed—not just as an heir, but as a mate.

His control slipped, and he slammed his fist into a half-collapsed wall. Pain shot up his arm as debris rained down, the impact sending dust and ash swirling around him like accusations.

"What am I supposed to do?" The question directed as much at himself as at his wolf.

"Face her," came Orion's immediate response. *"Stop hiding in pain."*

A piercing, restless energy vibrated beneath his skin. He needed to move. To do something—anything—to keep the surges of guilt and anger at bay. Kai shoved a broken plank of wood off to the side, the sharp splintering sound cutting through the night air. His fingers burned from the rough edges, the grit clinging to his hands as he forced himself to focus on the physical task.

The faint crunch of footsteps behind him pulled him out of his thoughts. He didn't have to turn around to know who it was. The cloying, floral edge of her perfume had already given her away.

"So, this is where you've been hiding." Ava's voice sliced through the stillness, sharp as the silver that had wounded their pack.

Kai straightened, hands tightening into fists at his sides. "I'm not hiding."

She laughed, a short, bitter sound that grated on his nerves.

"No, of course not. You're just out here, alone, in the dark, while everyone else is inside—while *I'm* inside—dealing with the aftermath of the night you walked out on."

Kai faced her. Something darker than frustration twisted her features, arms crossed like a shield over her chest as she stepped closer. The tension radiating from her shoulders made the space between them feel electric, dangerous.

"I needed air," he said, each word measured and flat.

"Air." she repeated, voice dripping with sarcasm. "How convenient. Because Kai, the ever-brooding future Alpha of Bloodstone, just couldn't stomach a room full of wolves counting on him."

The accusation hit hard, but Kai refused to let it show. He turned back to the pile of debris, crouching to pick up another broken plank.

"What do you want, Ava?"

"What do I want?" Her eyebrows shot up, voice climbing with each word. "I want to know why the hell you think you can just disappear. Do you have any idea how humiliating it was, standing there alone while Darius practically crowned *her* in front of everyone? Did you even think about what that did to me? The damage you've caused?"

A muscle ticked in his jaw. The familiar pattern of the past week—her demands, his deflections, silences that stretched to breaking—threatened to repeat itself. Every day he'd swallowed the truth that sat like a stone in his throat: he wanted Lena.

"Damage?" The word came out sharper than intended. "What are you really talking about, Ava?"

"I've known you since we were pups, Kai. Don't insult us both by pretending you don't understand." She stepped closer, ice bleeding into her tone. "What do you think everyone thought when they saw you leave me there? *I'm* supposed to be the one by your side. I'm the one who's *always* been by your side, and you made me look like a fool."

"You introduced yourself to Alpha Caleb as my girlfriend," Kai snapped. "You put me in an impossible position. Do you have any idea how much damage *you've* done to Bloodstone's standing with Crescent Fang and Moonshadow by lying about our relationship? Their trust in me isn't a guarantee, Ava."

Her lips curled into a bitter smile. "I was protecting you," she said, tone syrupy and mocking. "I didn't want Caleb and the others to think—" she paused, voice dropping to a whisper. "That you're not taken care of because your 'mate' is more interested in politicking with the 'favored alpha' than standing with you."

Kai recoiled as if struck. "Protecting me?" A snort caught in his throat. "You *embarrassed* me" His voice dropped to a low growl. "And yourself."

"Why do you even care so much about what Caleb thinks? Is it because of *her*?" Ava's voice broke on the word, but she pressed on.

"You're so damn enchanted by your perfect fated mate that you can't even see what she's doing?"

His gaze darkened, shoulders squaring. "This isn't about Lena."

"Isn't it?" Ava shot back. "She's leaving tomorrow. Do you really think she gives a damn about you? About Bloodstone? Yeah, she's helped this week, but when she leaves, it'll be to Moonshadow. *Her* home, not yours."

"That's enough," Kai snarled.

She ignored him, her words spilling out in a torrent.

"Do you even realize what you're throwing away? For a nobody female and an alliance with a forgotten pack?" Her voice faltered for a moment before hardening again. "You're going to lose me, Kai." She fixed him with a possessive, defiant stare. "And when she leaves you behind? You'll have nothing."

Her words wrapped around his guilt like a noose, tightening with each breath. He took a step closer, green eyes no longer defensive but burning with something new—the first spark of defiance.

"I'm not losing anything, Ava," His voice was cold, though exhaustion dulled its edge. "You're pushing, pulling, *forcing*...just like everyone else." He gritted his teeth as he stepped back. "And it's ruining whatever was left between us."

Her mask slipped, anger flashing raw and unfiltered. "I've weathered every storm with you. Elias's death, the rogues, every Goddess-damned thing this pack has thrown at us since we were pups. And her? You've known her for a month. You really think she's the one for you?"

"How long will you let her chain you with guilt?" Orion's tone dripped with disdain for Kai's former lover.

"This isn't about her," Kai repeated. Resolve threaded through his voice where there had once been doubt. "It's not about my dad, or Caleb, or anyone else. It's about *us*. And right now, you're destroying our friendship because you won't acknowledge the truth." He met her gaze without flinching for the first time. "I care about you, Ava," he said, voice quieter but unbending. "But you are *not* my forever."

Ava's gaze locked onto Kai with predatory focus. The air between them pulsated with unspoken words, the silence crackling like the moment before lightning struck.

"You're a coward." Each syllable calculated to find purchase in the fractures of his confidence. Her eyes never left his face, as if searching for the wound her words would open. "And she's not good for you, but you're too terrified of disappointing Daddy, too afraid of actually being the alpha you were born to be, to see what's right in front of you."

He saw her declaration for what it was: the desperate final play of someone losing their grip. Still, her accusations slid beneath his skin like splinters. The tension between them thickened, breathing, expanding, nearing the point of combustion.

"She's wrong." Orion assured. *"You're not afraid of losing her. You're afraid of letting yourself heal, letting yourself be happy."*

Kai stood motionless as understanding crystallized within him—sharp-edged and painful, but undeniably clear. His gaze dropped, not in submission as she might believe, but in recognition of a truth he'd been avoiding.

"Maybe I am a coward, Ava," he said quietly, meeting her eyes again. "But not for the reasons you think."

The transformation that swept across her face was instant—practiced vulnerability hardening into something bitter and ugly. In that moment, the mask fell completely.

"You'll regret this," she spat, each word both promise and threat. "When she's gone and you've lost everything, you'll regret it."

The statement hung in the air like a challenge, and for a moment, Kai felt a pang of doubt. This wasn't how he'd wanted things to end. Despite everything, he'd hoped to salvage something of their friendship. He remained silent, staring at the ground as Ava turned and walked away, her footsteps fading into the distance.

He let his legs fold beneath him. His back slid down a scorched beam until he hit the ground, ashes rising around him in a small cloud that settled onto his shoulders alongside the bite of her parting words.

Orion's presence settled in his consciousness like an anchor in rough waters.

"Let her go, Kai. Then you'll see what you've been blind to all along."

CHAPTER FIFTY-ONE

LENA

S unlight streamed through the high windows, casting golden patches over the long oak table where Lena sat. Her fingers tightened around the steaming cup of tea in her hands, the scent of chamomile and honey rising with the heat, its warmth doing little to ease the chill settling in her chest. The dining hall was quieter now, though the emotion of last night's rituals hovered like a shadow.

Beyond the windows, Bloodstone's packlands stretched out, still battered but *alive*. Wolves moved about, tending to the aftermath of the rogue attack, their movements steady and purposeful. The distant sound of hammers and saws drifted in, a rhythm of rebuilding. There was a resilience here that humbled Lena, but today it only underscored the ache in her heart.

Elara shifted beneath her skin, her presence a tangle of conflicting instincts.

"We could belong here," the wolf whispered. *"With time. With healing."*

Lena pushed away her wolf's musings. This wasn't her home. It likely never would be.

"Lena." Darius's warm voice broke through her thoughts.

She turned to find the Bloodstone Alpha standing a few steps away, his normally authoritative pine scent tempered with exhaustion. Gratitude crossed his features, but there was something else too—something more profound.

"Alpha Darius," she greeted, voice holding strong despite the emotions tangling inside her. She set her cup down, inclining her head in respect.

"None of that." he waved off her formality as he stepped closer. "You've earned the right to call me Darius." He took the seat across from her. "Are you about ready to leave?"

She nodded, meeting his gaze. "I am. My pack needs me. Cian's ceremony is in three days."

The corner of Darius's mouth lifted. "Of course. Ever the responsible one." His smile faded, replaced by a solemn expression. "But I couldn't let you leave without thanking you properly."

Her brow furrowed. Darius had expressed his gratitude multiple times throughout the week, but she remained silent as he continued.

"You've been more than I could have hoped for. The way you've supported Bloodstone, carried its weight..." His voice caught, and he paused, hands resting on the table. "You stepped into a role that isn't even yours yet, and you did it with grace and strength I can only marvel at. It's more than I could've imagined. You've surpassed every expectation."

His recognition tested the fragile dam she'd constructed around her emotions. The mate bond pulsed beneath her skin, an uncomfortable throbbing that spread from her chest outward. Darius was right, but she knew she couldn't stay. The sincerity of his praise made the truth she needed to share feel even heavier.

Swallowing hard, she pressed her fingernails into her palms to ground herself. The pain helped focus her thoughts, pushing back the burning behind her eyes.

"Bloodstone is full of incredible wolves," she said softly, voice steadier than she felt. "They deserved every ounce of effort I could give."

He studied her, green eyes sharp but kind. "I meant what I said last night. You will be an extraordinary luna. Knowing that Kai has you by his side makes me feel good about stepping down."

The words pierced her like a blade between ribs. Her fingers curled around her cup, knuckles white against the ceramic. A cold sweat broke across her skin despite the warmth of the tea seeping into her palms. She took a steadying breath, fighting against the tightness in her chest, and stated with quiet determination, "Darius, I need to tell you something."

Worry lines appeared around his mouth. "What is it?"

"I can't be Luna of Bloodstone." Her words faltered despite her best efforts to remain composed. A tremor coursed through her body as she spoke the truth aloud, her wolf whimpering in response. "I won't be coming back after the ceremony."

The silence that followed was thick, weighted with the implication of her words. The steady tick of a distant clock punctuated the stillness.

Darius stared at her, expression unreadable, but the scent of his distress hit her, sharp and acrid. "What are you saying?"

She forced herself to meet his gaze, hands trembling so badly she had to set the cup down before she spilled its contents. Her mouth had gone dry, tongue sticking to the roof as if her body was physically rejecting the words she needed to say.

"I've done what I can here, but I can't... I'm not coming back."

His jaw ticked. "I know things haven't been easy between you and Kai, but—" He stopped himself, hands clenching into fists on the table. His voice softened, almost pleading. "He is worth it, Lena. The bond is worth it."

She felt the truth of his words resonate through her entire being, the mate bond humming in agreement and sending a wave of longing so strong it made her dizzy. Kai was worth it. The bond, worth everything. But *their* bond was broken, jagged at its edges, and every moment she held on while he was so torn only cut deeper into her soul. Love wasn't supposed to feel like this. She couldn't let it consume them both.

She blinked rapidly, fighting back tears. A shudder ran through her as she tamped down Elara's urge to flee, to find Kai, to beg him to choose her.

"He is worth it," she agreed, voice barely above a whisper. "But the male I fell in love with in Moonshadow isn't the one I've seen here. Kai needs healing, Darius. He needs space to find himself, to figure out what he needs—what he wants. I can't be part of that and the bond is only making his pain worse. It's making *my* pain worse."

Darius's shoulders sagged as if her words had hollowed him out from the inside. The wooden chair creaked under his shifting weight. For a long moment, he said nothing, gaze fixed on the table where a patch of sunlight illuminated every grain and knot in the wood. When he finally spoke, his voice was low, almost broken.

"I wanted so badly for him to have everything he deserves, to know what I know—how the love and bond with his fated would complete him, make him the best alpha he could be. I didn't realize I was taking away his chance to find it on his own."

His admission was raw, laden with years of regret, striking something deep inside Lena. Maybe, just maybe, this moment would be a turning point for Kai—a chance to find himself without the pressure of the bond or his father's expectations clouding his path.

"It's not forever," Elara insisted. Her presence surged with the fierce certainty that only a wolf could possess. *"He will choose us freely. When he's ready. When his heart is whole again."*

The thought brought a flicker of solace, but it wasn't enough to fill the vacuum that had formed inside her. Lena couldn't share her wolf's certainty, couldn't risk her heart on maybes. She needed to leave. She couldn't come back—for both their sakes.

She reached across the table, grasping Darius's hands. "Take care of him. Not as his alpha, but as his father. Let him figure Ava out on his own. Don't push him, Darius," she pleaded. "If you force him the way you did at the Summit, you'll only break him further."

He nodded, regret and resolve warring in his expression. "I will. You have my word."

"Thank you," she whispered. She hesitated, thumb brushing against the back of his hand. "Be happy, Darius. For your pack. For Kai. For yourself."

A ghost of a smile, tinged with sadness, crossed the alpha's features. "You're remarkable, Lena. Perhaps more than Kai deserves right now, but I'll hold out hope that Selene will guide you both back to each other, will guide you back here."

She didn't respond, couldn't bring herself to. She couldn't let that hope root inside her because there was no guarantee that Kai would make it through, that he would truly choose her. Instead, she nodded. Her quiet acceptance the only answer she could give.

CHAPTER FIFTY-TWO

KAI

K ai's night had been restless, his dreams haunted by fractured images of Ava's accusatory stare and Lena's distant gaze. Each fragment clawed at his mind and heart, leaving him raw and unsteady. The ache beneath his ribs had become a constant companion, a dull throb that tightened with every breath. When he finally dragged himself out of bed, the sunlight streaming through the cracked window seemed almost cruel, mocking the turmoil that churned inside him.

Kai ran a hand through his hair, the strands falling messily into his eyes. Ava's voice echoed relentlessly in his mind: *"She's leaving tomorrow. Do you really think she gives a damn about you?"*

He wondered if Ava was right. Lena had every reason not to care. He'd resisted her from the start. Pushed her away even after she offered him patience, kindness, and understanding.

Why wouldn't she leave? Move on with someone who'd give her everything I'd refused?

The bitter fear that she would—and should—move on ripped at his insides, threatening to take root. He paced the room as his mind conjured images that contradicted Ava's poison.

Lena's gentleness when she asked about Ava. How she'd been curious without judgment, wanting to understand rather than accuse...

She had every right to hate him for what happened the last night of the Summit, yet she hadn't. She'd given him space to figure it out, even though it hurt her.

The images in his mind shifted to Moonshadow.

The way Lena stood up to her father, defending him when he hadn't deserved it. As if she'd known instinctively that he needed someone to fight for him in that moment...

Their first run together—her vulnerability after they'd made love...

Kai hadn't forgotten the way she'd looked at him that night, like he was more than the sum of his failures.

Those memories alone were enough to carve an empty space within him. The pain intensified as other moments crashed through his defenses in rapid succession.

Lena's attempts to comfort him in the aftermath of the rogue attack...

Her touch when her father delivered the news. Her insistence on being there for him so he wasn't alone...

Her time in Bloodstone. She hadn't hesitated. She'd cared for his people, even when she didn't have to. She cared for him, even when he didn't let her...

The evidence was overwhelming: Lena had shown him in a thousand ways how she felt about him, that she saw him.

Ava was wrong. He knew that now with an ache so sharp it felt like it might split him in two.

But Lena was still leaving.

Orion growled, the sound low and reverberating. *"You can't fix it if you let her leave."*

Kai yanked open a drawer, movements clumsy as he searched for a clean shirt. His hands trembled. His breath came in short, uneven bursts. The room felt too small, the air too thick.

He needed to move.

To act.

To stop her.

Orion's presence was steady in the back of his mind, a grounding force amidst the chaos. *"You panic because you know what you're losing."* There was no judgment in Orion's tone, only the brutal, primal honesty that wolves possessed.

Kai froze, grip tightening on the edge of the drawer. He swallowed hard, throat dry. Tension radiated through his body, coiling tighter with each heartbeat until his ribcage felt like an iron vise being cranked shut.

More memories flooded him—not of Lena's actions but of the way she made him *feel*—consuming him with their intensity:

The rightness of her in his arms when she'd thrown herself at him that first night, like she belonged there. The way his wolf had stilled, satisfied in her presence, as if he'd been waiting for her all along...

The flash of possessiveness and jealousy that burned through him when he'd seen her with Jace or Ryker. How he hated how natural their connection looked, how easy it had seemed between them, because he'd wanted to be the only one who could bring her that kind of ease...

The quiet, grounding warmth of her pinky hooking with his. That small, simple gesture that anchored him in ways he couldn't explain...

Or the way her voice would soften when she called him "mate," as if the title was a promise, not just a fact...

The overwhelming need to give her everything when they made love—the way she unraveled beneath him and pulled him apart all at once. He'd wanted to give her every pleasure, everything she deserved, because in those moments, nothing else in the world felt as right as her...

Kai's heart stilled, the depth of his feelings for Lena overwhelming his system. She'd given him everything, and he'd given her so little in return.

Orion's voice came again, softer this time, a nudge rather than a push. *"You love her."*

The declaration knocked the breath from his lungs.

Love.

The realization triggered an avalanche of truth: it wasn't the bond. It wasn't Selene's will. It was *Lena*. Her fire, her strength, her kindness. The way she saw him—not as the alpha-heir, not as her fated, just *him*. It had always been her.

Kai stumbled back, pressing a hand to his chest. His heart thundered beneath his palm, each beat pulsing with the truth he'd been too afraid to face.

I love her... I love Lena.

"Find mate," Orion urged. *"Talk to her. Before it is too late."*

The desperation in Orion's voice propelled Kai into motion. He grabbed his jacket and bolted for the door. He didn't know what he was going to say, but he had to find her.

He sprinted up the stairs and down the hallway, boots thudding heavily against the hardwood floor. His mind raced, the realization of his love for Lena fueling his urgency. He skidded to a stop outside the door to her guest suite, hand hovering over the handle for a moment before he knocked.

The door opened, and Ryker's broad frame filled the doorway. The Moonshadow Beta-heir's expression was stony, his normally soft brown eyes cold and hostile.

"What do you want, Bloodstone?" Ryker's tone was clipped, devoid of the camaraderie they'd once shared. The last time he'd called him "brother" felt like a lifetime ago.

Regret washed over Kai, the reality of his mistakes pressing heavily on his shoulders.

"Is Lena here?" he asked, voice tight with urgency. "I need to talk to her."

Ryker crossed his arms, glare icy. "Why should I tell you?" He leaned forward, dropping his voice to a dangerous growl. "So you can rub your girlfriend in her face again? Haven't you hurt her enough?"

The accusation cut deep. He stepped forward, his desperation breaking through.

"Please," he said, alpha confidence stripped away, leaving only raw desperation. "I need to talk to her before she leaves."

Tense silence filled the space between them. Kai nearly withered under Ryker's gaze. Finally, Jace's voice broke the stalemate.

"She's in the dining hall," Jace said from inside the room, voice measured and deliberate in that way that always made him sound older, wiser. "Saying goodbye to some of the pack members." He paused, then softer: "Don't waste this chance, Kai."

Relief escaped Kai in a quick exhale, the knot in his chest loosening just slightly. "Thank you," he said, glancing at Ryker. The Moonshadow Beta-heir's gaze remained icy, a reminder of how much Kai had to make up for.

Without another word, Kai sprinted toward the exit. The hallway blurred around him as he ran. Each stride burdened by everything he'd left unsaid, everything he still had to say.

Kai pushed open the doors to the dining hall, the creak of the hinges barely registering over the rush of his breathing. The quiet murmur of the pack moving about their day filled the space—clinking plates, the scrape of chairs, and the soft hum of conversation—all faded to static the moment he saw her.

Lena.

She sat across from Darius, their heads tilted toward one another as they spoke. Sunlight poured through the windows behind them, bathing them in a warm, golden glow. Kai stood paralyzed, unable to command his body forward.

They looked so natural together. Darius, who so rarely let his guard down, wore an expression that was almost gentle, and Lena... Lena was radiant. Her posture was as poised as ever, but faint shadows under her eyes betrayed her exhaustion. Despite it, she carried herself with a strength that drew in everyone around her, including his father.

A blade of regret twisted between his ribs. She'd done that. Lena had drawn something out of Darius that Kai had never been able to. Without even trying, she'd bridged a gap he hadn't imagined possible, simply by being who she was. The realization burned through him, leaving an ache in its wake.

"Look at her," Orion said, his earlier urgency tempered by affection. *"She brings out the best in him. Imagine what she could bring out in you."*

Kai's fists clenched at his sides. He didn't need the reminder.

What could we be now if I hadn't fought the bond at the start? Mated? Marked? Whole?

Sorrow bore down on him like an avalanche, but it wasn't enough to hold him back. He forced himself to move, legs feeling like lead with each step. His pulse quickened, every nerve in his body felt taut, stretched thin as the distance between them closed.

Both heads turned to him as he stopped a few paces away from the table. Darius's expression shifted, his guarded mask slipping back into place, but it was Lena's gaze that stole his breath. Her golden-brown eyes met his, and in the space of a heartbeat, he thought he saw something flicker there—hesitation, maybe regret, but also quiet strength. The kind of strength that had always drawn him to her.

"Can we talk?" The words came out sharp-edged and too abrupt, nothing like the practiced, careful way he'd imagined saying them.

Lena's brow furrowed, but she nodded. "Of course." She spoke with that careful neutrality she used when bracing herself.

Darius stood, placing a hand on Lena's shoulder before stepping aside. His father's departure left the air between Kai and Lena crackling with tension.

His jaw worked as he tried to form words that wouldn't come. His hands curled into fists at his sides, nails digging into his palms. Orion was there, his presence like bedrock beneath shifting sand, his voice cutting through the static in Kai's mind.

"She is home, Kai. Stop running from what's meant for you."

Throat dry as sand, he faced the female who held his heart, his future, and his very salvation in her hands. The realization surged with stunning clarity—there were no more masks to hide behind, no more excuses to make.

His next thought burned through him like wildfire, consuming everything but this single, desperate truth: *I can't lose her. I won't let this be the end. Not when I've only just found the courage to begin.*

CHAPTER FIFTY-THREE

LENA

The buzz of conversation around them grated against Lena's frayed nerves like shards of glass. The warmth of afternoon sun seeping through the tall windows was oppressive. Normally, the golden light would bring her peace, but today, it only amplified the storm swirling inside her.

The dining hall felt like a fishbowl, noise and movement magnified under an invisible but suffocating scrutiny. Lena felt as if every curious glance and whisper between pack members was aimed at them. The reality of their impending, indefinite goodbye pressed down on her like an immovable boulder. This moment needed to be theirs alone—not something for the pack to dissect.

Then, she looked at him.

Kai's emerald-green eyes, filled with something raw and unspoken, locked onto hers. Vulnerability and guilt etched into every line of his face.

Elara's growl was soft but insistent. *"He's hurting. Mate hurts for us."*

He's ending it, Lena thought, numbness spreading through her chest.

She'd expected this was coming, but the reality of it still felt like a slap. Breath caught in her throat, she had to remind herself to exhale. Her trembling hands curled into fists beneath the table, nails biting into her palms as she steadied herself and stood.

Her voice, soft yet firm, broke through the heavy silence between them.

"Maybe we could step outside? Get some air?"

KAI

He trailed Lena through the hall, each step echoing with a sense of finality. His breathing became shallow from the pressure of unspoken words building inside him. As they emerged onto the patio, the warm sunlight and gentle rustle of leaves faded into the background, overshadowed by the pounding of his heart and the desperate need to speak.

Orion's presence pulsed against his consciousness like a second heartbeat, urgent and insistent.

"The bond is strained. I can barely feel my Elara."

Kai stilled as the words struck home. Orion's tone softened, but his voice was still laced with a quiet desperation.

"Don't let her leave without telling her the truth."

Kai studied Lena's posture, gaze drawn to her arms curled defensively around her middle as her eyes fixed on some distant point. The emotional distance between them yawned like a chasm, its depths uncertain and daunting.

His voice cracked as he spoke, the words tumbling out in a rush. "I'm sorry," he began, the apology raw and unvarnished. "For everything. For failing you." He took a step closer, hands flexing at his sides, as if grasping for something to hold onto. "When you return, I want us to have the chance we deserve. To start over as mates, as your boyfriend, as whatever you need." He swallowed hard. "Please."

LENA

She turned to face him, face blank, mind reeling as his words hung in the air. The afternoon heat intensified, pressing against her back like a physical force.

His voice had trembled, emerald eyes glistening. She felt like she was drowning in the depths of his yearning. She'd expected him to end things, to walk away, but this...this was something else entirely. Her hands fidgeted at her sides as she struggled to find her footing. She felt torn in two, pulled between hope and self-preservation as his words sank in.

She let herself remember the countless times she'd longed to hear him say these things. Now, after everything they'd been through—the hurt he'd caused with the distance he created, and the insidious presence of Ava—it was too little, too late.

"Kai..." She swallowed hard, forcing herself to steady. "I'm not coming back."

The confession erected a wall between them, and Lena felt the sharp hint of tears pricking at the corners of her eyes. She watched as his face fell, searching hers as if hoping to find a glimmer of doubt, but her resolve remained firm.

Elara's presence flickered in her mind, voice trembling with anguish. *"We're hurting them. I sense my Orion's panic. Do we have to leave?"*

Lena hesitated, heart leaden with the gravity of her decision. *"We have to, Elara. We can't keep going on like this. The bond... It's not enough."*

"Our bond was broken from the start." Her voice wavered as she continued, "As much as I love you, it's destroying us... It's destroying me."

KAI

The words slammed into Kai like a riptide—pulling him under, stealing air from his lungs and leaving him gasping. A cold sweat broke out on his forehead, trickling down his temples like icy fingers. The sound of his uneven breaths filled his ears as his ribcage pressed inward, each inhale scorching lungs struggling to draw air.

She's leaving me...

"No," he choked out, shaking his head. "We said we'd take things slow. I can do better. Just...don't give up on us."

"Fight for mate." Orion's energy was a steady ache.

Kai scoured her face, frantic for any hint of uncertainty. She stood rigid but fragile, like glass about to crack. Her hands clenched into fists at her sides, shoulders rising and falling in an unsteady rhythm. Her beautiful, golden-brown eyes—red-rimmed and brimming with tears—held a world of sorrow. Her cranberry and rosemary scent, now tinged with bitterness, wafted up, making his gut twist with anguish.

I'm losing her... The thought screamed through his mind, fueling his desperation.

"You're crying because you don't want this," he pressed on, panic spilling over. "Please, Lena. We can fix this. You can't mean it."

His hands shook as he reached for her, wrapping his pinky around hers. A gesture they'd used so many times to stay connected. One that now felt like his only lifeline. He needed her to feel it. To feel the connection, the *rightness*, between them. He needed her to hold on.

"You can't give up," Orion urged. *"Prove it to her."*

"Let me come with you." He scrambled, grip on her pinky tightening. "I don't even need to pack. We can go right now." He pulled their hands up and pressed them against his heart, eyes never leaving hers. "We can talk on the way. Or Ryker and Jace can ride with us. It will be so good to be back home with you. I'll help with Cian's alpha ceremony, and then we can help Cian and Lyric plan their mating ceremony."

He leaned forward, forehead touching hers. "We'll keep working on us. And when you're ready, we'll come back here. Mated and marked. We'll take our place as the next Alpha and Luna of Bloodstone."

Lena's silence crushed him. He could barely hear her breathing. He lifted his head to meet her eyes. Her steady gaze driving home the truth he didn't want to face.

This can't be happening.

His legs gave out, the bond flaring painfully in his chest.

"I love you. Not because of the bond. Because of you." His voice dissolved into raw pleading. "*Please* don't leave me. I can't do this without you."

LENA

A crack split through Lena's chest as she gazed into Kai's face, heartbeat faltering before resuming with agonizing intensity. She kneeled in front of him, wrapping a trembling hand around his. The rough texture of the stone patio beneath her knees ground into her skin. A physical manifestation of the pain reverberating between them.

Her voice broke as she whispered, "I'm sorry. I love you, too... I'm so sorry."

The words felt like a betrayal, a cruel twist of the knife she'd already plunged into his heart. As she looked into his eyes, she saw the desperation, the fear, the *love*.

It was the love that nearly undid her, that made her want to retract her words and fall into him, but she knew she couldn't. In that moment, Lena realized that leaving Bloodstone wasn't enough.

Because Kai would never let *her* go.

Ava would never let *him* go.

And the more they all held on, the more heartbreak it would bring.

Lena recalled the promise she made to herself the night they'd returned to Moonshadow: *I won't sacrifice myself to save him.*

I have to sever the bond. The thought echoed in her mind like a death knell.

Elara erupted into a cacophony of panic and despair. *"No, no, no, Lena! Please, don't do this!"* Then she called to Kai's wolf: *"Orion! Orion, help me!"*

Lena felt her wolf's terror and desperation, a panicked spiral threatening to consume them both. The sound of Kai's labored breathing was a brutal reminder of the pain she was causing him. She tried to block out Elara's cries, but they pierced her mind like a thousand needles.

"My mate! Don't take my mate away, please!"

Steeling herself, Lena spoke the words she knew would change everything. "I, Lena, daughter of Alpha Raelen of the Moonshadow pack, reject you, Kai, Alpha-heir of the Bloodstone pack, as my mate." The rejection words tasted like ash, bitter on her tongue.

As she spoke, Lena felt the bond between them begin to fray, like the threads of a rope unraveling. Each strand that snapped sent a searing pain through her body, as if layers of her skin were being peeled away in slow, excruciating strips. The sensation radiated outward from her sternum, each thread's separation leaving raw, exposed nerves in its wake.

Elara's wails grew louder, more frantic, as the wolf thrashed in Lena's mind, fighting violently against what was happening. *"Orion, please! Don't let me go!"*

Lena steeled herself, knowing she had to see this through. She had to cut herself free, no matter how much it destroyed her.

KAI

Orion's anguished howl erupted in Kai's mind, a raw, guttural cry that shook him to his core. *"Elara! Elara, no!"*

The sound of his own broken breathing filled his ears as he pressed his forehead to Lena's, his sobs tearing through him like a storm. "I...can't. I... please..." he pleaded, head shaking with every word. "Don't do this to us. I love you, Lena. You're *mine*. Forever."

Lena's hands tightened around his, her fingers tracing soothing circles on the backs.

Orion rattled in his skull, screaming at Kai to hold onto his mate. *"No, Kai! Please! Don't let her go!"*

Lena's voice cut through the chaos. "Please, Kai, set us free. Release us from this pain."

She looked at him through unshed tears, and Kai felt himself crumble. He saw the pain she was trying to escape, the pain *he'd* caused her.

Kai knew he'd never been worthy of her love. He'd resisted her from the start, let fear overwhelm him in Bloodstone until he'd detached from her completely. Every bit of pain she'd suffered because of him flashed through his mind, and the enormity of his regret tore through him, obliterating his resolve.

I can't hurt her anymore. I won't.

He swallowed hard, forcing the words out. "I...Kai...Alpha-heir of the Bloodstone pack...accept your rejection."

The bond didn't merely snap—it detonated.

A crushing force like an anvil slammed through his ribcage, cracking bone and pulverizing his heart into splintered fragments. Each breath became agony as the void where their bond had once pulsed expanded, devouring him from the inside out. Blood thundered in his ears, drowning out everything but the sensation of his core being hollowed out. Kai collapsed, clutching his chest as Orion's presence began to fade with an anguished roar, leaving him gutted, adrift, and utterly alone.

LENA

Lena leaned in, hands shaking as she cupped Kai's face. Her thumbs brushed away the tears streaking down his cheeks. Her own tears fell freely now, each one feeling like a piece of herself breaking away.

"I love you, Kai." Her lips quivered as the words fell between them. "I love you so much. Please...heal. Fix things with your dad. Make a decision about Ava. Set the male I fell in love with in Moonshadow free." She forced herself to finish, her tears mixing with his as she pressed her lips to his one last time. "Be happy."

Lena tore herself away from him, unsteady legs barely holding her weight as she struggled to her feet. Every step away from Kai felt heavier than the last, as though the bond, even in its broken state, was physically pulling her back to him. Her chest ached, the severance leaving a void, a raw absence that felt too immense to comprehend. The urge to run back to him, to take it all back, clawed at her with each step, but she kept moving. She bit her lip hard enough to draw blood, willing herself not to turn around. If she looked back, if she saw him crumpled on the ground, she knew she would falter.

Just get to the Jeep, she told herself. *Hold on a little longer.*

Her vision narrowed, the world around her fading into muted blurs. All she could see was the Jeep parked in front of the dormitories, her father and packmates waiting for her. Raelen stood by the driver's side, worry lining his face. Cian, Ryker, and Jace stood near the vehicle, their postures tense. As she drew closer, Lena registered the curious glances and whispered conversations from nearby Bloodstone pack members. She didn't acknowledge them. Her focus was on reaching the Jeep.

The sound of footsteps reached her ears, and she lifted her head enough to see Ryker and Jace rushing at her. The fear and concern etched into their faces intensified her agony.

"Lena?" Ryker called out.

She didn't make it. Her knees buckled, and she collapsed into their arms. "Not here." Her hoarse voice barely audible. "Please...just get me to the Jeep."

Ryker's arms tightened around her as he and Jace lifted her to her feet. Her breaths were uneven, fighting sobs that threatened to break free as they guided her the last few steps.

Raelen ran to her, pulling her into a tight hug. "My Lena," he murmured, voice thick with sorrow. "I'm so sorry. It's going to be okay. We're going home."

She didn't have the strength to respond.

Her father helped her into the back seat, arms steadying her as Ryker and Jace climbed in on either side. Cian stood frozen near the door, a single tear sliding down his cheek as he looked at her. She couldn't bear to meet his eyes. To see the sadness and empathy in his gaze.

To see the fresh mating claim mark on his neck.

As the doors closed, Lena sank into the seat, mind spinning. She barely registered the sound of the engine roaring to life or the Jeep shifting under the weight of her father and Cian climbing in. Everything felt distant—muted—as the realization of what she'd done began to sink in.

She slipped inward, searching desperately for something—anything. *"Please...Elara,"* she pleaded into the thunderous silence of her mind. *"I need you. Now more than ever."*

There was nothing. No warmth, no steady presence. Only the sound of her own voice, echoing lonely in her consciousness. The wolf who had been with her since she was sixteen—integrated into her breathing, her heartbeat, her very thoughts—had vanished. The stillness in Lena's mind was absolute, like plunging into deafness after a lifetime of constant, comforting sound.

As the Jeep's tires crunched over the gravel border of Bloodstone's territory and turned onto the main road, the finality of her choice settled in.

The dam broke.

A wail ripped free from Lena's throat, raw and violent. Like a banshee's cry ricocheting through the Jeep's interior.

Jace pulled her into his lap, arms wrapping around her as she shook. Ryker leaned in, enveloping them both in his protective embrace. Their whispered reassurances were drowned out by the sound of her own sobs.

The rumble of the Jeep, the whispers, the echoes of her tears—all faded into the background as Lena finally gave in to the emptiness inside her.

KAI

Kai remained where Lena had left him—crumpled on the patio, head bowed—as the sum of all his failures broke him. The sun on his skin felt cold, an unnatural chill settling deep into his bones.

For years, Orion had been his center—his strength, his anchor. Now, the space in his mind where Orion once lived was filled with nothing but stillness. An oppressive quiet that Kai couldn't bear.

The severed bond left his chest not merely hollow but collapsed. As if his ribs were caving inward without Orion's presence to help them hold their shape. Each heartbeat sent shock waves of pain through the splintered remains where his core had been. The ache reverberated endlessly, each echo weaker than the last, like a dying pulse. Sounds muffled and distorted as he lay there until all he could perceive was the haunting silence in his mind—a silence with weight and texture, suffocating him from within.

He didn't hear the heavy footsteps at first. It wasn't until strong arms wrapped around him that he recognized his father's presence.

"I'm here, son," Darius said. "I've got you."

Kai's sobs broke free as he let himself be pulled into his father's embrace. "She's gone, Dad," he cried, voice raw. "Orion's gone. I have nothing. I am nothing."

"You're not nothing, Kai." Darius's voice cracked as he tightened his hold. "You're my son, and I'm here."

Kai's body felt limp, senses blurring as Darius lifted him, cradling him like a child. The courtyard, which had once felt like home, now felt impossibly large and unbearably empty. He barely registered the pack members lowering their voices, bowing their heads as they watched Darius carry his prone body.

By the time they reached his suite, Kai's senses became nonexistent. The colors of the world dulled, the edges fading into darkness as though the bond's severance was pulling him deeper into an abyss.

As Darius settled him onto the bed, Kai's thoughts grew disjointed, mind splintering into a thousand shards of pain and regret. He barely felt his father's hand, a steady weight on his shoulder.

"Rest now," Darius murmured. "I'm not leaving you."

Kai's final thought before the darkness consumed him entirely was a faint whisper, a name that felt like both an anchor and a blade in his chest.

Lena.

Acknowledgements

This story has lived in my head for years, sparked by a yearning for more each time I picked up a shifter romance. I'm still in awe that it's transitioned from a figment of my imagination formulated by so many "GAH! I wish..." moments into a living, "breathing," tangible thing. That said, I owe an immense debt of gratitude to the people who've helped turn this fever dream into a reality.

First and foremost, my sincerest and deepest appreciation for my husband. You've been the best co-conspirator and sounding board. Thank you for always saying "yes, and," for reading spicy scenes aloud (yes, you can keep calling it your "length"), for assisting with endless hours of "research," and for being the kind of partner who makes fiction pale in comparison. You are my Asher. You made this not just something I could do, but something I did to the very best of my ability. Less than three.

Next, to the M&MS—Manuela, Miranda, and Stephanie—this story exists because someone asked, "Would you rather wake up in your underwear at work or naked in the forest?" and the response was, "Well, are there werewolves, and is one of them my fated mate?" That question sparked an entire conversation about lycanthropy lore and my desire to see something different in paranormal romance tropes. I spent a month word-vomiting ideas onto the page, then another eight months making them real. SURPRISE!

Thank you as well to my Inkitt readers, you were my alpha group. I am eternally grateful for the safe space you provided to share my words and your feedback that transformed a linear progression of events into the book *FATED* is today. I hope you enjoy how the story evolved based on your reactions and comments.

To my beta readers—Aimee, Audrey, Luna, and Mira—your responses to these characters and this world encouraged me to move forward and share it beyond our circle. A special shout-out to Kelsey, who not only beta read *FATED* but provided developmental editing support and helped me navigate plot lines I was wavering on.

To Clara, my brilliant editor, who makes me better and inspires me to write more. When the revision process felt overwhelming or that voice in my head whispered, "The whole thing is stupid. Stop acting like it's going to be this epic exploration of fate and choice—it's werewolf smut," I would pull up your first round of feedback and read what you said about my characters and world.

To my cover artist, Sienna Arts, thank you for bringing not just this story, but my entire brand to life through beautiful imagery. I cannot wait for our next collaboration.

To Amanda, one of my dearest friends, who has never read paranormal anything or romance but dove headfirst into the messiest Google Doc imaginable. Somewhere out there, someone is holding this book or reading it on their Kindle because you said, "Publish it so I can add it to my Storygraph. And hurry up with Book 2, because I need to know what happens next!"

Last, but certainly not least, you, dear reader. Thank you for taking a chance on someone new. I hope that you'll stick with me to see how this story ends.

Oh, and Mom? I warned you...

ABOUT THE AUTHOR

Adeline Bryant lives in Minneapolis, MN, with her husband and their two feline overlords. Armed with an advanced degree in education and an endless supply of imagination, she has always been fascinated by the transformative power of stories and the bonds they create.

A longtime enthusiast of high-fantasy and paranormal romance, Adeline is drawn to intricately built worlds, enigmatic characters, and prophecies that make you question everything. *FATED*, her debut novel, was inspired by her fascination with lycanthropy lore—especially its connection to mythology and paganism, the complex dynamics of packs, the pull of fated mates, and the eternal dance between destiny and free will.

When she's not writing, Adeline can usually be found devouring books, rocking her signature red lipstick, and shamelessly belting out Taylor Swift songs. She firmly believes that every great story deserves a bottle of wine and a healthy dose of magic (and smut).

Coming 2026

CHOSEN | Book Two in the Bonded Legacy Trilogy

After the summit, everything changed. Each of them made a choice. Now they must live with the consequences.

Caleb chose to end Crescent Fang's isolation, trusting the collective to protect his pack's future. But reintegration is messy, and leadership comes at a cost. He's fighting for political influence—and for the male he loves—even as fate delivers him a mate who may tear it all apart.

Lena chose to reject Kai, walking away from a love that felt doomed from the start. She told him to heal. To be happy. But the price was steeper than she ever imagined—Elara's voice silenced forever, leaving a hollow echo where her wolf once lived. Now, wolfless and unmoored, she's dragging everyone around her into the wreckage.

Kai accepted Lena's rejection, letting her walk away when every instinct screamed to fight. Now his wolf is gone, his heart is shattered, and he doesn't know if he can move on. He may have been born to lead—but without Lena and Orion, what's left to fight, or even live for?

But Caleb, Lena, and Kai aren't the only ones facing the fallout.

Asher has always been steady. Loyal. Sure of his love for Caleb. When Caleb's mate emerges, and shares no bond with him, the foundation of everything Asher believed crumbles. As jealousy and fear threaten to poison what was once certain, he confronts a devastating question: is love enough to make it work—or was he always just meant to be Caleb's beta.

Ava spent years shaping a future by Kai's side. She fought for it. Bled for it. Then Lena blew it all up. With Lena gone, Ava has a chance to reclaim what was stolen—if she can piece Kai back together. But as long-buried secrets claw their way to the surface, Ava realizes that some truths are powerful enough to destroy not just bonds, but entire packs.

If *FATED* was about facing destiny... *CHOSEN* is about what happens when you try to make your own.

CHOSEN is the second book in the *Bonded Legacy Trilogy*, a lush paranormal romance featuring intricate pack dynamics, an escalating rogue threat, a white-hot why-choose dynamic, and the fight to course correct in the wake of heartbreak.

For release updates and exclusive Bonded Legacy content, visit https://addiewrotethat.com/

Connect with Addie

Thank you for reading! I'd love to connect with you and hear your thoughts.

Stay Updated!

Visit **https://addiewrotethat.com/** for updates on the Bonded Legacy Trilogy, behind-the-scenes looks at the writing process, and exclusive content and character insights!

Join the Pack!

instagram.com/addiewrotethat

Love FATED?

If you enjoyed this book, the greatest gifts you can give an author are:

A review on Storygraph, Amazon, Goodreads, or your favorite book platform.

Telling a friend about the book.

Posting about it on social media with #BondedLegacyTrilogy and #FatedNovel.

Your support means everything and helps make books like *FATED* possible.

www.ingramcontent.com/pod-product-compliance
Lightning Source LLC
Chambersburg PA
CBHW020012120726
47903CB00004B/1248